THE LAST LIBRARIAN

THE LAST LIBRARIAN

BRANDT LEGG

LAUGHING RAIN

The Last Librarian (Book One of the Justar Journal)
v2

Published in the United States of America by Laughing Rain

Cataloging-in-Publication data for this book is available from the Library of Congress.
ISBN-13: 978-1-935070-12-2
ISBN-10: 1-935070-12-6

Cover designed by: Jarowe and Eleni Karoumpali

PUBLISHER'S NOTE
This book is a work of fiction. Names, characters, places and incidents are products of the author's imagination or are used fictitiously. Any resemblance to actual persons, living or dead, businesses, events or locales is entirely coincidental.

BrandtLegg.com

This book is dedicated to Teakki and Ro

"People can lose their lives in libraries. They ought to be warned."

SAUL BELLOW

CHAPTER ONE

Monday, January 29

After all the remarkable changes which had occurred during the decades since the Banoff, it seemed strange that 2098 would long be remembered as "the year of change." For on a cold January morning of that year . . . the revolution began. No one knew it then because it started, as revolutions often do, as something quiet and almost routine.

There was no way Runit Happerman, a bookish, cautious, single dad two weeks past his forty-third birthday, could have had the faintest idea he would be at the center of the storm.

As he commuted to work on that frosty morning, through the gleaming city of Portland in what they now called the Oregon Area, his thoughts were on the book he'd always wanted to write, about the days before that terrible five-year period when everyone died. "The Banoff," as it had come to be known in the new-language, brought the human race as close to extinction as it had ever come.

The Banoff plague had struck with the suddenness and fury of a fatal car crash. Hundreds of millions died in the first months, the only bright spot – if you could call it that – was that the virus went from incubation to death in less than a week. As the relentless and efficient killer swept the globe, universal terror, grief, and mayhem followed. It became impossible to keep up with burning the bodies and dealing with contamination, and in the end, billions were lost. Chaos ensued, and war broke out.

But instead of the zombie-apocalypse many expected, those in charge actually managed a miracle. With the population more than halved, it was as if humanity had been given a fresh start. A reset. From the pandemic death and nightmare, a near utopian world emerged.

Nearly seventy years had passed since the Banoff war ended. The present society, in which Runit lived, was as near to perfect as anyone could imagine.

Even Runit, who would soon be unemployed, couldn't complain. A new job would be found for him, maybe in education, and the news hadn't been unexpected. For many years he'd been the head librarian at what recently had become the last library in the world. There were digital-drapes, as they were called, where people could download books, movies, music, whatever data they desired. But a true library, in the traditional sense of what they once had been, and what his still was, with physical books, would be extinct as soon as he closed the doors, in ten days, for the last time. There had been two other libraries still operating in the countries formerly known as Australia and Belgium, but in the prior couple of years the government had closed them, just as they were going to close his.

He split the white shells of pumpkin seeds in his mouth as he wondered why the Aylantik government couldn't have left just his library open as a kind of museum. It had been his secret hope, ever since they shut Belgium down. As he sat at his antique desk, he recalled what a famous author from the previous century had said.

"Without libraries what have we? We have no past and no future."

Runit shelled another seed and whispered to the stacks of

books that filled his office. "Where are you when we need you, Ray Bradbury?"

The librarian's office was cluttered and often disorganized, but each time he entered it, he was home. His soul came to life amongst the familiar friends, both read and unread. He moved a finger and the flash repeated.

"To: Runit Happerman, Head Librarian, Portland Public Library. From: Multnomah County Board. The Board has been notified by the Aylantik Government that the Portland Library will be permanently closed ten days from the above date. A meeting will be held on the Field today at ten-hundred to resolve pending issues. Closing will be facilitated by the AOI."

He swept empty pumpkin seed shells into a recycling bin and shut off the flash. He didn't want to hear anymore. The AOI seemed overkill for a simple job of shutting down the world's last library.

The AOI, an acronym for Aylantik Office of Intelligence, cast a shadow over the otherwise sunny post-Banoff world, but someone had to enforce the peace. They were headquartered in the former US capital of Washington, D.C., but there were no longer any separate nations, and the AOI had facilities worldwide. A few of the old country names remained to identify zones, but otherwise, since the initial, chaotic, half-decade that followed the Banoff, Earth had been run by a unified government known as Aylantik.

Runit looked at the photo of himself and his late wife Harper, kept propped on his cluttered desk. She still looked young and beautiful, and although he was by no means old, the ten years since her death had been stressful, as attested to by the lines on his face and the early gray in his otherwise thick, sandy brown hair.

Harper had loved him as a librarian, but she'd be pushing him to finish his book now. He mused to himself that before the Banoff, he would have probably been hired by a bookstore. But they didn't exist anymore either.

The last one had, coincidentally, also been located in Portland, a mere five blocks from where his library stood. It had been called Powell's City of Books, and was once the largest in the world. For almost fifty years before the Banoff, Powell's had been a haven for book-lovers, and had even lasted a few more years afterwards. The old bookshop's cavernous home, twice renovated, like most of the city's older buildings, was now powered by solar, wind, or one of the many other non-fossil-fuel sources. Sometimes, when he walked past it, he tried to imagine what it would have been like. All those physical books for sale. People actually used to have shelves full of them in their homes. Even children had apparently been allowed to have many books all their own.

The Banoff had changed more than just the way books were read. From its ashes arose the greatest ever civilization. The Earth united as one nation, known as Nusun. Runit's parents, born post-Banoff in 2034 and 2037, had him in 2056. He'd grown up hearing his grandparents' stories about life before. Many were hard to believe, but as he studied the old volumes housed inside his historic library, he discovered that the world which existed prior to the Banoff was far worse than they had described.

For thousands of years, wars had been almost constant. And for some reason during the last century, humans had ripped coal, oil, and natural gas from the earth to power their industry, electrical grid, and transportation instead of using the free, abundant, and renewable solar and wind, which the planet now used exclusively. Runit marveled at how relatively recently things had been so awful. But at least back then, people had valued libraries.

Why can't they just leave this last one alone?

A dusty old plaque hung on the far side of his cramped office. He hadn't read it for years, but suddenly it had new meaning.

"Libraries should be open to all—except the censor. We must know all the facts and hear all the alternatives and listen to all the criticisms. Let us welcome controversial books and controversial authors." – John F. Kennedy, October 29, 1960.

He reflected on the former President of the United States, a nation that no longer existed. The famous leader had also been an author, and the only President to win a Pulitzer Prize. Just over three years after he made that statement, an assassin's bullet found him.

Runit shook his head and thought, *What a strange past that we have twisted into this curious present.*

CHAPTER TWO

Nelson Wright, a contentious novelist, came into the library, as he did most mornings. He'd written six bestsellers at his favorite table on the second floor, near one of the giant high arched windows and always said, "I do my best writing surrounded by books, feeling the danger, hope, and potential in them."

Nelson, a throwback to Hemingway, Fitzgerald, and Capote, attracted admirers and high-end social invitations as much for his intellect and fascinating conversation, as for the cloud of controversy that followed his work.

Runit had been trying to write a novel for years, but he didn't get the same inspiration from the walls of books, perhaps because he was responsible for them. Telling the typically cranky Nelson the tragic news would be an ugly affair.

"Morning, Runit," Nelson said, inhaling deeply that flawless blend of paper, ink, and age. The scent of a million books.

Although just eight years the librarian's senior, Nelson looked much older, with his perpetually messy hair and a face full of blond and gray stubble. Nelson ate the wrong foods, drank a bit too much, and even smoked "bacs." Cigarettes hadn't been manufactured since the Banoff, but private farms produced a similar tobacco product, without the filter, that was longer and thinner than the old-fashioned kind. Nelson's sister said bacs were the reason he'd never married.

He regularly got in trouble with the medical monitors, who routinely fined him for exceeding weight limits. The fees were part of the new world, and Nelson cursed them every time they sucked the funds from his bank account, often enough, since assessments hit anytime someone went over by three kilograms. He generally kept between five and nine above ideal weight. Ten kilograms meant detainment at a state-run health and fitness facility, known as "Hops." Hops were no fun, a cross between boot camp, high school, and a bankrupt resort, where some of his favorite things – such as doughnuts, pizza, liquor, and bacs – were forbidden.

In contrast, Runit appeared lean and muscular and wore the same size clothes as his eighteen year-old son. The librarian's dreams of one day publishing and emulating his friend's writing success would likely never happen. Even if he could get a book done, he only wanted to write about life before the Banoff and, for various reasons, those books never sold.

"Before you disappear back there, I've got some news," Runit said, as they stood in the antique lobby of paneled wood. Next to them, the base of the grand double-staircase of white and gray marble led to the upper floors.

"No," Nelson moaned as he raised an eyebrow. "They're closing you down?"

"Yeah," Runit answered, not surprised at Nelson's guess. The surprise was how long they'd let the library remain. No one knew why Portland's had been left open so long.

"Damn them!" Nelson shook his head. "Closing the world's last library."

Runit nodded, the sadness hitting him anew. The three-story central library building, which occupied an entire city block and included a sprawling subterranean level, had been like a home to him.

Nelson opened and closed his pudgy fists, as if ready to hit someone, or something. "When?"

"I got it across the flash this morning."

"No, I mean how long do we have left?"

"Ten days."

"Then the time has come," Nelson said, pulling out a bac. "I need to show you something."

"What?" Runit asked, waving a finger at the bac before Nelson could light it.

"A torgon tragedy worse than the death of the old languages," Nelson said while absently putting away his bac.

Shortly after the Banoff, a new global language, created by computers, had been introduced. The language, dubbed "Com," contained many English words, but its simple design and logical structure made it entirely different and easy to learn.

Com, now universally spoken, had replaced all others as the world's only language. One of the primary reasons physical libraries had died out so easily was that not many people could read the old books without a special computer interface. Everything had been translated into Com and was available digitally. The paper editions were considered obsolete.

The prior, now-useless languages weren't taught in cyberschools. However, in spite of laws prohibiting it, both Nelson and Runit had learned English from their respective grandparents. Many in that former generation had clung to the old ways, but they were all gone now, as no one born before the Banoff was left, the oldest having lived only to age eighty-two.

"What tragedy could be worse than losing the last library?" Runit asked, ignoring Nelson's use of the word "torgon," an unofficial profanity.

"Something far more important is at stake than a magnificent building full of books?" Waving a hand, as if to dismiss his beloved library, Nelson said, "All human knowledge that existed prior to seventy-five years ago is about to be lost."

Runit stared.

"And I have proof."

CHAPTER THREE

Nelson took the lanyard from around his neck. It held a marble-sized Information Navigation Unit. INUs had been invented a few years prior to the Banoff by a man named Booker Lipton.

To call an INU a computer would be like referring to a spaceship as a paper airplane. When first introduced, INUs were the diameter of a basketball, but a miniaturization race during the intervening decades resulted in ever-smaller forms. Seven companies now made them, but the original firm, Eysen Inc., still dominated because of an uncanny ability to innovate and develop advancements years ahead of their competitors. Nelson allowed the INU to float between them. The solar-powered, levitating INUs projected holographic controls and images, both two and three dimensional, in any size and up to fifteen meters away.

After a quick series of hand gestures, pages from one of Nelson's own novels were projected in the air. "See there?" Nelson asked, pointing to a guilty sentence as if it might attack them.

"What?"

"This paragraph used to finish with the words, 'To what end,' right there." He stabbed his finger rigorously through the illuminated words.

"It still does," Runit said.

"No. Read it again. Now it says, 'To *that* end.' See?"

"It's a typo Nelson." Runit turned away, anxious to get to the long list of tasks required to close the world's last library. *Where would they store the books?* he wondered.

Nelson grabbed his shoulder, pulling him back around. "It is not a torgon typo!" He growled. "They've changed all the meaning, don't you get it?"

"It's one letter."

"It's *my* letter and they know how dangerous it is."

"Who is 'they'?"

He glared at Runit. "Who do you think?"

"Well then, *they* could be hearing this now. Doesn't that worry you?"

Nelson smiled gruffly. "No, I got a Whistler."

"Oh, great. Now you've broken the law. Do you *want* to go to prison?"

"Tell me this, Runit. Why are Whistlers illegal?"

"Because they block AOI monitoring."

"And why is that so bad?"

"They need to know about potential criminal activity. It's one of the ways our world is so peaceful, as opposed to how it was before the Banoff."

"Well I'm not a terrorist, so they don't need to know what I'm doing every minute."

Runit stared at him, concerned.

"You're worried the AOI will find out I have a Whistler and that you knew about it?" Nelson asked, trying to read his friend's expression.

"No." Runit's eyes glazed into a faraway look, thinking of his late wife. "I remembered something Harper used to say after reading a pre-Banoff book. 'More powerful than armies and police, stronger than guns and bombs, words are what change the world, and that is why they're always a threat to those that rule with corrupt ways.' Nelson, the AOI doesn't think you're a terrorist. They monitor people like you because you're something far more dangerous than a terrorist. You're a writer with the power to influence people."

"A writer can only spread ideas. People still need to think about them, draw their own conclusions," Nelson snapped. "I'm no threat."

"All it takes is an idea. Harper always said that too. It's rarely the person with the idea that causes any trouble. Ideas get out there, take on a life of their own. They infect people."

"I miss Harper. She was a good woman."

"Best thing I ever did was marrying her."

"I can't believe how long she's been gone."

"Grandyn was eight. He just turned eighteen a few months back." Runit tightened his lips. "Damn . . . It's been ten years since the accident."

"She was right about ideas. They do infect people. And books and other writings do spread them. Maybe that's the real reason they've closed all the libraries. One thing our elected officials have shown is they're torgon good at stopping the spread of infections." Nelson took the lid off his large paper coffee cup and poured in something from a silver flask he'd fished from the pocket of his long wool coat. "There's no difference between a disease and a contrarian idea, once the epidemic gets started, things will never be the same."

Runit shivered. The heat in the nearly two-hundred-year-old building had never worked very well, but today he felt colder. His friend made him nervous. It wasn't Nelson's rebellious nature, or even that he had an illegal Whistler. It was because Runit reluctantly shared his friend's views.

For decades peace had reigned. The pre-Banoff plights of hunger and poverty that had been a scourge for millennia didn't exist anymore. They were living in a utopian society, but something gnawed at him. He just didn't know what it was or why. Runit, a scholarly skeptic, always needed convincing.

"I've got a meeting in an hour with county officials. I need to get ready," Runit said.

"Wait. You may think changing one letter in my book was a typo, but it's more sinister than that. By making the 'w' a 't,' the entire meaning is transformed. 'To *what* end' leaves the passage open. It's wild and revolutionary. While 'To *that* end' is finite and controlled." Nelson looked at Runit, his fiery eyes slightly bloodshot.

"Maybe, but it's ambiguous. If it happened at all, it's likely just because they don't like you."

"Really? Then they don't like a lot of people, because I started looking and there are others. Don't you see how tempting it is? They can change everything if there are no physical books to verify what was actually written. And not only that, they know everything we've read. What we haven't read, what page we stopped on, what words you looked up, everything, everyone has read—"

CHAPTER FOUR

Runit looked around the library for a moment as if secret agents from the AOI might be hiding behind the shelves. "Who else don't they like?"

"Shakespeare," Nelson said, knowing the impact that would have on the librarian.

Runit, an expert on Shakespeare, pulled his own INU from around his neck and set it floating in the air. "What play?"

"So far, I've found twenty-six lines changed."

Runit looked surprised and doubtful.

"Check out The Tempest, Act 1, Scene 2, 'Hell is empty . . .' "

"Come on, no one could change that," Runit said. He gestured around the glowing pages and soon the famous line was burning through the air in front of them. "Hell is empty and all the devils in fear." His mouth hung open on the final word. "But it should end with 'all the devils are here!' It has always been that way, for nearly five hundred years. Why change it?"

"Because, damn it. 'The devils are here,' can be interpreted to mean those in charge are corrupt. 'The devils in fear,' is something entirely different.

"Who?"

"Only the AOI could do it."

"Why not a hacker?"

"Because it isn't just a few lines. There are entire books that are missing or changed."

"What books?"

"Do you remember *The Hunger Games*? It came out in the early part of the century."

"Vaguely," Runit said.

"It was actually a series of three books. The first appeared in 2008. It was a huge seller. Movies were made."

"Right, dystopian. A greedy few ruled the impoverished many. Government-sponsored kid death matches for entertainment."

"Correct. Well, pull up the book."

Runit found it in his INU. "*The Hunger Games*, by Suzanne Collins. Here it is. What page?"

"It doesn't matter. Open anywhere."

He motioned and a random page opened up. Runit stared disbelievingly, and then checked other pages. Finally, he looked back at his friend.

"*The Hunger Games* is a book on nutrition!"

"Startling, isn't it?" Nelson asked. "The real book is gone forever. Replaced by a glorified cookbook. The movie doesn't exist anymore either, and the sequel, *Catching Fire,* has become a home safety manual. The final book, *Mockingjay,* is now about the language of birds."

Runit moved his fingers through the projected images of his INU until he found what he was looking for, then stormed silently from the room. Although he hadn't stated his destination, Nelson knew Runit's purpose. As a librarian, he always counted on books. A physical copy would put things right. It might take him a while to find such an obscure title.

The old writer added a bit more "tonic" to his coffee and zoomed his sister while waiting for the librarian to return. Phones had long been replaced by INUs and 3D representational communications. Like a turbocharged video chat, "zooms" were the norm, instead of traditional voice "calls."

"I've told him," Nelson said, when his sister's image appeared projected from his INU.

"I thought you were going to wait until . . ."she said, looking around the library. The INU's 360-degree cameras provided a view as if she were actually in the room, instead of just her holographic avatar.

"I did."

"Oh no . . . They're closing it sooner than we thought."

"Yes. Ten days."

"Will he help?"

"I'm not sure. He has fear."

"Don't we all," his sister said. "Where is he now?"

"Verifying the crime. Oh, here he comes. I'll zoom you back once I know," Nelson said, closing his fingers to end the zoom.

As expected, Runit had an antique copy of *The Hunger Games* in his hand.

"I had to get it from the lower level storage, but I can tell you there are no torgon recipes in this book!" He slammed the volume on the table in front of Nelson as if it had done something wrong. "How many more?"

"Who knows? Hundreds. Thousands. Probably many more than that," Nelson said.

"We're living in the longest period of peace in human existence. We enjoy the highest standard of living in history. Everyone is happy. Why censor books?"

"None of the reasons I've come up with are very friendly."

Runit stared at him, shaking his head. His mind traveled some of the same paths his friend had already been down. "Don't they think somebody will notice?"

"No one could prove it without physical books."

"There are collectors who have books," Runit said.

"Not many. And where do their loyalties lie?" Nelson asked.

"It's been more than fifty years since the government implemented the materialism reforms, which included the personal property limitations and possession taxes."

"The World Premier at the time said that it was all in the interest of environmental and resource protection," Runit said.

"Yeah, and they told the people physical books weren't needed anymore because everything had been made digital, and digital is forever."

"It was an easy sale. Especially with the promise that there would always be libraries in the big cities." Runit sighed. "But, as you well know, almost no one comes in anymore."

Nelson smiled sadly. "I count on the solitude."

"Twenty some years ago, when they started closing the great libraries around the world, no one really even cared. And now, after more than six hundred years of public libraries, I'm the last librarian."

CHAPTER FIVE

Nelson looked at Runit gravely, Do you recall the lines from Orwell's 1984? 'Every book has been rewritten, every statue and street building has been renamed, every date has been altered. And the process is continuing day by day and minute by minute. History has stopped. Nothing exists except an endless present in which the Party is always right.' He could have been talking about the world today. Runit, we've got to get the books out!"

Runit held up his hands and slowly spun 180 degrees, gazing at endless shelves of books, then turned back to the grumpy author. "Moving all these books would be impossible, and definitely illegal."

"It is our moral duty."

"It would get us a very long prison sentence."

"Only if we get caught."

"Caught? There are close to nine hundred metric tons of books in this old building, filling thirty-three kilometers of shelves. It can't be done. Not without people noticing. It would be a monumental task to do in the light of day." Runit couldn't help but laugh. "I mean, where would we get all the boxes?"

"Where's your courage?"

"I'm not going to prison because of rearranged letters in a few books."

"It's not merely a 'few books.' It's George Orwell, Vonnegut, Kafka, Saint-Exupery. Here's a list of thirty-two pre-Banoff authors I've identified, and forty-six post-Banoff books."

"I'm just a librarian," Runit said, barely glancing at the names glowing in the air in front of him. "And I'm not even that for much longer."

"You're not just a librarian, you're the *last* librarian. A responsibility comes with that. You have to take care of the books."

"What can I do? You think we can simply move all of them? We'd never get more than a few dozen boxes out before the AOI showed up."

"We'll find a way." Nelson rolled an unlit bac between his fingers. "They must be saved."

"It cannot be done."

"I thought you loved books."

"I do."

"Did you notice this author on the list?" Nelson pointed to the name. "Ray Bradbury."

"Which one of his books?"

"Do you have to ask?"

"*Fahrenheit 451?*"

Nelson nodded.

The irony was too much for Runit. "It was one of Harper's favorites," he whispered. The memory of someone he loved so much strengthened him in the way that only pain can.

The classic book, one of many she loved, was a sentimental favorite. It described a time when all books were banned and destroyed, but a small group of people memorized entire books in an effort to save them.

"Harper definitely loved that book. I recall many wonderful conversations with her about it when I was writing *Characters*."

"Your book about the novelist whose characters took over his life? She loved that one too."

"I based the character of Zinn on her."

"I know." Runit stared out the arched windows between the shelves on the other side of the room. "Harper had a way of penetrating a person. It wasn't so much the ability to understand them, although she was good at that. Once you met her, you felt her in every part of your life. The day after we first met, I flew down to San Antonio for a conference. That evening I walked over a bridge and knew she had been on that same bridge before, that it had been important to her. Harper confirmed it when I got back. She'd been there a few weeks earlier, and always went to that spot to think . . . crazy. And it happened all the time." Runit clenched his fists. Missing Harper occupied less time than it used to, but her absence left an unending echo in his heart. "Whenever I read a book," he continued slowly, "I could feel what she would have thought about it. Still, ten years after her death, I know what she would say to every question I have. How she would react to any situation. She was more than a person. Harper was part of nature the way rain and wind are. She was an experience, and everyone she knew swam in her existence."

"I certainly did," Nelson said. "She had that kind of presence. I mean each time I saw her, I felt as if my life changed."

"Yes," Runit said quietly. "Imagine living with that . . . and then . . . living without it."

"You're a strong man, Runit."

"Not really. I've just been keeping it together for Grandyn. How do you survive losing a mother like that?"

"It's probably only possible if a kid has a great father."

Runit cupped his hand to close his INU without returning his friend's smile. "We have to let the books go. Grandyn may have made it to eighteen, but he still needs me. I can't wind up in prison, or worse."

"Harper would look at it differently."

"Don't tell me what my wife would have done."

"You know I'm right."

"Of course I know. But she had a different kind of bravery, one that I've never been able to grasp."

"Grandyn inherited that from his mother. Why don't you ask him?"

"I'm not going to involve him in this. It would destroy his life. Do you think Harper would want that?"

"I think she'd want her only child to have a meaningful life, not one chosen by an overly cautious father."

"Damn you, Nelson! You know I've been gutted. Ten years raising Grandyn, trying to do what she would have wanted, hoping to get it even close to right. How dare you cite her name? And then dumping this 'save the books' trip on me. Who the hell am I to save the books? Why would I question the government? They seem to be doing a fine job keeping the peace. The world is pretty damn wonderful, if you ask me."

"Who are you? As soon as the library in Belgium closed, your fate was sealed. You're the last librarian. It's up to you. It's not just books. Movies and music are also being changed and disappearing."

"Oh, I suppose you want me to save them too?"

"No, the music will have to fend for itself. Songs have long been lost in digital wastelands."

"I've got a meeting to prepare for. Just leave me alone."

"Go then. I'll be here when you finish."

A couple of hours later, Runit found Nelson in a corner of the grand building.

"How'd the meeting go?" Nelson asked.

"Not good," Runit said. "'Read the best books first, or you may not have a chance to read them at all.'"

"Why are you quoting Thoreau?"

"They're going to burn all the books."

"A real-life *Fahrenheit 451*." Nelson pounded the table, glaring out of bleary eyes.

"Yeah, too expensive to move them. They said they're obsolete anyway. Still, they don't want the plan announced or acknowledged in case there are any sentimental bibliophiles out there who might raise a ruckus."

"*Obsolete?*" Nelson roared.

"They stated it as an obvious and emotionless fact. The same thing was done at the other libraries. A laser-controlled interior burn is conducted, and then the building is leveled. This one is almost two hundred years old. It'll be replaced by a fifty-two story glass tower."

"Are you going to let them burn the books, Montag?" Nelson asked, calling Runit by the name of the protagonist in Ray Bradbury's classic.

"Is your Whistler still active?"

Nelson nodded.

"Would it really be possible to get them out?"

Nelson, calm for the first time since they had started talking, nodded slowly. "I have a plan."

CHAPTER SIX

Lance Miner, the ultra-wealthy pharmaceutical tycoon, looked into the lights of his Information Navigation Unit and smiled, pleased the world's last library would finally be dark, and sent the report to another section of his advanced and over-worked INU. He flipped an old silver dollar, a relic of the pre-Banoff days when physical currency still circulated.

"Hell," he said as it landed on tails. His tired routine told him the library situation might require more work than it should. Heads meant easy, tails meant work. But the coin was sometimes wrong. *No one cares about books made of paper, they don't even read the digital ones that much these days,* he thought. And he'd seen the data. The AOI traced every sentence read, when a reader started or stopped, what they highlighted. In 2098, there is no privacy, and secrets are only good for a trip to prison or a death sentence.

If all went well, the library closure wouldn't even make the news. They didn't need any sentimental rabble-rousers getting in the way. Portland wouldn't miss the worn out relic. The world didn't need physical books anymore, and keeping the place open was an outrageous waste of money.

That was what the Aylantik government had told the county

officials. In reality, the closing had nothing to do with budget cuts or progress. Rather, shutting down the last library would bring to fruition a scheme to consolidate power that had been decades in the making.

"We must fight for peace," Miner said to himself. "Stability has to be maintained at any cost."

He moved a few fingers near the glowing orb and a three-dimensional full color world map appeared. After expertly manipulating the projected light, Miner quickly scanned through the twenty-four regions into which the globe had been divided by the founders of the Aylantik government.

Miner's friend, Polis Drast, was the AOI Pacyfik regional head. Although their friendship had always been a strategic relationship, he actually liked the guy, and Drast did a more than competent job in a difficult position. The Pacyfik included the western portions of what were formerly known as Canada, the United States, Mexico, and extended down through the South American continent. For some time, the Pacyfik had been a source of concern for the government. While there hadn't been any recent trouble, the area held a large population of readers, writers, artists, and other creative occupations, long known to contain a higher percentage of non-conformists. Miner referred to them as "Creatives," and his tone always left no doubt about his feelings toward them, as if he was using profanity.

The Pacyfik also had its history held against it. The Banoff consisted of two events: The nearly two-year pandemic, and the three-year war, which started during the second year of the plague. The major pockets of resistance had come from within the Pacyfik region, and they rallied mightily against the Aylantik coalition, which had been comprised mostly of former US and NATO militaries. The Aylantik were eventually victorious, and had since presided over seven decades of peace and prosperity.

Miner's interest in politics and world affairs had served him well. A fourth generation billionaire, he had expanded his vast family fortune in the world's leading industry, pharmaceuticals, through lucrative deals and patent fights. At his birth, Pharma-Force, Inc., the conglomerate controlled by his family, had been the world's ninth largest drug company. It now ranked number one.

Miner waved his arm through the air and a series of virtual monitors, or "AirViews," lit. The holographic AirViews, like just about every other digital component, were touch-controlled and linked to the "Field," the name given to what the Internet had evolved into – an all-encompassing grid that connected each aspect of daily life across the planet.

Miner flicked his pinky slightly through a view of global news and rolling rows of up-to-the-millisecond updates on the world financial market. Earth's population basked in wealth. Some had more than others, and some a lot more than others, but things were good for almost everyone.

Sarlo, a fit woman in her thirties, entered his office, ignoring the breathtaking Parisian skyline filling the window behind her boss. PharmaForce had offices across the planet, each looking out on a stunning scene, and when people commented on them, Sarlo liked to say, *"Lance collects panoramic views."*

Working for one of Nusun's wealthiest men might sound like a dream job to some, but Sarlo knew the reality – stress. And although her good-looking boss often said, *"Money comes cheap,"* she disagreed, believing the cost of wealth to be high. *It's just paid for by body and mind.*

"Yes, Lance?" she said, attentively. In her nine years at Phar-maForce, she'd gone from star-struck to disillusioned to great respect and admiration, but lately it had caused her some anxiety. Big things were happening, or about to, and Lance Miner was a "Force."

They traveled together regularly, but he had never made even the slightest inappropriate gesture toward her. Miner had long been happily married, with three children. His thick gray hair seemed to make him more attractive, but it was his face that made the fifty-eight-year-old command the attention of both men and women.

His features appeared so perfect that rumors abounded about his billionaire parents selecting each gene. He'd heard the talk, and it amused him because he knew it wasn't true. *"I'm just naturally handsome,"* he'd say, whenever there was an opportunity.

Sarlo had married and divorced during her time employed by PharmaForce, but she now had an understanding boyfriend who could handle her crazy schedule. Or, at least, so she hoped. Sarlo worried that it would get old for him too, but she wanted her job more than any man. The power, action, and stress were irresistible. She'd been a cheerleader and model before being recruited to be Miner's assistant. He preferred to be surrounded by beautiful people. *Insisted* on it, actually. But he also demanded brains, and Sarlo did not disappoint in that department either.

"Are they here?" Miner asked.

"Yes. Everything is ready."

CHAPTER SEVEN

Lance Miner's grandparents had been among the founders of the new world immediately following the Banoff. The founders had, in fact, saved the world from certain destruction.

When the pandemic began in 2025, eight billion people lived on Earth. By 2029, with the plague controlled and the subsequent war ended, the population had been shattered, with fewer than three billion remaining. More than two billion had died during the first year of the pandemic. Nearly three were lost in the next. If it were not for the inoculations developed jointly by the nine pharmaceuticals, including PharmaForce, the human race may have become extinct. The current population stood closer to 1950 levels. Strict controls had kept it steady for decades.

"I ought to be nervous," Miner said, smiling. Admiring Sarlo's perfect bronze skin and long brown hair was a good distraction from her lips and peanut-butter-colored eyes.

"That would be a first," she said.

When her boyfriend had asked what the legendary businessman was really like, she told him that Lance Miner possessed two traits that made him successful: brilliance and vision. She left out the third secret ingredient. Miner could be startlingly ruthless.

Today would be one of those times. They'd been preparing for it for more than a year. In the end, whenever she doubted his motives, Sarlo repeated her boss's mantra. *The ends justify the means.* The world had become a wonderful place. She, like most, understood they were living at the pinnacle of human history.

Miner's family, along with the other founders, hadn't just stopped the pandemic that was wiping out humanity. They had won the final war, drafted the new Aylantik constitution, and had restored order to a world spiraling toward anarchy and Armageddon. But maintaining the peace, even with a single government ruling a united Earth, was surprisingly far more complex than it had been in the pre-Banoff years.

The economy drove everything. In her college economics classes, Sarlo had learned about the old systems of capitalism and socialism, after which their full-opportunity economy had been modeled. *"The economy keeps the peace,"* Miner always said, *"and pharmaceuticals make the economy."* She knew it to be true. The pre-Banoff world had churned with poverty, hunger, desperation, revolutions, and war. They had none of that now. Even crime was almost nonexistent, and her boss was a major reason things were so ideal.

Miner still sat on the A-Council, and regardless of the other global governmental titles including the World Premier, the A-Council still held the real power.

"The General?" Miner asked.

"Yes."

"And the Premier?"

"Yes, Lance, they're both here, and waiting. Being late isn't a good start."

"Then let's see if we can make history."

CHAPTER EIGHT

Nelson looked around the room to make sure no other library patrons had entered. The library's staff of seven employees and a dozen volunteers were spread throughout the building. The big room was empty except for Runit and Nelson.

"We can't take all the books. While I'm making the arrangement to move them, you sort and decide which are the most important works to preserve. No sense taking a copy of a pro-government history book, romance novels, nature books, or other stuff that they'll never change."

"How is it going to be possible to move them undetected? It would take a million trips in LEVs."

It was the first time Runit had wished for the days when automobiles still drove on concrete and asphalt, and fossil fuels could power giant engines capable of carrying large heavy loads. Instead "LEVs," or Levitating Electro Vehicles, pronounced "lev" as in levitate, were light, driverless, car-like machines, equipped with small wind turbines and solar panels, that floated above solar powered roads embedded with an infinite amount solar panels.

"We'll need trucks, which means using the magna-lanes," Runit added. "That means permits."

The outermost lane of most roads were reserved for trucks, which required more energy and magnetic-assisted generation to allow them to carry bulk and weight.

"There's a bottling company next door. I know a guy there. He'll help us. The trucks sit empty for some hours during the night before the predawn loading for their early deliveries. We should be able to get it done in three or four nights, depending on how many trucks we can use."

"You've already talked to someone?" he exclaimed in his loudest whisper.

"There isn't much time."

Runit paced away, hands in the air.

"We can do this, Runit."

"We're going to prison."

"No."

"Okay then." Runit stormed back to the table. "*You're* the mastermind. We have the trucks for a few hours. Where are we taking all these books?" he whispered.

"To the Interstate. There's a freight service center where we can transfer them to empty fruit trucks."

"Fruit trucks? Another friend?"

"Sort of."

"Why will they be empty?"

"Heading south, back to the orchards."

The Aylantik government had contracts with several major companies in the space industry to control weather. They'd been doing it successfully for more than fifty years, but advances were slow. The best case was in the regions with mild winters, where they could maintain a year-round growing season, adjusting temperatures a few degrees and increasing rainfall.

"I'm no transportation engineer, but don't companies backload trucks once the cargo is offloaded so they don't drive empty trucks hundreds of kilometers?"

"Usually, but not with fruit. Some kind of health regulation."

Runit suddenly stopped as it all caught up with him. Something had been amiss for so long that he'd almost accepted it as normal, but it never felt right. Perhaps it had been his late wife's independent spirit, or the fact that his was one of the few jobs tied to the last century, but he never felt he fit in. He often thought, *The world seems like a giant jigsaw puzzle with the last piece missing.*

"Charles Dickens," he began in a whisper.

"What?" Nelson asked, thinking Runit had said, *"Call all chickens."*

"Dickens could have been talking about 2098. 'It was the best of times, it was the worst of times.' There's such a thing as *too* perfect."

"Yes," Nelson agreed. "How do they keep it so good?"

Runit looked down the rows of bookshelves, thinking for a moment that the ghosts of all those dead authors might wander in and tell him the answer, how to make it right, what to do. Long seconds passed, during which he returned to the present reality.

"Okay. Tell me this," Runit said, turning to Nelson. "If we take four nights to move the books out, what do we do during the day when someone comes in to request a book?"

Nelson waved his arm in a sweeping motion. "Do you see anyone here? I think we can risk it."

"That's a big risk."

"We'll figure something out," Nelson said, as if placating a child. "There's no choice. We have to do this."

"Of course there's a choice."

"What? Let them burn the last books on Earth? Cede control of the intellectual and artistic legacy of human history to an elite few whose aims we don't even know? Shoot, I'd rather do *self-immolation.*"

"That might be an easier way to die than crossing the AOI."

"Exactly my point. Why are the books so dangerous to them?"

CHAPTER NINE

The library had for a long time exuded the energy of a museum rather than an active center for community and learning. Runit felt partially to blame, but hadn't known what to do, but steal the books? That was way beyond atoning for mistakes he'd made as a librarian. "Why us?" he asked, as if really saying, "Not us."

"Because we're here. Because we understand the stakes," Nelson said, with the impassioned bravado of an angry poet. "The collective works of our species must be preserved."

"At great risk."

"Yes."

"We could lose our lives to an AOI laser, or land forever in an Aylantik prison."

"Yes, but what else would you do with your life? Finish your book? Or, like most people, be content being babysat, left to watch and generally obsess about sports and entertainment stars? It's all fluff. People waste their lives on fluff." Nelson opened a view into his INU. "But you're one of the bright ones, aren't you? You follow politics and the news. Well, I have some *news* for you. It's theatre. Sports heroes, film celebrities, rock stars, politicians, controversies of all sorts filling the daily news cycle, it's all just different channels of the same show. *Distract and keep them happy.*"

Runit glanced at his friend's Information Navigation Unit as if something inside might explain the ramblings. "What are you even talking about?"

"Save the books, and your life will have meant something. Let them burn, and it was just frittered away."

"Grandyn means something."

"What do I mean?" Runit's son asked, entering the cavernous room.

He looked like a younger version of his father. Thick sandy hair, worn a bit longer, a bit wilder than his dad's, but with the same intense look, like something had bothered him, perhaps more angst in his expression, but not much. They both had gray-blue eyes, keen and expressive, but what people always remembered was the Happerman smile. If it could be coaxed, seeing Grandyn or his dad smile was like going to a party.

"Grandyn, great to see you," Runit said, shooting Nelson a "shut-up" look.

"Dad, did you forget we're having lunch today?"

"Yeah. No. I guess I did."

Grandyn laughed. "Nelson, want to join us?"

"No," Runit answered for him a little too quickly.

Grandyn looked from his dad to Nelson, who'd been like an uncle to him his whole life. He wanted Nelson as a buffer, knowing he and his father would have the same argument about him going to college in the fall. Applications were due in a few days, and Grandyn was trying to stall until the deadline passed.

"I'd love to," Nelson said, grinning at Runit.

Nelson loved Grandyn, loved seeing that smile, and he saw it a lot. Nelson had been the counter to Runit's attempts to rein in his rebellious son since his wife died. He had been almost a surrogate mother, not because he and Runit were best friends, but because Nelson had loved Grandyn's mother too.

"Uh, Nelson. Another time, huh? Grandyn and I have something important to discuss."

"Dad, let him come," Grandyn said in a tone that told Runit he might skip the meal himself unless "Uncle" Nelson were allowed to attend.

He glared, irritated at Nelson. "Fine, but you're just an observer."

Nelson widened his eyes and then winked at Grandyn. "Sure, that sounds like me."

"Where are we going?" Runit asked, grabbing his coat.

"Pizza?" Nelson suggested hopefully.

As they emerged from the ancient building, bright evidence contrasted nearly two centuries of differences from the library's stuffy interior and the wonder of Portland 2098, which waited on the outside. Towers of impossible shape and structure competed in a skyline which rivaled many of the best in the world.

Great silver spinning buildings, looking more like gigantic drill bits, controlled by a magnificent feat of engineering, allowing every unit a continuous 360 degree view, no matter which "side" they started on. Other office and residential structures seemed more like massive glass kites, and several resembled huge metallic flowers or entwining vines climbing to the heavens. Even the city's many bridges flowed across the rivers as if they'd grown there, shaped by the wind and colored by the environment.

Cleverly concealed solar cells and wind turbines powered everything, from the glittery buildings to the sleek light-up roadways. Signage appeared only as needed, projected into the air in proper size and color, as if the world were designed for each inhabitant. Storefronts and ground level structures took advantage of construction materials, which allowed them to change as often as desired to suit promotions, seasonal needs, aesthetics, or simple preference.

The same advancements allowed most clothing, made from Tekfabriks, to change color and design as frequently as the wearer desired.

Runit looked into the sky as drones silently flew in the air-path, a kind of computer-controlled lane for the microcrafts which transported small goods, data, and monitored everything from air quality to bot, android, cyborg, and human movements. The flashy and fast world outside the library always made him anxious, as if he were trapped in an Arthur C. Clarke or Isaac Asimov novel.

The AOI's nearly infinite camera network, officially known as "Key Efficiency Locating Artificial Intelligence Safety and Monitoring System," was often referred to simply as "Seeker" by the general population.

Seeker recorded them leaving the library. Facial recognition matched, and the system's algorithms quickly assigned a risk level to the group. Only Nelson had any idea that such a thing was happening. Runit and Grandyn had a vague knowledge of cameras, but were oblivious to the profiling. Their meeting that day achieved a level four risk. A number low enough not to be tagged, but uncomfortably close to a five, which would have garnered extra attention. Normally, a father-son lunch would have been a zero. The elevation to a four came because books were involved, and mostly because Nelson was, by himself, a level three. If Nelson's sister had joined them, which she never did, the meeting would have actually prompted a live agent response. She was a four by herself, making the group an unacceptable eight.

Peace came at a price. War was easier to avoid than terrorism. The latter required constant monitoring. Who wouldn't give up all their privacy in exchange for peace? Hardly anyone remembered it any other way. The cameras were so small and advanced that only a few knew that they were everywhere. Seeker was an intricate network of hundreds of millions of micro cameras recording in real time. Cross-indexing and risk analysis happened instantly, with constant revisions and action assessments. AOI teams were always ready. The zero tolerance policy for threats to tranquility had served the Aylantik government, and the citizens of a united Earth, very well for more than two generations. Upcoming events would cause the footage of them leaving the library, and their subsequent meetings, to be reviewed by many humans. But by then, things would be spinning out of control.

CHAPTER TEN

The open-air rooftop pizza restaurant, located a couple of blocks away from the library, had excellent food. But, surprisingly, that's not why Nelson often chose to eat there. The restaurant, through a fluke in its design, proved a rare weak spot for Seeker. Its cameras were present, but one of the more dangerous aspects of Seeker was its ability to read lips, and that didn't work here.

The system was controlled by Design Taught Intelligence, or "DesTIn," an advanced artificial intelligence program which, oddly, had difficulty being accurate within areas of thermal air-movement. Since the eatery made use of large vents bringing heat from the building to create a wall of warm air against the cold damp January temperatures, it wreaked havoc on the Seeker surveillance system's DesTIn. A glass roof kept the rain out, but created another challenge for Seeker, as it monitored conversations through people's INUs. Angled glass, covered with raindrops, was also problematic. Even without his Whistler, the pizza place was one of the more secure public spaces.

Nelson was happy to see his preferred table available. The hostess ushered them to the private spot, located on a narrow overhang. They had all seen the panoramic view before, but looking at the Willamette River, dramatic at its confluence with the Columbia River, was always compelling. On rainy days the overhang could get misty, but today, Mt. Hood's dramatic beauty stood as if guarding the city. Grandyn pointed out the snowcapped peaks – Mt. St. Helens, Mt. Rainier – rising from the distant horizon like mystical white spirits. In the closer distance, a troop of perhaps eighty AOI agents flew in formation with only the aid of lightweight turbo-jetpacks on their backs. It was such a common sight that they hardly noticed.

Runit wasted no time bringing up college, and Grandyn, just as quickly, defended his position. "Dad, I don't want to do anything that a degree will help."

"As you've said before, but you still haven't given me an acceptable answer of just what it is you do want to do." They'd covered this ground on many occasions, but this time was different. The deadline was upon them, and they had a witness.

"I don't know yet. Why do I have to know? I'm only eighteen."

"Runit, he's had a job for three years. He's responsible. Why not let him take some time away from the classroom?"

"I didn't ask you Nelson."

"Dad, I love working outdoors. Maintaining the trails for the Parks Department makes me feel like I'm part of the environment."

"Great. Maybe you could move up in the Parks Department, or even get into the Forest Service, but that takes a college education. Environmental sciences, arborist, I don't know, but everything I can think of that you're interested in requires some kind of degree. You may like what you're doing now, but basically you're just a laborer. You're too smart for that, and believe me; when you get a little older, you'll get tired of the physical work."

"I'm not worried about that now."

"No one ever worries about that stuff when they're young."

"So why are you expecting me to be different?"

"Because you're *my* son."

"Oh, and who are you, dad? You're a librarian. A dinosaur."

Runit stared at his son silently with watery eyes and a clenched jaw before finally managing a quiet and steady response. "That's out of line."

Nelson nodded his agreement.

"Well, sorry, but . . ." he stammered. "I mean, sorry, Dad. Noble profession and all, but you're like the last one. What I'm saying is that it may be fine for *you*. It's just that I'm looking for something academics can't give me. My life is not in a book."

"Fine, but until you know what you want, you need to follow the course."

"I know what I don't want," Grandyn said. "I don't want to follow the course."

The waitress glanced over. Nelson also liked that the pizza place was one of the small percentage of restaurants that still used human servers. Most had shifted to some form of mechanical: either bots, cyborgs, droids, or drones. Nelson motioned that they still needed a few minutes. None of them had even looked at the virtual menus floating a few centimeters above the table.

"You have no idea what college can give you," Runit said.

"It can't give me adventure."

"So that's what you want? Adventure? Take the summer and go on a hike through the Rockies. Or if that's not enough, how about the Andes, the Himalayas?"

"We don't have money for that," Grandyn said.

"I'll borrow it."

"I can kick in some," Nelson offered.

"I'm not starting out my life in debt."

"It'll be my debt so long as you agree to go to college."

"Dad, that doesn't work for me. Maybe fifty years ago college made sense, but now knowledge is so instant. I just feel that continuing my education on the Field would be like going on a hike in a tuxedo. It's overkill for what I want to do. "

"'You can never be overdressed or overeducated,' Oscar Wilde," Runit said.

Grandyn shook his head, having long grown tired of his father's propensity for quoting authors. "'I have never let my schooling interfere with my education,' Mark Twain," Grandyn shot back.

Nelson laughed. "Touché."

"You want adventure? 'Education is the cheapest ticket you can ever buy for the greatest adventure that is life,' Willy Stuyvesant."

"'Self-education is, I firmly believe, the only kind of education there is,' Isaac Asimov," Grandyn said, glaring.

"Runit, he learned it from you," Nelson said, laughing harder. "Better quit while you're ahead."

"He's not ahead," Grandyn corrected.

"I lost my job today," Runit said.

His triumphant voice was suddenly defeated. "Oh no, Dad. Really?"

Runit nodded.

"Why didn't you say something?"

"I just found out."

"Damn," Grandyn said. "Dad, I'm really sorry. Are they closing the library?"

"Afraid so."

"Isn't there anything we can do?" Grandyn asked.

"No. As you just pointed out, it's the last one. Not a surprise really."

"Wow." Grandyn shook his head. "What are you going to do?"

"I don't know. They haven't sent me my option list yet, but for the first time since I got out of school I'm grateful for the zero unemployment policy. There was a time in the world when jobs weren't guaranteed."

"I know. We studied it in school. But getting a job from the option list isn't great either."

"At least I'll earn a living. I've been a librarian for twenty-three years. There aren't many people looking for that kind of experience."

"It's a hard way to make my point, Dad, but I want to do something that's exciting and isn't ever going to be deemed obsolete."

"I'm just trying to avoid your working from the option list yourself. Most people have a degree."

"I'm starving," Nelson said, and they all quickly agreed on their choices.

For fifteen minutes they discussed old times at the library. Grandyn had taken his first steps there and learned to read English and Com, even some older Spanish. When the pizza came, the tension between Runit and Grandyn had eased.

"So, pretend for a minute that I don't somehow convince you to attend college. What will you do?"

"Maybe it's a bad time to tell you, but I don't want you to worry about me." Grandyn looked from Runit to Nelson. "I'm thinking of joining the AOI."

Runit coughed to avoid choking. Nelson dropped a piece of pizza into his lap.

"Why would you do that!?" Nelson asked, beating a still stunned Runit to the question.

"You've heard their commercials: Adventure, Opportunity, Income." He downed a gulp of soda. "You remember my buddy, Trig? He signed up last summer after he graduated and loves it. It's an exciting career."

Runit and Nelson exchanged glances.

"You can't do that Grandyn," Nelson said.

"I thought Dad might not be thrilled, but I didn't expect *you* to be against me on this Nelson."

"I'm never against you, Grandyn. But you can't."

"Why not?"

Runit shook his head at Nelson.

"*What?*" Grandyn demanded.

"Because they won't take you?"

"Why not?" Grandyn repeated.

"No!" Runit snapped at Nelson, half raising out of his seat.

"Because they don't take people related to enemies of the state."

CHAPTER ELEVEN

Grandyn looked questioningly at his father.

"Nothing has happened yet," Runit said. "And it probably won't." He shot Nelson a deadly look.

"What. Are. You. Talking. About?" Grandyn squinted at both men.

"Nothing," Runit said while Nelson looked around cautiously and triple-checked his Whistler.

"The library is the last collection of physical books left and they're going to burn them."

"What?" Grandyn gasped. "Who?"

"Stop," Runit said. "I don't want him involved."

"How can he not be?" Nelson asked.

"Grandyn, the AOI is changing the contents of the digital books, and the only way to prove it, or stop it, is to save the physical books."

"And Dad's doing that?" He turned to his father. "Are you going to save the books?"

"I haven't decided."

Grandyn stared at his father for a moment. "How can you even hesitate if this is true? *Is* it true, Nelson?"

"I'm afraid it is more than true."

"Dad, your life has been books. Wait . . . why is the AOI even doing this?"

"We aren't entirely sure," Nelson said. "To stop dissension, to protect secrets, to control information, to lower the collective intelligence, all of the above?"

"My father, brave and true." Grandyn whispered the words Runit used to say to him when reading him bedtime stories as a little boy. "How can you hesitate?" he asked again in a shaky voice.

"You don't understand the risks involved," Runit said defensively.

"I can imagine the risks of inaction," Grandyn said.

"I promised your mom I'd protect you."

"Don't use me as an excuse." Grandyn held his father's gaze. "And Dad, is that really what Mom would want?"

"She'd want you safe."

"In a world without books?"

"Nothing is more important than your safety."

"Don't hide in that. I'm not a kid anymore. Your job is done." His look softened for a brief second. "But if the world isn't what it appears, if something is wrong and we can fix it, I'd rather be brave and true than safe."

Runit, Nelson, and Grandyn spilled into the library, still in the midst of their heated debate. It had continued in clipped and cryptic bursts since they had left the pizza place.

"Not here, not here," Runit whispered loudly as two stray patrons turned to see the source of the noisy disruption in the suddenly "busy" library.

Nelson and Grandyn followed him to a long, narrow room on the lower level which could have also served as a bomb shelter.

The 12,000-square-meter, three-story limestone building had been listed in the Register of Historic Places since 1979, and had undergone three major renovations in its nearly two-hundred-year existence, but the old place always seemed cold, even in summer. Labeled boxes of books and metal filing cabinets filled the room.

"He's not helping, and I don't even want him to know another thing about it!" Runit blasted as he shut the door.

"You can't stop me Dad."

"The hell I can't! Not a single book leaves this building without my participation."

"You'd sacrifice the books?" Grandyn asked.

"To save my son? I'd sacrifice everything." He paused. "And that *is* being brave and true."

"Listen to me," Nelson began. "We don't have to get caught. Our lives don't have to be ruined."

"What do you think the AOI is going to do when they discover we stole all the books they intend to destroy?" Runit shot back.

"They're going to burn them in the building. We're not taking *all* the books. The AOI guys come in and see a bunch of books on shelves, I doubt they're going to do an inventory."

"What percentage of books do you think we need to take?" Runit asked, calming down.

"You're in a better position to answer that than me, but I'd say as many as 70 or 80,000 titles," Nelson said.

"We've got over a million books," Runit said. "Maybe they wouldn't miss eight percent."

Nelson smiled. The world was about to change and all because of some library books.

CHAPTER TWELVE

Lance Miner turned up the rocking music and danced Sarlo around the office for a couple of minutes. "I never thought they'd answer today," he said, finally releasing her.

Sarlo sat down in one of the leather chairs, a little breathless. "They know a good idea when they hear it."

"Damn right!"

He relished the new authority granted by the A-Council. Their agreement to his proposal did more than give him significant power to attack his and the Council's rivals. It also signaled that nothing could defeat him in his bid to be the next A-Council President. That essentially meant the tycoon would rule the world, though he dared not say that out loud. Even the "elected" World Premier, chosen by the planet's 2.9 billion citizens, secretly answered to the A-Council. No Premier had ever been elected who had not first been selected by the secretive group. And, as Council President, Miner would effectively be making that choice, something he'd been longing to do for years. The ideal candidate would be smart, respected, and most of all, *obedient*. He had the perfect person in mind.

Still, there were many issues to deal with in the meantime. Most on the Council were advocating loosening the restrictions that had been in place since the Banoff, but Miner wanted a harder line. The most controversial of those was "41," named for its Constitution item number, which stated that each person was allowed only a single offspring, meaning a couple could have two children, but the limitation remained for life no matter how many marriages, or even if the child died.

The founders were concerned with population control for many reasons, risk of another pandemic and chief among them, limited resources. The Constitution held eighty-eight items, and most were restrictive in nature. But because that document had produced a near-utopian society, few were ever challenged. Even 41 had spawned a mini-industry of brokers willing to find buyers for your bearing-rights. If you didn't want a child – ever – you could sell your right to have one for as much as twenty thousand digis.

The restrictions weren't Miner's only concern. There were also rivals to the Council's power, including Eysen, Inc.'s CEO, Spencer Lipton II, usually referred to as "Deuce." His holdings went well beyond being the world's largest Information Navigation Units maker—Eysen INUs were considered the best—and included an interest in many leading technology companies across multiple industries. For decades there had been challenges to the Council's power, but not from the masses, to which the A-Council was only a rumor among the conspiracy theorists and Creatives on the fringes. The threats had come from fellow billionaires and, even subversively, from Lipton, the world's wealthiest man and only other trillionaire besides Miner. The Aylantik system favored the rich, but that didn't mean they always agreed. The government was more window dressing than a representative democracy. Corporations had long replaced nation states as the power centers.

"What about Lipton?" Sarlo asked.

Miner had invested heavily in Eysen's rivals in an effort to drain some of his seemingly infinite revenue stream, but it seemed impossible to catch the reclusive trillionaire in INUs. Deuce Lipton's massive StarFly Corporation also ranked number one in the world's fourth biggest industry – Space. In the past sixty years, it had grown into a vast segment of the economy. Space involved everything – exploration and mining, satellites, defense, science, tourism, etc. – and StarFly had divisions in all of them. Unlike Miner's public companies, none of Lipton's wealth was tied to the world stock market. His firms were all privately held.

"It's astonishing his family has survived. Why my grandfather didn't have his grandfather killed is beyond me," Miner said in a tone as close to anger as he ever got.

"Your grandfather did things like that, did he?" Sarlo asked, knowing the answer.

"Everything was at stake. Do you know that they offered his grandfather, Booker Lipton, a seat on the A-Council? And the son-of-a-bitch turned it down. He's the only person who ever said no to the Council."

"I know."

"Why would anyone turn down a position on the Council?"

"I think you know the answer."

"It doesn't matter. I'm going to use the new CAAP Board to finally rein Deuce in."

Miner rubbed his hands together. Corporate Assets Acquisition Parity, CAAP for short, was the gift the Council had given Miner. It would allow him incredible power to slow, and even stop, many of Deuce's business activities.

Miner sat behind his desk and began filling the space with AirViews from his INU. "And when Deuce resists CAAP looking at his holdings, and our new requirements for approval before any acquisition, he'll challenge the CAAP Board, and therefore, the A-Council. The public is going to love it!"

For the first time since the Banoff, the government would begin to analyze and curb corporate activity, specifically when acquisitions of other companies or assets would give a corporation an unfair advantage. The A-Council members and their friends would not face much scrutiny, but their competitors would endure much higher taxes and oversight.

Sarlo once again brought up her biggest concern for the scheme. "But even with the Council agreeing to let you form the new board, we don't know how they will deal with his violations and refusal to comply."

"The Premier will announce the CAAP Board later this week, once they find someone from the Economic Chairman's office to run it." Miner couldn't be the public face of Corporate Assets Acquisition Parity Board because of the obvious conflict of interest, but he would be in charge behind the scenes as the CAAP's liaison to the A-Council. "Deuce is obviously our first target, but it'll take months and months before we're ready to charge him, by then—"

"You'll be Council President, and soon after you'll have Polis Drast in as World Premier," Sarlo finished his sentence, knowing the plan too well.

"Clockwork."

"But they didn't give you everything," she said as AirViews interacted with holograms and light-forms depicting every possible outcome with CAAP in place. Most of the millions of outcomes led to disaster for Deuce Lipton, many even had Miner's greatest rival winding up in an AOI prison.

"That was another mistake I'll remedy once I'm in charge," Miner said, speaking of his request to have AOI remove Deuce pre-emptively. "They don't fully understand the threat he poses."

"To whom? You or the government?" she asked slyly.

"Hell, soon there won't be a difference."

"That may be why they didn't grant that proposal." She

glanced at the scenarios being crunched and quantified and saw a miniscule, but worrying, percentage showing Miner in ruin.

"I didn't push. I barely have the votes to get the presidency as it is. I don't want to jeopardize that, but I may just do it myself."

"You're not serious? You know what happens if you defy the Council and act autonomously."

CHAPTER THIRTEEN

Runit scanned the shelves. "It's a lot of books to move," he said, looking from Grandyn to the endless volumes filling the place, then back to Nelson. "And what happens if they come in with a list of specifics books—the ones we've taken—and they aren't there?"

"I doubt very much the guys they'll send in to do this are readers," Nelson said. "Of course they won't miss ten percent. How many books are down here in storage?"

"More than that," Runit said absently. "Still, generating the list of which 80,000 books we want and then pulling them is a huge undertaking."

"That's why you need help," Grandyn said.

"I guess there's nothing suspicious about you hanging around the library. You grew up in this grand old building," Runit said. "But you're to be nowhere near this place once the first volume goes out the door."

"Deal," Grandyn said.

"Not so fast," Runit said. "This is big stuff. I want one more concession." He put a hand on his son's shoulder. "You get those applications in."

Grandyn grimaced. "If that's what you want. But filling out the paperwork doesn't mean I'm going to college."

"At least it extends the deadline for us to be able to finish the debate." Then he looked at his son. "Does this 'not wanting to go to college' have anything to do with Vida?"

"Dad, my girlfriend, you'll be happy to know, agrees with you. Vida thinks I should get a degree."

"Well," Runit said, smiling, "I've always liked that girl."

Grandyn looked at his father and smiled.

Runit tipped his head slightly to his son and gave half a wink.

Grandyn nodded back and let his eyes linger on his father's for a second.

Runit understood the profound thanks his son had just given. It was an incredibly tough decision to allow his son into this thing, but three things made it easier: he trusted his son completely, and knew Grandyn was both smarter, and tougher than himself.

"Okay, now that we have that little bit of business out of the way," Nelson said, taking advantage of the temporary peace, "do you think we can get started on the monumental task of saving humanity's written treasures?"

"I can link a listing of our titles to your INU, and you can help tell me which books to mark," Runit said to Nelson. "But it's going to take a lot longer than we have."

"I think we can automate it somehow. There are whole categories we don't need to even look at," Runit said.

"We need someone to write an artificial intelligence program to sort, you know like DesTIn," Grandyn said. "The system could generate a list of books given the right parameters." Design Taught Intelligence,"DesTIn,"an advanced artificial intelligence program, was used to power the Seeker surveillance algorithms and thousands of other things throughout Nusun.

"Do you have any idea where we can find such a person?" his father asked.

"I don't."

"You might, if you were in college."

"Hey, that argument has been shelved," Nelson said. "Runit, please leave that alone until we get through this." He widened his eyes at his friend.

Runit nodded.

"Besides, I think I know the perfect person to do the DesTIn program."

"Seriously? Who?" Runit asked.

"Blaze Cortez," Nelson said.

Cortez, a famous and eccentric inventor, had created the DesTIn. But he owed more of his fame to his stunning brilliance and outrageous personality. Always controversial, and with a natural ability to offend, Blaze somehow managed to parlay those difficult traits into a talent for brokering deals. He seemed to have contacts in every governmental office, all the great universities, and any corporation that mattered.

"How do you know Blaze Cortez?" Grandyn asked.

"Forget it," Runit said. "I've heard he's connected to the AOI."

"It's not true," Nelson said. "I've known him for years."

"How well?"

Nelson fumbled for his bacs again before recalling the rules. "I-I met him at a party four or five years ago," he stammered.

"And have you seen him since?"

"No."

"He won't even remember you."

"Blaze Cortez remembers everything. They say he has an implant."

Tens of thousands of people, known as "Imps," had nano-computers, INUs, or other processors implanted into their brains. The transformation often left eerie effects, such as making them secretive, cold, and distant, resulting in Imps being shunned, and even feared, by respectable society.

"If he's really an Imp, that would make him all the more dangerous. Anyway, there's no way to find a guy like that."

"Not true. I know Deuce Lipton."

"Now you're friends with the world's richest man? Did you meet him at the same party?" Runit asked with a smirk. "Have you seen *him* since?"

"It wasn't at a party. I was doing a reading last year in San Francisco. He came up to me afterwards. Said he'd read all my books."

"All of them? I haven't even read them all."

"I wish that were true. You've actually read them all *twice*. How else could you point out the parts you didn't like so easily."

"Well, there really aren't that many parts I don't like," Runit said. "And, I admit, I may have read a few of them more than once."

Nelson flashed a rare smile. "Anyway, he's written me several times since. Not over the flash. Instead, a courier drops by an envelope. Always a few typed pages, signed with a scrawled 'DL,' nothing more." Because of AOI monitoring, a minor industry had grown around old-fashioned couriers delivering messages in a variety of untraceable ways.

"What do his letters say?"

"Mostly observations about my books. He really likes them. The man *gets* my work."

"You're so full of surprises." Runit looked at his old friend. "But I'm not surprised. Brilliant writers have often attracted an impressive, if not odd, assortment of fans. But tell me this. Who else do you know?"

"That's the wrong question. It should be *what* else do I know."

"Tell me," Runit said.

Grandyn never took his eyes off Nelson.

Nelson leaned close to Runit's face and then whispered, just loud enough that Grandyn could also hear, "You have to understand. They aren't rearranging the words for no reason. Deep motives exist for distorting the meaning of these works. It's a complex mess, but the changes leave a pattern as to exactly why, and what I'm seeing is very disturbing."

"There's a thin line between genius and madness, my friend."

"I see no line." Nelson stared at him until Runit's expression finally matched his in seriousness, then added in a grave, yet barely audible, voice, "We *have* to save the books. They're everything we are. They alone can bring the answer."

Runit nodded. "This thing we are about to do . . . I'm afraid we can't even imagine the trouble it will bring."

CHAPTER FOURTEEN

Nelson drove to Seattle. In the days before LEVs, the trip would have taken more than three hours. Now, with self-driving LEVs, he'd arrive in just under two hours, by about sixteen-hundred, which meant Nelson could be back home by eighteen-hundred, nineteen at the latest. Vehicular accidents and traffic were something the generations since his grandparents knew little about. The onboard-computers, equipped with DesTIn advanced artificial intelligence and Sophisticated-GPS, allowed all vehicles to float along the solar-roadways in the most efficient manner.

The City was home to many large corporations, two actually predated the Banoff: Boeing and Amazon, both competed with Deuce Lipton. The Aerospace maker was a competitor to StarFly, manufacturing satellites and space vehicles. Amazon didn't sell physical books anymore, but they had become by far the world's largest retailer. Amazon also made an impressive array of gadgets, including their own Information Navigation Units, marketed as "Fire INUs."

Nelson didn't expect Deuce Lipton to be in Seattle, but it was his closest office, and asking for the trillionaire's help could only be done in writing. Zooms and the flash system could not be trusted. They debated using a courier, but they weren't all trustworthy.

Lipton was the wealthiest man in the world, but no one knew for sure how much money he had. The old ways of measuring wealth had vanished with paper currency and exchange rates. These days, digis were the only legal tender. All of it was kept track of on the Field. Of course, holdings of land, companies, and stocks also still factored into a person's wealth, but one thing hadn't changed. It all came down to power.

Deuce Lipton had been born owning more power than anyone in history, with the possible exception of some long-forgotten Egyptian pharaoh. His grandfather was the legendary Booker Lipton, a man already fabulously wealthy when he created the first Information Navigation Unit, known as the Eysen-INU. These remarkable tech spheres completely destroyed the personal computer, tablet, and smart phone markets within a few short years. It took more than a decade before any other company came up with a reasonable competitor to the Eysen-INU. Even now, the half dozen other Information Navigation Unit makers combined only accounted for a third of the world's market.

Booker Lipton, a black man, back when race still mattered in the world, had made many enemies, but he owed that more to his ruthlessness as a businessman and a clear distrust for the government. He often said he knew corruption had existed everywhere because he'd bribed half the officials in the world. But the elder Lipton was also a paradox, whose deep spiritual beliefs drove him much more than a greedy pursuit of wealth. Booker had funded a group called the Inner Movement that, prior to the Banoff, sought to change the world from a materialistic, personality-based society to one rooted in love while living from the soul.

Then the Banoff happened, which not only interrupted the IM's plans, but also disrupted the track of human evolution and advancement. When more than half the species dies in the space of two years, an indelible mark is left on all who come after. The catastrophe gave rise to the Aylantik, which most agreed, that even with its faults, was superior to the old world and far better than the horror that might have easily followed such a devastating event.

Nelson wrapped his gray wool scarf around his neck against the damp January weather as he crossed the parking lot of Eysen, Inc.'s sprawling Seattle campus. He cleared security easily. One of the guards had actually finished Nelson's most recent book the night before, which proved to be just a foreshadowing of the cranky writer's good fortune that day. After giving his name and telling the receptionist that he simply wanted to leave a note for Mr. Lipton, she asked him to wait. After twenty-five minutes, he considered asking her what exactly he was waiting for, when an Asian-looking man approached.

"Nelson Wright, Mr. Lipton will see you now."

"He's here?" Nelson asked in disbelief, thinking he would have shaven off his stubble and put on a fresh shirt if he'd known there was a chance to see the trillionaire.

"Yes. He has read your note and would like to talk with you, if you have a moment."

He looked to see if the Asian man was joking. "Who wouldn't have a moment for Mr. Lipton? I've got all day."

The man smiled and bowed slightly. "Right this way, please."

After surviving a maze of secure doors, facial recognition scans, and two elevator rides, Nelson was left alone in a round waiting room that, although lit, featured an incredible planetarium on the ceiling.

Nelson lost himself in the stars. After almost ten minutes, Deuce Lipton entered the room, gliding across the floor, his legs fluid as if he might have been a dancer. "Nelson, I'm so glad to see you again," he said, placing his hands together and bowing his head slightly, in greeting. The custom of shaking hands had ended during the Banoff plague. "Sorry to keep you waiting."

Nelson had slid down in the chair during the star show and

almost tripped getting to his feet. Deuce, tall and wearing old-fashioned faded blue jeans and a dark, natural fiber shirt, appeared as a time traveler.

"Mr. Lipton, thank you for seeing me. I didn't expect—"

"Please, I prefer Deuce." He sat down across from where Nelson had been sitting.

Nelson was struck anew by Deuce's eyes, an intense shade of blue rarely seen on someone primarily from African descent. Nelson recalled reading that Deuce's maternal grandmother was from Norway.

CHAPTER FIFTEEN

The lighting inside seemed to change with Deuce's words, presenting stars or glowing colors depending on the context of what he said. "Nelson, do you know Fermi's Paradox?" he asked, as the vastness of the universe appeared above them.

"Yes," he said, a little surprised at the off-topic query, but he had read that Deuce had a great interest in space, and of course owned StarFly, the largest company involved in the various off-Earth industries. "With the infinite size of space, where is everybody?"

"Correct. Here it is, 2098. I've got bases on the moon and Mars, we've identified thousands and thousands of planets orbiting stars that should be able to support life, and undoubtedly millions more must exist among the trillions of stars in the observable universe," he said, motioning to the stars above them. "Yet no evidence has been found. No contact made."

"I believe we're looking in the wrong way."

"My grandfather thought that also. He followed the Transcension Hypothesis originally put forth by John Smart, a futurist born in the latter half of the twentieth century. He speculated that all of the advanced civilizations capable of reaching us have evolved so far beyond us that they've vanished within themselves to another dimension, a higher realm."

"Yes. I've read similar theories, but the AOI has done a fine job of suppressing debate and discussion on topics such as these."

"Yes, they have. Why do you think that is?"

Nelson shifted, uncomfortable answering without his Whistler, but surely Deuce's office was safe. Unless he'd walked into a trap. "Even before the Aylantik came to power, well prior to the Banoff, there have been those who sought to prevent the masses from looking within."

"Why?" Deuce pressed.

Nelson looked around and absently reached for a bac, but stopped before his fingers touched the pack. "B-Because," he stuttered, "that's where the power is."

Deuce held his gaze until Nelson, uncomfortable, looked away.

"Enough about everything. Let's talk about something much simpler . . . the matter you came to see me about today."

"I'm still in shock. You must have fifty offices around the world, and—"

"Yes, a happy coincidence that I happened to be in Seattle. And it's good you came to see me about this."

Nelson returned to his seat. "I know how you value books. I've always appreciated your interest in my writing. But I didn't think of actually involving you in our little project."

"Yes, I read your note. You'd like me to help you get in touch with Blaze Cortez."

"That's right. I believe he could create the DesTIn program we need."

"To cull the most important ten percent of more than a million books . . . that would be a large set of variables, and you are correct, it would require an AI source that only DesTIn could deliver. What kind of timetable are you working under?"

"Very short. Less than a week."

Deuce nodded, as if this short deadline could be doable. "And your note didn't say why you're doing this, 'project' I think you called it."

Nelson didn't know what to say.

Sensing his quandary, Deuce rescued him. "This has something to do with the closing of the library in Portland?"

"Yes, but how do you know about the closing?" Nelson asked, afraid he'd made a huge mistake. Of course Deuce knew. He could easily have been involved in making the decision to shut it down. For all Nelson knew, it could have been all Deuce's idea, but Nelson also had knowledge that Deuce and the AOI were not exactly friends.

"The subjects of information dissemination, education, and the preservation of art and ideas are ones that interest me greatly." His blue eyes focused like a laser on Nelson.

Nelson studied him. A large part of his success as a writer came from his ability to create believable characters. He owed that skill to a gift for reading people, for summing up all their traits in a few well-chosen lines. Deuce Lipton may have been insanely wealthy and wildly powerful, but he was still just a living, breathing collection of neurosis, baggage, bad habits, and unresolved issues like the rest of them. Nelson went with his intuition.

"We have that in common."

"Once you identify the books you want, does your plan include 'checking them out' from the library in the next nine days?"

Nelson nodded slowly.

Now Deuce studied Nelson. After some time, he stood and paced the round, windowless room. Nelson shifted uncomfortably in his chair, unsure if he should also stand, or stay seated.

For a moment, Deuce stared past Nelson, as if watching a movie that only he could see.

Finally, Deuce spoke.

"We tried to get the books out in Belgium. The mission failed."

It was the last thing Nelson expected to hear, and it both emboldened and devastated him. If Deuce Lipton had sought to save the books, it proved the critical importance of Nelson's objective. Yet the fact that the richest and one of the most powerful people in the world had not succeeded at doing the very thing they had just undertaken, meant the odds of succeeding were terribly slim. *It doesn't matter,* he thought. *The books must be saved.* He didn't know it then, Deuce actually agreed with him, but for *very* different reasons.

CHAPTER SIXTEEN

Deuce looked past Nelson, as if he could see a thousand miles, or a thousand years into the past.

"Why did *you* want to save the books?" Nelson asked, trying to ascertain if Deuce knew about the changing words.

"Same reason I keep gold and other physical assets. The 'virtual' world is not a place that feels very secure to me. It's too difficult to tell what is real. It's too easy to manipulate reality across the digital Field."

"I always thought you controlled much of the Field."

"It is too big for anyone to control. Once upon a time, there were safe places where one could keep a grip on things, but those days are long gone," Deuce said, still pacing. "That was before AOI and the war." He stopped and stared into the faux heavens above them.

"What war? We've had peace for seventy years," Nelson said.

Deuce did not immediately answer. Eventually, he sat back across from Nelson. "I wish I could help you more, but you have no idea of the complexities that exist within this simple peace." He said the last word as if growling out the word "piss" in disgust.

"Your note asked if I could get you in touch with Blaze Cortez. Are you sure you want to swim with the sharks?"

Nelson felt suddenly lost. A moment ago he sensed Deuce might get involved, providing a lifeboat, joining them in their attempt to rescue the books. Now, he realized he'd somehow botched the conversation and Deuce was throwing them overboard, "to the sharks" as he put it. On top of that, the powerful trillionaire seemed angry with him.

"I know enough to know we can't do this without some powerful help," Nelson said almost pleadingly.

"You have no idea."

"Will you help us get the books out?"

"No. That is not possible."

"Then, if you won't help, I have no choice but to seek the assistance of Cortez." Nelson pushed a hand through his shaggy hair. "I met him a few years back."

Deuce raised an eyebrow. "He has no loyalties."

"Is it true he's worked with the AOI?"

"Blaze Cortez has worked with everyone." Deuce stood up and pressed a button on a narrow gold wristband that Nelson had not noticed before. The stars above faded, replaced by images of Blaze and various buildings. The entire room became an INU display.

"Normally, within a few minutes, I could give you the current location of just about any person on the planet. Cortez, however, is a special case. His DesTIn expertise allows him to vanish in ways we mere mortals find most difficult."

"Does the AOI have the same system as you? I mean, can they also locate us anytime, anywhere?"

"Not quite as fast, not quite as reliably, but they can find you if they want you."

Nelson shivered. "Can they even track you?"

"You ought not to ask so many questions, Nelson."

"Sorry. Just the curious writer in me."

"Yes, but remember that what you might disguise as fiction will be understood as fact by those searching for the truth."

"I'm counting on it."

"The AOI and I have considerable history. They may not know where I am at any given time, but let's just say they know how to reach me."

Nelson considered this. "Are things . . . bad?"

The two men each knew things that the other didn't, but they shared a common knowledge that the wonder of their time wouldn't last forever, and it might not even be true.

"I've been in this business a long time," Deuce said, "and I've learned that the only thing more dangerous than asking questions is getting the answers."

Nelson nodded. He took what Deuce had said to be a yes. Things *were* bad.

Deuce looked up at the image of Blaze. "I tried to hire him a long time ago, but he's always preferred to be freelance. A few years back I even offered to buy his company, hoping to acquire his talents that way, but again, he refused. As I said, Blaze has no loyalties, and I value loyalty above all else." Deuce eyed Nelson, then continued. "But nobody does DesTIn like Blaze. It's in part his system that allows me to remain somewhat invisible."

Nelson thought about asking Deuce why he couldn't develop a DesTIn system as good as Blaze's, considering his vast wealth and his own corporations that were leaders in most tech industries, but decided he'd asked enough questions. Then, images suddenly appeared in the air above them that made him not only doubt their ability to save the books, but he wondered if he'd be in prison, or dead, by the end of the day.

CHAPTER SEVENTEEN

Polis Drast, AOI head for the Pacyfik Region, stared into the illuminated aura from his Eysen-INU, carefully considering the colors on the map that stretched from what used to be South America up to the Alaskan wilderness. The red areas, level-fours and fives, were not his greatest concern. He knew those hot spots and had plenty of resources in place to handle anything. The yellow-lit pockets, however, kept him up nights. There were too many of them, and the unpredictable nature of the level-threes presented challenges that could easily upset the delicate balance that kept the world one step ahead of what he feared most: a collapsing peace and a long spiral toward war . . . or worse.

He focused his deep blue barracuda-like eyes on details as the INU spun more AirViews into being. The vivid-holographic-displays floated all around, filling the space, revealing more profiles of possible troublemakers, instigators, and schemers. There were thousands who had been identified and were under increased monitoring, one mistake and one breath away from elimination by the AOI.

His favorite DesTIn-enabled bot rolled up. DesTIn had allowed bots and other AI-sourced machine assistants and servants to become near-human-like in their ability to "think" and communicate, yet found them far more advanced than their biological counterparts in their usefulness.

The bot displayed Drast's image. Mirrors had been replaced by digital-reflects long ago, providing complete 360-degree views of any part of one's body, with full magnification available, as well as hundreds of lighting filters. His dark hair had just a few touches of gray. It was short, but not too close, still enough to slick back with product that didn't look slick but kept everything in perfect place – a handsome politician. He'd come a long way from the Wyoming Area farm where he grew up, the eldest of two boys. Anyone who studied facial recognition and genetics would recognize that his clean-cut and polished looks belonged to a rugged, mountain man who would put up a tough fight and might be just as comfortable saddled up on a horse as sitting among floating INUs and AirViews. His Tekfabrik suit immediately changed to a more formal pattern and began a light temperature reduction, as he was about to speak with his boss.

"The Field-View is live," a digital voice announced as his regional map was replaced with images from the other twenty-three AOI heads, along with the AOI Chief. He was surprised to see the World Premier's Security Chairman also present. In his seven years as Pacyfik head, he'd never known anyone from the WP's close staff to attend.

The Chief and two-thirds of the AOI heads were women. Being white also put Drast in the minority, but in 2098 skin color wasn't the issue it had once been for the world. There had been much blending. The majority of people were a varied and lovely light shade of brown.

The AOI monitored the Field, Seeker, and many other factors, then continuously dissected and assimilated the resulting data in a massive DesTIn-based system which allowed the government to anticipate trouble before it occurred. Nusun may have been led by humans, yet Design Taught Intelligence, "DesTIn," and other advanced artificial intelligence programs actually ran the world. Incredibly complex algorithms interpreted voice tone, speech patterns, body language, word choice, and interactions of the planet's 2.9 billion citizens.

Privacy, an antiquated idea, didn't hold the same romantic notion it once had. Still, most people were completely unaware of how sophisticated the system had become, and how devastatingly heavy-handed the AOI could be if you were thought to be a threat to the peace. Only thirty-eight percent of those arrested were given a trial, as the Aylantik Constitution did not guarantee this right. Many charges allowed no trial option, just a straight shot to prison or execution, and both of those carried a wide spectrum of variations in the exact implementation of the punishment.

"We begin with the Pacyfik," the Chief said. A perpetual hardness in her expressions, even when smiling, seemed to fit her job as the world's number one enforcer. A short, military-style haircut, always kept a dusty shade of brown even though she was close to sixty, completed her tough demeanor that was neither cultivated, nor contrived, but rather totally natural for the one-hundred-push-ups-and-fifty-sit-ups-a-day, highly intelligent leader of the AOI.

"Thank you, Chief." Drast was not surprised, nor unprepared. He delivered an eight-minute summary of the current state of his slice of the world. Most of it had been routine. Drast, like all regional heads and the entire AOI, held a tight grip.

"The library closing in Portland," the Chief began. "Is it anything to worry about? We had a few issues in Belgium last year."

"I've studied both the Belgium and Australia closings, and other than Deuce Lipton dabbling in bibliophilia, it was textbook, no pun intended."

"No pun, I'm sure," the Chief retorted. "However, although we never uncovered Lipton's reason for trying to obtain those books from the Belgium library, knowing the man as I do, it would be foolish to assume he is simply a wealthy bibliophile pursuing a hobby."

"Seeker has reported nothing concerning Lipton and the Portland library."

"Good. But Seeker isn't foolproof, particularly when it comes to Deuce Lipton."

"All indications are for a quiet ending to that chapter . . ."

The Chief cleared her throat at Drast's second attempt at levity. "See that it remains quiet then."

"Chief, is there anything more to this than a library closing?" he asked, eyeing her carefully.

She paused, perhaps for a fraction too long, "Only that it is the last library, and located within a Creatives-heavy section of the Pacyfik."

"I'll give it extra attention."

"Good," she said, flipping her hand to change her Information Navigation Unit displays. "Chiantik."

Drast relaxed as she called the next region and began shuffling his INU until he reached an open AirView connected to a subordinate. He sent him a flash to pull a full risk assessment on the library closing.

Drast was relieved when the Chief closed the meeting with her standard, "Peace prevails, always." He immediately double-checked the Seeker and ran complex crossing reports on Portland. He assumed the Chief's interest was due to Lipton's attempt to interfere with the Belgium closing. Deuce Lipton had always been a difficult and delicate matter for the AOI, and the tensions went well beyond the simple fact that the Aylantik government considered the world's wealthiest man to be a renegade.

There were rumors, which Deuce was fully aware of, that the AOI had something to do with the death of his father. Even the prior generation, Deuce's grandfather, Booker Lipton, had history. The A-Council, which had formed the AOI from the wreckage of the world's intelligence agencies that existed prior to the Banoff, had offered Booker a seat on the Council, and he'd turned it down. The suspicions between the Liptons and the government, Drast had heard, had even existed earlier, but in the post-Banoff world, Booker's rebuff of the Council had cast the die for seven decades of distrust.

The Chief was being careful, but not overly cautious. She knew it would be difficult for Deuce to interfere with Portland's closing without being detected. Still, she considered seeking permission from the Council to brief Drast on the ultra-classified Data Arts Correction And Revisions project. DACAR had been going on in some form for four decades, and even she hadn't fully been brought up to speed, but she knew enough to know it was nearing completion. The closing of the final public library merely signified the culmination of the A-Council's mission to remove any intellectual threats to their power.

DACAR had long been at the center of the A-Council's three-pronged arsenal to counter or suppress any mass opposition before it took root. The other components were simply dubbed "Removal" and "Surveillance."

The Council had learned, from the centuries that led up to the Banoff, that fear did not represent a long-term strategy to manage a population. They wanted everyone happy.

CHAPTER EIGHTEEN

Blaze Cortez owed Deuce a favor, or he was just curious by nature. Either way, he agreed to meet with Nelson. Even with a Whistler and all of Blaze's tricks, the conversation needed to be in person. Blaze got word while somewhere in Mexico, but he had a plane and a pilot so logistics never bothered him. They set the meeting for 2300 that same night at the Portland airport.

Nelson would be exhausted – his bedtime typically hit between 2100 and 2200 – but he couldn't disregard "the winds of fortune," as he called his string of luck that day. First convincing Runit, then actually sitting across from Deuce, and finally Blaze Cortez flying to Portland to meet with him? He took the successes as a sign that he had a solid plan with "right" on his side. But the high level of interest, coupled with the jarring images he had seen at Deuce's office, confirmed what he'd suspected all along: closing the last library was about far more than just books.

Blaze's long, chocolate-brown hair fell just below his shoulders with strands crossing into his eyes, which he occasionally brushed away. A short mustache and trim goatee framed a nearly constant sly smile, giving the impression that Blaze knew something no one else did. And he probably did, thought Nelson.

"Drinks?" Blaze asked even before saying hello.

Nelson wasn't put off, remembering him as being gruff, and Deuce had warned him that Blaze's social skills were "somewhat unique." Still, it seemed as if Blaze had no memory of their previous meeting.

"Sure."

"My grandparents were Spanish. Yours were apparently bakers in the old US Midwest," he said, poking a finger into Nelson's doughy belly.

"Uh, no." Nelson tried not to sound irritated, a state he often resided in.

"Did I offend you Baker-Boy? Tsk, tsk. But you're descended from paper-white folks?"

Nelson gave a confused nod.

Blaze ordered drinks. Tequila for himself and water for Nelson. "I just think you should watch the calories. Have you ever been to one of the fat farms? They aren't very friendly."

Nelson caught the waiter and changed his water to a rum and coke.

"Okay, but I'm already questioning your ability to do what you say."

"Why is that?"

"You're clearly a sloppy, and therefore reckless, man, Nelson. I don't like messes."

Nelson fought his temper. "I assure you I am neither." He stared into Blaze's eyes. The irises resembled a sandstorm.

"We'll see . . ." He took a pen-sized device from his coat pocket, placed it on the center of the table, then found another object the shape and thickness of two quarters and put them down in front of Nelson. "Place your INU on top of this." He pointed to the little round disc.

Nelson did as he'd been told.

"You have my time as a favor to Deuce. However, getting my commitment is something entirely different. I'm leaving as soon as I finish my drink," Blaze said as the waiter set the glasses on napkins and left them alone. "Unless you've convinced me by then."

"Do you recall that we met at a party in Santa Fe some years back?" Nelson finally asked.

"Of course I do. You were a few kilos lighter then, but still eating more than your share. Black button-up shirt and a black leather sport coat. Did you dress that way hoping it would make you appear slimmer, or were you just trying to be cool? Neither worked."

"What is the fascination with my weight?"

"It is not fascination, it is an admonishment. Was I not being clear? Forgive me Baker-Boy, but I prefer precise over nice. I've read some of your books. You write well. In fact, your prose reads as if it were written by a lean, muscular man younger than yourself. Is that where your energy goes? Your will power?"

Nelson stared at him, considering options. Some would leave at the insults, others might hurl some back. There might have even been a compliment in there somewhere.

Nelson took a gulp from his drink and smiled. "Were you this way before the implant?" he asked.

Blaze squinted, unfazed. "Do you know why people get them?"

"Because they want to be smarter than they are. Smarter than the rest of us."

"They want to be like me." Blaze's smile widened. "I helped develop the first ones. My artificial intelligence DesTIn technology is still used in them. Nothing better out there. So the rumors began that I have an implant, but I do not."

"Then you just happen to remember what a person you only met briefly four years ago was wearing?" he asked, refraining from calling Blaze an "Imp," the slang for people with implants. Imps had become quite common in the past twenty years, with their numbers exploding during the prior decade due to reduced cost and increased availability. Several communities had sprung up around the world where the elite, often odd, thinkers gathered.

"That's not unusual. If, however, I could tell you that you were drinking fruit juice with a straw, that you had a cut on your right hand, that your fingernails were too long, that you signed a book for a woman in a hideous green dress using a silver pen that wrote in black ink and that the woman had on a brown scarf that made her look like a Boy Scout in drag, and that the party had two bartenders, both were clearly of Hispanic descent, their names were Roberto and Martin, and would you like to know how many drinks they served?" Blaze paused.

"Why do you deny you have an implant?"

"Why do you deny the obvious?" he said.

"Which is?"

"That I don't *need* an implant. I have tuned my mind so that it's vastly superior to yours, and everyone else's for that matter." He downed the remaining liquid in his glass. Nelson noticed a gold and black ring on his right hand. It caught his attention because men rarely wore rings anymore. "And you have not convinced me to help you Baker-Boy. Quite the contrary, in fact."

CHAPTER NINETEEN

Nelson, anxious to get the meeting back on track, tried again. "Let me buy you another drink . . . please."

"The first was surprisingly adequate. Yes, I'll have one more," he said looking into the INU and noting the time. They'd been together less than fifteen minutes. Nelson signaled the waiter to bring another round. "But you shouldn't. Does it bother you to eat more food than you need? What if we hadn't conquered hunger?"

"But we have."

"People like you could send us to the pre-Banoff days."

"I need a program that can determine which books out of 1.6 million are worth keeping," Nelson said, deciding it was foolish to spar with a man like Blaze.

"Because?"

"The government is closing the world's last library of physical books."

"And this is important why?"

"The books will be gone."

"So?" Blaze asked with faux fascination while the waiter replaced his empty glass. "We already have everything that has ever existed digitized."

"Yes, but—"

Blaze took a large sip from his drink and pointed to it as if it were an hourglass.

"They can change those," Nelson said slowly and quietly.

Blaze nodded, while rubbing his hand on his chin thoughtfully.

"Who are *they*? And why would '*they*' do such a thing?"

"I have a theory. There are 2.9 billion people on the planet, yet most of the wealth is controlled by less than one percent of the population. Something like twenty million super wealthy."

"Like our pal Deuce."

"And you."

Blaze laughed. "Me? No you've got me mixed up. Deuce is a trillionaire, and most of the folks you're talking about are billionaires. I'm just an average poor old millionaire."

"Yeah, I've read all about you. Public estimates peg your worth at six hundred million, but you're a genius at DesTIn and concealment. Many believe you're actually a billionaire with a substantial amount of billions."

"And what do you believe, Baker-Boy?"

"It doesn't matter. Either way, you're in the super-wealthy one percent."

"Then let me hear your theory about my little club of millionaires, billionaires, and Deuce."

"My theory is that the one percent or, more precisely, the top one percent of the one percent, are actually running the world. The government, elections, and the other trappings of our glorious worldwide democracy are merely theatre."

"An illusion?"

"Yes."

"A good one."

"If by good you mean that it is effective at fooling most of the population."

"That is what I mean."

"Does it fool you, Blaze?"

"Ah, but you forget I am in the one percent."

"But are you in the one percent of the one percent?"

"That is quite a question for you Baker-Boy. Because if I am and you're right that my club is secretly running the world, then you'll probably not wake up in the morning," Blaze smirked, then finished his drink. "Might not even make it home tonight."

"I have no idea how much money you have Blaze, but I have two reasons to believe that you're not going to turn me in to the AOI."

"I'd love to hear them."

"You're too smart for that game, and I'm guessing you'd not get along with whatever kind of group is in charge. I think you know about it, but you prefer to stay on the outside and play the game."

"A writer's mind is a dangerous place to sit and think Nelson."

"I also don't believe Deuce would let me meet with you, if you were going to have me killed."

"Are you and Deuce that close, that he'd be worried about keeping you alive?"

"He likes my books."

"Ah, yes, the books. So this global conspiracy of super-rich tyrants, what do they want with all the books?"

"I don't know. But there is something in some of them, maybe a lot of them, that can damage those in power, possibly unravel the whole thing."

"Do you ever look at the polls? Are you aware that the citizens of our sweet little planet are almost unanimously happy? Life is good. Seventy-five years ago, before the Banoff, this would have been considered a utopian world. We have no war, no hunger, no poverty, and disease is almost completely under control."

"I know."

"Disease is almost completely under control," he repeated, "after billions of our ancestors died of Banoff plague! And we live without war and virtually no crime. Who cares about a few damn books?"

"*They* do."

CHAPTER TWENTY

Blaze remained silent for a moment as he peered into the projections from Nelson's INU. Then he made some gestures above the pen-sized object he had set on the table earlier. "Tell me exactly what you want the program to find."

"You'll help?"

Blaze pointed to his empty glass. "You're out of time. Talk fast."

After Nelson's explanation, Blaze frowned. "You're asking me to design a program in less than twenty-four hours that is capable of assessing the level of contentious ideas contained in each book? One point four million books?"

"Can you do it?"

"If I could, I believe the AOI might pay handsomely for such a program." His expression did not change. "Is Deuce sponsoring you?"

"I don't know," Nelson said, unsure and worried.

"You ask for something, a thing only *I* can provide. Do you not think I deserve payment for such a product?"

"Of course, but—"

"But? Do you realize the danger? Do you imagine that your

little Whistler will keep the AOI from descending on you with laser bullets, wiping the imprint of your life from the digital world as if you were never born?" His voice had not risen, he had hardly moved, yet the tension in his speech built like a frantic native drumming. "The books you've written will vanish and burn, along with your library. They can take everything with one click. *Ev-er-ry-thin-g!*"

"That's why I came to see you."

"Of course it is, but I am not a charity. I don't give a damn about you, or *your* books, or a *million* books. I serve only myself. The world is only here to make me comfortable, do you understand?"

Nelson swallowed hard, his mouth suddenly dry. He simply nodded.

"Good. I can do this for you. *I* will give you *everything*, but you'll pay me ten million digis upon delivery." He stared at Nelson.

Nelson nodded hesitantly.

"Are you saying yes? Because I'm not feeling confident in your answer."

"I'm not sure I can."

"Then I'll seek payment from the AOI."

Nelson could not conceal his fear. His eyes darted around the room as if agents might arrest him any moment. He licked his lips repeatedly.

"Don't worry, I probably won't mention your name . . . initially."

"Maybe we should forget the whole thing. I'm sorry to have wasted your time," Nelson finally managed to say.

"Too late for that Baker-Boy. I've already started work on it. I've got half of it designed in my mind. And besides, are you going to move a million and a half books, then find a safe place to hide them *all* because you aren't sure which are the important ones? Or maybe you'll try to do the separating by hand."

"I don't know."

"Don't think Deuce is going to help you. The AOI knows every time he takes a leak. He may have the world's biggest fortune, but he's a prisoner to the shadows." Blaze stood. "A bunch of books aren't worth the risk to Deuce. He learned that the hard way already."

"You have so much money, why do you need another ten million?"

"It's true, DesTIn has been good to me. Developing the best advanced artificial intelligence program in existence has helped me stay within that one percent you're so worried about. But my life style is expensive. It's cheap to live average, that's the design. But I am different, and I mean to walk that edge to a lighted place."

"You've lost me."

Blaze laughed. "Of course I have. Baker-Boy, you know nothing about me. What you read on the Field isn't who I am." He sat back down and leaned close, so close that Nelson could smell him, lime and salt-air. "I see visions you cannot imagine," Blaze whispered. He scooped up the disc and pen-objects. "You'll have the product in twenty-four hours, probably less. And the money will be ready?"

"Uh, uh," Nelson hesitantly coughed.

"You get the money, or you're going to have a torgon problem much larger than which books matter."

He left Nelson sitting there with the drink check and mentally drowning in terrifying thoughts of the AOI coming for him.

CHAPTER TWENTY-ONE

Driving home from the airport, Nelson thought again about what he'd seen on the screen at Deuce's office, images of AOI raids and its secret prisons. There had also been scenes of executions, all by lethal injection, which really got to him. Hundreds had filled the air above them. Deuce wouldn't tell him how he'd obtained the images, but they were frightening.

"Still want to steal library books?" Deuce had asked.

Nelson had heard all kinds of things about the AOI, even knew some things first hand, but seeing it happen was like discovering that your best friend was a serial killer.

"A peace maintained by that much death is a false peace," Deuce had said. "You want to change the world, stick to writing books. Taking the ones that have already been written will just get you killed, and the peace will go on and on and on."

Deuce had stared off as he said it, as if trying to wade through a complex world of betrayals and false illusions that Nelson knew little about, at least outside of books. But Nelson might know more than he thought.

Nelson shook off the nightmarish images Deuce had showed him as his tired mind returned to Blaze. It was true that the world seemed a wonderful place. Certainly in all of recorded history it had never been better. Even with the prisons and executions, they paled to the millions lost to wars prior to the Banoff. They were enjoying an unprecedented stretch of peace, along with full employment, almost no crime, and no poverty. Even the environment had not been in such good shape for at least three centuries.

Once Earth's population had been more than halved by the Banoff, the carbon footprint of humans became manageable. Then, with the implementation of tough environmental laws, things had improved rapidly. Fossil fuels were phased out and banned, new rules made it illegal to manufacture anything that could not be recycled, and solar, wind, and other renewables powered everything.

Other than the AOI, which generally didn't interfere with most people's lives, there were few things to complain about. Lack of privacy was the most common gripe, although people generally agreed it was an easy trade for their utopia. Besides, no one alive really remembered what it had been like before the Banoff.

Nelson only knew from his grandparents and books. Back then one could assume conversations would not be monitored, and that every association and connection would not be tracked and analyzed. But as many said, and Deuce so clearly pointed out, "peace comes at a price."

There was another source of criticism against the Aylantik regime, stemming from the government's policy of discouraging the formation of religious organizations. Many of the people in the raids Nelson had viewed in Deuce's Seattle office belonged to religious groups worshiping in secret.

Ironically, it had begun just prior to the Banoff when the Catholic Church had collapsed in scandal. Within months of that shocking development, most governments around the world had revoked tax-exempt status for all religious institutions. Then, in the disarray following the massive deaths of the Banoff plague and the Aylantik-Pacyfik war, most churches, as well as just about every other institution, crumbled. The few remaining religious organizations were made illegal in the new constitution. The state allowed people to continue to worship however they saw fit, as long as it was not done in groups. The early Aylantik government took the position, still held seven decades later, that organized religions encouraged separateness. And while Aylantik was trying to save and unite a wounded and scattered world population, it had determined that separateness would only encourage war.

The Aylantik constitution also limited freedom of the media, but most saw that as a good thing. It had long been a less than trustworthy source of information. In the years since the Banoff, the constitutional restrictions, combined with instant communication and sharing through INUs, a lack of crime, and the absence of war, relegated the media to a few small and basically irrelevant phases on the Field.

None of that mattered to Nelson as the road took him home. He had less than twenty-four hours to secretly raise ten million digis. Impossible. And even if he did figure out how to get the money, he felt as if he'd just made a deal with the devil. Blaze Cortez might even be worse though, because he was real.

Runit would already be asleep. Nelson wanted to wake him and tell him all his news, but it would have to wait until morning. That is unless Blaze turned him in before dawn. If that did happen, he hoped they'd kill him in his sleep. Then what would death bring? One of the novels he'd written featured a man who died, but instead of blackness and nothingness the man found everything. He had appeared in a colossal, glowing world in which nothing existed except energy, love, and forms of thought. Nelson had never really been satisfied with his description of that vision. The book had actually been his worst seller, but it brought him his most loyal fans and his first notice from the AOI.

Much had changed in his life since then, since his eyes had been opened by the accidental writing of a cult classic. If the AOI had never bothered him he wouldn't have known what he knew, and certainly he wouldn't be trying to save the dusty old books from a forgotten library.

But they *had* bothered him.

As his car pulled into his driveway, so close to sleep, his final thoughts were of his sister as he typed into his Eysen-INU, "If I die tomorrow, I know that an endless and beautiful world of light will be waiting. And in that place of everything and nothing, I will finally feel full."

CHAPTER TWENTY-TWO

Tuesday, January 30

Runit arrived at the library early so he'd have an hour before staff showed up, and another hour until the public would be allowed in at ten hundred hours, but it was usually closer to lunchtime before patrons straggled in, and rarely more than a few.

Runit walked through the canyons of books, wondering which ones contained secrets that the government wanted silenced. He hadn't slept well, imagining the holocaust that awaited the 1.4 million volumes in his care. The books had, at times, been a burden to him, but never more than now. Yet he believed in them, and in what they offered humanity.

"Books are more than words, they're dreams, ideas, and answers, and that is why they fear them," he said to himself.

Perhaps he wasn't as devout a follower of books as Nelson, probably because he'd never published one himself. His resentment of that fact caught in his throat, taking him by surprise. In his own way, he'd shared the wisdom of the books with thousands through his role as head librarian, but that hadn't been enough, even if it had led him to this point in time where innocence could fade into the intelligence of disobedience, and thus change his destiny. Maybe now, with the library closing, he could finally write his own book. A single story always festered in him: a hero of the pre-Banoff wars realizes peace is unattainable in the corrupt world. No one would buy it, but he could write it anyway.

As he descended, he counted the ninety-two steps of the main staircase, as was his habit. A kind of silent meditation. He scoured the shelves for important work, filling boxes, but after almost an hour the task overwhelmed him. It would be impossible to find and save the books that mattered most, the ones that could change people, transform a society, and threaten a government.

At zero-nine hundred, as other staff members streamed in, he zoomed Nelson over flash, waking him with a quote from F. Scott Fitzgerald.

"So we beat on, boats against the current, borne back ceaselessly into the past."

"Reading Gatsby? Always a good idea. What time is it?" Nelson asked sleepily. His INU glowed with Runit's image. Nelson didn't motion on his video link, so Runit could only hear him.

"Just past nine."

Great, less than fourteen hours to live, he thought. "Sorry. I didn't sleep much." He slid out of bed, still groggy and stiff. "I'll be there in an hour."

As the zoom ended, an older volunteer, a woman in her sixties, told Runit there was a large delivery at the back door. Runit was puzzled, as nothing was expected. The loading dock went months with no action. The truck driver had already unloaded six large cartons. Four of them were one meter by one meter. The other two were slightly smaller. Runit had never heard of the company from which they originated, but he signed for them anyway. As the truck pulled away, Runit opened one of the bigger ones and saw some sort of machine. He was looking for a manual or paperwork when a man climbed up on the dock, startling him.

"Runit Happerman?" The guy checked his Information Navigation Unit and confirmed Runit's ID. All INUs had a built in Facial Recognition Identification Grid system, or "FRIDG."

"Yes," Runit answered hoarsely, scared the AOI was already on to them.

"Message for you." The courier handed him a plantik sleeve. The naturally derived plantik had replaced plastic sixty years earlier. The sleeve had a tamper-proof code.

Runit thanked the courier and waited until he was out of sight before taking out his INU. There was a code waiting on his flash-view. He touched the plantik code panel in the proper sequence and it opened, allowing him to pull out the paper inside that otherwise would have turned black and disintegrated.

Strapping machines delivered. Best way. Approximately twenty-five books per bundle. No signature.

It took Runit almost half an hour to unwrap and wheel in the four strapping machines. Each was about the size of a three-drawer filing cabinet turned on its side. Luckily, they had legs and casters, so once unpacked they were easy to move. The other boxes contained large spools of black, one-inch-wide plantik strap-ping. He assumed that the "gift" was from Deuce Lipton. Nelson must have made contact.

Things are looking up, he thought. The strappers were actually a huge gift, since part of his fitful night had been spent trying to figure out where to get thousands of boxes, and then how to get them into the library without attracting notice. Problem solved.

Once back inside, the same volunteer found him and reported that Nelson was waiting. He checked the wall clock and saw that it was quarter to ten. *Nelson made good time,* he thought.

But the man waiting wasn't Nelson. It was another courier. And he wasn't waiting to see Runit, the volunteer had misunder-stood. He was waiting *for* Nelson.

"He'll be here soon," Runit said. "If you want to leave the message with me, I'll be sure he gets it."

The courier tried to suppress a smile. "I prefer to wait and deliver it myself."

Runit nodded, not surprised, but worried. He recalled the plot of some mystery novel he'd read years earlier. In it a courier worked as a paid assassin. *Could the AOI already know?*

CHAPTER TWENTY-THREE

It was twenty minutes before Nelson pulled into a space half a block from the entrance. Runit had been pacing out front. He helped Nelson, who was juggling two cups of hot something and a box of doughnuts.

"Aren't you worried about the weight limits?" Runit asked, motioning to the doughnuts.

"It's the last thing I'm worried about. In fact, if I hadn't been so distracted about being executed for treason before the government could send me to a fat farm, I'd have bought a second box. Maybe some ice cream."

"There's a courier waiting for you."

Nelson stopped. "Why? Who sent him?"

"I have no idea. You know how couriers are."

"Blaze Cortez wants ten million digis."

Runit felt sick. "What?"

"By tonight . . . or he's selling the program, and us, to the AOI."

"I knew that bastard was a bad idea," Runit said, as he put his foot on the concrete bench etched with "Mark Twain." Twenty-two benches surrounding the giant library were inscribed with the names of great authors.

"He's more than a bad idea. Blaze is psycho."

"I'm getting Grandyn out of town."

"Don't worry. I'm going to drive back to Seattle and talk Deuce into giving us the money."

"He was there?" Runit asked.

"Yeah. You won't believe it. He tried to do the same thing in Belgium." Nelson shuffled his box and picked out a doughnut, offering one to Runit.

"What do you mean?" he asked, shaking his head to the pastry.

"When they closed the library in Belgium. He tried to get the books."

"That explains the strappers."

They were walking again. Runit told Nelson about the delivery, and he agreed that they had to be from Deuce. Certainly Blaze hadn't sent such a gift. They stopped at the steps. Nelson was nervous about what the courier's message would say and who had sent it. Just then, Runit reached the same conclusion Nelson had the day before.

"If Deuce Lipton couldn't save the books . . ."

"This time it's different."

"Dangerous words for gamblers, investors, and criminals."

"Good thing we're none of those."

"We're all of those."

"What are we investing in?" Nelson asked, conceding that they were in fact gamblers and criminals.

"The future," Runit said. "You may be doing this for the past, but I'm doing it for the future. Grandyn's future."

Nelson nodded. "When Deuce went for the books, he thought the government had considered them to be just trash, that no one cared about books anymore. We know differently."

"And that makes it easier?" Runit asked.

"If we can get the DesTIn program, we can do this."

"Assuming Cortez doesn't turn us in just for his own amusement."

"Yeah, assuming that."

Runit didn't know how Design Taught Intelligence, but knew that advanced artificial intelligence programs, such as DesTIn, were the only chance they had at finding all the important books in time. They headed up the outside steps. A minute later, the waiting courier FRIDGed Nelson, matching his image stored in the Facial Recognition Identification Grid database, then delivered his message, and departed.

Nelson read the paper silently, stunned by the message. He read it again. Then, as if to see if the words were real, he spoke them out loud to Runit.

"Funds received. Even untraceable. Impressive Baker-Boy. Fully operational DesTIn Program will be delivered by sixteen hundred hours today. Do you trust me?"

Miner looked over at Sarlo and clicked his old US silver dollar on his desk. She knew the coin well. It had belonged to his father and grandfather before him. The worn date could still be read "1988," the year his family reached billionaire status after buying up cheap securities following a stock market crash in '87. They hadn't looked back since.

"Hell, there is so much they don't know," he said, responding to her assertion that the Council knew everything. "As advanced as our tech is, there's plenty happening that we know nothing about."

Sarlo looked out over Paris, perhaps the least changed skyline since the Banoff. The Eiffel Tower still dominated. It's one of the things she loved most about the city. The rest of the world had moved on to laser-lit, silver polymer, space-age-inspired malleable skyscrapers, but Paris remained Paris.

"Risky to assume they'll miss something that could . . ." She paused to choose her next word carefully. Although Miner had a board of directors, a staff of attorneys, and other advisors, because she had been involved so closely with his deals and strategy for all these years, Sarlo occupied a unique position. ". . . potentially destroy you."

Miner squinted at her and quietly slapped the silver dollar, which had been spinning on his desk. *There is also a lot that Sarlo doesn't know*, he thought.

"And just how do you see that playing out?" he asked, adjusting his custom-made Tekfabrik slacks. He preferred to wear his in the old style so that he looked how a businessman would have in his grandfather's era at the beginning of the century.

"A portion of the Council, one of their many 'subcommittees', would convene an emergency meeting and debate your unilateral action. Because there are those who already deem you dangerous, they would likely rule that you're indeed a threat to the Council's power and they would remove you from the Council." She took a sip of water, his favorite, imported from the Arctic at one hundred thirty-one digis a liter. "And then, after a few tense weeks, maybe a month, you would die in your sleep."

Miner nodded. "I suppose it would go something like that . . . *if* they found out." He smiled smugly. "*If* I hadn't made a fortune on secrets, *if* there was anyone better at controlling secrets, *if* they didn't know I was already more powerful than they are."

"Well, Lance, that's one of the differences between us. I don't like playing with *ifs*."

"You might, *if* you were as good at it as I am." His smile widened.

"So you're going to have Deuce Lipton killed?"

"Of course not. I don't do that sort of thing."

She ignored his unconvincing denial. "Why now?" She looked out over the view of the city and watched as two of StarFly's mighty space vehicles broke from the distant horizon and headed for orbit. Another sign – or warning – she thought. No one was ever far from Deuce Lipton's influence.

CHAPTER TWENTY-FOUR

Sarlo stole another look at the incredible Paris skyline.

"We are at a crossroads," Miner said, ignoring the view and playing with his silver dollar. "There is no one left who remembers life prior to the Banoff."

"I guess that's true."

"Seventy-three years since the plague began. The oldest Banoff survivor died three months ago."

"Why does that matter?" Sarlo asked. "She would have been eight or nine when the plague hit. Not likely to have many substantial memories."

"Uh-huh. But she would have been thirteen or fourteen at the end of the war, and in those first five years as the Council established the constitution and Aylantik government, she would have been in her late teens."

"Who was she?"

"She was no one. She didn't matter. But her generation was a potential problem."

"Maybe sixty or seventy years ago, but not recently."

"They were the connection," he said, thinking about the name given to that final generation by the first Council. "Proof."

"The connection to the pre-Banoff world. So what?"

"So it doesn't matter now. That is over." Miner waved his arm. "What we are left with is Deuce."

It drove Miner insane that there were things only Deuce knew. Secrets unknown to Miner and the Council were dangerous. And worse, Miner believed it didn't work both ways. There were no secrets known to Miner that Deuce did not also know. For more than a century, companies owned by Deuce, or his father and grandfather before him, had made the majority of the surveillance equipment used to monitor the masses. It made the impending confrontation between the two titans all the more treacherous.

"What is it about Deuce? After all these years with you, I only know that you hate him, that he is not on the Council, and therefore a threat to it. But there must be something else, great or small, that drives your vendetta against him." She sat on the corner of his desk, a series of large metallic slabs that looked like a modern art sculpture.

"Isn't it enough that he threatens the Council, and therefore the stability of the entire world?"

"Yes, that would be enough for how the Council views him, detached and serious. But you're more passionate in your feelings."

Miner smiled. "Can I help that I'm passionate?" He stood and walked to the window. "Do you want to know what makes me crazy? With all the Whistlers, jammers, and false frequencies we put up, I still can't be one hundred percent sure that he's not able to somehow tap into my operations, see my flashes, even hear this torgon conversation."

"Then why do we talk here?"

"Because there is almost nowhere to go. Maybe the mountain forests are safe, but we can't go out there every time there is something sensitive to discuss." He flipped the silver dollar in the air, caught it, and turned it over on his wrist. "Heads. Back when coins still existed, this would have meant to go with my brain. Stick to the plan."

"I know, and tails meant take a chance."

"I have to assume if he could hear us, I'd be dead."

"Okay, but are you really willing to risk your rise to Council President and the appointment of your choice for World Premier, just to kill him?" She pushed away a lock of brown curls and adjusted her blouse.

"No," Miner said without hesitation. "At least not yet. And not because I'm scared. It's because I'm brave. I know what needs to be done to keep the peace. It's not all automatic, as you know. We had thousands of years of war, poverty, and destruction before the Aylantik system saved us from ourselves. The human impulse toward screwing it all up is still very strong."

"So you think that Polis Drast is the answer? You can choose anyone on the planet to be World Premier, and *he's* the one?"

"He's perfect, for many reasons. No one knows the security of the Pacyfik region better than he does, he is completely devoted to the stability and peace of Aylantik at any cost, and he knows of the Council's existence."

"And most important, he is a friend and gets your greatness."

"Well, that never hurts." Miner laughed. Then a zoom came through on his INU. The auto-filter meant it could have only been one of six people: the World Premier, the President of the Council, Polis Drast, his wife, Blaze Cortez, or Sarlo. The pulse told him which.

He moved his hands across the beaming light streaming from the small unit. His was not manufactured by Eysen, Inc., for obvious reasons, making it one of the few times in his life Miner had settled for second-best.

Sarlo excused herself. He wouldn't have minded if she stayed, but she had lots of work to do, and they would discuss the call later anyway.

"Blaze, I didn't expect to hear from you so soon," Miner said as the DesTIn expert's face came through, floating above Miner's desk like a colorful ghost.

"Does your man Drast have any idea what's going on in his own backyard?" Blaze asked, sweeping his hands to reveal a satellite map. "There's a potentially cataclysmic problem in the Pacyfik."

CHAPTER TWENTY-FIVE

Deuce walked through the dense silence of the giant coastal redwoods. Ever since childhood, whenever things got difficult, he retreated into the ancient redwood forests. Lately, they were one of the reasons he could so often be found in his San Francisco or Seattle offices.

A quick Flo-wing flight and he could be in his beloved trees. A Flo-wing might be described as a descendent of the helicopter, but there had been much crossbreeding along the way with small jets and even aerospace. Deuce's own StarFly Corporation made the best, but other pre-Banoff plane manufacturers, Boeing and Lockheed Martin, sold more. The supercharged flyers were capable of high speeds and great distances, as well as vertical takeoffs and landings. The high-end models also featured luxurious cabins, galleys, and communication-entertainment centers. Every self-respecting billionaire executive owned at least one.

It had been Deuce's grandfather, Booker Lipton, who'd first taken him to the redwoods, and until his death, Deuce's father continued the tradition. Deuce saw those two great men in the contours of the bark and heard their voices in the mist. He missed his father, but Booker's influence on his life was certainly more profound.

Booker had been a legendary figure in the pre-Banoff world, and still held a strong mystique in some circles. A ruthless businessman, regularly at odds with the former US government, he had supported controversial organizations, and was said to have brought about the downfall of many once considered infallible institutions. Even before Booker's company released the Eysen-INU, he'd been one of the wealthiest people in the world. But the Eysen-INU, as the world's first Information Navigation Unit, made him rich and powerful beyond almost any measure. Its technology was so advanced that now, more than eight decades later, it was still the standard. Not bad for a poor black kid who'd dropped out of high school.

The redwoods made Deuce feel small. Their humbling nature soothed his stress and changed his perspective. In the silence of the forest, he found mindfulness an easy practice. He'd spent time on the moon and loved the stars, was even contemplating visiting StarFly's Mars operations, but the redwoods were an integral part of him. Deuce looked at the centuries that had passed between the ageless trees as if he could see time itself. His thoughts went to his lineage.

During the tumultuous days following the Banoff, Booker, along with his wife and their newborn son, had disappeared. They hadn't surfaced again for more than a decade. By then, Deuce's father was eleven years old, and the Aylantik government had managed to impose peace and calm on the world. Deuce's father had been educated by tutors, but learned his most important lessons at the side of his father. Deuce took a similar path to knowledge. His skin didn't hold the same darkness of his father's, even though his mother had been of African descent. Her line deviated through several Scandinavian branches.

Booker had continued to stay mostly out of public view, and could go unseen for years at a time. Eventually, in 2060, by then in his late eighties, he had disappeared for good, his body lost at sea while sailing to one of the many private islands he owned. Deuce had always suspected Booker checked out on purpose, having no interest in the ailments of old age. Deuce's father was another matter.

Five years after the boating accident that claimed his grandfather, Deuce's father died at forty from a sudden, inexplicable disease that took him from perfect health to death in two awful weeks. Deuce had been just nineteen. The loss of his mentor and best friend had sent him into a dark place, which he still battled thirty-three years later. The passing was made even more difficult with the weight of the world's greatest fortune thrust upon him, an unprepared teen.

Then came the horrible realization that his father had not simply contracted an extremely rare disease in a nearly disease-free world. He never told anyone of his suspicions, including his future wife and children, but he believed it had been murder. It would be years before that theory would be confirmed, and even longer until he could seek revenge. The decades had not eased his pain, nor borne forgiveness. "Time is a funny thing," his grandfather used to say and, in this case, time had hardened his resolve for retribution.

But the forest softened his pain. The presence of the trees and their conversational sounds, brought him serenity as nothing other than the stars could do. There is wisdom in every leaf. A secret code, created long ago, that could not be understood, only felt. "It wasn't just that they robbed me of a father," Deuce whispered to the magnificent trees. "They stole something irreplaceable from the world . . . truth."

Deuce had been extremely careful, most would say completely paranoid, since his father's death. His companies were at the forefront of technology, and much of it was employed to keep the famous CEO safe. He ran corporations hardly anyone knew existed, and other companies that were known, but with his ownership concealed. His empire, revered by some, feared by many, was even more massive than anyone could comprehend. The A-Council didn't even know its true scale, but they did know two things.

He either had to join them, or be destroyed. The planet could not support them and Deuce lipton much longer.

CHAPTER TWENTY-SIX

Deuce checked his INU. No connection to the Field. Everything in the world had a link to the Field. Even in the middle of the ocean one could check their flash or place a zoom. The super satellites orbiting the planet made sure no one was ever out of touch, or untraceable. But in spite of the wizardry of technology that could create human replacement organs and limbs, that had built and populated manned bases on the moon and Mars, which were also connected to the Field, there were places on Earth that inexplicably could not reach the Field, most of them heavily forested areas, and no one knew why. The redwoods seemed impenetrable by the Field, or any other part of the spectrum used in modern communications.

Heavy mist continued to come off the nearby Smith River, and more rolled in from the ocean. The trees absorbed the moisture as easily as humans breathed air, one of the things to which they owed their great size. Deuce loved to see them that way, as if rising like giant reeds from an endless gray lake. He wandered, recognizing each tree he'd known for more than half a century. How many people, he wondered, were incapable of finding their way without GPS assistance? He checked the time, realizing he'd lost track of it. Looking up, cataloging the trees, calculating the distance he still needed to cover, Deuce walked purposely toward the southwest.

Along with the wealth, Deuce had inherited a pure devotion to nature. Whenever surrounded by wilderness, his thoughts would turn to the irony of the Banoff, which had nearly wiped out the human race. Even before the devastating plague, humanity was on a collision course with annihilation. Global warming, water table and ocean contamination, air pollution, nuclear war, and the assorted ailments of over-population were creating an acidic-toxic stew.

"It was only a matter of time," his father had said.

But the Banoff had saved the planet. By suddenly reducing the world's population by sixty percent, scarce resources became plentiful. That, combined with the complete elimination of fossil fuels and making non-recyclable products illegal, reversed global warming. The world since had indeed become a wonderful place in which to live. The Unified Aylantik government meant no war, and although the AOI could be heavy-handed, the peace had been kept, and everyone was happy.

"At least they think they are," Deuce said to the trees, finishing his thoughts.

Then, emerging from the silvery cloak of floating water particles, the reason he had come appeared. An old man with smooth, mud-tinted skin, wrapped in cream-colored linen that couldn't possibly be warm enough against the January chill, smiled and moved toward Deuce in a way that made him appear part of the fog.

"It's been a long time, my friend," said the old man, extending his arm.

"Too long," Deuce agreed, hugging him, alarmed at his thinness.

The old man's dark face showed pain. "There's trouble coming."

"I know. It's why I wanted to see you."

"I can be of no help. It is impossible to change the change."

"There is a way, and you can help."

The old man pushed back his hood. "How?"

"By telling me why Aylantik wants to destroy all the books." He knew the man would know about the library. Somehow, he always seemed to know what was really going on in the world.

The old man barely smiled before staring off, as if looking for a specific tree. He contemplated for more than a minute. Deuce was used to this, and waited as if time had no meaning.

Finally, without making eye contact, the old man said, "There is too much power in books that they cannot control."

Deuce, disappointed in the answer, found the old man's eyes, and then said, almost angrily, "That's not the real reason."

More silence.

"Then tell me," the old man said. "Why do you think they're doing it?"

"Sure, they'd like to limit the amount of discontent that people consume in books, but most of the old paper copies they're after aren't even read anymore. There probably aren't more than a handful of people who have even thought of them in decades. And if anyone checks them out, the AOI will know." Deuce paused as the fog became a light, misty rain. "It would actually make more sense to keep the books around, track anyone who looks at them, and then pick those people up for interrogation. There has to be more to this."

"It's about one book," the old man said.

"What?" This had never occurred to Deuce. "One? Then why don't they just pull that one and destroy it?"

"It's not that simple. The book they're seeking doesn't even really exist."

CHAPTER TWENTY-SEVEN

Runit stared at Nelson. "Blaze Cortez actually asked if you *trust* him? Let me see that," Runit said, grabbing the message. Nelson, lost in thought, easily let it slip from his hand. "Nobody trusts this guy. Everyone knows he's the most notorious scoundrel since Rhett Butler."

"That's just like a librarian to compare a real person to a fictional character," Nelson said. "But in this case, you might have made a good one. Rhett Butler worked both sides, but in the end he was basically a good guy."

"Is Blaze 'basically a good guy'? Because we have more than just the books riding on that assessment. It's our lives, Nelson, and Grandyn's too."

"If we can't trust him, why hasn't the AOI stormed the library yet?"

"Maybe they're on their way."

"Then we shouldn't have long to wait before we get our answer. Doughnut?" Nelson held the box in front of Runit, who shook his head.

"You keep up with the doughnuts and you're going to get picked up for weight issues. Then you'll be no use to us."

Nelson pulled a half-eaten, glazed-cruller away from his mouth, looked at it as if he were saying farewell to a lover, tossed it back in the box, and pushed it across the table. "From now on, I'm by the book." He grimaced at his own unintentional pun. "Every hour counts until they shut us down, so let's make a plan. We can't afford to waste this day waiting for the DesTIn program."

"Or waiting for the AOI to burst in."

During the next few hours they developed a set of procedures that would be used to pull and strap the books. They made a list of a hundred books to test their system. Symbolism not lost on the librarian, nor on the bestselling author, they pulled *Fahrenheit 451* first. *The Call of the Wild, The Catcher in the Rye, Animal Farm, 1984, The Adventures of Huckleberry Finn, For Whom the Bell Tolls, The Little Prince, The Autobiography of Malcolm X, Invisible Man, Beloved*, books on Thomas Jefferson, Spartacus, Pancho Villa, Stepan Razin, Gandhi, Martin Luther King, Jr., works by Howard Zinn, and a host of other free thought and spiritual books made their list. They broke for food, happily delivered by a local health spot fully approved by the Aylantik Health-Circle. After lunch – Nelson had a salad – they pulled, strapped, and delivered four bundles of books to the back door.

"I talked to my contact at the bottling plant. We might be able to get four thousand books on each truck," Nelson said, lighting a bac as they stood on the loading dock, speaking in hushed tones.

"That's not enough," Runit said, pulling his coat tight against the damp cold.

"I know. If the DesTIn identifies a hundred thousand books, we're talking about twenty-five trips. The fruit trucks can handle a hundred thousand plus in one load, but it'll take four nights to get all the books to the service center."

"It's too risky. We need to do it in one night."

"Removing the books from the building and then getting them out of Portland is obviously the scariest part of this," Nelson said, exhaling a long stream of smoke. "Even if we could get twenty-five beverage trucks in one night, it would be too much activity. Seeker would analyze the scene and wake a real-life agent."

"Our luck won't hold for four nights."

"I know. It's about twenty-minutes to the service center. Without traffic we should be able to make it in more like sixteen or seventeen. If we get good unloading time, we could do two trips per truck, which could cut it down to two nights."

"Better, but where is all the manpower coming from to load and unload trucks illegally?"

"What about your volunteers?" Nelson said, lighting another bac.

"A good group of people and booklovers all, but I doubt any of them would be willing to go to prison to save them. Plus most are in their sixties. A bit rigorous."

"What if they didn't know they were breaking the law? We tell them that the library is closing and they're moving all the books to storage, but that we need to do it at night in order to avoid protesters about closing the world's last library."

"Some of them would want to be among the protesters," Runit said. "But if I'm behind the move, they might go along. Yes, it might just work." He looked at Nelson. "You're pretty good at this criminal activity. Maybe you missed your calling."

"Hey, I write fiction. I'm just working my way through the plot that is my life."

"It's *our* life, now, so write a good ending," Runit said. "Did either Blaze Cortez or Deuce Lipton offer a theory as to why the Aylantik government wants to destroy the books?"

"Blaze doesn't care, wouldn't say even if he knew. Deuce on the other hand, he's angry about it. I mean, he didn't *say* that, but he is. The guy comes across as cool as a northerly breeze, but underneath, at least about the AOI, he's a boiling caldron of rage."

"I'm glad to hear that. I'm angry too," Runit said. "But does he know about the content being changed?"

"He didn't say, but how could he not. His company makes the best selling INUs, he owns StarFly, not to mention dozens of other hi-tech giants. This guy knows everything that's happening . . . about anything!"

"And yet he is not using that great might to save our books." Runit waved his arm up to the library building.

"*Someone* paid Blaze the ten million."

"Maybe, or Blaze could be lying. He's known to do that. It's surprising he hasn't been knocked off. I mean the guy is the world's most famous rogue. But even if someone did give him that money, maybe it wasn't Deuce."

"Oh come on, who else do you think paid him? Grandyn?"

"No one else knows."

"It was Deuce." Nelson shot him a serious look. "He's happy to let us do the grunt work."

"Happy for us to take the fall if the AOI finds out," Runit said. "Let's get back inside. We've got an impossible task ahead."

"Really optimistic, Runit. You know, I've heard you tell Grandyn a thousand times since he was a little boy that nothing is impossible--"

"Secretly moving a hundred thousand books in the dark of night with Big Brother and the Gestapo watching is as close to impossible as I'd ever like to get . . . but I'm doing it because I believe what I've told Grandyn, and I'm doing it so Grandyn can have a future by knowing the past."

"I know," Nelson said quietly. He crushed the bac under his heel and followed Runit inside the library.

CHAPTER TWENTY-EIGHT

Grandyn and his girlfriend, Vida, were waiting for them on the main floor of the library.

"Vida's going to help," Grandyn said as soon as he saw his father.

"Help with what?" Runit asked.

"Pull books," Grandyn said. Vida smiled.

Runit looked at Nelson, who shrugged. "Grandyn, let me talk to you alone."

"Dad, she knows. I told her."

"Both of you in here, right now," Runit said, pointing to a small meeting room. Nelson followed them into the glass-walled space and closed the door.

"What were you thinking?" Runit began. "Don't you care about her?"

"I love her," Grandyn said. Vida, a beauty of Brazilian descent, squeezed his hand.

"But you've put her life in danger."

"My life is with Grandyn," Vida said, her slight Latin accent stronger with anger. Accents were rare two generations after the new language became mandatory, but they still occurred occasionally, as if a genetic trait.

Runit rolled his eyes. "You two are eighteen. You don't know enough about life to make these kinds of choices."

"Don't pull that parent-babble on me, Dad. You raised me too well. You've taught me about life, but you always seem to forget that. I know what I'm doing."

"Damn it, Grandyn. I may have taught you, but you have to live it to really know it."

"That's what I'm trying to do." He looked at his father. "Let me live it."

"We need help," Nelson interjected. "There are a million books to get through."

"I'm a good worker, Mister H," Vida said, shifting in her faux, black leather jacket. "And, actually, I'm nineteen."

Grandyn laughed.

"She already knows," Nelson added.

"Yes, she already knows," Runit repeated. "This is crazy."

"Let's get to work," Nelson said, clapping his hands.

Until the DesTIn program arrived later, there wasn't much to do, so they cleared out the room next to the loading dock to be used as a storage space for books between loads. They also set up the strapping machines in two alcoves in the main hallway of the lower level. Still debating how much to tell the staff, Runit put out a story that a number of books were being transferred to a nearby university, but was vague about the reason.

Nelson walked up the street as an excuse to smoke, but he also picked up and consumed a couple packs of peanut butter cups. He felt guilty. Not for the calories, but because he hadn't told Runit everything about the meeting with Deuce. He'd mentioned the planetarium and Deuce's failed attempt in Belgium, but held back the information about the prisons, raids, and executions. Nelson had no doubt that if Runit knew about the brutal tactics of the AOI, he would cancel the whole operation.

Nelson felt especially bad about involving Grandyn and Vida, but Runit's role ensured that Grandyn was already in jeopardy. Once Grandyn told Vida, she had to be let in or they risked a leak. Even if the books weren't saved, their lives would be threatened anyway.

Deuce and the old man strolled through the ancient, majestic trees.

"Please make me understand."

The old man stopped and looked carefully at Deuce. "You sound like your father. He always surprised people by asking questions. A man in his position, the wealth and power, people like that are often afraid to admit they don't understand. Your father wasn't one of those. He always questioned."

"You have also spent your life questioning."

"True," the old man said, the lines in his face a mix of happiness and something else, maybe regret, "but differently."

Deuce nodded respectfully. He loved the old man more than anyone, other than his children, and their time together was rare and always too short. They walked in silence, unbothered by the rain as the trees took most of it.

Finally, just when Deuce was going to bring up the books again, the old man spoke.

"The books were a detail no one really thought about, but those types usually are trying so hard to catch everything that they miss something. And in this case, the something turned out to be everything."

Deuce smiled to himself. He was no closer to understanding, but he'd had many conversations like this with the old man, and out of the confusion and vague references clarity would eventually come. The old man simply had a different way of seeing things. That was one of the reasons that Deuce so valued his counsel.

"Does the Aylantik government know the *book* doesn't exist?"

"I'm sure they do."

"Then why are they looking for something that isn't real?"

"Oh, I never said it isn't real." He wagged his finger, lecturing an overconfident student. "It is very real indeed. But it's not real in the way you imagine, manufactured with paper and ink."

CHAPTER TWENTY-NINE

A volunteer found Nelson on the lower level and informed him that another courier was waiting at the main desk. Nelson arrived breathless from the stairs. After checking his image in the Facial Recognition Identification Grid database and deciding he passed his FRIDG, the courier handed him a small package the size of a pack of playing cards. It had come from Blaze, and contained a tiny INU insert known as a "slide." He took it to Runit's office where they installed it on a new Information Navigation Unit, purchased specifically to run the program. It had already been loaded with the complete library catalog. The program began scanning immediately.

"I still don't know how this is going to work," Runit said.

"It goes onto the Field and finds the book, matched to title by the ISBN, and then searches for text which fits a complex criteria that may be objectionable," Nelson said, reading from a projected manual.

"But if the book has already been changed?" Runit said.

"That's the beauty. Blaze has designed a system that can detect revisions, which adds to the criteria. It won't show specific deletions or additions, but any book that has been revised that fits into other categories will also be tagged."

"Blaze got this done pretty fast," Runit said.

"I know what you're thinking."

"Yeah, that he probably designed the system that the AOI used to find the books they changed in the first place."

"He might have."

"Who else?"

"I don't know. The government has thousands of engineers on staff that could create something like this. But we have the best."

"Anyway, we have the books. The *real,* non-tampered ones with ink printed on actual paper."

"Look, it's giving live updates. It's already found more than eight hundred 'revised' books. And another three hundred that are 'at risk.' Let's start pulling."

They printed the first list and divided it among the four of them. After an hour, two things were evident: Grandyn and Vida were faster than Runit and Nelson, and they needed more people. Runit put two of his favorite – and trusted – volunteers onto the task of pulling books. Nelson, the slowest, moved to strapping and called his sister to help. Runit and Nelson were in the book storage area when she arrived.

Chelle Andreas entered the dark, dingy room in the bowels of the 180-year-old library building and it was as if the ceiling had opened, allowing a sunny spring afternoon to burst through. Her movie-star looks were at once disarming and intimidating. Wispy, long, blonde hair floated, and a bubbly smile, dimpled cheeks, and inviting eyes said "air-head cheerleader." But with a closer look, Runit saw something he'd never noticed during the few brief occasions when they'd met years earlier. Those sparkling eyes held a steaming fire, an intense something that took him a moment to shake and longer to place.

Anger. The beautiful and alluring woman was furious.

Other than their fair complexions and the fact that they both favored natural fibers over the popular transformable Tekfabriks everyone else wore these days, Nelson didn't seem to have much in common with his sister. She still carried the name of her dead husband, a man Runit knew almost nothing about. They'd married eight or nine years ago after meeting somewhere in old-Asia, now mostly part of the Chiantik region. She'd been working in banking since finishing graduate school. Runit figured that would have been six years earlier. The couple had lived in Hong Kong for several years before her husband died. Nelson had reminded him it had been three years since it happened, and Chelle had been living in Europe during the intervening time. This was her first trip back to the Pacyfik.

Runit took Chelle's hands between his and stared thoughtfully into her eyes. "I'm sorry about your husband."

She kept her hands in his and held his gaze for longer than appropriate. Chelle gauged men easily, the way pretty women get used to doing, to weed out the takers. She recognized her pain within him, a mirror of the loss. His wife had just died the last time they'd seen each other, but Chelle had been younger then and didn't grasp the extent of what that kind of thing could do to a person. They had met just a few times, and she didn't realize he'd only been half alive at the time. Even now, his recovery nearly a decade on, she saw what she'd missed then – heroic courage.

"Thank you, Runit." Her bright smile faded to a softer one before it retreated altogether. "And I . . . never properly acknowledged your wife's passing. I didn't understand, you see." Her eyes teared.

He shook his head. "No one really does, do they?"

"Not until they row that boat alone."

"It's better that they don't."

Chelle nodded. Their eyes fought parting a second longer.

She took his breath, and he had no idea that his impact on her was equally vibrant. She had met an honorable man who seemed to possess a bottomless depth of knowledge – not the scientific or even scholarly type, but rather the emotional. She had been around the world, a whirlwind of intrigue and adventure, and while Runit Happerman had rarely ventured more than five hundred kilometers from home, he had traveled through books. Chelle could feel his experience, although he had done most of it through his mind.

Runit remembered Truman Capote's words. *"She had only one flaw. She was perfect, otherwise she was perfect."*

That is a dangerous thing, he thought.

Nelson cleared his throat. The two people he knew and loved best in the world had just shared a moment. He'd been an observer of human nature all his life, known for his uncanny ability to capture characters so vividly in his writing that they became real to his readers. He could see that a storm had just brewed.

CHAPTER THIRTY

Miner ended the awful call with Blaze, now having more concern about the possibility of war than he'd ever had. Blaze had delivered the news of a "potentially cataclysmic problem in the Pacyfik," and it all originated with one single woman. He believed she could bring the end to the unprecedented period of peace which made their world such a glorious place.

"The woman must be found and destroyed," he said to himself.

Miner told Sarlo to make arrangements for them to fly immediately to New York. His supersonic jet would have them there in less than ninety minutes. They quickly boarded the Flo-wing that was always on standby. Nineteen minutes after finishing with Blaze, he sat across from Sarlo in the taxiing jet. He stared out the completely transparent sidewall across the wide-angled wing, woven of a combination metal-polymer-Tekfabrik. It was the latest model in a long line of corporate jets, which now resembled something sleek like the old stealth fighters from the pre-Banoff days, except new materials made the walls and ceilings transparent so that, during the day, the fuselage was basked in natural light, and at night the stars felt touchable.

He turned back inside. His INU had already linked with the plane's system, so the interior had been personalized to his current mood. All the colors had been softened, the AirViews faded, and the audio reports muted. Vitamin-and-antioxidant enriched air was pumped through the cabin, but the automated efforts to soothe him were having little effect.

Sarlo could see her boss was terribly agitated, and wished she'd been on the call. Once they were in the air, she finally asked for an explanation.

"We have a major problem in the Pacyfik," he said, more calmly than she expected.

"Major?"

"It could lead to revolution."

What Blaze had told him gnawed at his stomach, but the things he'd only alluded to were making him nauseous. His health sensors silently alerted his INU and moments later a bot appeared with a tray of PharmaForce pills.

He brushed them aside. Sarlo smiled to herself. The irony always amused her. Lance Miner, CEO of the world's largest drug maker, never took medication. Still, she could tell by what pills had been offered just how he felt and she measured her words, deciding not to bring up the A-Council. Sarlo knew the Council feared revolution more than anything else. They controlled the economy, and therefore the world, but the one thing that could cause it all to come crashing down was an open revolution. Pacyfik always seemed to be seething under the surface, and revolution would surely lead to global chaos because the world was so small.

"Is it PAWN?" she asked, referring to the league known as People Against World Nation.

The group had long been rumored to exist, but nobody knew for sure, not even the Council. Yet, even without evidence, they had treated PAWN as a real threat since the Aylantik and Pacyfik war ended seventy years earlier. She doubted a revolutionary organization could stay in stealth mode for the better part of a century, and personally didn't believe it was real, but she respected the Council, which had dedicated great resources to defeating the invisible enemy.

"Yes, it's PAWN," he said, staring out the clear wall distractedly, hands working a mini-AirView.

"Is there proof?" she asked skeptically.

"Blaze says that—"

"Blaze Cortez?" she interrupted. "If PAWN exists, then *he's* probably one of them."

"I don't disagree with you, but I can't risk it. And, I might add, if PAWN exists, they likely think Blaze is part of the AOI."

"My point exactly. He can't be trusted," Sarlo said. "So you informed the Council of the threat?"

"No. I want to investigate it myself first."

The strategy didn't surprise her. If there were, in fact, finally proof of PAWN's existence, it could be a powerful discovery. Peace threatened would be a galvanizing force. "Knowledge is power" was one of Miner's favorite axioms.

"Investigate what?" she asked.

"The woman."

Sarlo, slightly frustrated, sighed and did not inquire further. Miner, clearly distracted by whatever information Blaze had conveyed, did not yet seem ready to share it, his mind still processing. It wasn't her style or place to try to pull it out of him one word at a time. Curiosity was something Sarlo could easily control, especially when she'd been swept away on this flight, again at the last minute.

Her boyfriend had been planning to cook a nice dinner, then dancing, and a romantic evening afterwards. She loved to dance, especially with him, but that would all have to wait. Sarlo closed her eyes, but couldn't resist wondering what woman had so bothered the great Lance Miner.

Could PAWN be more than legend? Did a *woman* lead the secret and dangerous organization? Were they ready to finally strike back at the Aylantik government? Why now? Part of her disbelief in PAWN stemmed from doubts that any group could muster enough support for a real revolution when the world appeared so happy and content. In the years before the Banoff, when most of the global population lived in subpar conditions, hunger, poverty, and debt, not more than a small percentage ever seemed to complain, much less try to stage a real revolt.

CHAPTER THIRTY-ONE

As Sarlo drifted off, Miner was working his Information Navigation Unit like a magician, whirling AirViews, holographic projections of 3D multicolored satellite maps, and people's faces sliding in and out of data streams. The INU did lightning-fast computations and probability tests leading to DesTIn-builds that portrayed arrests, battles, losses, and gains. Miner could push his every theory, answer even the most outlandish questions, and the response filled the air all around him, smothering him in a reality that he had feared since childhood.

The odds of peace lasting as long as it had were already astronomical. The chances that it would continue were not much different from the Earth getting struck by an asteroid. But that would be easier to defend against. Deuce Lipton's StarFly Corporation had seen to that more than a decade earlier. After all, space defense was part of the world's fourth largest industry. Ironically, AOI and internal security actually ranked nearer to tenth. Miner had argued against that complacency for years. Once he became A-Council President and was able to anoint Polis Drast as World Premier, he could finally get the priorities straightened out, but would it be in time? His INU cast doubt.

And it wasn't just the woman. Miner had known Blaze a long time, and something between the lines bothered him. The woman wasn't the only problem in the Pacyfik, but she might well be the key. As he thought more about it he became increasingly worried, but decided that the woman would know. She wouldn't just be able to tell him about the underbelly of the Pacyfik. She could tell him so much more.

Miner spoke toward his INU as it opened communication with his head of security. "I need a crew to the Oregon Area."

"Damn Pacyfik. What is it this time?" his head of security asked. The man had been with him nearly twenty years. Before that he'd been in AOI, served most of it in the Pacyfik. Lance Miner, like Deuce Lipton, had a private security force that functioned as part intelligence agency and part special ops commandos. Both men employed more than ten thousand in their units. Miner suspected Deuce might have closer to twenty thousand, and often worried that the break of peace might not come from Pacyfik rebels, PAWN, or even the deep Chiantik region, but rather as a war between corporations. If that were the case, it would most likely be Miner and Deuce as the generals, and it might wreak far more destruction than a PAWN uprising ever could.

Miner explained briefly what he needed as the security head asked all the right questions. Miner had a secure link into his INU, and would monitor the progress in real time. It would require AOI-Seeker data, but that wouldn't be a problem. Polis Drast would be Miner's next call.

"We'll find her," the security head said at the end of the call.

"I know you will," Miner said. "And, I'll say again, she must be unharmed."

"I am clear on that sir."

"Good. You bring her to me, day or night, the moment she is found. I must talk to her in person."

"Understood. But sir, do you really believe this woman is still alive? It seems rather incredible, if you don't mind me saying."

"She's alive all right. She's been keeping me up nights for years."

He brushed his hand and closed the connection. He looked out of the transparent fuselage, noting how much the planet had changed since the Banoff. There were massive tracts of land returned to their virgin state and gleaming solar-powered cities, clean, precise, and efficient, where everything ran through and by the Field and the people were healthy. All of it brought about by the Aylantik, the A-Council, and PharmaForce. He saw Karst, the third largest city in the world below. It didn't even exist sixty years ago, and now it gleamed as a model to everything humanity had always strived for.

"Who has been keeping you up?" Sarlo asked groggily as she woke from a nap.

"I don't know her name. I don't even know what she looks like. Can you imagine that? In this day and age, when everyone's every move is recorded and analyzed, not knowing what someone looks like?"

"How is that possible?"

"I hardly know a thing about her, but I can feel her."

"Does your wife know?" Sarlo regretted her attempted levity the moment the words escaped her mouth.

"Damn it, I'm serious! This woman is the devil."

"The devil?" She knew Miner well enough to know he wasn't religious, and the irony almost made her smile, as Lance Miner had been called the devil on many occasions himself, but his last outburst sobered her.

"Who is she?" Sarlo asked quietly.

"We'll know soon enough."

"What has she done?" Sarlo tried one last time.

"She leads PAWN."

"So, it is real?"

"As real as earthquakes, volcanoes, and floods."

CHAPTER THIRTY-TWO

Deuce tried to calm himself in the ancient trees. Holding onto the connection they held to his past, his father, his grandfather. "Then what?" he asked. "What kind of book could be so powerful?"

"This book was created from breath and memories, from air and time, dreams and vision. It is of truth and stars. They're, unknowingly, actually seeking a belief."

"A book about belief?" Deuce asked, trying not to sound stupid.

The old man nodded. "But not *about* belief, it is *of* belief."

"How do you know all this?"

"I've read this book, or rather, part of it." The old man stopped and stared at Deuce. "I read it with your father, and he read it to you."

"To me?"

"When you were very young."

"I don't remember," Deuce said, thinking of his father.

"But it's still with you. Your mind has it." He turned and started walking again. "Some books are so alive that they never leave you. They only change you."

The two men walked on in silence until they came to a tree known as Lost Monarch, by mass, the largest tree on Earth. They sat on a nearby fallen trunk and gazed in awe. Although both had seen it many times before, it always stunned them anew. Like seeing the Grand Canyon, it didn't matter how often it was seen, the majesty would still take your breath.

"You see, the root of their problem may be a single title," the old man began, "but it has been referenced in many works, before and after its publication. The basic principles of that which they seek have been woven into the texts of thousands of other books, but they don't know which ones. The only way to stop the ideas of that one book from disrupting their regime is to destroy them all."

"Where did it start? What is the original title?"

"Even that is hard to say, but the contents were the collected papers of a man known as Clastier."

The name sounded familiar to Deuce, as if he'd heard it in a dream.

"My father had the originals once, but they were lost with him, or to time." He paused and stared at the great tree for a long time. "Perhaps that is the same thing."

Deuce looked at the old man, and saw deepening age: drooping lips, sunken temples, brittle nails, and his bent body seemed to surrender to the memory of a once strong and confident stance. But what concerned him most was the fatigue in the eyes he'd always known and trusted so completely. He couldn't imagine losing him.

"The AOI doesn't even know you exist. Why do you insist on staying in hiding?"

"I'm not hiding." He stood up, suddenly looking younger. "Is that what you think?" He shook his head and shot Deuce a scolding glance. "I'm living how I choose, not within a system designed to make us forget." The old man sighed, and then walked to Lost Monarch and pressed his brown, leathery hands onto the thick bark. He closed his eyes, meditating. A few minutes later, he turned back to Deuce. "I am *not* running, I am seeking. I am *not* hiding, I am finding."

"Where do you go? What do you do?"

"I'm just dancing with time, and occasionally wrestling with it. Like my daddy used to say, 'Time's a funny thing.' But I'm not laughing." He sat next to Deuce again. "It's almost over."

"What? Are you sick?"

"My body is tired. I'm ready to go."

"What are you talking about? I can get you the best doctors."

"You should know better than that. Besides, I want to go. This earthly world is a burden and," he hesitated, "I was born just after the last revolution. I'd kind of like to miss the next one."

"But I need you."

"You'll be fine." He put his rough hand on Deuce's shoulder. "You've inherited the best of your father, and me."

Deuce looked at his uncle. "I hope so."

"Do you know the real reason my parents disappeared during the Banoff?"

"My dad always said it was to protect him." Deuce's eyes softened at the mention of his father.

"Booker had a vision, before the Banoff, of his two sons. So as soon as your father was born, they dropped out of sight. Sure, my dad had many enemies, but the real reason was that they wanted me born in secret."

"Why?"

"His vision was of two sons, one running his business empire and the other pursuing his other interests – the spiritual side."

"So that's why you never went into business. Did he leave you anything?"

"He made sure I wouldn't have to worry about money, so I could devote my life to the study of the universe and the soul."

"But you gave up the power and fortune. Is that what *you* wanted?"

His face broke into a huge smile. "Oh, yes. The only thing I would have wished different is that my brother could have joined me on my quest."

"Why couldn't the two of you have done both?"

"Booker tried to do both, but business held him back from his spiritual pursuits. He didn't believe it was possible to do both."

"Do you?"

"I think anything is possible, but I have yet to find a way to reconcile the two."

"How much time do you have left Uncle Cope?" He looked lovingly at the face of a man who knew the past, Deuce's only link to it. "Life is unfair."

"Whines the trillionaire." Cope laughed. "Weeks, maybe months. Whatever it is, I got a better deal than your father. He got the money, but only had forty years. I've had seventy-two, and I got everything."

Deuce often saw the Lipton money as a burden, but he knew his grandfather saw it as a way to change the world, and that was what he wanted to do. "The world is not as simple as it looks."

"Sure it is," Cope said, rubbing his straggly gray beard. "It's only about perception."

"That's beyond me."

"Perception again."

"What about truth?"

"Depends on perception."

"You've never really said if you think my dad was killed."

"And now that I'm dying—"

"Don't take your knowledge with you."

"I never told you what I thought because I didn't want you chasing ghosts, seeking revenge. It doesn't matter what happened. My brother is dead."

"But someone can be held accountable."

"Karma will take care of that. You just worry about living. Life is too short for retribution, grudges, and hate. Forgiveness is a beautiful power."

"Not telling me what you know about his death is tantamount to an answer. You know that, don't you?"

"Yes."

CHAPTER THIRTY-THREE

Wednesday, January 31

Runit and his team had worked late into the night, and would have slept in the library but for the risk that Seeker would see their failure to go home as an anomaly and possibly alert Portland-based AOI agents. It might also go unnoticed, but with the library closing and all the high level interest, they couldn't risk it.

Chelle passed Runit on the stairs. "I love your library," she said. "I can see why Nelson likes to write here. Excitement is hidden on every shelf."

"Isaac Asimov once wrote, 'It isn't just a library, it is a space ship that will take you to the farthest reaches of the Universe, a time machine that will take you to the far past and the far future, a teacher that knows more than any human being, a friend that will amuse you and console you -- and most of all, a gateway, to a better, happier, and more useful life.' But you know what?"

"Tell me," Chelle said, as if waiting for a great secret.

"During all my years in this grand building, I've come to the realization that Asimov actually understated it. In truth, a library contains the entire universe, and each book is a portal to a different world."

"That's exactly why they want it destroyed," Chelle said. "There's too much at stake if we learn too much."

Progress was slow, even though they arrived early that morning in order to try to get deeper into their task. They had eight days remaining until the closing. Runit thought he could get more done if he didn't work anywhere near Chelle, his fantastic distraction. He decided that his son should be free from Vida's charms as well, so he planned to station them in different parts of the building when they arrived later. Nelson's attention seemed diverted only by food and the fictional characters running around in his head. The unfinished manuscript he'd interrupted for the closing crisis was to be another in his popular corporate espionage series.

"The characters are harassing me. They're impatient. They want me to help them out of their messes," he claimed more than once.

"They're not real," Runit told him.

"I know that. I'm not crazy. But *they* think they're real. So do me a favor and tell them, and while you're at it, ask them to let me sleep!" He poured hot coffee down his throat and Runit noticed what could only be doughnut crumbs on his coat, but didn't say anything. They would likely all be in prison before the weight-police came to get Nelson.

"It's going to take ten years to finish this," Runit said.

"We've got to get more of the staff involved."

"Too risky. They aren't idiots."

"We're all idiots," Nelson murmured. "Come outside so I can smoke. You know, it's ironic that in like a week they're going to torch this place and you still won't let me smoke inside the damn building."

"It's a health issue, not your topic, I know."

Nelson yawned, and Runit did the same a second later. They

were hashing out a way to get the entire staff to help and weighing the dangers when Grandyn appeared, jogging up the marble steps."

"Why aren't you in school?"

School had also changed dramatically since the Banoff. At first, students were isolated from one another as fear of another outbreak kept parents cautious. The Internet allowed distance-learning to flourish. As the Internet morphed into the Field and everything became connected, that became even easier, but students were floundering. With the success of the Aylantik Health-Circle and great pharmaceuticals preventing another plague, students eventually returned to classrooms, albeit very different ones. Instructors from around the world lectured and taught across the Field to thousands of students at once. Classes ranged in size depending on age level and location, and each highly paid instructor had staff available to assist. The local gathering of students, still called schools, were mostly monitored by cyborgs and bots, with one human director acting as Dean or Principal.

"It's raining," Grandyn said, as if answering a silly question.

"And they're cancelling school now because of rain?" Runit asked, still lost.

"Dad, remember? They've been waiting for a rainy day to do the test."

"Oh, right. TreeRunners."

Grandyn shook his head, annoyed. "I just stopped by to tell you I won't be able to get back here until dark, but Vida will be here right after school."

"Can you skip it?" Nelson asked. "Clock's ticking and we need all hands on deck."

"Nelson, aren't authors supposed to avoid clichés?" Grandyn asked.

"Only when writing."

Grandyn nodded. "If we need more help, I can get as many

TreeRunners as you need. Well, at least a dozen." The group, like a combination of an intellectual fraternity and an Eagle Scouts program, had been around for at least fifty years, though no one knew for sure. The first clan was said to have begun in the Rocky Mountains, but soon spread across the globe.

Runit was about to turn down Grandyn's offer until he remembered the oath. Grandyn had been a TreeRunner since age five, and he'd known the other kids in the wilderness program all that time. Each year they renewed a blood oath of loyalty to each other. Their bonds were made even tighter with rugged camping and hiking trips, where survival skills and an appreciation for all things nature were forged into their being. They stayed in until age twenty-five, but the friendships lasted a lifetime. Former TreeRunners were always sought after for the best jobs from top corporations because of their loyalty, leadership, and discipline. They were especially favored by AOI because of their extensive training. Each year in the program the difficulty level of the tests grew more arduous, but no one ever quit because the group supported each other completely. They'd even carry someone many kilometers if necessary.

Today, Grandyn would do a ten-kilometer run through dense forest in heavy rain. The TreeRunners actually got their name from the ancient art of racing at full speed through trees, practiced by tribes of the American Northwest. The grueling run, done barefoot, tested speed, endurance, and mental skill. Spectators were not permitted. Only fellow TreeRuners would see the feat. Next year he'd have to do it blindfolded.

"Would they do it?" Runit asked.

"If I asked," Grandyn answered.

"And they'd keep it absolutely secret?"

Grandyn gave him a that's-another-stupid-question look. "Of course."

"No questions?" Nelson asked, knowing the answer.

"There should be no doubt about the oath," Grandyn said. "Their silence is guaranteed."

Runit silently thanked his wife. It had been her idea to push their young son into the elite wilderness fraternity. It had done much to shape Grandyn into a responsible, confident, and resourceful young man, and now a corps of energetic, trustworthy youths was about to help save the books.

"Please, ask them," Runit said.

"You got it Dad. Order in a stack of pizzas. We'll be here around dinner time."

CHAPTER THIRTY-FOUR

As promised, Vida showed up after school. Runit sent her to work with Chelle. The two tall women discovered they were both black belts in karate and endurance hikers, each having recently completed the Pacific Crest Trail. They immediately became friends. Vida admired Chelle's "tough spirit," and desperately wanted a role model. Her parents had gone through an acidic divorce, and seemingly cared only about how Vida could be used against the other. Her mother, not especially bright, frequently lost jobs, and had twice been sent away to the fat farms. Her father, a scoundrel, had been juggling young girlfriends even before the marriage ended, while staying buried in debt.

"Are you going to college?" Chelle asked as they pulled books in the same section. She enjoyed Vida's accent. It reminded her of a friend she'd had in the Chiantik region.

"I don't know. Money's tight." Although the Aylantik government paid full tuition at any college that accepted you, housing wasn't included. "Even if I can get into Portland State, I'd have to find a place to live."

"Your folks?"

"No."

"Sorry."

"Anyway, Grandyn doesn't want to do college, so I might follow him."

"Following a man is not always a good idea," Chelle said. "But, I must admit, sometimes it is . . . if there is love."

"There is." She smiled, maybe blushed, but her cocoa complexion made it hard to tell.

"Are you being careful?"

"Oh yeah. We don't want kids."

"Ever?"

"Never," Vida said firmly. "I'm even considering selling my bearing-rights."

"Don't," Chelle said, suddenly angry.

"Why not? It's just free money. I told you we don't want kids."

"You're too young to decide that much of the future."

Vida didn't respond. A few minutes later, the silence had grown uncomfortable, but Grandyn came in with a boisterous group of TreeRunners. Upon seeing the thirteen highly trained, energetic young men and women, Chelle realized that the young could, in fact, decide the future. She hurried to find her brother.

Deuce sat quietly in the Flo-wing on the short flight to his San Francisco office, his thoughts heavy with the reality of soon losing his uncle. The man, more than just the last link to his father and grandfather, had been Deuce's spiritual compass throughout his life. Now, about to embark on the most challenging time the world had known since the Banoff, Deuce wasn't sure if he possessed the fortitude not only to survive the coming changes, but to actually lead the way.

The question was moot, he thought, recalling the plaque that had hung in his father's office. *"Circumstances define the man. No one wakes up and decides to be great. It's the events he's thrown into that determine if he is truly great. Survive or not is to be great or not."* The quote had been attributed to the Old Man of the Lake. Deuce never knew who that was, but knew Booker had given it to his father. Soon, the changes were going to begin, and Deuce would have to deal with them, ready or not. But so much depended on Portland.

His INU lit up the interior of his spacious Flo-wing. These aircraft were much quieter and faster than the ones his grandfather had known, and this one had been custom-built for him by a division of his giant StarFly Corporation. The very same company he had long been counting on to change the world. Though, the question now was, would there be enough time?

He watched the dazzling AirView displays that turned the cabin into a mini-Seeker monitoring station. All the activity taking place around the library came into view. AOI even had limited interior surveillance. For nearly a hundred years, companies controlled by the Liptons had been supplying government agencies with the world's most advanced spy, intelligence, and surveillance technologies. The advantages, aside from the profits and access to power, were almost limitless, especially the secret "back doors" that were always built into the systems.

Chicago85, the main company dealing with government contracts, could never be traced to him. It had been set up long ago by his grandfather, and still appeared to be controlled by the reclusive Mumford family. Chicago85 was his third largest asset after Eysen and StarFly, but all three of his massive conglomerates would be required to save the world from itself for the second time in a century.

Watching the busy library made Deuce even more concerned. He immediately dispatched a courier to Nelson as he watched him smoking a bac on the loading doc. *How could so much hinge on a ragtag bunch of bungling book people and teenagers*, he wondered. It took him less than four minutes to identify all fourteen teenagers, and it delighted him that thirteen of them were TreeRunners. Very few people knew he'd been a TreeRunner as well, and once a member of that fraternity, always a member. *They might pull this off yet*, he mused.

CHAPTER THIRTY-FIVE

The final teen in the group that worried Deuce was Vida Mondragon, a pretty girl from a broken home. After cycling through a few frames from his INU, it appeared obvious that she and Grandyn were an item. *Vida might be the weak link here*, he thought. Deuce's hand whisked through the air and full data scans came up on Vida, her parents, extended family, friends, including a past boyfriend, and every teacher she'd ever had. Another hand gesture and an employee received the assignment: dig into everything Vida.

Chelle Andreas was another matter. Aside from being Nelson Wright's sister, she was Beale Andreas' widow. He already knew plenty about her. There weren't many men Deuce respected more than the late banker.

Banking had evolved into something more specialized than in the pre-Banoff days. Because of the Field and the end of paper money, all banking was digital. It became more generic and less profitable until the rise of the power bankers. A handful of shrewd and well-connected individuals brought the "dealing" back into the industry and spawned a new elite class of brokers. These firms had important clients, and one of the most impressive rosters belonged to Beale Andreas.

The wealthy sought him out not just for his connections, but also for his ability to both find money and identify the right places for it to go. But perhaps the thing to which he owed most of his success was charisma. Everyone had adored the charming man, which was the reason his ending came as such a shock.

Along the way, Beale himself had become rich. He counted among his friends the likes of Lance Miner, Blaze Cortez, and most of the world's elite, including Deuce. That combination of relationships proved to be the key to his success, and also his undoing. Beale learned many secrets in his dealings, and eventually he heard the wrong one. When he was killed, Chelle had surprisingly been spared, although stripped of wealth with the tiniest gesture into an INU glow. The fact that she'd been allowed to live appeared to rule out the AOI as the responsible party, but Deuce understood the vast complexities. He also knew the secret that had gotten the banker murdered.

Deuce hadn't been surprised to see her show up at the library. Even if she had not been Nelson's sister, since her husband's death she'd grown increasingly important in the underground movement. And Chelle Andreas seemed to be at nearly every hot spot in the past thirty-six months. Somehow, she had avoided detection by the AOI, which made Deuce wonder if she had a protector. That, along with her blonde athletic beauty, the battles waging in her eyes, and the secrets she must know, all left him uneasy.

He'd learned from his grandfather, during a long ago walk in the woods, that there is no such thing as coincidence. It had been no accident that Blaze Cortez had met Nelson at a party any more than Deuce's showing up at Nelson's reading had been random. The current upheaval had been building for a long time, but more than that, it had been predicted, and the participants in the know had been preparing.

He looked back at the library and zoomed in on the woman that connected so many of the players, admonishing himself for not knowing the answer to his nagging question. "Who is Chelle Andreas, really?"

But he couldn't watch Seeker anymore. There was a more pressing concern. Lance Miner's latest trick could become a problem if not dealt with soon. The Corporate Assets Acquisition Parity Board would be introduced in two days by the World Premier, and then the public would expect results.

"CAAP must be stopped *before* it is announced," Deuce told one of his trusted vice presidents, in charge of a division of his mighty BLAXER security company. He knew that the proposed Corporate Assets Acquisition Parity Board would cause more trouble than even Lance Miner planned.

BLAXER created by his grandfather a hundred years earlier, provided defense, safety, and protection to clients worldwide, but essentially it was really a private army, and a very large one, second in size only to AOI's.

"I understand," the VP replied. "It's a lot harder to put the genie back in the bottle than to just bury the damn bottle in the first place."

CAAP would be a major distraction at a time when Deuce needed complete focus, but more than that, it would act to polarize him from the public, and even from his few allies within the government. The timing was awful, but that, of course, was exactly how Lance Miner had designed it.

"Does this warrant assassination?" the VP asked.

"Possibly, but those are so damn messy. Better left to the AOI," Deuce said. "Yet there certainly needs to be a removal. I can think of no other way to derail this thing, now that it's gotten Council approval."

His thoughts returned to Chelle. *What secret is keeping her alive?* he wondered. It wasn't the same secret that had gotten her husband killed. She knew something else. Now that she'd involved herself with the Portland Library, he would need to have a talk with the beautiful widow, and he'd have to be extremely careful.

"Sir, my orders?" the VP asked, bringing him back.

"Sometimes secrets get you killed, sometimes they can save your life, but secrets can also make extremely powerful weapons," Deuce said, and then laid out his plan for the VP.

CHAPTER THIRTY-SIX

Thursday, February 1

They had made some progress last night, but this would be the first real test, as only seven days remained. The advanced artificial intelligence program Blaze had created from DesTIn, had identified 112,804 books. So far about 4,300 had been removed.

"We've got to pull and bundle at least sixteen thousand books every day," Runit said to Nelson during a bac break outside. "It's a tough deadline."

"We have a better chance of making it now because of the TreeRunners, but still, even if we do get them all pulled, the books will need to go out Monday and Tuesday night," Nelson said.

"That's cutting it too close."

"I studied the DesTIn program a little more and discovered that we can prioritize the list based on an endless number of factors."

"In case we don't get them all?" Runit asked, his eyes closing. He'd already been having nightmares about the books – more than a million – that would be left behind . . . and burned. He saw it as a barbaric atrocity. Sure, those lost volumes would "always" be available digitally, but as he'd told Nelson early on, "An ebook is like having a photo of a dead loved one. It's convenient to look at and it will stir the mind, but it doesn't breathe."

"We'll get them all," Nelson said.

"I've got to put the full staff on this today. They've been buying the story that we're moving books to a university," Runit said, "but by tomorrow there'll be so many books off the shelves that they'll start to notice."

"Can they all be trusted?"

"Do we have a choice? What if the book we don't get a chance to save turns out to have been the one that could have changed everything?"

"DesTIn should help us avoid that."

"What if DesTIn gets it wrong?"

They decided to bring the others in, not because there wasn't risk, but because they would probably find out anyway. "Better to control the message," Nelson said. Runit called a staff meeting and informed them of the library closing. The news surprised no one. They'd been expecting it since Australia closed and knew it was only a matter of time once Belgium went. Still, the mood in the room turned solemn and many shed tears. Confusion took over after Runit explained the need to keep the news absolutely confidential and that no one outside the staff could know.

"Why does it need to be secret?" someone asked among the questioning faces.

"We're afraid of protests," Runit answered. "Ours is now the world's only library, after all. Hopefully these last remaining physical books can be preserved. We've made arrangements to have a large part of the collection housed at Portland University. The rest will be put into storage."

"Oh good," one of the older ladies said.

"But the government isn't excited about the university deal," Runit explained, "so the books need to be moved before word gets out. If this becomes a political issue, who knows what they'll do with the books?"

That seemed to satisfy everyone, mostly because they'd known and respected Runit for so long. Also, no one had reason to believe anything nefarious was happening.

"We have work left to do, and I'm counting on your help."

Each staff member and volunteer received an assignment, and work began. For the first time since he and Nelson had decided to take the books, he believed they might pull it off.

Then his INU lit up red. The color, at least that shade of it, had long been reserved for urgent government directives. He looked around and saw several other people getting code reds as well. His stomach tightened. He should have known the AOI would find out.

Nelson rushed toward him. "Damn this timing," he said, but Runit ignored him, still trying to look over the flash. He read it twice before sighing in relief. The Health-Circle, which administered all health matters for the Aylantik government, had issued an urgent directive that all citizens needed a booster shot.

Ever since the Banoff, disease had been essentially kept in check by the diligent efforts of the pharmaceutical industry, their inoculations, and booster shots. The return of the plague to finish its deadly work of eliminating the human race was a fear that still gripped the populace. The giant pharmaceutical companies had obtained savior-like status, and many of their corporate leaders were seen as folk heroes in the eyes of the public. War and poverty were minor compared to the Banoff plague.

Although the private sector had taken on all research and testing, the government's Health-Circle still had final approval on all new drugs. The process had been streamlined, and usually took less than a week. Studies had shown that the Banoff pandemic had been catastrophic, partially because the correct drugs were not available due to bureaucratic red tape. Ever since then the government, pharmaceutical companies, and medical professions had operated as a triad partnership concerning the world's health. Every policy decision had the underlying tenet: preserve the species; another pandemic must never occur. The strict health regulations in place allowed no exemptions.

The Health-Circle emergency directives were rare, usually once every couple of years, but citizens were expected to drop everything and comply within eight hours or arrests would follow quickly. Even though the system was startlingly efficient, this would take the whole team out for three or four valuable hours. The volunteers, TreeRunners, staff, everyone would need to report to the nearest health station to wait, get their shot, and then rest for ninety minutes. But there was nothing Runit could do about it. Not only was it illegal to refuse, resulting in immediate imprisonment where you'd receive the shot anyway, but the Health-Circle had obviously identified an imminent risk. That was their task. They'd kept the world healthy for decades, and people rarely questioned the Health-Circle. They were revered and praised, but Runit cursed the timing. At least they could go in shifts.

Runit worried about missing future boosters, in case the AOI found out about the books and they had to go into hiding, but then Nelson assured him that a small black market existed for boosters. Thinking about it later, Runit wondered how many people could possibly need boosters outside the system. How many "outlaws" were running around in the shadows with so little crime in the world? And how did Nelson know these people? When he asked, Nelson brushed him off.

"I discovered some things while researching a book. It's an interesting story. I'll tell you later."

Runit began thinking about which book Nelson had been researching when he discovered the black market, but he couldn't remember any plot that would have resulted from that. His thoughts were interrupted when he wound up in the same group with Chelle, heading to the health station. She sat close. He liked it.

They talked quietly as the LEV navigated the streets. One of the library volunteers, an older lady with nearly blue hair, smiled at them. He nodded back politely, enjoying Chelle's warmth. He was glad Grandyn would be going later.

"Shots make me nervous," Chelle said. Her hair brushed his face, smelling of snow and tangerines. "Sorry." She smiled.

"It only hurts for a second," he said lightly.

She started to cry.

"What's wrong?" he asked.

"Will you just hold me? I'm so embarrassed."

Runit took her in his arms. The blue-haired lady blushed and turned away for a second before retuning her gaze with a shy smile.

Chelle held onto Runit so tightly that the back of his neck and left wrist where her hand pushed into his flesh were suddenly hot and sweaty. She cried. He didn't know what to do, so he just held her and let her sob softly into his shoulder.

CHAPTER THIRTY-SEVEN

Forty-eight hours before the World Premier was scheduled to give his speech announcing the Corporate Assets Acquisition Parity Board, Lance Miner left the meeting with him, satisfied that all would go well. CAAP had the potential to take a big piece out of Deuce Lipton's fortune, and Lance smiled at the thought of Deuce's reaction, knowing the money would be the least of his pain. The CAAP initiative would cost Deuce something much more valuable than wealth: time. Deuce would become so mired in regulatory fights and popular protests that he'd be unable to get in Lance's way for a very long time.

On the other side of the continent, Deuce, although not quite smiling, could certainly have been described as happy. Everything had been put into place. In an hour, a top BLAXERs representative would be meeting with the World Premier. He wasn't aware that Miner had just left the same office, but it wouldn't have made a difference anyway. Things were not going to go Miner's way.

Deuce's son, Twain, a lanky, twenty-six-year-old, tech-geek, stopped by to see his father. He was another reason Deuce favored the San Francisco office. His twenty-one-year-old daughter, Tycen, was in college there, and his son worked in nearby Cupertino.

Deuce had tried to entice him to join the family business, but Twain was determined to make his own way, and Deuce loved him for it. They mostly talked about the three overlapping subjects that fused their passions: space, Eysen-INUs, and other technology. Twain may not have wanted to live off the family fortune, but that did not mean he didn't want to change the world, and he believed Earth could only be changed from space. Unfortunately, there wasn't time for one of their lively discussions today. Deuce had requested Twain's help.

"You and your sister may be in danger."

"Aren't we always?" he asked, motioning to his security detail outside the door. It wasn't something he liked, but it couldn't be avoided.

"I saw Uncle Cope yesterday."

Twain's face brightened. "I wish I'd known, I'd love to see him. How is he?"

"He's fading, I'm afraid. Maybe we'll arrange a get-together this weekend."

"Fading?"

"He says he doesn't have much time left."

"Damn." Twain chewed on the inside of his lip as he did whenever something upset him. Uncle Cope had been almost a mythical figure in his childhood. He and his sister called the old man "UC" as in "you-see" because of his philosophical ways and seemingly magic ability to know their thoughts. "Please, let's go see him today."

"Not today, but this weekend for sure. In the meantime, he has insights about trouble coming. I'm currently involved in helping some people defy the government, and at the same time my old nemesis, Lance Miner, is escalating his crusade."

"Dad, you've got all the money in the world. Why can't you just be content to enjoy it?"

"With great wealth . . ."

"I know, 'comes great responsibility'," Twain said, using his fingers to put quotation marks in the air.

"Right." Deuce smiled, knowing his son had heard that line a hundred times. "So, will you consider taking a leave of absence?"

"No."

Deuce looked at him pleadingly.

"Is it really *that* dangerous right now?" Twain asked, softening.

Deuce held out an Eysen-INU, which projected a large image of his wife, Twain's mother. "Please, Twain," she said from a secluded island.

"No fair getting Mom involved," Twain said, smiling. "Okay. I guess I can work from one of the islands for a while."

"Thanks," Deuce said.

"But you knew I'd be a pushover. You really asked me here to get me to convince Tycen, didn't you?"

"Yes, please," his mother said. "You know how Tycen is. But she'll listen to you."

Their daughter shared Deuce's love of the wilderness, including the oceans. She'd been to every island the family owned, a considerable accomplishment, and was taking a double major, marine biology and business. Deuce had been grooming her since her tenth birthday to take over the vast Lipton Empire, and although she loved spending time at one of their islands, especially during winter, she loved college too, and did not like being told what to do.

"She's not going to go for it unless you can show her a real life threat," Twain said.

"Just try," Deuce said.

"She'll listen to you," his mother repeated. "She always does."

Sarlo ignored the sweeping nightscape of Manhattan, no longer even one of the world's fifty biggest cities, but still breathtaking.

"Care to dance?" Miner asked.

"I think I might enjoy a spin," Sarlo said, smiling. She had worked almost as hard as he had on the Corporate Assets Acquisition Parity Board scheme, and finally it was about to happen.

She'd been Miner's first zoom after the successful meeting with the World Premier, and the normally reserved Sarlo had actually squealed. The pressure and stress would finally ease. After all these years, they now had the upper hand on Deuce Lipton. That triumph, coupled with Miner's impending rise to President of the A-Council, meant good days ahead. A lot of them.

"Let's drink a toast," he said, as the song ended and he swooned her in a dramatic dip.

She stood, catching her breath. "Maybe we should wait on the toast until after the announcement."

"Damn it, Sarlo, you're always too cautious. Let your hair down," he said, laughing. "The only thing that could stop CAAP now is if the World Premier dies in his sleep tonight."

She made a scared face. "Stranger things have happened."

"True," Miner said, pouring two glasses. "But I have access to his health records. He's in top shape. And hell, even if he kicks in the night, we'll have the Vice Premier announce it after a few days of mourning. It would make him immediately popular. We're there. We did it. Drink up."

They clinked glasses.

"But we do have some unpleasant business to address, don't we?" he said after gulping his drink.

"Unfortunately, yes. The woman in Pacyfik."

"Yes, the real reason we're in New York in February," he said as if it were a prison sentence. "What did you find today?"

Sarlo looked out the fifteen-meter wide window. Aside from Paris, Manhattan had, more than any other city, retained its pre-Banoff appearance. Many of the new towers caught her attention with their shiny finishes and daring architecture. Some resembled silver lollypops or flameless torches, tubular shapes that left one amazed, even an inverted pyramid the color of a blue autumn sky. Sarlo adored the stunning "sky-bridges" which connected multiple buildings across city-block distances, and used them whenever possible. But below all that, the old New York City remained like an anchor sunk in the sea of time.

"There are many stories about that woman Blaze spoke of, but nothing concrete. It's more like . . ." Sarlo hesitated.

"What?"

"It's more like a legend."

"I don't believe it! Blaze Cortez says she's real, says she's in the Pacyfik Northwest and that she has a torgon following."

"We have more than a hundred and fifty people working on it," Sarlo said. "They're spreading money and intimidation around the region like manure. If it's true, we'll find her." She looked at Miner, waiting until their eyes met. "But tell me, Lance. How could this woman possibly be alive?"

CHAPTER THIRTY-EIGHT

Chelle had managed to stop her tears by the time they called Runit for his shot and she released him. Once in the examination room, the nurse FRIDGed him, carefully checking his image in the data base, and then administered the needle. He grimaced for a split second, but his mind was too occupied with Chelle to even notice the nurse's routine words.

Nelson's beautiful and normally strong sister had been in his arms for almost twenty minutes. They had exchanged only a few whispers during the entire episode, but Runit felt it had been the most sensual experience of his life. As her scent of snow and tangerines still covered him, he relived their "conversation." They had been silent for at least five minutes after she'd told him to just hold her.

Finally he had asked, barely audibly, "Are you okay?"

"No." She breathed the word as if it had seven letters and each represented a different form of desperation.

"What can I do?" he'd asked, careful to avoid the blue-haired lady's stare.

"This." And she held him tighter.

All he could feel were her hands on his wrist and neck, her

breath in his ear and her body pressed into him. Damn the shots, he thought, he hadn't ever wanted a woman more. Not since the first time he'd met his wife. But Chelle's magnetism overpowered him. Something mysterious about the woman spun his mind, and her touch, so completely erotic, made him feel stoned.

"I need to move," he said, wanting to free his wrists.

"Don't," she said, again making the word sound like one he'd never heard before, as if it might have three syllables.

"Okay." Even then, he tried to shift slightly.

Somehow, all that did was allow her to get closer, which made their contact even more intense. She was crying softly and he couldn't tell if the wetness he felt on his ear was her tongue or her tears.

"I need you." Her words came on a hot breeze, felt only by him.

He stuttered, incomprehensible for a moment.

"Runit, don't let me go," she whispered.

"I won't," he said, determined that if he did nothing else in his life, he would not let her go until she again felt safe. Those had been their last words until word came through on his INU that the doctor was ready. He didn't want to go, but she assured him she'd be okay.

Runit rolled down his sleeve after the nurse put a small bandage on the spot where she'd poked him. Leaving the office, he passed Chelle and told her he'd wait for her.

He climbed back into the LEV and pretended to scan his INU, but the blue-haired lady returned and started talking to him anyway.

"Is she okay?"

"Oh, yeah," he replied, giving a reassuring smile to the old woman, who had been a volunteer for three or four years. He hardly knew her. "She's Nelson Wright's sister."

"Oh," she said, impressed.

"Terrified of needles and lost her husband not too long ago. Bad experiences in medical facilities."

"Oh, my. How awful."

Runit nodded and went back to his INU after giving the lady a look of agreement, as if it had been quite awful but now everything was just fine. Scanning the flashes that had accumulated during his time away, he determined that nothing seemed important. He allowed his thoughts to drift to the woman who had suddenly consumed him.

Each time they were together it felt like a life was at stake, and he didn't know whose. But he needed to save whose ever life it was, especially if it turned out to be hers. Chelle had a power, something that created a new way of seeing the world. He'd wanted to save the books; they had long been his life. He needed to do it simply because destroying them was wrong. He believed in books, more than in people, because everything was discoverable within the pages. Read and think, and one could understand.

People were much harder to grasp, with Chelle being the most impossible. But she wanted to save the books too. He would have been getting the books out anyway, he'd been doing it, but Chelle brought the passion to the cause. Somehow she made the books alive. To Runit, the books were people. People about to be murdered.

The future was at risk without the knowledge from the past, the *true* knowledge. Runit remembered the philosopher Santayana's warning, *"Those who cannot remember the past are condemned to repeat it."* No one should ever have to live in the pre-Banoff world again, with its wars, pollution, and poverty. He thought of something else Santayana had said and shivered.

"Only the dead have seen the end of war."

Yes, he knew the books had to be saved, and he had more than just an interest in the future. He had Grandyn. He would do anything he could to save them. He'd known that even before Nelson convinced him they could do it. Yet the mission suddenly became more important with Chelle Andreas involved. He couldn't explain it, but it was true, and he sat there trying to understand why.

His mind swirled in confusion, as he waited in the LEV. *Could I love this woman I hardly know? Every man who meets Chelle must fall in love with her. But she seems equally captivated with me. Is that possible? A librarian. The last librarian? What will I be in a week? Where will any of us be?*

Runit missed his wife every day. The decade since her death sometimes seemed like ten minutes. He'd dated over that time, though probably not enough. He'd been careful not to get involved, making a conscious decision not to let anyone interfere with raising Grandyn exactly as Harper would have wanted. But now Grandyn was eighteen and Chelle had arrived on the scene. The encounter in the LEV actually made him feel guilty. If they'd been alone on the ride to the medical station, he was sure they would have had sex. Even though he was at least a decade older, she seemed to want him even more than he wanted her. He might have risked arrest for her if she'd insisted on not getting the shot.

Maybe she'll come back to my place after we finish pulling books tonight, he thought. They'd be exhausted, but passion is the second most powerful stimulant, with fear being the first, and there was no shortage of that.

His Information Navigation Unit suddenly brought his attention back as it glowed with an important flash. He moaned as he read it, devastated. A few seconds later, Chelle entered the LEV. Runit motioned his fingers to open an AirView that allowed her to read it. Upon finishing, she closed her eyes in apparent defeat. But when she opened them a moment later, instead of the tears of frustration he had expected, her eyes glared with an inner fire that startled him.

She gave the voice command to engage the LEV that Runit had been too distracted to give. "We'll make it," she said as she moved her fingers around her own INU, notifying Nelson, doing some kind of calculations, scanning her own flashes, and a lot of other things. But Runit had no idea what. She seemed completely transformed from the woman who had ridden over with him. Now she was a commander in charge of a mission.

He wanted to discuss it, whatever *it* was, that they had shared, what they'd felt together, tonight's plans . . . but she was all but ignoring him. He didn't understand at all, but he knew that any "relationship" conversation would have to wait. The flash had taken precedence with the news that their near-impossible task had just grown impossible.

As they rode back to the library on that cold Thursday evening, he read the flash again and wondered how they could possibly have everything out by Sunday night. The schedule had been changed, and the AOI crew would arrive two days earlier than originally planned. At dawn on Monday, they would burn all the books.

CHAPTER THIRTY-NINE

Nelson, a bac hanging from his lips, met Runit and Chelle outside on the library steps.

"We can do this," he said.

"How?" Runit asked, sounding more irritated than he should have, subconsciously blaming Nelson for being Chelle's brother. "Do you have to smoke all the time?"

"Relax, Runit," Chelle said, barely squeezing his shoulder as she passed him on the steps. "Nelson has always had reasons for wanting to kill himself. We don't need to interfere."

Oddly, Runit felt better, but her sway over his emotions bothered him. *You're not a dumb teenager with a crush*, he silently admonished himself.

Chelle exchanged a quick glance with Nelson, but Runit missed it. Chelle's nod had been almost imperceptible.

"I just received a message from Deuce. I sent word back with the courier."

"What did his message say?" Runit asked as they pushed through the front doors.

Nelson stayed behind for a couple of seconds and inhaled two more drags from his wonderful bac.

"Good news, bad news."

"Yeah, you know what Kurt Vonnegut would say. 'The truth is, we know so little about life, we don't really know what the good news is and what the bad news is.' I find it often applies." Runit then realized Nelson had remained outside.

"Come on," Runit said, going back out after him. "What did Deuce say?"

"Wait until we're inside and I'll show you." Nelson stamped out his bac and followed Runit into the library. Then he led Runit and Chelle to a small empty room usually used for preschool reading circles.

"Why here?" Runit asked.

"Because this is what Deuce sent." Nelson laid four sheets of 11x17 paper on a table. "They're all the Seeker locations that impact the library."

"Wow," Chelle said, her expression simultaneously showing awe and concern.

"You won't believe how many cameras there are inside and outside of the building," Nelson said, "but this room is clear."

"How are we ever going to get the books out of the building?" Runit asked. "Even if we had a month, they'll see every move we make."

"That's why he sent it," Nelson answered. "All we have to do is obscure the one covering the loading dock during the few hours of the load out."

"It isn't that unusual to have a Seeker camera go out," Chelle said, surprising Runit with her knowledge. "The library is certainly on a heightened watch list, but it's probably not on any of the security-risk lists. That designation is reserved for power plants, tech centers, AOI facilities, and government offices, et cetera."

"What line of work are you in again?" Runit asked Chelle.

"Long story."

"I've got time," Runit said.

"No, you don't," Nelson said.

"Well, it's just she knows stuff about AOI and Seeker that I've never heard before," Runit said.

"There are a lot of things you don't know," Chelle said. "Not everything is printed in books."

She had almost offended Runit, but her smile disarmed him, and then she took his arm. "Don't worry, you're a smart man. I have a feeling that by this time next week you're going to be teaching me stuff about the AOI."

Nelson laughed.

Runit ignored him and looked into her eyes, as if to ask if she were just toying with him, trying to remind her that he too had lost a spouse and that they were both fragile and should treat each other gently. Only Chelle didn't seem fragile *or* gentle. His confusion heightened when she returned his gaze with an "I'm serious and I want you" kind of a look. But it didn't matter that he didn't understand. It's what he wanted, and he didn't mind a little emotional turmoil on the way to wherever they were going, as long as they got there together.

"On the message you sent back to Deuce, what did you request?" Chelle asked her brother.

"What do you think? I pleaded for help. He employs an army."

"Even if he wanted to send a thousand people," Runit said, "those papers on the table say it's impossible. Look at all those Seeker camera locations. You don't think they'd pick up on the extra activity? They may even be able to identify his people. Wouldn't that be great?"

"Not after Belgium," Chelle said. "We can't risk a repeat."

"Were you there?" Runit asked Chelle, suddenly worried he had missed a big piece of what was going on. "Were you at the Belgium closing?"

"No." She blinked, looking a little offended. "But I know what

Nelson told us, that Deuce Lipton tried to save the books and in the end they were all lost. Wouldn't you agree that we don't want to lose the books *this* time?"

"Yes."

"Look," Nelson said, "I talked to my contact at the bottling plant. We can have seven trucks on Saturday and Sunday nights, starting at nineteen hundred hours. We can even have a few on Friday night if we're ready, but there aren't as many available because they preload their Saturday morning deliveries for weekend events."

"What about Grandyn getting more TreeRuners?" Chelle asked.

"No, it's already too risky. They're just kids," Runit said.

"It's their future we're fighting for," Chelle replied.

"Why do you think they're trying to change the books?" Runit suddenly asked her.

"They're afraid. It's the same as it always has been. A corrupt leader needs to control what the people think so they don't revolt. There are three ways to do that: don't allow them to learn anything that counters the official line, bombard them with propaganda disguised as news, and finally, give them a distraction, usually an enemy."

"Why would anyone want to revolt?" Runit asked. "Don't get me wrong, I'll do anything to save the books, but what if the government is trying to stop some very bad group from disrupting the most peaceful and abundant society the Earth has ever known? What if we are inadvertently helping to destroy all that goodness?"

"All that goodness?" Chelle laughed. "If it's as good as it seems, it'll be strong enough to withstand a few controversial books. Wouldn't you agree?"

"Yes, I would," Runit said, charmed all over again. "But only if we can get them out in time."

"Well, there are three of us in this room who aren't pulling books right now," Nelson said. "We've got about eight hours left today. Let's go pull some torgon books!"

They spread out to different parts of the building. Runit wandered down the aisle where biographies were – there were thousands to be pulled there. While trying to shift emotional gears, he thought about spending the night with Chelle but knew, given the crisis, it was not practical. At the same time, because of the crisis he wanted it even more.

What is it about that woman? he asked himself.

Deuce was asking himself the same question about Chelle as he watched his intercepted Seeker feed and read the request from Nelson. There were holes in her bio over the past few years, including times when she had vanished altogether. That was not an easy thing to do in the Aylantik, post-Banoff world. All financial transactions were instantly traceable, and the Facial Recognition Identification Grid system made moving about without leaving a trail nearly impossible, but she had been invisible nonetheless. Perhaps she'd been camping in the woods somewhere and living off the land, he thought, because without truly incredible connections, she couldn't have pulled off that kind of disappearing act.

Then again, with her late husband's roster of banking clients, someone might be helping her. But why? And who? Lance Miner always topped his list when something suspicious was going down, but if that were the case, her aiding the library heist didn't make sense. She could have gotten her brother out of there and blown the whistle at any time. Unless . . . He suddenly stood and paced.

Unless Lance Miner *knows* about the book.

Deuce realized he would probably not be getting much sleep that night, maybe not much until Monday. And somehow, even with the CAAP issue erupting tomorrow, he needed to get as many of his people surreptitiously down to that library as possible.

CHAPTER FORTY

Grandyn and his band of TreeRunners were working so fast that Runit thought they might actually pull it off. The young crew did even more once the library closed for the day, when they could crank the music. Runit worried about Seeker cameras, but they were careful around the sensitive areas, and Chelle assured him that the advanced artificial intelligence program monitoring the interiors, also based in DesTIn, would, if anything, assume the crews were preparing for the library closure.

Runit wondered if Blaze, with his hands in the AOI's DesTIn-based tools, could be ready to sell them out. "What if Seeker's algorithm refers that question to a human?" he asked her as they passed in historical fiction.

"I know a good lawyer," Chelle said, winking.

Alone again, Runit chastised himself for allowing Grandyn to be involved. His late wife, Harper, would have seen it the other way. "Kids need to live, take chances, learn at their parents' side," she often said. "I don't want our son growing up sheltered and afraid. Grandyn needs to be tasting all that life has to give, running fast, falling down, and jumping back up." Harper would have been fine with him skipping college. "Pursue your dreams, no matter what anybody says," she would tell Grandyn, when he was still too young to even know what she meant.

Runit rounded a corner and found his son making out with Vida. They heard his approach and broke apart, giggling. "Not going to find many books that way," Runit said lightheartedly.

Grandyn stepped aside and pointed to an overloaded cart. "Dad, we're just trying to slow down a little so we don't totally embarrass you and Nelson. You guys are not very good at this."

"I thought librarians could pull books in their sleep," Vida teased. "But Mister H, you're kind of sleepwalking up these aisles."

"You're right, Vida," Runit said. He checked his list and saw an easy section ahead – history. There were a ton of books in there, close together. "You two split up again, like you're supposed to be, and we'll have a little contest. First one to a hundred books."

"Gets what?" Vida asked.

Runit touched his INU. "I've got ten digis."

"Cool," Grandyn said, grabbing his INU. "I'll put in ten."

"Winner take all?" Vida asked. "I'm in." Her INU lit and she sent the funds.

Runit nodded, smiling. He knew he'd win, but he'd buy them a pizza or something with the loot. "One, two, three, go!"

They split up, and fifteen minutes later Runit already had forty-four books. But then he pulled *A People's History of the United States* by Howard Zinn. It had been Harper's favorite. The memory sent him back to her rants on the pre-Banoff world. They had made Runit laugh so hard he'd end up crying. He smiled, flipping through the pages.

Harper had been a history professor specializing in the world before the plague. But in another life, she could have been a stand-up comedian. She had a talent for making the most serious situations seem ridiculous. A particular favorite target were the justifications for war during the prior few centuries.

"Sending young people to die over money, oil, lines on a map, tea, and taxes is kind of like shooting chickens because you don't like the price of eggs," she'd say before launching into a presidential tone, delivering actual lines former world leaders had used to justify war. It always sounded rather ludicrous and comical all those years later. Runit often wondered how it seemed to the citizens who had actually lived through those crazy times when war was entered into so easily. Harper had also written many serious papers on pre-Banoff conflicts and fiscal policy. She'd not been a fan of the economic systems favored in that age, nor the present one. She had done detailed research, linking every major war in history to money.

"How could there ever be a real moral reason for war?" Harper would ask rhetorically. "It always comes down to someone's greed. History is populated by the distorted tyrants and corrupt businessmen willing to trade a cup full of blood for a purse filled with gold. Prior to the Banoff, the world spent trillions every year on weapons. What does that say about our species? How can we evolve to something higher when we insist on killing one another for profit?" And after one such diatribe, she had ended with the whispered question, "And what do we spend today to keep this cheated peace?"

He recalled a conversation in which Harper had cried over the issue of prison reform. "In the pre-Banoff days the United States had millions in prison, but at least they had a chance. The Aylantik government doesn't believe in large prison populations. They just execute people."

"But drugs were illegal pre-Banoff, and with the poverty issues of that time, it's no wonder they had millions in prisons. The AOI might be harsh, but they keep the peace. And they do have people in prison, at least a hundred thousand," Runit had said, then added the foolish comment, "They only execute the really bad ones. It's not that many."

"I cannot believe you just said that." It had been the harshest expression he'd ever seen on her face. "Who decides how bad is bad?" she continued, glaring at him almost like a stranger. "Of course, the Aylantik government doesn't release execution figures, but some estimates have it as high as twenty thousand a year."

He dug in deeper. "Whose estimates?"

"Monitoring groups."

"Those groups aren't even legal. Those people could wind up in prison themselves."

"Or maybe they'll be executed too." Her tone was brittle.

"The figure isn't anywhere near that high. It couldn't be."

"Maybe not the legal one, but they have other ways to remove troublemakers."

She didn't get the chance to elaborate because just then, Grandyn and some friends had come home. He was eight. They wanted snacks and help fixing a broken remote control car.

Harper was dead two days later, and now, after seeing the Seeker diagram, he thought desperate things and had a horrific realization that even in its vile blatancy he wanted to deny.

CHAPTER FORTY-ONE

Grandyn found Runit sitting on a stack of books, crying softly. He looked at the book in his hands and nodded. A similar copy of Howard Zinn's *A People's History of the United States* was in his night table at home, only it didn't have a cover and the spine had been chopped off. Partly destroying a book avoided the heavy possessions-tax, especially the particularly high ones levied on books. It had belonged to his mother. No one knew where she had gotten it. Grandyn had read it many times, mostly to feel close to her, but he didn't really understand why it was so important to his insightful mother. It covered about five hundred years of what Grandyn considered ancient history. He didn't get why anything that had happened before the Banoff mattered. Everything he'd read about it made those years sound barbaric.

"Come on, Dad."

"Sorry."

"It's okay." Grandyn always broke down a little when his father cried. "She'd be glad about what we're doing, wouldn't she?"

Runit wiped his eyes. "She sure would. Your mom would have led the fight to save these books and she would expect us both to work around the clock to do it."

Grandyn embraced his dad. They were close, but the hug still surprised Runit, and he fought a fresh wave of emotions. He rallied quickly when Vida came laughing around the corner, pushing a cart.

"Looks like I win," she said. "You can count them, but I can tell you there are actually a hundred and four because I'm just that good."

Grandyn had about eighteen before he went to see if Runit even had a chance to beat him. He hadn't counted on getting stopped. "Okay, baby," Grandyn said to Vida, laughing. "I guess you're buying dinner."

Nelson crowded into the tight aisle. "I've been looking all over for you."

"Is everything okay?" Runit asked. "You look stressed."

"Don't I always?" Nelson said humorlessly, ignoring the fact that his friend appeared to have been crying, after he saw the book in Grandyn's hand. "I just need a bac. But actually, I have good news."

"What a welcome change," Runit said, as Grandyn loaded the books his dad had pulled onto the cart.

"We can do a few test runs tomorrow night," Nelson said. "I've just zoomed my friend, totally encrypted. He's a driver for one of the fruit companies. He can meet the beverage trucks and run the load to Talent."

Talent, a tiny town in the southern portion of Oregon Area, had long been a barely noticeable speck in the agricultural district. Its roots went back to its days as a stop on the Southern Pacific Railroad in the late 1800s. The small, residential community had grown between the larger cities of Medford and Ashland, but following the Banoff, it had become even smaller. With the vast population reductions and realignments of borders, much of suburban land, in growing centers around the world, was returned to agriculture, the southern portion of Oregon Area being one such region. Massive tracts of land, measuring thousands of acres, were farmed by small cooperatives that sold to the huge agro-corporations that made up the world's second largest industry, controlled by billionaire rivals of Lance Miner and Deuce Lipton.

"And where are the trucks going in Talent?" Runit asked.

"I know someone who has land outside the orchard and vine-yard district who can hide them," Nelson said. "He has a big old barn."

"What about Seeker?" Runit asked, growing used to Nelson's convenient network of contacts.

"There's hardly any monitoring in those rural areas," Chelle said, joining them as Vida struggled to navigate the cart out of the cramped space. "There are more cows than people down there, and it's surrounded by Mandated-Forests."

The Aylantik government had set aside huge swaths of forested lands around the world, known as Mandated-Forests, in order to help reverse the greenhouse effect left over from the mass polluting days, prior to environmental reforms.

The conversation shifted back to beverage trucks and the magna-lanes. The larger fruit truck would be ready to take the test load to Talent on Friday, and again with the full loads on Saturday and Sunday night. Nelson had everything covered. There were even empty cattle trucks on standby, but everyone was hoping to avoid them for obvious reasons. Then they all scattered back to work, except for Chelle.

Suddenly they were alone, and Runit asked what he had wanted to know since they were at the medical station. "Why were you crying?"

She looked at him as if she might burst out laughing, then she stood very close so that only an inch separated their faces. The proximity made it hard for him to focus on her, but that scent of snow and tangerines pulled him in. It took great concentration not to kiss her. Chelle's whisper stole into his mind, sounding like a secret shouted in the dark.

The moment broke like a pebble thrown into still water as her hand touched his. He shivered.

"What do you believe in, Runit?"

He backed up a few inches, trying to focus on her face, but she moved with him.

"Can you confess to me now the things that keep you awake?" she asked, in an even softer voice. "The thoughts that hold your whole heart?" He could feel her warm breath on his lips.

"W-What are we talking about here?" Runit stammered.

"The only thing that matters. The only thing I ever talk about . . . everything."

"Yes," he said, almost able to taste her tongue. "I believe in everything."

"Do you?" She laughed. "I bet you do."

"But, uh, I think the first question was mine."

She pulled an imaginary thread off his shirt. "Really, what was that again?"

"You cried," he reminded her.

She stared into his eyes. "It looks like you might have been crying too."

His eyes watered at her perception. "Sometimes I think of her," he admitted. "After she died, I tried not to cry . . . I was afraid if I started, I wouldn't be able to stop."

"I know," she sighed. Chelle's own eyes teared up as they stood mirroring each other for a moment. "My husband, I hear his voice. Every day I can hear his sweet, crackly voice. He spoke in a deep tone that sounded like an on-air guy." She looked down the aisle. "And I always expect him to come walking up to me. Like he's going to be around every corner. Three damn years later, and I still think he'll be right back."

"How did he die?"

Chelle stared at him, that angry fire he'd noticed when they were reintroduced flaring.

"AOI," she mouthed.

Runit gasped. It was the last answer he would have imagined. "But he was just a banker."

"Are you *just* a librarian?" she snapped.

CHAPTER FORTY-TWO

Friday, February 2

Before the sun rose over Oregon Area's Cascade Mountains, an elite unit of Lance Miner's dark army landed at a local airport and drove into the countryside. They had reason to believe that the unknown woman, the alleged leader of the rumored revolutionary group thought to be called PAWN, might be in the area.

Polis Drast employed many tactics to keep the Pacyfik's Creatives and other potential revolutionaries in line, but informants proved to be the most effective. The only problem with his spies was that they tended to be unreliable half the time, and when they did have a fact of value, they'd treat it as such and trade it to multiple parties until it became worn and useless.

Drast knew Blaze Cortez to be a regular buyer of anything useful. Several of his purchased spies had been caught with restricted information originating from Drast's own paid informants. But, as often as not, Blaze could be counted on to provide the AOI with remarkable data.

On the sprawling AOI campus in the dry California Area farmland south of Sacramento, a city half the size of its pre-Banoff heydays, aircraft-hanger-sized data centers handled infinite amounts of Seeker-generated feeds from the Pacyfik region. Every day billions of bits were recorded, assimilated, and interpreted. The facility also housed training centers for intelligence and police units, active AOI military squadrons, and a fifty-two-hundred-person public relations department.

Drast preferred the company of DesTIn-based bots to that of humans, mainly because they were predictable and completely trustworthy. Logic and loyalty were two of the three things he valued most. The third might surprise his old friend Lance Miner, but Drast also prized love. He knew people were capable of incredible things in the pursuit of love, but most people didn't see that side of Polis Drast. They only knew of the first two of his three guiding principles.

"The world is a complicated place," Drast told a human lieutenant as they stood in the glowing shadows of endless images and data streams. "The smartest animal on Earth is also the least trustworthy. You can bloody well guess what a tiger will do, or a grizzly bear, or even a damn shark, but most humans? Hell, they can't be counted on except to cut your throat . . . and they do that with a torgon smile on their face."

"A bit cynical aren't you, sir?"

"When you've seen what I have and know what I know, you'll call me a realist. If I were really a cynic, I'd have shot myself long ago." He smiled and swept his arm across a group of INUs, causing the room to become an interactive series of floating AirViews showing real-time footage of several AOI teams, as well as Miner's unit. The sightings of the woman they were all seeking had come from dubious sources.

Drast told his top people that he didn't buy the stories, but if she *did* exist he believed she'd have to be in the southern part of the Pacyfik, down around old Ecuador, Peru, maybe even Brazil. There were vast, sparsely populated areas down there among the mountains and jungles where she could hide.

The Amazon Rainforest had dramatically increased in size

during the last seven decades. Ever since the Mandated-Forest program was put in place, the greatest wilderness on Earth, previously raped by human activity, had rebounded faster than anyone had expected. It now covered more than twice as much land as the former United States. The AOI knew the remoteness of the area had attracted small colonies of "Rejectionists," as they referred to the unorganized populace who rejected Aylantik rules and modern society. Those people, who dropped out of sight to live off-grid, were a rumor the government never confirmed, and the topic remained high on the lengthy media no-coverage list.

Yeah, she could get lost down there for years, Drast thought. *But not up here.* In spite of the huge forested tracts and low populations, there were regular patrols, satellite surveillance, and robotic sweeps. *She could never have gone undetected all this time.*

Even with his confidence, the possibility ate at him. Polis Drast's rise to power had not been bold and imaginative; it had been steady, calculated, and done with careful consideration of whom to court and whom to screw. Lance Miner would soon make him World Premier, but a major flare-up in his region before then would destroy that and unravel all his hard work. And if the woman was real and wasn't found soon, then his nightmare scenario might come true.

He placed a zoom to Blaze Cortez.

"Mr. Premier," Blaze said, smiling as his image projected out of Drast's INU.

Drast smiled. "A bit premature for that Blaze." He paused as Blaze seemed preoccupied with his hair, pushing strands here and there. Drast didn't understand why Blaze didn't just cut it into a proper style.

"You're probably right, Polis . . . anything could happen between now and the selection, er, c-section, uh, erection, no, that's not it, what's it called? Tax-collection, no, oh silly me . . . e-lec-tion."

"Your maturity has always been diametrically opposed to your supposed intelligence," Drast said, angry he hadn't been able to ignore the jab.

"Election," Blaze repeated. "A funny word. E-lec-tion. Say it very slowly and it sounds disgusting. But if you say it just fast enough it almost sounds real, like it might even be legitimate."

"Torgon-off!" Drast said impatiently. "There's not time for your sophomoric drivel. I've zoomed for a favor."

"I'm sure you have. You want to know about the woman. I gave the man holding your leash all I have. If you need more, you can find it yourself. She's just one single woman. Can't the elite AOI manage the task?"

"How much?"

"For what?" Blaze asked, sounding confused.

"For her damn location."

"I'd always thought you believed her to be a myth. And now you want an address?"

"Listen to me Blaze. You may have convinced Lance that she's real, but I think this is another one of your shakedowns." Drast clapped his hands together and stomped around the life-sized projection of Blaze as if he might start taking jabs like a boxer. "For all I know, you've taken this fairy tale and perpetuated it all these years so that you might make a play and disrupt the election."

Blaze laughed. "You give me too much credit, *Mr. Premier*. I suppose you might blame me for the Aylantik and Pacyfik War, and other events that happened before my birth. Maybe even the Banoff itself was my fault."

"Damn it, what do you want?"

"Do you know that in Spain, one thousand years ago, they called money dineros? A more beautiful word than digis, wouldn't you say? Pesos or marks, rupees or rubles, francs or even dollars! *Sólo el amor al dinero puede destruir el alma.*" Blaze paused his manic rant and stared through at Drast, as if trying to see the smallest detail in his face, then continued. "Forgive me, your Excellency, you most assuredly don't speak Spanish . . . not that Com, our modern language, isn't useful in a utilitarian kind of way, but it lacks a certain grace or heart. Do you speak only Com, or are you a truly educated man? No? I thought not. Allow me to translate. 'Only the love of money can smother the soul.'"

"I'll give you one million digis for her location."

Blaze stared unblinkingly. "You want me to remove the only thing that stands in the way of your ascent to the throne, that which would cement you into history, and the offer you propose is an amount that I spend on Field advertising *every week*?"

His image disappeared as Drast's INU went dark.

Drast's fingers worked furiously until he had an AOI captain online.

"Issue an arrest for Blaze Cortez."

The captain stood speechless before coughing out the words, "What charges?"

"Obstruction of an AOI investigation, treason, espionage . . . that should get you started. But don't worry, I'll think of more."

CHAPTER FORTY-THREE

Runit arrived first. The TreeRunners, having decided to skip classes that day, showed up a few minutes later. The rest of the staff and volunteers staggered in between zero seven hundred and eight hundred hours. All of them were exhausted and worn out from pulling and moving books late into the previous night. Even the TreeRunners were in slow motion. Chelle and Nelson showed up together late because Nelson had insisted on getting doughnuts and coffee for everyone.

"I tried to dissuade him," Chelle said, tossing Runit a banana. They had not slept together, hadn't even gotten together for a drink, and he was glad. It would not have been a good first date – too tired and too stressed. "It's organic," she said. He looked at it a little more closely as he peeled it.

Organic produce, although not illegal, was no longer certified by the government and extremely hard to find. The giant corporations managing the world's food supply and Aylantik government research had long ago shown post-Banoff pesticides and fertilizers to be entirely safe. PharmaForce even had a division involved in the consortium that manufactured the products. That, coupled with the Health-Circle endorsement, convinced all but Rejection-ists that chemicals in food were safe.

"Thanks," he said smiling. "I won't ask."

"It's how my big brother bought my silence on the doughnut issue. He knows a guy who knows a guy . . ."

"I'll bet he does."

"How's it taste?" Chelle asked.

"Amazing."

"Way different than the GMO ones," Chelle said. "You can taste the rain and the sun in it, can't you?"

"Yeah, imagine if we could grow these," Runit replied. "Cicero once said, 'If you have a garden and a library, you have everything you need.' But what if you have neither?" He tried to savor the fruit and the moment with her, but the walls of books were closing in, and having a building filled with TreeRunners during school hours made him more nervous than he'd been since the nightmare had begun.

"Don't worry about the AOI," she said, as if reading his mind. "All the TreeRunners are seniors. They're allowed to fulfill classes independently over the Field without attending their groups."

"I know, but it's a change."

"It's a small risk," she said, as they grabbed a cart and headed into the fiction section.

"All these small risks add up to danger," Runit said.

She turned to him. They were alone in an aisle. "You're a man filled with courage. Let it surface. Let it guide you."

"Even if that were true, I can't afford courage when Grandyn's life is at stake."

She put her hand on his heart. "His life is at stake either way. Don't you see? If you act from fear, you reduce his chances. You must act with courage. It's the only way."

"I wanted you to see what real courage is, instead of getting the idea that courage is a man with a gun in his hand. It's when you know you're licked before you begin but you begin anyway and you see it through no matter what," Runit recited.

"*To Kill a Mockingbird*, by Harper Lee."

"Yes, that's right," Runit said, surprised. "You know it?"

"Only because it's one of Nelson's gazillion favorite books. He made me read it when I was a teenager. Of course, I loved it and read it several more times."

Runit nodded. "Anyway, I get what you're saying. But courage is a scary thing, especially when love is involved."

Grandyn and Vida delivered carts to Nelson, who was working one of the strappers on the lower level. "Are we going to make it?" Vida asked Nelson.

"I don't know, but we'll probably get close enough," Nelson said, chewing a wad of spearmint gum.

"It's so weird," Vida began. "I was just outside and everything seems so normal on the street. Everyone is busy like it's a normal day. It's like the same old happy world out there, but inside there's this tension, this pressure. Are you guys really sure about all this?"

Nelson did not slow his strapping, but glanced at Grandyn, the kind of look one gives when they've just heard gibberish from a mentally unstable person. "Vida, do you know what a serial killer's neighbors say when they're interviewed after some horrific crime?"

She shook her head.

"They say, 'Oh, Mark seemed like such a nice quiet man, he always smiled, even helped out during the snowstorm,' or whatever."

"And your point?"

Nelson shot another look to Grandyn, who was smiling.

"My point, sweetheart, is that the world may appear all quiet and happy and peaceful, but there is a cold-blooded killer underneath all that, just waiting to strike."

Vida laughed a nervous laugh. "So you're saying you're sure about taking the books?"

Nelson let out a sigh and nodded, closing his eyes for a moment. "Yes, Vida, we're doing the right thing."

"Okay, you're the smart ones."

Nelson thought of Blaze Cortez, Deuce Lipton, and a series of other famed billionaires, plus a lot of unknown wealthy people. "No, sweetheart, we aren't the smart ones. We're the dumb neighbors who woke up to the serial killer too late."

CHAPTER FORTY-FOUR

Lance Miner stared at the new report projecting from his Information Navigation Unit as if he were rapidly bleeding to death. He started to yell, but panted instead, trying to catch his breath.

Sarlo burst into his office, ignoring the view of Miami's skyline and the morning sun sparkling on the ocean backdrop. "The Flowing is waiting," she said.

"You saw?" Lance asked weakly.

"Just now."

"This is the work of Deuce Lipton," he said, snatching his INU and heading toward the door.

She followed. "It would seem so."

He turned back, almost knocking her over. "I should have killed him! Damn it, why didn't my grandfather kill Booker Lipton so that this torgon rat bastard was never born?"

"Let's find out what happened?"

"I'll tell you what happened. Deuce paid the Premier to resign."

"But we've still got the Vice Premier, and he can announce CAAP." The Corporate Assets Acquisition Parity Board was so close to reality, Lance could almost taste the unlimited power he was about to wield, yet he could feel it slipping away.

"Maybe, but do you think Deuce didn't think of that already? The Vice Premier will probably drop dead of a heart attack at the swearing-in ceremony."

"That would be risky for Deuce to try," Sarlo said in her calmest voice.

"Deuce Lipton's middle name is "Risk." Hell, this could be the start of a torgon coup!"

While in flight to Washington, Lance zoomed Drast.

"Why is he resigning?" Drast asked. "This can wreck our timeline."

"That's for sure. Depending on whom the rising Premier picks as the new Vice Premier, we could have a complicated mess to deal with."

"You're thinking Deuce did this?"

"Damn right he did!" But as the shock had worn off, Miner couldn't be sure. "Although as I think about it, there are at least twenty people who are going to be hit hard by CAAP."

"How did word get out?"

"You tell me."

"Well, I've already got a warrant out for the biggest info-broker in the world . . . Blaze Cortez."

"You have what? Damn it, Polis, what were you thinking? Cancel that now."

"Let me tell you what he did first."

"I don't care what he did. You do *not* arrest that man. I'd prefer it if you didn't even offend him."

"If you're not on offense, then you're playing defense," Drast said. "We need him under control."

"I don't need you quoting the unofficial AOI motto to me. You think of Cortez as a nuisance? Well, he's anything but that. Blaze Cortez is the fulcrum on which our fragile peace rests."

"How so?"

"Because there are two sides battling for the future of our society. Two sides that are heading toward an open war," Miner said. "Up until now we've managed a secret war that has maintained the illusion of peace. And an illusion of peace is as close as we'll ever get to real peace, so long as money is involved."

Sarlo's eyes widened at her boss's admission, but by moving her hands across the glowing reports revolving around her INU, she pretended not to be listening.

"If we go to an open war," Miner continued, "then we have already lost. The Aylantik coalition's grip on power depends on peace. So, if that peace is broken, our defense of peace will cripple us."

"And Blaze Cortez?" Drast asked impatiently, his voice rising.

"Cortez is the battlefield of the secret war. The Aylantik wants to keep things as they are, the others want change, and the desire for change is a powerful force, one we have been fighting for decades. But Blaze Cortez wants something different from either side . . . he wants whatever works for him. His interest isn't in the Aylantik or in the changers, he's in it for the money and power he can get out of it. Both sides use him, and our battles are won and lost in his activities. If Blaze has a good day, peace continues."

"And if he has a bad day?"

"Peace continues. He's the ultimate neutral party because he doesn't care, and yet he has the power to matter in the conflict. Historically, war was fought on battlefields and then in back alleys and dark night encounters of spies. Then we went to boardrooms and the cyber world, but today we fight a war within the sphere of one man's life."

Miner thought he may have overstated this. He didn't think Blaze deserved that much credit or power.

"But he can't be trusted," Drast said.

"Of course not! Now pull that warrant. It's not as if you would have found him in the first place. You can't even find a single woman with a thousand agents."

"We're getting closer."

"How do you know?"

"Because I know where she slept last night."

"So she's alive?" he exclaimed.

"Well, at least the rumor of her is alive."

"What's that supposed to mean?" Miner waved off a cyborg server offering a drink from the Flo-wing galley.

"I'm not convinced that some rogue pocket of Rejectionists or Creatives isn't keeping this false legend alive."

"You think she's an urban myth?" Miner laughed. "Are you willing to bet your future on that assumption?" His voice grew more agitated. "Are you willing to risk the future of *humanity* on your little hunch?"

"We're following up. We're pursuing every lead. If she's out there, we'll find her."

"I know you're working it Polis, and I hope you're right. That she isn't real. But even that would present a situation. Why is there so much chatter flaring up about her now? If Rejectionists, or Creatives, or so help us, PAWN, is using her as a rallying point or some kind of a symbol, then we've still got a big problem."

"There is nothing of size. We'd have detected it."

"Lance," Sarlo broke in, "the Vice Premier is on."

"Keep me updated. And as the Chief says, peace prevails, always," Miner told Drast, as he ended the zoom.

"Maybe we'll get some answers," Sarlo said.

"From the Vice Premier? More likely lies."

CHAPTER FORTY-FIVE

Drast zoomed Blaze Cortez. "Why do you think I'd want to speak with you after you tried to arrest me?" Blaze asked in an amused tone.

"How do you know about that?" Drast asked, annoyed by Blaze's smirk.

"Please." Blaze twisted his head, so that his cheek touched his shoulder, his long brown hair dangling in his face. "I knew about your issuing the warrant before you knew."

"Very funny."

"Oh, not really. Well, it is to me, but for you it's very sad. Of all the many things I know, which is nearly everything, one thing I don't know is what it feels like to be as inept as you are." Blaze smiled for only a second. "Could you tell me, Polis Drast, what is it like to be deficient in intelligence?"

Drast could have grown angrier. Instead he laughed. "You'll never know."

"Of course, you're quite correct."

"I need her location."

"Yes, you do. But you're wasting my time. It is so frustrating speaking with those such as you."

"Tell me what you want."

"I already have everything."

"Everyone wants something."

"That is not the case, Polis Drast, but you're close. *Not* everyone *wants* something, but . . . everyone *needs* something."

"Fine, Blaze, what do you *need?*" he asked, watching the DesTIn-expert precisely shell and eat peanuts in a way that seemed intent on bothering Drast. It was working.

"Something you're not in a position to give."

"Damn it." Drast punched his hand. "And you say it's frustrating talking to *me*."

"She is within mere kilometers of your forces at this very moment and yet you will not find her."

"I don't believe you." Drast imagined watching Seeker footage of Blaze arriving at an AOI prison, restrained, and beaten. He desperately wanted to incarcerate this man.

"I don't care."

"You're the least trustworthy man on the planet."

"I assure you that title does not belong to me."

"Prove it." Drast changed his Tekfabrik to all black and adjusted his collar.

"I have nothing left to prove, but I'll tell you something just because it gives me pleasure to aggravate you." Blaze tossed a peanut in the air and caught it in his mouth before continuing. "The woman's influence extends well beyond your region."

"Until I am World Premier, only the Pacyfik concerns me."

"Hmm. Trouble in another region might even work in your favor. Perhaps you're smarter than I give you credit for . . . perhaps not." Blaze shelled more peanuts and ate them as if there were nothing tastier in existence, throwing shells on the floor and sucking the salt with a mouth-smacking sound.

"I've been exhausting myself trying to wring any truth out of your lies."

"Any kind of thinking must be exhausting for you. But I'll tell you, trying to comprehend my intentions or thoughts might cause your brain to hemorrhage. Oh, but you have connections at PharmaForce. They'll get you the right pill. Might even save your life."

"Last time," Drast sighed. "What will it take to get her location?"

"I have three bits of data to insert into that tired mind of yours, Polis Drast. For starters, she wasn't where you think she was last night, and I suggest you rethink your position about events outside the Pacyfik mattering to you. She has more power than you might believe . . ."

"How could she?" Drast asked. "Even if she is alive, she is only a myth."

"You poor, dear man."

"Where is she?"

"I will give you my demands tomorrow. If you can meet them, I shall provide her exact location, down to the square-meter."

Lance watched the Vice Premier's face projected from his INU. He knew the man well and didn't particularly trust him.

"The Premier has only cited personal reasons, more time with family as the reason for his resignation," The Vice Premier said.

"I know that much," Miner said impatiently. "But surely you've been briefed on the Corporate Assets Acquisition Parity Board?"

"Yes, I have, Lance. But CAAP will have to be shelved for a few months."

"What? Why?" Miner demanded. "The A-Council has approved it."

"I'm aware of that, but things have changed since the approval. Don't worry. I'm sure we can get CAAP back on track in the near future," the Vice Premier replied in the smooth tone of a seasoned politician. "Right now we have other concerns, and there's the matter of continuity. CAAP is just too politically sensitive in this climate."

"What are you talking about? If you want to be endeared to the masses, go after the wealthy."

"The masses aren't the ones who keep the world calm," the Vice Premier said, echoing words Lance had said before the Council many times.

"Like hell they aren't," Miner said, knowing he sounded hypocritical. "It's a small crime that grows into a scandal."

"We'll have to continue this later Lance. I'm about to be sworn in."

Lance stared at the space above his INU where the image of the Vice-soon-to-be-Premier had been.

"It's just a delay," Sarlo said. "We'll get in to see him tomorrow. We can rally the Council."

"This is a failure that will make me look weak in front of the Council. Damn Deuce Lipton."

"Be careful Lance," she said, busily motioning around her INU.

"I'll make sure CAAP will still happen," he said, glancing out into the sky as they flew over Savannah, Georgia.

"Instead of a distraction for Deuce, it may become one for you."

"That's just what Deuce wants."

She nodded.

"Any luck getting us in to see the Premier? I want to know how Deuce got him to resign."

"He's not willing to see you," she said, working AirViews that were filling the air in the small cabin around them.

"I'm sure he's not."

"Lance, the A-Council President is on," she said, pointing to his INU.

"Tough break, Lance," the President said.

"I'll say," Miner shot back coolly, knowing the President was secretly amused and probably in on the operation that had cost him his dearest project.

"You've still got the votes. We'll get it back on the agenda in the spring."

"It'll be too late," Miner said.

"For what?"

"Deuce Lipton is funding rebels. By spring we could be in an open war."

"I know your theories Lance, but you have not one shred of proof. Nothing. And on top of that, if Deuce were to fund rebels he'd be cutting his own throat. I know the man well. He's only interested in peace. He may not be on the Council, but he is not undermining the Aylantik government. Deuce profits from the status quo more than any of us."

"You're wrong," Miner said.

"I don't think so, but if you have a case, bring it to the Council and we'll reconsider your previous requests to eliminate Deuce. In the meantime, you'd better be certain nothing happens to him. The ramifications from Deuce's death would be far-reaching and destabilizing to the entire world. But particularly to you. You'd be the prime suspect, and the Council would not be forgiving. Not in the least."

CHAPTER FORTY-SIX

Deuce Lipton watched the library through Seeker, as well as several other feeds not available to the AOI monitoring system. For more than fifteen years he had been slowly hijacking Seeker feeds. The process required incredibly complex programs, total access to AOI systems, and patience, all of which he had.

His crew would begin arriving at the library in a matter of minutes, and while he had committed more than a hundred people to the operation, fewer than a quarter would be able to work inside the building. They would straggle in over the next few hours disguised as plumbers, technicians, delivery people, and patrons.

The day, so far, was going according to plan. The World Premier had shocked the entire planet, and especially the A-Council, by his sudden resignation, thus delaying the expected Corporate Assets Acquisition Parity announcement. With Deuce's access to Seeker, and the even more powerful tools of direct satellite surveillance, including the 'silver bullet,' as he called his covert Eysen-INU monitoring, he had enough secrets to easily persuade someone like the WP to resign.

The WP was so corrupt, normally he might have ignored Deuce, but Deuce had things on people the WP cared about. Ultimately, the same tactic had convinced the Vice Premier that he should not back CAAP either. However, the A-Council would not take the defeat indefinitely, for even those on the Council who had only reluctantly backed Lance Miner's latest scheme, agreed on one basic tenet of the A-Council's By-Laws: the Council must always prevail.

Today's bold maneuvers had been risky, and they would buy him only a few months at best. But he only needed a matter of months. After that, CAAP would be the least of the Aylantik governments concerns.

As Deuce watched the happenings at the library in real-time, another AirView showed an AOI report on PAWN. He almost smiled at the irony of the name, because in recent days he'd felt locked in a chess match with Lance Miner, the A-Council, Blaze Cortez, and a revolutionary woman he knew too little about. In truth, Miner and Deuce had been locked in a duel since birth, but the minutes were ticking down toward checkmate, and he was less sure than ever that it would be his king standing at the end.

He saw Chelle and Vida together in a reference room. They seemed to wind up in each other's company often. These two women worried him, unpredictable and influential in their own ways. Each could affect the outcome, and anyone with that power needed to be watched and possibly "ended." Because of the Eysen-INU stations in the room, he could hear the conversation.

"Have you thought more about it?" Chelle asked as she pulled an old volume of pre-Banoff prison poetry she'd been trying to locate.

"Yeah, and you've made me question my decision, but I still need the money."

"There are other ways to get money."

"No way I know of to get that kind of money fast."

"There are."

"They can't be legal," Vida said, moving a small stack of books onto a cart.

"Don't kid yourself. When society is this out of whack nothing is legal, least of all the laws which govern us into submission."

"Kind of a harsh view."

"Hardly." Deuce noticed Chelle's fists were clenched. "They know everything we look at on the Field, they know how long we're looking, everything we read, everywhere we go, whom we talk to, what we say, whom we love, and what our weaknesses are. Someone is listening to us this very minute, do you realize that?"

Deuce actually jerked away from the AirView and looked over his shoulder.

"If they were listening to everything in the library, wouldn't we all be in jail right now?" Vida asked.

"It isn't just the AOI who listens, and the government doesn't always have to arrest a so-called criminal to punish them."

Deuce was growing more worried about Chelle with each passing, tension-filled second.

"What would I have to do?" Vida asked slowly. "For the money I mean?"

"Keep a secret, memorize a few lines, deliver them at the right time, and then answer some questions. Like being an actress."

"Sounds easy enough. And for this *acting job*. . . how many digis will I receive?"

"Fifty thousand."

Vida stared at Chelle, mouth agape. "It sounded easy, but for that kind of money it must be dangerous. Why so much?"

"Because it *is* hard."

"And dangerous? I deliver a few lines and get enough money to change my future?"

"It's not dangerous, but it's important. That's why the money seems a lot. Those few lines won't just change your future, they'll change the world."

Vida started to laugh, but then saw Chelle's serious expression.

"And what are those lines?" Deuce wondered from his San Francisco office. "And to whom is she to deliver them?"

"You better tell me what I have to say," Vida said, "*before* I decide. I mean selling my bearing-rights may be something I regret one day, but it isn't dangerous." The system was so rigid that even with a second child, twins were not permitted. All pregnancies were monitored in the earliest stages and triplets or more were absolutely illegal.

"Good girl," Deuce said out loud to himself. "Let's hear this." He double-checked what he already knew, that there was no way the AOI could be hearing this conversation.

"I can't tell you everything yet," Chelle said, looking around the room. "Some things need to happen first, but I'll tell you this." She leaned close to Vida's ear and began whispering.

"Come on!" Deuce yelled at the AirView. He couldn't hear anything.

Vida's eyes widened. "I had no idea," she said quietly, pained by the disclosure.

"So you see," Chelle said, pulling away from Vida after a few moments of whispers, "you won't be in danger, but he is. And your words will be the thing that saves him."

"But how do I know?"

"Know what?" Chelle asked.

"How do I know that you're the one I should trust?"

Chelle smiled and put a hand on the younger woman's shoulder. "Because, my dear, before this conversation you didn't even know there were those involved who could not be trusted. If you couldn't trust me, why would I have told you?"

"I guess you're right," Vida said, smiling with an expression more of relief than of happiness. "But it's a big deal. I'm shocked."

"I know. You thought we were just saving the last books made of paper from the flames. But now you understand. The fire will take far more than our history, the thoughts, and ideas of great minds . . . If the books are burned, we don't just lose words, we lose the *truth*."

CHAPTER FORTY-SEVEN

A courier delivered a message to Nelson and then waited. Nelson found Runit pulling books in the vast fiction section.

"Novels hold more contentious ideas and contemplate far more truth than nonfiction," Runit said, looking up from a thick volume as he saw Nelson enter the aisle.

"That's why there are so damned many of them on the list. We never could have found them all without Blaze's DesTIn program," Nelson said.

"Neither would the AOI."

Nelson nodded. "I don't like to think about that too much. But I have good news . . . the cavalry has arrived."

Runit looked at him questioningly, even warily.

"Don't worry, old friend. The richest man in the world has not forsaken us." Nelson smiled. "Deuce Lipton has sent twenty-two people to help us finish this task."

"How does he plan to slip them past Seeker and the AOI?" he asked, looking around for Chelle, who usually expertly fielded such questions.

"He's smarter than we are. The courier who delivered this is one of his people. He'll do some tinkering with Seeker and the others will stream in as plumbers, techs, pizza guys, bringing real pizza I hope, and other assorted folks, including ordinary patrons."

"Sounds risky."

"I don't know how else we'll be able to do it," Nelson said gravely.

The remainder of the day was a blur of activity and stress with an unremitting drumbeat of intensity that Runit had never known. If an AOI official had come into the library, they would have all been shot on the spot. Seeker micro-infinite-definition 3-D-ready cameras were tampered with, replaced, and blocked in risky and suspicious ways. As near as Runit could tell, only half a dozen real patrons showed up that day, but it was impossible to be sure. One of them asked him why the place was so busy.

"We're involved in a major reorganization and book sharing program with the university," the librarian heard himself saying in his most official voice. It seemed to satisfy the person, but he still believed his arrest and execution were imminent. Runit muttered the words of Proust to himself as the person walked away. "If we are to make reality endurable, we must all nourish a fantasy or two."

Runit wandered into the library's basement to check the progress, and maybe to get lost. Nelson, working a strapper, glanced up as he saw him approach.

"Did you know Ray Bradbury wrote the initial manuscript of *Fahrenheit 451* in the basement of a library?" Nelson asked, as if they'd been in the middle of a conversation.

"Really?" Runit welcomed a diversion.

"He was poor and lived in a tiny house at the time. With the distraction of his kids, he needed a place to work. The library at the University of California in Los Angeles had a room in the basement with rows of a couple of dozen Underwood and Remington typewriters, which they rented for ten cents per half-hour. They actually had timers. So Bradbury pounded out the words as fast as he could type and finished the first draft in about nine days. In between, he would take breaks and wander around the library."

"Wow. I knew he loved libraries, but now it all makes even more sense."

"That was almost one hundred fifty years ago," Nelson said. "But it feels kind of like we've come full circle with old Ray."

"Bradbury once said, 'Without the library, you have no civilization.' I guess we're about to find out."

Later, Chelle brought Runit some dinner and he allowed himself a deep breath. All the activity had raised the temperature inside the building, and Chelle appeared in a tight black tank top and dark jeans. She handed him a wrapped sandwich. He recognized it as being one from his favorite deli around the corner. He peeled back the brown paper and smiled at his standard BLT with extra pickles on the side.

"How'd you know?" he asked, flattered she'd gone to the trouble to get his favorite.

"I saw it on an AOI report," Chelle said casually.

"What?" Runit stepped back, not appreciating the humor.

Chelle laughed. "Vida told me."

"Oh." He felt foolish. "You asked?"

"You're too stressed. The last thing we need is for the last librarian to have a heart attack."

"Thanks," he said, raising the sandwich in a little toast. After finishing his first bite, he said, "That deli has been there since before the Banoff. It's nice some things never change."

"This library has been here since long before the deli," she said.

That time he caught the irony.

CHAPTER FORTY-EIGHT

The first beverage truck rumbled to a stop against the loading dock's heavy, black, rubber bumpers. Once they had Grandyn's side platforms lined up well enough, the driver pushed a button, which raised all the panel doors. Then the chain began like a bucket brigade. It went with the bundles passing from one pair of hands to the next. Grandyn and three other TreeRunners worked the end of the line, a pair on each side of the truck. Grandyn threw a bundle to his buddy and tossed the next one into the cargo space. It took them a few minutes to get the pace figured out, but once they did they moved about four hundred books in sixty seconds, and had the first truck loaded in less than ten minutes.

Runit, Nelson, and Chelle took a break near a second floor window to watch the first loaded truck roll out. Nelson checked his watch. "Looking good."

"We've just committed the crime," Runit said. "Up until now we could have changed our minds, but now it's too late to turn back."

"One day we'll be celebrated as heroes," Nelson said.

Runit clutched his tightening stomach and stared as far down the darkened street as the beverage truck's headlights allowed, searching for AOI agents, local cops, the grim reaper, anyone who might torg up the plan, his life, and Grandyn's future. But only a routine Portland evening was out there, at least as best he could tell.

The drones – he didn't have the faintest idea what they did – thinned out slightly at night. The lit directional signage and lane lines dimmed on most of the roadways. Shopping districts, which had come in and out of style and necessity during the past seventy years, were springing back to life. A few blocks away, Runit knew people were strolling in and out of posh and glitzy techie boutiques that attempted to capture what vintage shopping was once like. And he could smell the restaurants. Even in the era of delivered groceries and prepared meals, people still went out to eat and drink with friends and family.

Turning to Chelle, Runit asked, "And what do you think? Are we doing the right thing? Are we heroes?"

"They fired first," she said coldly, then turned, grabbed a cart, and pushed it back into one of the aisles. "And we're still way behind schedule. If we hope to get the rest of these precious books to safety, we need to be pulling."

Runit looked at Nelson questioningly.

"Don't take it personally," Nelson said. "She takes everything personally."

Runit nodded, but remained confused.

"Let's go check on the boys," Nelson said, fumbling for a bac. "It'll give me an excuse to smoke a quick one."

As soon as they got there, Runit instantly calculated that they would be able to do three runs per truck. The loading dock, thick with tension and books in the darkened evening, paradoxically also held a joyous, party-like atmosphere as a rebellious sense of expectancy surrounded the crew. The second truck, already half-loaded, sat ready to continue its noble mission. It was nineteen hundred hours, and as long as they were done before midnight there shouldn't be much trouble with Seeker, especially with the one key camera obscured.

"Good job," Runit said, smiling to Grandyn, who barely had a chance to acknowledge his dad while heavy into moving bundles.

"You heard about the World-Premier?" Nelson asked between drags.

"Yeah. Surprised he resigned so close to the end of his term."

Nelson stared at the ground, contemplating his glowing bac as if thinking about whether or not to tell Runit something. Runit, too busy watching the loading, missed it, and the moment passed. "We'd better get back to work before my sister comes looking for us."

"Sometimes I think she's mad at me, but I don't know what I did," Runit said, almost to himself.

"She's not mad at *you*, she's mad at the world." Nelson took a last drag and let the smoke come out of his nose. "Shoot, Runit, you're the first guy she's been nice to since her husband died. I'm pretty sure she likes you, and I'm damn sure you like her."

"I have to admit, I'm rather taken," he said, a little embarrassed.

"Just be careful," Nelson said, making eye contact. "The timing couldn't be worse."

"Because she's still mourning?"

"No. Because we've just started a revolution."

CHAPTER FORTY-NINE

The trucks drove the round trip in just over half an hour. With a short time to park on each end, ten minutes to load, almost twenty to unload, they were looking at an hour and ten minutes per run. With the additional help of Deuce's people it would still be tight, but for the first time they had confidence that everything would be out by the end of Sunday night.

By twenty-two hundred Runit was feeling almost relaxed, or was it exhaustion? It had been only an hour since he stopped regularly checking out the windows for AOI agents. Nelson had been useless for almost as long, as his flask had been emptied and refilled from the spare liters he kept in his LEV, and then emptied again. Runit found him asleep on the floor of the young readers' room.

The plumber, who had been the first of Deuce's people to arrive after the courier, ran into the room. "AOI agents are on the street."

Runit's knees went weak, but he managed to remain standing. *How could he get Grandyn out of there?* "What are we supposed to do now?" he asked.

"We must not panic," the man said, seeing in Runit's face that he was doing just that. "There's only one patrol so far, and we're trying to find out if it's routine or pointed."

"Meaning?"

"Are they focused on the library, or are they just in the neighborhood?"

"Have you seen Chelle Andreas?" Runit asked, suddenly wanting her AOI expertise.

"She's on the lower level strapping." The "plumber" looked at Nelson, passed out on the floor, and thought about the objectives Deuce had sent them in with: assisting with the removal of books and monitoring Chelle and Vida. He knew there was a possibility that he'd be ordered at any time to abduct, or even to kill Chelle or Vida. "Hold, I've just received information . . . The AOI patrol is not on us."

Runit noticed the plumber had not consulted an INU, and therefore must have an implant. This made him nervous and relieved at the same time. Imps were dangerous, too much information available to them, too machine-like, and why not? After all, they were Field-connected micro-computer processors with a neurological interface. Whenever anyone got an implant, which were expensive to install as well as maintain, they seemed to become less human. Their emotions took a backseat to the data driven power of the implant.

The plumber pulled up AirViews, which may or may not have come from his INU. Runit wasn't sure because he'd heard that people with certain types of implants could display visuals from optic drives imbedded in their wrists. The images immediately grabbed Runit's attention.

He recognized the building, only half a block up the street. The AOI agents left their LEV as another, larger one showed up. Four more agents got out of that one. The first two used a laser blast to blow in the front door without even slowing down. All six agents disappeared inside and, shockingly, another AirView, floating at Runit's eye level, displayed the interior scene. Before he could ask how, he became riveted as the AOI agents interrogated the three people they found. The questions lasted only about two minutes. Unfortunately, the images did not have accompanying sound. Then, without warning, the suspects were executed. At least that's what Runit assumed, as the agents pushed a silver, tubular device into the back of the necks of each of the two men and a woman, who instantly collapsed.

"Are they dead?" Runit heard himself asking the plumber, but he scarcely recognized his own voice. It sounded like he was talking from down in a sewer somewhere – hollow and muffled.

"Absolutely," the plumber said. "Better them than us." His hands were moving, punching virtual buttons and sliding images through more screens like a dealer in a casino. "Are you okay?"

Runit squatted on the floor. "Better them than us," echoed in his now aching head. "No," Runit said, "I'm not as accustomed to seeing people killed as apparently you are. Don't you realize what just happened? It's still happening, right now, only a few hundred yards from here?"

"Yes sir, I do."

"And what were those poor people doing?" Runit asked in a strained voice. "Probably something far less treasonous than us."

"We'll never know."

"Really? Something tells me your boss, Mr. Deuce Lipton, already knows."

"I'm sure he's working on it," the plumber said. "But . . ."

Runit didn't hear the rest. He was already heading to the lower level, to Grandyn. He passed Chelle on the way.

"What's wrong? What's happened?" she asked upon seeing his face.

He didn't stop moving "AOI."

"Here?" she asked, head darting, looking for threats, escapes, and answers.

"No." He slowed only slightly. "Busted . . . killed three people across the street, a few doors down."

"What side of the building?"

"Front." He stopped and looked at her as if she were a monster. "Didn't you hear me? The AOI, the ones we're defying, just killed three people. I *watched*."

"How did you watch?" Chelle asked, suddenly concerned that Runit might have been closer to the action than she thought.

"One of Deuce's guys had it on a screen."

She smiled. "Impressive."

"Look Chelle, I don't know what the hell you're really doing here, maybe you get off on this stuff, but I'm getting Grandyn, and he and I are getting as far away from the library as we can possibly go."

She grabbed him. "Stop."

"What? No."

"Runit, you can't go anywhere. Don't you get it?"

"No. I guess I don't. Why can't I?"

"Because there's nowhere to go."

CHAPTER FIFTY

Runit's heart started to race. He turned and stared directly at Chelle. Suddenly, he felt sick, the kind of tightness and trembling that attacks your stomach, bowels, and throat when fear introduces itself and it's so close you can actually smell the burning, decaying stench of its foul breath.

It had been a mistake going along with Nelson's scheme to save the books. He knew that now. He'd known for at least a day, although he'd been denying it. That there was more going on than just saving books. Most of all though, he knew it was already too late to turn back.

"I have to save Grandyn." He choked back tears. The promise to Harper to keep their son safe weighed heavy. "He's the whole world."

She threw her arms around him. "I know you think so, but Grandyn doesn't want to live in the world the way it is," she whispered.

Runit pulled away. "How do you know what he wants?"

"Because. It's. Not. True." She spat the words.

"What isn't?"

"The world."

"I don't have time for conspiracy theories. I'm going to get my son."

"It's too late." She pleaded with her eyes. "If you try to run, they'll find you and kill you both, just like those people you saw. Your only hope is to see this through. Stay with us."

"Damn it!" He slammed his fist into a stack of books, sending it toppling onto the concrete floor. "Why should I believe you?"

"Because you do."

He knew she was right, but admitting it made him feel helpless. Runit looked down at the books and saw an old copy of *How the Aylantik Coalition Saved the Human Race*.

Chelle saw him looking at it and laughed.

He looked at her, wanting to be disarmed by her, yet uncaring if she saw the scared desperation in his burning eyes, eyes that begged for truth. "Rummaging in our souls, we often dig up something that ought to have lain there unnoticed . . . Tolstoy," he said in a manner not inviting a response. "We're calling it a night."

She nodded and stood aside.

Thirty paces later, he found Grandyn sealing up the last truck of the night.

"Just in time," Grandyn said.

"You've worked hard," Runit said, trying to sound proud rather than afraid.

"The next two nights will be even harder, but we might just make it."

Runit thought Grandyn sounded old. He'd always been mature. Being raised by a single dad and the TreeRunners had both contributed to that. But now, with such stakes and the AOI killings he'd just witnessed, all of a sudden Grandyn seemed too old.

"I hope we get to find out."

"Something you want to tell me?" Grandyn asked, studying his father's expression, a face he knew so well.

"No. Nothing I *want* to tell you. But you know the risks. And it turns out those risks are even higher than I realized."

"It must mean all this work is worth it."

"Maybe." Runit looked at all the young people helping. He'd jeopardized their lives. "Wrap up. We need to be out of here in ten minutes."

"Is everything okay?" Grandyn saw the strain in his father's face.

Runit shook his head. "Ten minutes."

Eight minutes later, Grandyn joined Runit on the main staircase. They sat and talked as everyone else filtered out of the building. Soon only the plumber, Vida, Chelle, and Nelson remained, the latter still passed out on the reading room floor.

"Dad, in case you forgot," Grandyn reminded, "I'm eighteen."

"I know. What you don't understand is that when I look at you, I see you as eighteen, and twelve and ten and eight, six, three, a baby in my arms."

"It may surprise you, but I know you do. I can feel it. See it in your eyes."

"You got that sense of perception from your mom. She always knew what I was thinking."

"Stop trying to protect me. I've been well raised. I'm part of mom and you. Tell me what's going on. You're not just my dad, we're best friends."

Runit pulled Grandyn into a smothering hug, which his son fought only for a second. "The AOI just killed three people down the street," he whispered into his ear.

Grandyn broke free from his father's embrace. "Were they involved with us?"

"No. I have no idea who they were, or what they were doing, but it seemed like a mighty bold warning."

"If a building burns down on the next block, does that mean ours is next?"

"Maybe."

"We're just moving books."

"It's more than that."

Chelle and Vida walked up. "Are you guys ready to go?" Chelle asked.

"Dad was just telling me how serious this is, about the AOI killings," Grandyn said.

"What?" Vida asked, looking from Grandyn to Chelle.

"They should know," Chelle said, flashing a glance at Runit. "The AOI keeps the peace in a peculiar way. They kill anyone who disagrees with the Aylantik government."

Grandyn shook his head. "That's not true," he said. "There are plenty of people who speak out about stuff."

"Anyone who gets too close, or worse, gets even a small following, winds up dead." Chelle's tone was harsh. "Or do you think there are so few dissenters because everyone is so happy?"

"So they'll kill us if they find out what we're doing?" Vida asked.

"In a heartbeat," Chelle snapped. Runit shook his head slowly, not to disagree, but in his absolute dismay that he'd led these innocent children to slaughter.

The plumber ran up the stairs. "The AOI is going door-to-door."

"Torgon!" Runit groaned.

"How close are they?" Chelle asked.

"They're two buildings away. They'll be next door at the bottling plant any minute, then we're next." The plumber worked AirView screens as he walked. "We need to be out of this building . . . *Now!*"

CHAPTER FIFTY-ONE

Runit, Grandyn, Vida, and Chelle followed the plumber back down the stairs. They jogged until they reached the now closed bay door at the loading dock. Runit reached down to unlatch the old bolt.

"Wait," the plumber said, scanning AirViews and listening to instructions in his ear only he could hear. "No good. They have a LEV in back."

"What the hell are they looking for?" Runit asked, afraid of the answer. "Are they onto us?"

The plumber shook his head without answering. "Do it now!" he snapped.

"Do what?" Runit asked, confused.

"He's talking to someone else," Chelle said as they remained huddled in the lower hallway.

"Estimating," the plumber said, turning back to Runit. "They'll be here in six minutes."

Runit thought of his wife, saw her holding Grandyn as an infant, and thought of the post-Banoff author, De Elmers, who wrote, *"Nothing changes the world so much as the birth of a child."* If it were just him, he'd take up arms and push the AOI back with all he had, but there was Grandyn to think of. His world had changed, and now it was ending.

There could be no escape. *How the hell could a librarian be expected to outsmart the most powerful and sophisticated regime in human history?* he asked himself, disgusted. His next thought was of a road strewn with traps and obstacles. A gauntlet he could run, somehow save Grandyn, and go out in a blaze of glory.

But there was no road. He didn't have a gun or a weapon any more powerful than the words pressed between obsolete covers of old books.

"Can we get to the roof?" Chelle asked.

"Maybe," Runit answered, returning from his devastated reverie. "I mean, yes."

"No," the plumber said.

Runit looked at Chelle, assuming she might know if the plumber was answering her or giving orders via his implant across the Field. The plumber answered before she had a chance to figure it out herself.

"We have something. Everyone stay right here."

"But we only have six minutes," Runit said.

"Actually less than five now," the plumber said.

"Dad, maybe Chelle's right. As a kid I used to play on the roof. There are places we could hide up there."

"Go twenty-six!" the plumber barked.

Vida jumped.

"What's going on?" Runit demanded.

"They'll be here in three minutes," Chelle said.

"We just gave them a diversion," the plumber said, never taking his eyes off the screens floating around them. He spun it in the air so they could all see.

"That's AOI's Portland headquarters," Chelle said. "Did you do that?" She pointed to flames covering the front of the AOI building.

"It doesn't matter how it occurred," the plumber said without emotion. "All that I care about is if the agents who are about to leave the bottling plant come here or return to their own burning building."

"Is anyone in there?" Runit asked, motioning to the AOI headquarters in flames. "Did anyone die?"

"Who cares?" Chelle said. "If they find us, *we* die."

Runit nodded and looked at Grandyn.

The plumber switched the AirView to display a live shot of the front of the bottling plant. Grandyn wondered how they were getting the footage. "Dad," he whispered. "Where are all these cameras? How can we see it as it happens?"

The agents emerged from the bottling plant.

Runit, who still wasn't over seeing the executions inside the building the AOI had raided, didn't know how to answer his son.

"There they are," Chelle said. "I hope they didn't find anything suspicious in there. The last truck isn't back yet."

"They aren't looking for us," the plumber said. "They're looking for PAWN."

Chelle swallowed hard and clenched her fist.

Runit looked at Chelle, wondering if she knew what PAWN was since he'd never heard of it, and noticed her tense at its mention.

As the agents started toward the library, Vida pointed to the AirView. "They're still coming! They'll be here in a minute!"

"Calm," the plumber said.

A second later, one of the agents activated an AirView out of his INU and they began running. No one spoke. Runit didn't breathe as the agents ran toward the main entrance of the library and then passed it.

Grandyn looked at his father as he let out a loud breath, then back to the screen as a LEV pulled up and the agents jumped in, speeding away, presumably to the AOI headquarters fifteen blocks away.

"Let's get out of here," Runit said. "Grandyn, can you help me with Nelson?"

"Sure Dad."

They all went to collect the drunken author. Chelle talked nicely to him as Nelson partially woke and protested the move. Runit decided to take Nelson to his place, even though Chelle said she could handle him.

"We have to finish," Chelle said to him after Grandyn and Vida pulled away.

"I need to think about it," Runit replied.

"When Nelson wakes up, tell him I said to tell you about Belgium."

"Why don't you tell me now?"

"We can't stay here, and anyway, Nelson will do it better. He's the storyteller in the family."

"Am I going to like what I hear? Maybe I don't want to know."

"It doesn't matter what you want. The world is burning." She motioned to the smoke, visible in the moonlight, rising above the city. "And *you* lit the match."

CHAPTER FIFTY-TWO

Polis Drast had a dozen AirViews open as he watched the Portland AOI building burn. The media, already streaming images around the world, reported that initial assessments pointed to electrical causes, but Polis knew people would suspect otherwise. He'd learned that although most of the population remained happy in their oblivious state, there were always those who paid attention. They were the dangerous ones, the ones PAWN could recruit.

But right then the bigger question, which made him want to use all means necessary to find Blaze Cortez, was learning who did this. Blaze would know. *And that weasel knows the whereabouts of that woman likely responsible for this outrageous affront,* he thought. That's when the wave of fear hit him. The Pacyfik region had become a powder keg, which could easily destroy his chances of becoming the next World Premier. *If I don't handle this right, this could lead to an open revolt.*

The AOI Chief appeared in one of his AirViews. Drast sighed, seeing her expression. As always, it looked mean, and he thought her short "razor-sharp" hair, coupled with the pinched face, gave her the appearance of a Dobermann pinscher attack dog.

"Polis, what the hell is happening?" she snapped. "Is it PAWN?

Do you have a target list? What's the motive? Have arrests begun?" She fired off questions like a professional boxer hurling body shots.

"I'll be making a major arrest tomorrow," he said, hoping that Blaze Cortez wouldn't demand too much for the information. But whatever the weasel wanted, he knew he'd have to give. It wasn't just his political future anymore. The peace was at stake.

"*Tomorrow?*" the Chief snarled. "By tomorrow who knows what other damage they will do."

"I believe the firebombing was the direct result of terminations conducted tonight in Portland," Drast said. "A firebombing is unsophisticated and requires almost no planning. If this was anything more than a retaliatory strike, there would have been real damage."

"Because you think they have weapons?" she asked, concerned.

"As you know, large amounts of weapons were never accounted for after the Banoff."

The Chief, of course, knew this. But she, like so many in the AOI, preferred to believe that mistakes had been made seventy years earlier when the new constitution made gun ownership illegal and teams had rounded up, then destroyed, millions of firearms. A painstakingly tedious effort of matching registrations and other records had been undertaken to ensure that they got them all, but the results were less than conclusive. Still, she had difficulty believing that nearly three quarters of a century later, any kind of organized resistance could lay hands on a sufficient quantity to do any serious damage.

"Do you have this under control Polis?" the Chief asked, knowing AOI policy granted regional heads great autonomy. They were like naval captains. They ran their regions as they saw fit, but still answered to a supreme leader. The Chief was that leader, and wanted to be sure this ship didn't sink.

"Things will look much different by Monday," he assured her.

"Okay," she said reluctantly. "Keep me updated through the weekend. Peace prevails, always."

He took one more look at the fire, now under control, and then studied the images on another AirView. These showed the bios and photos of the three people killed earlier on his orders. His was a job of conflicting realities: kill, keep the peace, and provide the appearance of safety while combating dangers from all sides. The complexities of his role were impossible to understand, even by him.

The raid, in reaction to intelligence gathered in the search for the woman, had gone well until the fire strike. Their brain scans would be studied and their INUs downloaded into AOI super-processors. That information could prove invaluable, with or without Blaze's assistance. A team would normally work all night, but with the damage to the AOI headquarters, that would have to be done out of Seattle. Which meant results might not be available until late Saturday.

However, the fact that they were meeting proved PAWN was active, and the immediate retaliatory strike demonstrated something even more ominous. PAWN wasn't hiding anymore. They felt bold enough to start hitting back.

Times were changing. Drast knew he had to change them back to the way it had been, or at least change faster than PAWN, if he were to become World Premier, a job he would happily kill half the Pacyfik population to get.

The man actually responsible for the AOI firebombing, Deuce Lipton, stood surrounded by massive AirViews displaying the incident, making him feel as if he were in the middle of the fire. The move had been regrettable, but he'd been left with an awful choice: lose the library or allow PAWN to be compromised. He knew PAWN would get the blame, but the library was obviously too important to let go.

As he paced between the Seeker and media footage of the fire, he knew he'd made the right choice, but the AOI would now move swiftly to kill what they saw as a sleeping tiger. PAWN, no longer a rumor, existed in unknown form, and Polis Drast would have to find out how large a threat this rogue group really was.

Lipton looked like a crazed symphony conductor, his hands and arms moving wildly as he spun between AirViews. The measures he implemented, from the top floor of his secret San Francisco office, would change history. His grandfather, Booker Lipton, had taken the first steps nearly a hundred years earlier, and now Deuce had been forced to do what his whole life he'd been hoping would not fall to him.

In those few moments he had mobilized the BLAXERs, his private army. Tens of thousands of "security experts" around the globe would now be on stand-by. Assets were transferred and contingency plans, involving products his companies had already supplied or would soon be supplying to the AOI and Aylantik government, were initiated. Deuce glanced past the floating AirViews to a far wall where portraits of his father and grandfather hung.

"No turning back now, gentlemen," he said out loud. "It has begun."

CHAPTER FIFTY-THREE

Saturday February 3

Runit woke to the smell of coffee and toast. The familiar surroundings of his home on the outskirts of the city seemed suddenly strange. With all that had happened, it felt as if he'd been away for a long time. Nelson, who'd been too drunk to go home alone, had bunked at Runit's. He looked much worse than he felt, judging by the way his fingers swiftly worked over the virtual keyboard.

"Aren't you hung-over? How can you write?" Runit asked.

"Hangovers are for college kids," Nelson said in a raspy voice. "If I don't write every day, I'll die. Not all at once, but a little at a time as the words clutter and clog my creative arteries until suddenly, in a quiet moment, I shall cease to breathe."

Runit knew the feeling, that part of his soul had been strangling him for years. "You missed some scary stuff last night."

"Oh?" Nelson asked, glancing back at his AirView of words, realizing the rest of the day and part of his inspiration would be lost.

"The AOI busted some people across the street."

He shifted uncomfortably. "Who?"

"I have no idea. In case you've forgotten, I'm just a simple librarian."

"Of course," Nelson said theatrically, "the *last* librarian."

"The AOI executed people . . . a few hundred meters from where we were stealing books. They were going door-to-door . . . Nelson, the AOI was on the library steps last night heading for our torgon door!"

"Who was executed?" he asked, a note of desperation in his voice.

"I don't know," Runit repeated. "Could it be friends of yours?" Runit suddenly had that realization again that he was missing something. "Chelle said you should tell me about Belgium."

Nelson shot a quick, surprised glance, then stared into the adjoining room, wrapping both hands around his hot mug of coffee as if it were the only thing in the world keeping him warm, thawing his blood. The half-knowing of the world's secrets had left him so cold and empty.

"We live in a crime," he mumbled to himself. After a long moment, he went to his coat and rummaged in its many large pockets until he found a pack of bacs.

"You can't smoke in here," Runit said.

"I torgon know – damn torgon well – I can't smoke in here!" Nelson exclaimed as he contorted in such a way that could only be described as climbing into his coat, then headed for the back door. "But if I'm going to tell you about Belgium, I'm gonna smoke. So if you want to hear what I have to say, you'll have to follow me out into the cold."

The patio was small, but the view was large. The Portland skyline guarded the distant horizon. The morning mist had danced crystal-like as the sun managed to find a few openings in the threatening clouds. Nelson sat on a bamboo-framed chair made from ecofabric and put his feet up on an old wicker chest that must have predated the Banoff by fifty years. Runit stood, still spreading jam on a bagel, and waited until his friend inhaled enough smoke to engage a reluctant section of his brain.

"Belgium is no easy topic," Nelson finally said in a bluish-gray exhale. "Are you sure you're ready to hear it?"

"Chelle thought I was."

"It's my guess that she wanted me to tell you about Belgium because you were talking about quitting. Am I right?"

"I watched those people die."

Nelson raised his eyebrows. "Tell me how you managed that and are still here talking to me. Unless you're dead, in which case I am too and this is not at all what I expected."

"Are you making light of this!?"

"What else would you have me do, Runit?"

Nelson jumped out of his chair and threw an angry look at Runit, then walked the perimeter of the small, fenced yard. It had once been a glorious garden of vines, shrubs, and flowers, but since Harper's death Runit had let it go wild. Even the two apple trees and a plum tree had become tangled in the weeds. But Runit loved it there, and it reminded him of Harper. The house sat slightly elevated above the sloping lawn, so a fine view of the beautiful city was always there, even over the weathered, slat-board fence.

Nelson returned, satisfied that no neighbors could overhear them. He sat down again, pulled off his now-damp shoes, and lit another bac from the end of the spent one. "If I didn't allow my humor to occasionally spare me from the insanity of this world, I would forget my place and either start giving suicidal speeches, or worse, I would become part of it."

"One of Deuce's guys, the plumber, let me see it on his INU. I watched them kill those people." Runit shook his head. "Why *shouldn't* I quit? They were coming for us. They were going to kill Grandyn and me the same way."

Nelson wanted to talk about what else Runit had seen. He'd already figured out that Deuce was tapped into the Seeker system, and he'd seen enough similar AOI actions while visiting Deuce's Seattle office to know how Runit felt. He needed to talk to the plumber. He needed to see the footage and confirm what he already believed. That the three people Runit had watched being executed were good friends of Nelson and Chelle's. But all of that would have to wait, because he had to convince another friend not to give up. He had to shatter what was left of Runit's world and tell him about Belgium.

He dug into another pocket of his long black coat and found the flask.

"The thing is," Nelson said, pouring the last of the 'tonic' into his mug. "You and Grandyn are already dead."

Runit looked down at the disaster of a man. The old author appeared haunted by every character from every book he'd ever written, and probably even more by the ones yet to escape his head. "Explain it to me slowly," he said, trying to contain his anger and unquenched fear.

The mist turned to a light rain, and Nelson was glad for the opaque Plantik sheets that covered the patio. Still, he was cold, and some of the wet from the grass had left his socks damp. "Let me smoke inside. I'll sit next to the window." His look, pleading and cranky at the same time, somehow convinced Runit.

"Fine."

Nelson almost smiled as he grabbed his shoes and pushed inside. He pulled a wooden chair to the bay window that offered the same view of Portland and turned the crank to open the glass. He remained standing, put one foot up on the chair, took a long drag, and considered his words.

"The last library in old Europe, as you know, was in Bruges, Belgium. The librarian, his wife, and their two daughters died seven weeks after the library was closed."

CHAPTER FIFTY-FOUR

Runit's mouth opened, but he couldn't force anything out.

"Australia too. And the nine before those. As near as we can tell, it has always happened. Within weeks of a library closing, the librarians and their families die. So you see, you really are the last librarian. The others are all dead."

"Is this true?" he whispered.

"I'm sorry to say it is. But that's not all. There was something different about Belgium. The part that Chelle wants me to tell you."

"How do you know all of this?"

Nelson inhaled deeply, as if the smoke were life-sustaining. Then he regarded his bac lovingly, all the while thinking, *How much to tell Runit?* Nelson had been over these conversations dozens of times, scripted them in his author's mind, but real life often brought surprises superior to those any writer could imagine. He didn't want to tell him much more. Not until all the books were out.

"You're part of some kind of underground, aren't you?" Runit pressed.

"Deuce Lipton wasn't the only person who tried to save the

books in Belgium," Nelson said, exhaling far less smoke than he'd taken in.

"You've answered my question by ignoring it and by telling me someone else wanted the books. Was it you?"

"Friends of mine. They had a few people on the staff helping." Nelson shivered involuntarily. "That's the thing. In Belgium, in the end, all the staff, volunteers, anyone associated with the library, were killed." He noticed a photo of Runit, Harper, and Grandyn taken on Oregon Area's coast. He recognized the cliffs and rock formations.

"Torgon. And no one noticed?" Runit asked, dry mouthed. "How do they cover up a mass murder like that?"

"You know how they do these things. People disappear, people die of 'natural' causes, and anyone left alive is consumed in fear."

"No, I don't know how 'these things' work. Why would I know? I'm not a spy or a revolutionary, I'm a damned librarian!"

"I guess you didn't know . . . but now you do."

"You want to overthrow the Aylantik government, don't you?"

Nelson stared out the window.

"Damn it, Nelson. When this started you said it was the books, but the books aren't the real objective, they're just a part of the game. I never would have gotten into this if you'd told me the truth in the beginning."

"I told you about the discrepancies and the manipulations. You knew I knew Blaze Cortez and Deuce Lipton. All the pieces were there for you, you just didn't put it together . . . because you didn't want to know."

"How dare you?" Runit grabbed the bac from Nelson's hand and tossed it in a glass of water. "How dare you put Grandyn and me in this kind of danger!? And what are you thinking? Do you really want to end the longest run of peace in human history because you don't like someone editing your damned books!?" Runit shouted in a tone of anguish.

"Peace at gunpoint is not peace."

CHAPTER FIFTY-FIVE

Lance Miner paused at the window of his penthouse office and gazed out at the old capital city of Washington DC. Its core skyline had remained almost unchanged for more than a hundred years, while Rosslyn, Alexandria, and Arlington, Virginia had merged into a major city of gleaming skyscrapers fused with solar-glass, laser electricity, and super alloys. Much of the land beyond had been returned to agriculture, and the rural population levels were closer to those of the first part of the twentieth century. He continued walking the perimeter of the eighty-seventh floor, enjoying the three-hundred-sixty-degree view. Finally, he heard the voice he'd been waiting for.

"I think you should reconsider your choice for World Premier," Blaze Cortez said through his INU as an AirView opened, allowing a virtual Blaze to take the scenic stroll with him. "That is, assuming you still get to choose. Things sure have gotten messy fast."

"Blaze, you overestimate my enemies."

"Really? Are you sure?" He pushed his hair back out of his eyes. "Deuce Lipton is a formidable foe, but he's overplayed his hand by forcing the Premier to resign. That action directly defied the Council and shows he's scared, and if he's scared, he's vulnerable."

"Maybe, but being scared is not always a sign of weakness, it could be— "

"In my experience only two kinds of people show no fear. People who are crazy, and people with nothing to lose."

"Deuce is neither of those."

"Ah, maybe. But it depends on how you look at it. His perception of reality might be slightly different from ours, and that could fit any definition of crazy. A man who has everything may believe there is nothing to lose." The virtual Blaze stopped, spun around, and smiled at Miner. "The thing is, my friend, Deuce may not be your greatest enemy."

"The woman."

Blaze nodded.

"Then tell us how to find her . . . please."

"I was ready to do that this morning, but now I'm not so sure."

"Nearly any accommodation can be made. I'm certain we can make an exchange that would prove most rewarding to you," Miner said, looking past the translucent version of Blaze Cortez to the Washington Monument, currently celebrating two-hundred-fifty years since construction of the obelisk began.

Oh, the world was so different then, but yet much the same, he thought, *intrigue and profits colluding in the run-up to a civil war*. That war actually delayed the opening of the five-hundred-fifty-five-foot monument, still the world's tallest stone structure. It had been built to honor the leader of another revolution against the world's greatest power. *Can I avoid this revolution?*

"That's just it," Blaze said, breaking the silence. "You can't give me what I want. Only by withholding the information can I hope to gain an advantage."

"And what is that?"

"A shift."

"Hell, you mean a revolution."

"A shift can occur by many means."

"We'll find her anyway."

"You haven't so far, and you've had years."

"We didn't know she was real before."

"And now you do? Then the question is . . . will you get her in time?"

"Blaze, I've always valued our relationship, and I have the highest respect for your calculating mind, but I'd be remiss if I didn't warn you. Do not wind up on the wrong side of this situation."

"I never do."

Miner zoomed Drast as soon as Blaze's image faded out. "Cortez still isn't willing to give us her location. Something else is happening. You need to request an immediate AOI troop buildup. Sweep your damned region! That woman is the tip of an iceberg, and I want it melted."

"That may give the appearance that I don't have control of the region."

"So does a firebomb at AOI regional headquarters. So will a war starting in Oregon Area."

"Okay." Drast's frustration with the search for a single woman had grown complex. Everything could just slip away. His recent conversation with the AOI Chief echoed in his head. The region suddenly seemed to be a tinderbox, and the library was a problem. He'd take care of that, as soon as he finished with Miner.

"Use my people, break legs, intimidate, rape, plunder, and pillage, I don't care. But *find* that woman before she finds us."

CHAPTER FIFTY-SIX

The flash message felt like a kick in his gut. Runit looked up from his Information Navigation Unit and saw Chelle. The two of them had been working the rare stacks on the upper floor. He had hoped to be in a different part of the building, away from her, yet wanting to be with her at the same time. The latter occurred when Nelson suggested they re-prioritize and all the adults moved to the section of the library housing most of the pre-Banoff books. Once there, Chelle just seemed to find him.

He wanted to believe it was because she liked to be near him too, but part of him worried about her knowledge of the surveillance systems, the AOI killing her husband, and all that had occurred in Belgium. He didn't know if he could trust her. He didn't know if he cared. Chelle Andreas might be very dangerous for him, but he hadn't felt this alive since Harper died, and even then . . .

Chelle read the fear on his face. "What's happened?" she asked, moving toward him.

"The county just notified me that the burn will take place on Sunday instead of Monday. The AOI will be at the library Sunday morning. Why do they keep moving the burn up? We're dead."

"No," she said. "We'll just have to get them all out today." She checked the time. "We've got fifteen hours until midnight. We can make it."

"Only if you can defy the laws of physics and the AOI patrol doesn't return."

"Have you always been a pessimist, or is that something new?" she said lightly, but with a stern stare.

"Forgive me, but I only get that way when I'm breaking the law, smuggling contraband, involved in a treasonous conspiracy, and watching people getting executed across the street."

"I think you got that way when your wife died."

Her comment bit him, and he had to resist the urge to lash back. But he thought too much of her to risk an argument, and in any case, he knew she was right. Life had indeed gone gray when Harper died. He'd even thought of suicide, and might have followed through with it if it hadn't been for Grandyn.

His son saved him, not just because he needed to take care of him, but because his son shared much more in common with his mother than he did with Runit. His rebellious streak, determination and passionate extremes, intense creativity, commitment to a cause, all had come from her. In his son, Runit saw a faded reflection of his wife, as if she were still alive inside him somehow. When Grandyn spoke, particularly on serious topics, Runit heard Harper, as if distant music, still talking to him.

"Let's go tell Grandyn that we'll need all the TreeRunners that he can get, and maybe Deuce's plumber can bring in more people," Runit said.

Chelle smiled. "See, I knew there was a fighter in there somewhere." She brushed her palm over his heart. "I'll go tell Nelson."

As he headed to locate his son, Runit felt as if he'd been fighting through a weird dream. He recalled Mark Twain's words, *"Truth is stranger than Fiction, but it is because Fiction is obliged to stick to possibilities; Truth isn't."*

CHAPTER FIFTY-SEVEN

Grandyn thought he could get four or five more TreeRunners. The plumber, after contacting Deuce, said ten additional people would arrive in the next few hours. It still seemed impossible, but like his mother, the more difficult the challenge, the more resolved Grandyn became.

"They aren't burning these books!" he'd said through gritted teeth as he heaved another five bundles onto a cart bound for the back door staging area.

Runit caught up with Nelson in the long storage room on the lower level. The space had once been offices, back when the library needed a bigger staff to serve several thousand patrons a day. Now they were lucky to see that many in six months. And, of course, Runit thought, *No one will ever read in this building again.*

"What are these books?" Nelson asked, leafing through an old, leather-bound volume.

"They're the private collections. After the Banoff, when book ownership became so expensive, many families and private libraries donated their books. Without any budget, it took decades for volunteers to sort them. Many were discarded, but there are quite a few gems in there. "

"Are they in the system?"

"Not these."

Nelson squinted his eyes. "Are you serious?"

"Damn. In all the confusion I forgot that Blaze's DesTIn program will not have run these."

"Is there a list?"

"Nothing complete."

"Then we have to take them all," Nelson said, looking at boxes containing at least two thousand books.

"Didn't Chelle tell you?"

"Yeah, we've got to finish by midnight," Nelson said. "But we have to get them all. We don't know what they're after. There could be one paragraph on one page inside one of these antique books that changes everything." He blew dust off an old copy of *The Revolution*. "This was written in 1918 in Norway, the year after the Bolsheviks took power in Russia. It's a study of repression throughout the ages and analyzes revolutions throughout history, including the American in 1776 and right up through Russia's in 1917. And look at this," he said, holding up another thick volume. "This is an encyclopedic work on the true cause of every war ever recorded up through 1975. It's called, *The First Shot*. Ever hear of it?"

"No."

"Of course you haven't. They don't want anyone reading this stuff. Maybe they closed every library just to suppress these two books. Shoot, I'm going to hand-carry these out of here myself."

"I know." Runit thought again of the people he'd seen killed. He thought of his wife's copy of Zinn's book. "Change lies sleeping within books, just waiting for the covers to be opened."

"Exactly. Your life has been books. These two books have been in this building since before you were born and you've never read them!"

"Maybe because I'm not interested in revolution the way you

are." They'd been friends for decades, and Runit often tired of Nelson's romanticized notion of controversy.

"Yes, you are. You're just afraid of death."

"Afraid of . . . do you really want to talk to me about that?" Runit moved toward Nelson as if he might shove him. His face flushed. "I welcome death! There have been many days when I actually invited it, when I would have embraced it. You know what I've been through. I've had to hold it together for Grandyn. For my son. I can't just drink and eat my way through life the way you do!"

Nelson pushed a box in the direction of Runit, and two cartons full of books teetered off a stack and landed at his feet. "I'm a little bored with your damned 'poor-me-single-dad' routine. Do you think you're the only one who ever lost anyone? Maybe you think you have a monopoly on grief, but there's a world full of loss out there. Where is your courage man? Why haven't you written your book? Try creating something sometime. Risk it!"

"Torg off!"

"Damn it, Runit! Do something instead of feeling sorry for yourself."

"Mutsu, a post-Banoff author said in 2066, 'Creativity can't be coaxed, it is fragile and sometimes comes only when the world is ready; waiting until it is safe for it to grow into something great.'"

"Really? I see it another way. 'An idea that is not dangerous is unworthy of being called an idea at all.' Oscar Wilde." Before Runit could reply, Nelson added, "I think I agree with Kafka: 'We ought to read only the kind of books that would stab us.'"

"Writing isn't everything," Runit said quietly, reaching down to pick up the books.

"Leave them!" Nelson shouted. "They're going to burn anyway, right?"

"Why don't you face up to reality? Life isn't a novel."

"Wrong! Life is a novel that no one bothers to write down."

Nelson took a slug from his flask. "Maybe if you realized that, you'd be better at playing the part of the hero."

"Why am *I* the hero?" Runit asked, still picking up books. "Because I'm the last librarian?"

"Yeah. That's all that's required. You're in the right place at the right time. Don't you feel it? We're here at the crossroads of history. This is as great a moment as any of the ones in these books." He smacked his hand on *The Revolution* and *The First Shot*. "We can change everything. We can get it right this time."

Runit stared at him for a moment. "I may not have read *those* books, but I am a librarian, as you like to constantly point out, and I've read thousands of books. I was also Harper's husband, so I picked up a thing or two about pre-Banoff history, and I can tell you that the revolutionaries always think they're right. They always plan to make it better, get rid of the oppressors, and create a wonderful world. But you know something? They never do. They end up corrupt like the rest until someone comes along and throws *them* out, thinking they're going to make it better. Believing the same lie."

"Eventually someone has to get it right," Nelson said, taking another shot of liquor. "It might as well be us. We have to try to find the right path or we become complicit in the crimes against us."

"You tell me to *create* something. I've *created* a son. I've run this library and countless things have been *created* here under my watch. My library has helped *you* write *your* books. There are a million ways to *create*. It's not always typing words, painting pictures, or acting in a play. And you don't get to decide which is correct."

"Fair enough." Nelson said, sitting on the edge of a table and reaching for a bac. "But, Runit, you're just scared. They're going to burn these books. Nice and reasonable people don't do that. The perfect world they've given us is a lie, and there's a reason it's a lie."

"I *am* scared," Runit said. "And I'm brave enough to admit that. But you didn't see how easily they killed those people. True, I don't know what they might have done, but they never got a chance to defend themselves before being sentenced to an immediate and violent death."

"I knew them," Nelson said, lighting the bac.

"Who?"

"The people you watched die."

CHAPTER FIFTY-EIGHT

Runit looked at his old friend and wondered if he really knew him at all. "Why do you, a bestselling author, know people that the AOI executed without even bothering to arrest? Just how deep are you in this thing? Damn it Nelson, you tell me right now. What's going on?"

"We don't have time for this Runit."

"*Make* time."

Nelson lit a bac and tapped the air around his INU. Chelle's face came through. "We're up in the collections room. Would you mind joining us? Runit wants to know . . . everything."

"Can't we do this tomorrow?" Chelle asked Nelson in a businesslike tone. "We don't need any distractions until we get the books out."

"No," Runit yelled. "I'm tired of being lied to!" His outburst surprised himself even more than it did Chelle.

"I'll be right there," she said, disappearing off the AirView.

"I'd really rather you didn't smoke," Runit said. "I know they're going to burn this place tomorrow, but I'd rather not breathe in that poison."

Nelson took another drag without commenting.

A few seconds later, Chelle came into the room. "You're allowing him to smoke in the building now?" Chelle asked.

"No, he's just being rude."

"Put it out, Nelson," Chelle demanded, and her brother complied. "Now, please listen to me Runit. I know you're confused about all of this, but you're better off not knowing everything right now. You've already reached the point of no return, so it hardly matters when you get briefed. But I promise, as soon as the books are safely out of here, I'll answer your questions."

"No."

She looked at Nelson. He nodded.

"Have you ever heard of an organization called PAWN?"

Runit shook his head.

"For decades PAWN has sought to end the rule of the Aylantik government and the elite super-rich who control them."

"Why? I mean I know everything isn't perfect, but compared to the shape the world was in before Aylantik came to power, we're living in utopia."

"Before the Aylantik came to power was before the Banoff," Chelle said bitterly.

"Are you telling me that since the Banoff, there has been a group, PAWN, trying to stop Aylantik?"

"Yes." Chelle took his hand into hers. "PAWN stands for People Against World Nation. Even before the Banoff, there were those who sought to unite the world under one government. The Aylantik is just a front for the super-rich corporate owners who control everything."

"And the books?" he said, thinking he should pull his hand away but wanting to keep it there.

"There is something in them that Aylantik wants to suppress. Therefore, we must find it."

"But we don't know exactly what it is?" he asked, not believing they really didn't know.

"We're working on it," Nelson said.

"You both should have told me all this in the beginning," Runit said, yanking his hand away.

"Would you have gone along with us?" Chelle asked.

"Hell no!"

"That's why we waited to tell you," Nelson said.

"Well, good for you." Runit scowled at his old friend. "Is that how you generally get what you want? By deceit and trickery?"

"Desperate times," Nelson said.

"Yeah, well one day someone will write the history of what we're doing here and I sure as hell hope they get the facts straight." He glared at Nelson.

"Maybe you'll be the one to write it," Chelle said.

"Nah. I'll be long dead before they work out this tangled mess."

"I hope not," she said. "But you're right about one thing. It *is* a tangled mess. And once you learn more about it, you'll realize why we kept you in the dark."

"Real friends don't have to lie to each other to coerce them into doing something," he said, drilling another look into Nelson.

"Really?" Nelson shot back. "Then why didn't Harper ever tell you?"

Chelle let out a sharp sigh. "Damn it Nelson!"

"What? What did you say?" Runit gasped. "What didn't Harper tell me?"

"That she was part of PAWN."

"We don't need this now," Chelle said, shaking her head at Nelson.

"You better tell me what in the hell you're talking about Nelson, or I'll zoom the AOI myself right now."

"Harper was active in PAWN," Nelson said defiantly, taking another swig from his flask.

Runit just stood there, gaping for what felt like hours but was only a minute. Finally, with contorted facial expressions, something between pain and anger, he almost whispered, "Were you sleeping with Harper?"

"Oh, good God!" Chelle threw up her arms, exasperated.

Nelson looked confused, but didn't respond.

"You'd better answer me right now. Were you having sex with my wife?"

"How did this turn into a high school drama?" Chelle asked.

Nelson managed to get a bac lit and, with an exhale of smoke in a gravelly voice, said, "I loved her too you know."

"Yeah, I know that, but my question is, were you screwing her?"

Nelson's eyes filled as he found Runit's gaze. "It only happened once. She regretted it, I'm sure of that."

Runit's lips tightened and then quivered. He opened his hands and extended his fingers, then made a fist, glanced at Chelle's face to confirm she had known, then walked out of the room.

"Don't just walk out Runit!" Nelson called after him. "We've been friends too long."

"There is no friend as loyal as a book," Runit responded, barely loud enough to be heard, but Nelson recognized the words of Ernest Hemingway, and in them the hope that they might get past this.

Runit moved through the familiar confines of the library as if he'd been dropped on the surface of an unexplored planet. Nothing seemed recognizable. Even the air felt strange. He wanted to un-know everything he'd heard that day. The crimes and broken illusions pushed him into a wall of blinding fury. He expected tears, cornered in that dark part of the cold building which held centuries of lessons and emotion, but all that came was a silent chant from Lewis Carroll's *Alice In Wonderland*. "*I can't go back to yesterday because I was a different person then.*" He repeated it several times until he stumbled away, bleeding a bloodless pain that he wished would kill him.

He wandered until, coming to the lower level, he saw the only friendly face in a world suddenly lost. His son, the one all this effort was supposedly for, but now even that seemed in question. The crushing realizations of doubt piled in on him.

He didn't live in a utopian society. His life had been wasted on books. Friends used him and lied. His beloved wife was an adulteress, and beyond that, she was some sort of spy or secret agent for a clandestine revolutionary group bent on taking over the world.

"Dad, we're going to make it!" Grandyn shouted upon seeing him.

He watched his son push a cart piled high with bundles toward the back door. Grandyn's elation rallied Runit. He nodded and gave him a thumbs-up before going back upstairs to find Chelle.

CHAPTER FIFTY-NINE

Polis Drast looked over the maps lighting the tiles beneath his feet. Three INUs filled the room from floor to ceiling with projected images so that he walked in a real-time 360-degree view of wherever the action was. He zipped from the investigation at the charred Portland AOI headquarters to the wilds of Oregon Area's mountains, then to coastal cliffs of the southern Washington Area. The search for the woman leading PAWN had narrowed to four sectors in and around the Washington and Oregon Areas. Even without help from Blaze Cortez, they would have her by nightfall.

He tromped through the virtual room as troops arrived in the Pacyfik region's major cities. Lance Miner's warning that Blaze might be using the woman as a smokescreen concerned him.

No, he thought, *it terrifies me.*

Drast moved like a choreographed martial artist as he went from location to location, making the INU show him people and places, tapping Seeker and integrating data overlays, intelligence analysis, and probability projections. Polis Drast was more than a rigid policeman, more than a skilled politician. He was an INU wizard, and could glean more from the "mighty marble" than perhaps anyone other than Deuce Lipton.

His DesTIn-based assistant circled the room, its thin blue light signaling that an assessment was ready and waiting for engagement.

"What?" Drast shouted, arguing with DesTIn as if it were an angry spouse.

"War appears imminent," the digital voice said.

"Of course it is, but it needs to wait. I will never become World Premier if a war starts first. Particularly if it breaks out in the Pacyfik."

"PAWN is ready for war."

"I need to know how to stop it. Where do I send my troops?"

"All current deployments are on target. Our conclusions state that only the woman can delay war."

"And killing her?"

"Assures war begins before her body burns."

"So we must capture her alive. And then?"

"You lie and manipulate until she believes your intentions toward reform are equal to hers."

"Then we'll need full brain scans on her so I can understand what she wants."

"She wants peace."

"How do you know?"

"Because we are not at war yet."

"Perfect. I want peace too until it's time to kill all the scum."

Drast gave the order to send a Neuron-mite unit into the area where they expected to find the woman, and he wanted full brain scans to begin as soon as they found her. He also gave the verbal command to wipe the last fifteen minutes of memory from the DesTIn-based system. It was one of the reasons he liked DesTIn bots so much – loyalty was programmable.

The INUs floated and spun, and when he couldn't see it all fast enough, he danced and twisted as two more INUs shot across the space and zipped into place. Something was there in all the images and data formulas, and he had to find it.

Lance Miner had moved his operations for the moment to Denver. For reasons unknown, but most likely related to weather control, that city had grown when others had declined. Many population shifts had occurred around the globe and could easily be understood. Without oil and gas, Houston and Dallas had shrunk to population levels of the 1920s, and Texas, instead, had become one large-scale solar farm. Earthquake-risky Los Angeles had seen its number of residents drop by seventy-five percent since the Banoff. But, just as risky, San Francisco had maintained its pre-Banoff level, perhaps because much of the world's high-tech industries were still based in the northern California Area.

Sarlo entered her boss's office and stared for only a brief moment at the rugged, snow-capped Rocky Mountains stretching into a cloudless sky of deep blue. The majestic peaks seemed ready to push away the stars as soon as night came. Denver was her favorite office. Most people toiled away with digital views out their window, gorgeous, changeable, and super-high-definition, but Miner preferred real ones. "I can tell the difference," he always said.

"Why are we in Denver?" she asked.

Sometimes she thought she was in love with Miner, other times she thought him an egomaniacal monster bent on world domination. But she always thrived on his aura of power. She really was helping to rule the world, and that kind of drug is addictive beyond all reasoning.

"Research," Miner said, staring out the window on the opposite wall where he could see the skyline of glass needles and shiny silver spires that had been built mostly in the last four decades.

She had guessed as much. Denver was now a center for people

with implants. Not as big as the implant communities in old Mexico and Asia, but she suspected that Lance didn't want to be far away from the hunt for the woman. It amused her that Miner didn't trust communications channels enough to conduct his "research" over the Field. Instead, he almost always flew to the source.

"What are we researching?"

"PAWN," he announced. She had also figured that out, but what he said next shocked her so completely that she nearly collapsed. "And Booker Lipton's second son."

Sarlo thought she knew everything about Deuce Lipton, at least as much as her boss knew.

"Booker Lipton had another son?" she asked.

"Still does," Miner said, enjoying her surprise.

"You mean he's alive? Deuce Lipton has a living uncle?"

"So it would seem. Do you recall Booker Lipton's missing years?"

"Of course. He vanished for a decade after the Banoff," Sarlo said, easily recounting the long-memorized facts of the Lipton family.

"His wife gave birth to a second son during that time, Deuce's father's younger brother. And they kept him hidden. Kept it a secret."

"For seventy years?"

"Yes."

"How? Why?"

Miner looked at his assistant as if she'd asked him to explain where babies come from. "It's the Liptons."

She nodded. "Secrecy is their business, I know, but— "

"We just intercepted a conversation between Deuce's kids Twain and Tycen."

"That doesn't happen too often," she said, impressed.

"New technology. It's shaky, but it tracks and aligns with DNA, and once we have a link it's tough to beat."

"Whoa."

"Yeah, unfortunately it is still very buggy. Cuts out more than it's in."

"Do we have it on both of them?"

"Just Tycen at this point. But we'll get Twain too."

"And the uncle, I just can't believe it. Why so secret?"

"That's what we're going to find out."

CHAPTER SIXTY

It took Runit a while to find Chelle. The building was large, busy with activity, and he moved in slow motion. He finally found her on the main level, pulling books as if nothing had happened.

"Where's Nelson?" he asked.

"Outside. Smoking, drinking, reliving painful memories." She waved a hand dismissively.

"I want out of this."

She just looked at him.

"I can't escape, can I?" he asked hesitantly.

"No."

He stared into her eyes for a moment, and then beyond at the books and on into forever.

"We're doing a good thing here," she added.

"Do you remember when we were going in for the shots and you cried?"

"Yes, of course."

"And you held me?"

She closed her eyes and sighed. "I was protecting you." Her response was unexpected, and his confused look prompted her to take his arm. "Come with me." She led him to a small sitting area under one of the large windows. The chairs, large and soft, were meant for reading, and they both fit into one comfortably. "I gave you an anti-dose."

"What do you mean?"

"With a patch through your skin, at your neck and wrists. I gave you an anti-dose to counter the effects of the state's booster shot."

"Why?" he asked, the betrayal he'd felt earlier now compounded by this newest violation.

"The government is controlling and poisoning the population through the regular injections." She held his gaze. "No one is safe as long as they're getting the shots."

"Do you have proof of this? Because the last time I checked the health of the world, it was pretty damned good. There hasn't been a major outbreak since the Banoff, and every time something flares up somewhere, the Health-Circle comes up with a way to defeat it within weeks."

"Don't you find that suspicious?"

"Is there proof or not?"

"There is."

"I'd like to see it."

"Forgive me for not carrying it with me. But don't worry Runit, I'll make it a priority to show you the proof of the conspiracy even though you probably won't understand it or allow yourself to believe it."

"Why did you give me, what did you call it, the anti-dose? Why am I so important?"

"Because I care about you."

"Really? I wish that were true. Chelle, you have no idea how much I want to believe that. . . or maybe you do. Maybe that's why you've been able to play me so well. I simply would like to know why? For the books? No. . . there's something else."

"I get why you don't believe me. I do. We've had to keep a lot from you and—"

"And you've lied a lot, and for what? For your revolution? Well, do you know what George Orwell said? 'In a time of deceit, telling the truth is a revolutionary act.' This is the man that wrote *1984*."

"I'm sorry Runit, but I really hope you'll forgive me and trust me. My entire cause is about bringing out the truth."

"Ha! You really are a piece of work."

"That same day we protected Grandyn too. He was given the anti-dose. That wouldn't have happened. Grandyn isn't vital to the cause. But I made sure he was spared too because of my feelings for you."

"We thank you very much," he said sarcastically. "But for all I know you've put him at risk of death. I mean, Chelle, you're asking me to take your word over that of the Health-Circle, which has kept me healthy my whole life. And your credibility isn't exactly the most reputable at the moment."

She nodded. "You've had to learn a lot of unpleasant things today. But ask yourself how you feel when we're together. How you've felt from that first moment the other day, after I got back in town. Was I manipulating you into feeling that way? Was the attraction mutual?"

He stood there dry mouthed. She moved closer.

"Is the attraction . . ." her voice hushed in breathy syllables, "mutual? Is it?" Her lips were only inches away. "Runit, I don't have time for distractions. You're the very last thing I need in my rather complicated life right now. And yet, here you are."

"I don't know what's real anymore," he said, trying to mask his disappointment.

"Nothing is real other than the moment we're in. Don't you get it? Life is only about this."

She reached behind his neck and pulled him into a kiss. He wanted desperately to resist, to push her away and to yell at her for all the betrayal he felt. Instead, he returned the kiss as if her mouth was his only source of life-sustaining oxygen.

CHAPTER SIXTY-ONE

The plumber caught Runit and Chelle in their moment. He'd report their kiss to Deuce in a few minutes, but now, "Bad news," he snapped.

They were startled out of their passionate embrace. "What now?" Runit asked, annoyed on so many levels.

"I've just received reports that the AOI is on high alert in the Pacyfik region. They're mobilizing substantial assets, and extra units are arriving in Portland as we speak. Salem, Eugene, and Medford are also under similar scrutiny, but the whole northwest is lighting up. It's a massive buildup."

"They know," Runit said.

"It's a show of force," Chelle mused.

"Of course it is," Runit replied.

"No. What I'm saying is they do *not* know about *this* operation," Chelle explained, returning to her military-like persona. "They may know *something* is going on, but if they knew we were taking the books we'd already be in jail. They don't need to thump the whole region just to arrest us. No, I'd say with certainty that they do not know."

"I'd have to agree," the plumber added.

"Fine," Runit said, knowing he was far from the espionage expert in the conversation. "But how are we supposed to get the books out when AOI is all over the place?"

"We'll find a way," Chelle said.

"Is Deuce going to help?" Runit asked the plumber.

"I'm here, aren't I?" the plumber barked.

"I mean *more* help, now that the AOI is such a problem."

"We've got twenty-nine people in this right now. Mr. Lipton is taking a serious risk as it is."

"We'll be fine," Chelle said, as she pulled Nelson up on her INU. "What's the status?" she asked him.

He looked awful, a few drinks away from disaster. It took him several seconds to respond. "We're on track to complete the load-out by 08:00 hours Sunday morning."

She looked at Runit, and then at the plumber.

"We can't go a minute past midnight. We might have to leave some behind," Runit said.

"Not an option," Chelle said. "Runit, you've got to step up. These are *your* books. This is *your* responsibility. Put all that disappointment and disillusionment into this one task. Save the damned books!"

Oddly, her little pep talk permeated his numb psyche. "Nelson, send that run to my INU. I'm going to see where we are with the loading downstairs. Grandyn and his TreeRunners can find some extra energy for a few more hours," Runit said while jogging away and added, looking directly at the plumber, "Meanwhile, I hope we can count on Deuce to help keep the AOI at bay."

For hours they worked machine-like. Even Nelson switched to coffee and, with the help of a few additional TreeRunners, by 21:14 hours the DesTIn projections finally showed them completing the task before midnight – at 23:57 hours – although it would still be close unless they could get the numbers down even more in the next couple of hours. During that time, the news from the outside world worsened as reports of AOI checkpoints, arrests, and executions came in via the plumber.

"Why is the AOI so scared?" Runit asked Chelle as they left a brief update meeting.

"I don't know what has them spooked."

He looked at her doubtfully. "How high up are you in PAWN?"

"Not as high as you think."

"How high? Are you like a commander? A general?"

"They don't use ranks like AOI. They have numbers. Everyone is a number. The top leader is number one." She looked at him, as if telling him this much was a strain.

"Then tell me your number."

"I'm twelve."

"Wow," Runit said, impressed. He didn't think she'd actually be that high. "And Nelson?"

"He's two thousand something."

"Just how many are there?"

"More than eighty thousand."

"How on Earth has this been kept secret so long?"

"Because it's generational. Most of the members have been brought up in PAWN. Their parents and grandparents were members, and many, too many, have loved ones who were executed or imprisoned by the AOI."

"Do you have weapons?"

"Runit, are you with us?"

"Is there a choice?"

"Do you *believe* something is terribly wrong?"

That was certainly a statement he could agree to without any hesitation. "Yes, something is terribly wrong."

"And . . . ?"

"And, I'm with you. 'He had learned the worst lesson that life can teach – that it makes no sense.' Philip Roth," Runit said.

"Really, do you know what else he said? 'All that we don't know is astonishing. Even more astonishing is what passes for knowing.' See, you're not the only one who can quote dead authors."

He could not help but smile. Not loving her was kind of like not breathing, but only the latter would happen when he died.

"We're going to win," she said.

"Then you must have a lot of weapons, because the AOI is, by design, the ultimate force. We've got at least fifteen books on their history. They are what has kept the peace all these years, and they've done it by being without weakness, so that no one would ever challenge them."

"I know the history. Why do you think the revolution has taken more than seventy years to surface?"

"You said we're going to win. How soon?"

"Hard to say. Another year or two?"

"Two years after surfacing? That's a long time. At what cost will this victory come?"

"Victory always costs more than defeat, and change often commands a high price."

CHAPTER SIXTY-TWO

Exhaustion ran through the dimly lit library like an oppressive humidity draped across a tropical island before a hurricane. Runit checked the time; 23:18 hours. They had forty-two minutes until midnight. The stepped-up AOI patrols throughout the city had slowed the process, but still, they were going to make it.

Chelle had made sure to keep Nelson away from Runit, and neither of them had a problem avoiding the other. There wasn't the time to explore the past. All they could do was try to save it. It had taken a collective strength and mental stamina that could only be described as monumental to get the books pulled, bundled, and loaded. But Nelson, returning from an outside bac break, ran into Runit as he was checking the final loading.

"Do you ever do anything but smoke and drink?" Runit asked.

"Let's not do this now," Nelson said. "Please, tomorrow, when the books all are safe, I'll meet you wherever you want and we can have a good old-fashioned fistfight or a duel at ten paces, I don't care. But let's not endanger the operation and everyone in this building by losing it now."

"Spoken like a true coward," Runit said.

"One of the trucks just got stopped by the AOI," the plumber announced when he found Runit and Nelson at the backdoor.

Grandyn, who somehow hadn't heard his dad and "uncle" arguing, overheard the plumber. He looked to Runit with weary eyes, registering panic.

"Let's get out of here," Runit said.

"We've got just two more loads," Nelson said. "And the priorities got mixed up in all the confusion. They're important books from the private collections."

"Why'd they get stopped?" Runit asked the plumber.

"We don't know yet. Might just be routine. He showed them the live scene patched in from a nearby Seeker camera. The technology impressed Nelson, and the view of real-time events, pulled up on command, stunned Runit anew, reminding him of the executions he'd watched.

"I know we have nothing like the privacy our ancestors enjoyed before the Banoff, but this is astonishing. Do they watch me sleep?" Runit asked.

The plumber pointed to the AirView. The AOI agents were ordering the driver out of the truck.

"If they make him open the load-doors, we're dead," Nelson said. "It would take them about five minutes to trace all those books back here."

"Less," the plumber said as he talked into his wrist and used his other hand to manipulate AirViews, suddenly filling the air around them.

"What are you doing?" Runit asked.

"Getting people there."

"Are you prepared to start an open war based on this incident?" Nelson asked.

The plumber ignored him.

"We haven't authorized any kind of intervention," Runit said.

"Who are you to question it?" the plumber asked. "You're not in charge."

"Those are *my* books," Runit said.

The plumber looked at Nelson.

"Runit, what happens if they open those doors?" Nelson asked.

"Protecting the books is different from starting a revolution," he said, turning from Nelson to the plumber. "You, let me talk to Deuce!"

The plumber moved more screens and talked again into his wrist.

"The revolution started a long time ago," Nelson said.

"Maybe, but it's been a silent revolution until now," Runit replied, glaring at Nelson. "If his men engage the AOI at that truck, it'll be like we started it."

Grandyn, who hadn't missed a word as he put the pieces together, caught his father's eyes. The two had always communicated in a shorthand based on expressions and body language. Grandyn saw the strain in his father and knew, even if they survived the night, their lives would never be the same again. A few TreeRunners went by, and he wondered how many of his closest friends would die for this cause he didn't yet understand.

The AirView showing the stopped truck got buried behind other images for a moment as the plumber shuffled and danced through the data and images. When it surfaced again, an AOI agent could be seen conducting a FRIDG scan on the driver. He studied the man's face, then checked the details in the Facial Recognition Identification Grid data base.

"What do you think?" Nelson asked Runit. "Do you really think we can do this without bloodshed? Are you dreaming that this can somehow be won without violence?"

"It's been done before . . . a new world can be achieved."

"It's never been done on this scale," Nelson said. "We don't have that kind of time."

"Why not?" Runit asked.

Nelson wasn't ready to answer that, and certainly not without Chelle's approval. "Look," he said pointing to the AirView. "An

AOI agent climbed into the front cab of the truck and began searching it. "They're going to open the load!"

"Runit," a voice said from the plumber's INU. "This is not a good time to lose your nerve. But let me be clear. In no way do we need your permission."

The plumber looked at Runit and mouthed, "Deuce Lipton."

"They're my books," Runit said, surprised to be talking to the world's richest man.

"Do you want to keep them?" Deuce asked.

"We're in place," the plumber interrupted. "Engagement ready."

"What happens if you 'engage'?" Runit asked, borrowing the plumber's word.

"We might just get those books to safety and finish the job you started."

"If you don't need my permission, why are you talking to me?"

"Because you're right. This could escalate things to a tragic new level, and you deserve to be part of the decision."

"Are you seeing this?" the plumber asked Deuce.

The AOI agent had left the truck's cab and was now walking to one of the load-doors while another agent continued to detain the driver.

"I do," Deuce answered. "What's it going to be Runit?"

Just then Chelle came up, looked at the three of them gathered, and saw the scene on the AirView. She made eye contact first with Nelson, and then settled on Runit.

"It looks like they might be asking the driver for the locking-code," the plumber said, pointing to the agent by the load-door. "Do we have audio yet?"

Runit couldn't believe they were capable of getting audio. Chelle held his gaze, but surprisingly said nothing.

Would Deuce really leave this decision to me? he wondered.

"He's punching the code. He's about to open the load-door," the plumber said, raising his voice only slightly.

"Either way," Nelson said to Runit, "the war will go on. The difference is, will we still have the books?"

"He's opening," the plumber said.

"Runit?" Deuce asked.

Chelle remained silent.

"Do it!" Runit said, looking directly into Chelle's eyes.

"Go!" the plumber said into his wrist, and almost instantly they all saw the four AOI agents around the truck fall simultaneously. Another man ran up to the stunned driver and convinced him to get back into his truck. The man, one of Deuce's people, also got into the truck and they drove off. A LEV showed up a minute later and the four bodies were hurriedly loaded and taken away. One of Deuce's people was left behind. She got into the AOI vehicle and, once it was gone, the AirView showed the roadway as it would otherwise appear on a typical deserted late night.

Adjustments to the area's Seeker cameras would be necessary, but that would be done in minutes. "Thank you," Deuce said. "I hope we can meet some day in person." He was off before Runit could respond.

"I just killed those agents," Runit said, mostly to himself.

"You just saved my life," Chelle said, hugging him. "And everyone in this building, including Grandyn."

He nodded slightly.

"And the books," Nelson added. "You saved the last genuine books."

"Brave and true," Runit whispered inaudibly.

CHAPTER SIXTY-THREE

Drast got word of four missing agents thirty-two minutes after the incident. Hourly check-ins were automatic with all AOI on-duty personnel, but in heightened security zones, they were required every ten minutes. The vehicle turned up outside a bar several kilometers from where the agents had been posted. No one inside had seen them. Normally, this never would have reached Drast so early, but he'd asked for any and all abnormal issues to be sent to him immediately.

He looked at the report, let his INU run a couple million scenarios, and settled on the most obvious. The agents had stopped a vehicle carrying either some form of contraband, fugitives, or simply people acting outside the law. The stop went bad, and the agents were either abducted, or killed. The facts that their LEV had been taken from the scene and that Seeker showed no incident at all pointed to a high level of sophistication, possibly even a planned event. There was nothing in the agents' bios that made him doubt their loyalty, or to suggest that the hit was personal. Then there was the timing, with the firebombing and the stepped-up security level. He noted the location was not far from the burned-out AOI headquarters and zoomed Lance Miner.

"I think we have a problem," he said as soon as Miner's image came through.

"*More* trouble?"

After Drast finished his update, Miner zoomed Blaze Cortez.

"I thought you might be in touch, what with the growing mess in the Pacyfik and the government shake-up," Blaze said, smiling and releasing his hair out of a ponytail.

Miner smiled back. "I know you think this is a game Blaze, but there is too much at stake."

"Yes, there is, your control being the main matter teetering on the edge."

"I'm not talking about my power, damn it! I'm referring to the peace. We cannot be allowed to slide back into the brutal days of war."

"Pretend we haven't been at war since before the Banoff if it makes you sleep better at night. But a silent war, as the AOI has proven, can be far more brutal than a conventional one." Blaze moved several fingers and instantly images of the AOI arresting and executing people played behind him.

"You sound as if you care about something Blaze, but you and I both know that isn't true," Miner said, ignoring the unauthorized footage but quietly fuming. "The AOI has done what is necessary to keep peace. I know you to be a student of history, so surely you understand, even if you aren't happy about it, that peace is synonymous with prosperity."

"Your prosperity, maybe." Blaze slid his hand in a quick motion and the AOI images changed to PharmaForce factories cranking out bottles filled with pills, vaccines, and all types of medical formulations.

"Very amusing." Miner had known Blaze a long time, and had grown used to his eccentric and often antagonistic manners. "Tell me something. Why not just give me the woman's location? Do you think she can lead PAWN to some sort of victory? Against the AOI? It isn't possible, so why do you protect her?"

"Why can't you find her yourself?" he asked, stroking his goatee slowly, like a pet.

"She's good at hiding."

"Ah, she may have other talents too. Like being able to bring a fraudulent empire to its knees."

"Impossible," Miner repeated.

"Then why are you scared?"

"Name your price."

Blaze flicked the virtual controls before him and the air filled with charts and scans of Lance Miner's brain, accompanied by other health-related vitals. "Perhaps you're unaware of the fear in your eyes when you look in the mirror, but the data before you is irrefutable . . . you're hours away from outright panic."

"I don't believe you actually know her location."

"It should be enough that I confirmed her existence and told you she is in the Pacyfik, but I also narrowed it to the south-western portion of the Oregon Area. If you can't find her in an area of 42,504 square kilometers with the vast resources at your disposal, then your near panic is rightly warranted, because the woman can bring it all down." He switched the images to the burning AOI headquarters in Portland. "And when she does, the war that so terrifies you will be your worst nightmare. It will cost you everything."

Miner's INU went black and Blaze was gone.

Miner stared at the black INU for a long time. Somehow, Blaze had fried it, and it was in that moment that Miner realized that revolution was imminent. Blaze had always been difficult and might lack allegiance, but he was surely a profiteer, and his refusal to deal such a critical piece of information, which had value only until the AOI found her, made sense only if he had seen the future and it held a fractured world. Miner called Sarlo into his office.

"You look awful," she said, genuinely concerned, ignoring the nightscape skyline which looked like vertical columns of stars sparkling against the sudden blackness where the Rocky Mountains took control of the terrain.

"We have only one chance left to avert rebellion and war," he said. "We have to locate Deuce Lipton's uncle and find out what he's been doing all these years."

"Why? What's he got to do with PAWN? What about the woman?"

"Drast has to find her, if she is findable." He flipped his silver dollar, caught it, and slapped it on his wrist. He looked at the results as if he were reading tea leaves, looking for more than an answer. Miner hoped for guidance from a source in which he didn't believe. "We're the only ones who know about Booker Lipton's other son. The AOI, the Council, and even the evil torgon Blaze Cortez don't have this information."

"How do you know?"

"Because if they did, I would never have been allowed to find out."

"And you think it's no accident that he's surfacing now? That the Liptons have kept PAWN going all this time and that the missing uncle is the link?"

"Yes."

"The LEV is waiting," she said. "And I'll be very interested to see how you plan to get one of these implant people to help us find Deuce Lipton's uncle without revealing that information."

"So will I."

CHAPTER SIXTY-FOUR

The transfer of books from the beverage trucks to the fruit carriers had long been a source of concern for the planners because of the openness of the insecure transport center, but all the other possible locations were rejected for one reason or another. PAWN had managed to arrange for the service bay to be available, which provided privacy for the teams to unload the beverage trucks, as each arrived, into the larger carrier. Later, the entire cargo section of the fruit carrier would need to be craned onto a fifty-five-year-old Mack flatbed. Its converted engine ran on bio-fuel, and it had actual tires to navigate the tiny farm roads, which, although they had LEV lanes, had never been fitted with magna-lanes.

The AOI crackdown complicated matters further. Halfway through the deliveries, the transport center, with its convenient location near the Interstate and other major roads, became a temporary hub for the AOI teams. They floated in and out with increasing frequency. Deuce monitored the situation and searched for another staging area, but too many books were already loaded onto the transport. As it turned out, although nerve-racking, the AOI presence actually worked in their favor. As any good fugitive knows, the best place to hide is in plain sight.

The bustling transport center concealed their activities perfectly. The AOI agents coming in and out were busy coordinating and heading to their respective assignments. They weren't looking for people illegally moving books, a crime they didn't even know was taking place.

However, by law, self-driving trucks still required drivers, in much the same way planes flying on auto-pilot still required an actual human pilot in the cockpit. The beverage truck drivers, who originally agreed to some moonlighting for a few extra digis, balked at the risk of arrest, but the plumber managed to allay their concerns and they agreed to continue. Each driver was coached on all actionable precautions and what to do in case of trouble: "Shut up and wait for assistance to arrive." But those vague orders didn't help sway the underpaid drivers nearly as much as the large amount of digis moved into their accounts by one of Deuce's untraceable enterprises.

It would be the driver of the fruit carrier who would be the most at risk. His load would contain all the books, and he needed to take them from the openness of the Portland service center to their first hiding place in the rural growing district of the southern-most part of Oregon Area, between the Cascades and the Siskiyou Mountains. In his truck would be one of Deuce's BLAXERs, in case anything were to go wrong. Deuce would be monitoring the movements of the vehicle from satellites and drones. Additional BLAXERs would be on the road. Deuce had everything in place.

"This will *not* be another Belgium."

Miner and Sarlo enjoyed the gourmet food that the tech center provided, mostly seafood and vegetable dishes. Beef hadn't been available since the Banoff. Early on, it had been blamed for the plague, but even after that was disproved, the environmental impact of mass cattle operations had been made illegal by the reforms. Fortunately, the oceans had recovered quickly from the pre-Banoff years of overfishing and polluting. All kinds of genetically modified veggies made meals fresh and exciting, and fish had also been crossbred to yield large healthy varieties.

Imps, a socially awkward group even before their DesTIn computer brain interface implants, always insisted on the best food. They were strange in a number of ways, including their passion for chewing gum. Imps were sometimes affectionately referred to as vampires because the majority of them preferred working all night and sleeping during the day. Scientists were still unable to explain the phenomena.

By the time Miner and Sarlo completed seventeen interviews and decided on their candidate to find Deuce's uncle, it was nearly midnight. Miner zoomed Drast and requested an immediate profile on the Imp. Drast, up late with the growing militarization of large areas of his region, had no patience left for the background searching of an Imp.

"Anything that vampire can tell you, our people will be able to do quicker and more accurately."

"Your Imps haven't been able to come up with the woman's location. I want someone else working on this," Miner lied, but he couldn't risk Drast knowing about Deuce's uncle. "It's my ace," he told Sarlo. "It may be the one card that saves my hand."

"I'm not giving him clearance!" Drast barked.

"He said he doesn't need it."

"Of course he did." Drast rolled his eyes. "These Imps are all so arrogant, as if they were born with super intelligence. Buying a brain isn't the same as earning one."

"They have their place," Miner responded.

"The soonest I can get you anything on him is noon."

"Make it first thing in the morning."

"I'll do my best. We're stretched at the moment."

"I'll zoom you at 08:00 hours, so get some sleep. Peace prevails, always."

Drast flashed a fake smile at the motto that felt like a harassment. Those three little words constantly mocked him.

CHAPTER SIXTY-FIVE

With the last books safely out of Portland and the library quiet, Chelle found Runit sitting on the marble steps near the top floor.

"Everyone's gone," she said. "We have to go."

"What time is it?" he asked, staring glassy-eyed a moment too long, but she looked ravishing in the dim light. Soft and approachable, almost comforting. His eyelids strained, as if holding up the words he didn't trust himself to speak. The weight of moving the books was not nearly as heavy as falling in love . . . again. And that love felt like a high school crush – important to him, yet seemingly flippant to her.

"Just after 01:00," she said. "We can take my LEV. It will have us at the rendezvous point by 07:00."

"I'm not going."

"What? You have to." She sat next to him, their arms and legs touching. "Grandyn will be there."

"The AOI will be here first thing in the morning."

"I know, that's why we have to go. And with the crackdown, they may even show up earlier."

"But they won't miss the books we took. We've filled all the blank spaces. It looks as full as ever. Even Nelson said they would just send in some muscle to do the burn. How will they know if there are a million books, or nine hundred thousand?"

"Because, you keep forgetting that it's not just about the books."

"So?"

"You have to come."

"Don't you see Chelle? If I flee now, I'll be running for the rest of my life. Maybe I'll join you after the AOI burns all this . . . maybe. But Grandyn should come back. He's too young to spend a life in hiding. They won't know he was involved. He can still get into college, or even get that job he's been talking about. Maybe—"

"You're forgetting Belgium and the other libraries," she cut him off. "If you stay, Grandyn will be an orphan, and if he comes back, even to go to your funeral, he'll be joining you in the urn."

Runit had not just been forgetting about Belgium, he'd been subconsciously blocking it out. He suddenly looked horrified, as if it had hit him for the first time. Now with the books gone and the library closed, he realized that Grandyn would be sought and killed. Chelle gave him a minute to work it all out. "But where will we go?" he finally asked in a desperate, broken voice that sounded as if he'd been running a marathon.

"PAWN has places. You'll be safe."

"But Chelle, what will we do?"

"You'll help the cause."

"How?"

Chelle tried to remain patient, but worried the AOI could show up any minute. She didn't believe they'd wait until morning. "Please, Runit. I can tell you on the way."

Vida was already working on Grandyn about recruiting the other TreeRunners. Chelle had told her enough about AOI threats and tactics to terrify her, and the promise of money was merely a bonus to saving Grandyn. She'd still be paid well if Grandyn agreed and brought his clan into the rebel movement. The Tree-Runner oath made that group incredibly appealing. Even without Vida's prodding, their involvement looked assured. Grandyn, one of their own, was in danger, and they would have to oblige.

Runit felt as if the lump in his throat might strangle him. What had he done? But then, sanity swept through him like a monsoon.

He hadn't had a choice. The world had moved in on him. Even Harper had led him down this path. They were going to burn the books, the last books. He had to protect them. He was the last librarian, and now he had to keep on protecting them. And Grandyn would help.

"Grandyn can go. I'll stay through tomorrow. If I'm not here for the burning, they'll know something is wrong. They might even figure out we've taken books."

"It's too dangerous."

"You said yourself. If they suspected us, we'd already be in jail. But if I'm not here for my last day of work to help supervise 'the closing,' then they're going to start investigating and it may lead them to the books. This will all be for naught." He waved his hands around at the books.

Chelle couldn't argue with his logic, but she also knew what had happened in Belgium.

"Runit, they may just lock you inside the burning building." She could see in his face, tired and stressed, suddenly looking old, that he was considering it, but she still didn't think it was sinking in. "Don't you see? They've already signed your death warrant. The AOI agents who show up to burn the books also have orders to kill you."

"Maybe," he said, staring somberly. "But we don't know when they're going to execute me. Nelson said they usually make it look accidental. I have to stay to protect the books so they don't suspect we got some out."

"Yeah, poor librarian dies in library fire. A neat and tidy accident!"

He just looked at her.

"I'm sorry," she said quietly. His stoic bravery overwhelmed her, and she put her arms around his neck and kissed his cheek softly. The wetness of a single tear from her eye seemed to fuel their passions. "I don't want you to die," she whispered. "You're worth more than the books."

"History is replete with those who sacrificed for a greater cause."

"Is that what you want? To be a martyr?" She pulled back. "Do you even understand the cause?"

"No, I don't understand, and I definitely don't want to be a martyr. But I don't believe I'll die tomorrow. The risk and experiencing the uncertainty are my only sacrifice. I'm not foolish enough to think history will remember the last librarian. I just hope whatever it is in these books that is so important, is more than just the history everyone already seems to have forgotten."

Chelle touched his face. "Men like you . . . " She looked through the glass wall into all the books that remained, searching for words. "You're from an old romance novel I once read. Full of conviction and manners, ideas from another time, honor, courage."

Her lips found his and melted him as passion took hold of the remaining threads of his resistance. The frustration and fear, which had tormented him all week, shattered the doubt, the risk of another betrayal, and his uncertainty all fell away like broken bits of glass showering the grand staircase as he pulled her closer.

In the middle of the night, with only pale light seeping into their caress, they took each other into their lonely grief, and trusted that this time abandonment would not follow them. Perhaps between the touch and the breath, something would keep safe their race into the face and fury of a rebellion on the brink of eruption. In their stirring heat, the cold night and AOI were forgotten, and even the books, both condemned and liberated, vanished into whispered mist as they wrote an original scene, played a million times before, but never like this.

CHAPTER SIXTY-SIX

Sunday, February 4

For once, things went their way. In the early morning hours of an unseasonably warm Sunday, the books breezed down the Interstate as if it were a load of pears going to market. The fruit carrier, loaded with the cumulative core of humanity's knowledge, pulled into the old barn just before 06:00 hours. Two young men, dressed in a black Tekfabrik, closed the large wooden doors behind it.

The driver got down from the cab and looked around. He couldn't see up into the loft or he would have been stunned at the array of modern electronic gear located in the vintage structure. That wasn't the only thing out of place on the old farm. Twelve meters away, a Flo-wing sat under some nano-camo tarps that automatically changed to the surrounding landscape like a chameleon. The two men who closed the doors greeted the driver, smiling, then quickly injected him with a tranquilizer and held him while he struggled and finally slumped to the hard ground. Minutes later he was aboard the Flo-wing and immediately en-route to an unknown destination.

Two more vehicles arrived ten minutes later, followed by another Flo-wing, which brought a BLAXER crew of fourteen.

They would prepare the books to be moved again. Deuce wanted them out of there before the PAWN people arrived. Competing interests of the same cause, he thought, but he was determined to take no chances until he knew Chelle's ultimate goals.

The BLAXERs had brought new containers, developed after the Belgium fiasco. Constructed of carbon composite blends and Tekfabrik, they utilized the latest atom-displacing-adjusted-molecule technology, resulting in a forty percent decrease in the total weight. The added benefit of a video readout of the contents meant almost no sorting. It had been too risky to use them in the library, but now that the books had been safely evacuated, they could be used. Especially with the continuing journey, something better than bundle straps had been needed. The books were repackaged with military precision.

Deuce Lipton, watching it all happen on the floating AirViews in his office, smiled. The books were safe, at least for now. He'd won this round. Even managed to get almost five hours of sleep. Now, if the librarian lived through the day and the AOI didn't find the woman, he might even start making real progress.

Then, on his INU, he noticed his son and two security guards enter the building. Twain should have been on his way to the safety of a family-owned remote island, but instead Deuce had brought him back to do a job only a Lipton could do. The 06:30 meeting meant his son had been up early, and hopefully he could still make it to that island by the end of the day.

Elevators still existed in older buildings, but modern structures, like the one that housed Lipton's San Francisco office, used ultra-fast Q-lifts, which could span twenty floors almost instantaneously. It brought his son and his security detail to the top of the one-hundred-forty-three-story building in less than seven seconds. The BLAXER agents waited outside the office door.

Deuce hugged his son. "Thanks for coming."

"It must be getting serious."

"I need you to go to the redwoods and bring your uncle back here," Deuce said.

"Are you kidding?" Twain could tell his father was serious, but he knew his uncle would never come.

"I can't be off the Field. I need him here."

"Why?"

"Because they've found Munna."

His son looked at him. Munna was a name he knew well, but hadn't heard since he was much younger. "I've always wondered if she was real."

"I've told you since you were little that Munna is alive."

"I know, but . . ."

"Your whole life, I've never lied to you Twain. Never forget that. Everything I've ever told you was the truth. There is a sacred pact between parent and child."

Twain nodded. "Who found Munna?"

"The AOI."

"Oh no," he said, letting out a breath.

"They don't have her yet. They just know her vicinity. But for the first time ever the AOI believes she exists, and their trackers are closing in."

"Where is she?"

"Where do you think?"

"With the books?" he asked, already knowing the answer, but not wanting to believe it.

"Of course. She's on her way to them now."

"Why? Doesn't she know the risk?"

"I'd say she knows the stakes better than the rest of us combined."

CHAPTER SIXTY-SEVEN

Alone, on the gray stark morning, Runit walked through the grand old building slowly, soaking in the radiant energy from the condemned books. He vowed to preserve their memory. Although still unsure exactly how to do that, he knew that guarding the hundred-thousand-plus spared volumes was the best start, and being there that morning, in jeopardy, was the best beginning to that start.

His library, for it had belonged to him longer than his only son, longer than he'd been with Harper and, in fact, had occupied the greatest portion of his life, appeared brave and true. The columned archways held steadfast, like soldiers loyal to the written heritage of time. Windows filtered in opaque light as if secreting the contents of the remaining volumes out into the forever etherealness.

He stopped and sat on the marble steps between the second and third floors and thought of Chelle, but only for a moment. In an effort to shield himself from more pain, more loss should he never see her again, he denied the memory as best he could. He looked up at the ornate round skylight that had been there for a century and basked in its muted glow.

"Damn them for doing this," he whispered, then wondered fearfully if anyone could hear him. *What difference would it make?* he wondered. *I'm already a dead man.*

He looked around, trying not to glance at the Seeker cameras. They'd been so careful. Every possible precaution had been taken, and so far no one had been arrested.

Maybe they'd pulled it off. What about the missing AOI agents from last night? What if someone saw something? What if they noticed the missing books?

He double-checked the lower level. Grandyn had wisely remembered to get the strapping machines out on one of the last loads. A group of TreeRunners had carefully canvassed the entire building, searching for any large gaps on the shelves. It all looked fairly normal. For years he'd been bothered that they didn't have enough room for all the books they had, including the ones from private donors that didn't even show up in their system. Now that problem might be what saved them. The library still looked full, even with the absence of more than one hundred thousand books.

Still, Chelle's warnings troubled him. He could be dead in a matter of hours, and then how long would it take them to find Grandyn?

Suddenly, he saw the copy of *The Road* by Cormac McCarthy. It had been on the list, but no one had been able to find it. There it lay under some papers on his desk. Damn it! The story had particular meaning to him. The world as we know it ends, the mother dies, and a father and son wander through the wrecked landscape of what came after, looking for survival and hope. Who knew how the AOI censors would butcher the stirring father-son tale.

He didn't have much time. Finding one of Nelson's old doughnut boxes, Runit concealed the ninety-two-year-old book and carried it to his LEV along with an old sweater and an antique brass lion that had been in his family for years. He tried to look casual, and now, knowing where each Seeker camera was, he carefully avoided looking directly into any of the prying, ever-present, digital-eyes.

An hour later, his INU lit up, notifying him the "team" was minutes away. He met them at the front door. An amicable man with short pudgy fingers named Krucks, introduced himself as the agent in charge. Nine men in shiny silver flame suits entered the building behind him. The flame suits, he later learned, were fireproof Tekfabrik which, when worn with the appropriate headgear, would allow them to walk through flames of more than six hundred fifty degrees Celsius.

Krucks, dressed in relaxed black slacks and a gold shirt, explained that the special AOI crew had done this before. "They're trained for such missions." Two more men pushed a large cart filled with tanks and hoses into the lobby. Runit was horrified to think he was living through a real-life warped version of *Fahrenheit 451*. "They'll spray the target materials, in this case books, with Red-1953, a specially formulated agent made by PharmaForce. It is quite an amazing product. It will incinerate the target materials while leaving much of the surrounding area unscathed," Krucks added smiling. "Of course, the shelves will be badly damaged or lost, but we won't be needing those after the burn anyway."

"What about the building?" Runit asked, feeling queasy.

"Oh, it'll be fine. But I understand they're going to level it sometime this summer. They haven't decided yet, but the new AOI regional headquarters might be built on this site." He looked at Runit as though this might make him feel better. "Our other place was badly damaged recently, you know?"

Runit nodded as if hypnotized.

"Don't worry," Krucks assured him. "We've got two dozen agents on the perimeter in case someone decides to make any trouble."

"Trouble?" Runit asked.

"Just a precaution. We don't expect anything. No one cares about books anymore." He pulled one from a nearby shelf. "Talk about antiquated. These heavy, clumsy things became obsolete about a hundred years ago. Strange that libraries lasted all this time. You can fit a few hundred thousand digital versions of books in a standard INU." He patted his, and Runit noticed it was an Eysen brand. "And digital ones never wear out. The one thing the paper versions do better is burn." He smiled.

"Yeah," Runit said, silently recalling Dwight Eisenhower's warning, "Don't join the book burners. Don't think you're going to conceal faults by concealing evidence that they ever existed. Don't be afraid to go in your library and read every book..."

"Did you get everything out?" Krucks asked, sounding concerned.

"What?" Runit asked, feeling as if he'd just swallowed a mouthful of straw. *They know! Of course they'd known all along. We took over one hundred thousand books out in complete defiance of an AOI order. They're just going to throw me in with the books, burn us all. Maybe Grandyn can get away into the trees. The TreeRunners will help him.*

"Your personal belongings." Krucks smiled. "Did you get them out? You've been employed here a long time. I assume you've accumulated a few items along the way. Wouldn't want to see those burn too, would we?"

"No. I mean, yes, I got them," Runit said, unable to hide his relief.

"Good," Krucks said, still smiling. "Where are you parked?"

"Why?" Runit asked, full of straw again.

"Nothing really. We just have to check your LEV. Make sure there are no books," Krucks said, looking into an AirView that Runit couldn't see. "I can see you're not the foolish type, Mr. Happerman, but at some of these closings librarians have actually tried to take some of the old books with them. But they're government property. It's kind of funny when you realize they can read whatever they want on their INUs."

Runit nodded, thinking of the book in his LEV and desperately trying to figure out how to escape.

CHAPTER SIXTY-EIGHT

Krucks sighed. "Of course, the books still checked out will be collected over the next few days by local agents. Looks like there are only a few hundred. Not many people used this place anymore. Inefficient and cold," Krucks said, shivering. "At least until we start the burn." He laughed, as if it were a brilliant revelation. "Your LEV? Let's get that piece of business out of the way so we can enjoy the burn."

"Uh, this way," Runit said, pointing down the stairs leading to the lower level. Each step was like a ticking time bomb as Runit tried to figure a way out, to think of a stall, a way to contact Grandyn. He should have listened to Chelle. She knew the danger, had tried to warn him. Maybe she'll take care of Grandyn.

By the time they reached the parking area, Runit was trying to hide his perspiring, knowing it would seem odd on the cold February day. "Are you okay?" Krucks asked, noticing.

"Feeling a little under the weather. I didn't sleep well last night. The truth is, I'm going to miss all the old books."

Krucks smiled. "Of course you will, you're a librarian. Or should I say, the last librarian?" Don't worry, we'll be back inside in a minute. Although I swear it's colder in there than it is out here . . . at least until we start the burn." He laughed again, amused by his replay of his burn line.

They reached the LEV. Runit saw two nearby AOI agents and assumed they would be the ones to arrest him, maybe even just shoot him on the spot as he'd seen through the plumber's INU. Why did he take that book? His whole life had come down to this, executed for reading a Cormac McCarthy novel.

"This it?" Krucks asked, peering in the wide, clear, glass-like windows.

"Yes, this is my LEV."

"There's your problem," Krucks said in a serious tone, pointing inside the vehicle.

Runit looked back at the AOI agents.

"You had doughnuts for breakfast. That'll make anyone feel like dirt. They're just sludge in your system. Look at your health numbers, you'll see." He pointed to Runit's INU hanging around his neck. "Now, let's get back inside and start the burn."

"That's it?" Runit asked.

"Huh?" Krucks asked. "Unless you've got books strapped to the underside of this thing. But then it wouldn't be able to drive, so I think we're safe with you. Like I said, you don't look like the foolish type."

The team took less than an hour to set up, mostly moving things and checking their gear. They started on the top floor. Runit asked not to watch, but Krucks insisted. "As the head librarian, you'll have to sign off. It's a swear-and-attest-under-penalty-of-perjury thing. Pretty official."

Runit and Krucks donned special Tekfabrik jumpsuits, but they were well away from the flames. Runit stood under the domed skylight at the top of the grand marble staircase, which now seemed somehow cold and haunted.

Krucks called to him, "Come on, Happerman, the view is better from here."

Runit reluctantly joined him in the doorway that led to the special collections. He looked out at all the thousands of books he had failed to protect. Their death sentence came only because they weren't deemed controversial enough by Blaze Cortez's DesTIn program. But they were no less beautiful and fulfilling books, and the AOI could just as easily change their contents on all the digital editions to suit some future policy against interracial or same sex relationships. Perhaps one day somebody wouldn't like redheads and they would all be banned from books. Maybe anything that mentioned the former country of India would be erased, or the entire history of a specific war or financial crisis would be wiped from the recorded memory of humanity with the touch of a finger.

The flame-suit men sprayed Red-1953, which turned out to be neon-red-colored sticky micro-pellets, across all the books. To Runit, it looked like they were bleeding. As Krucks promised, the men were fast and efficient, and the Red-1953 didn't even create any dust or haze like Runit had assumed it would.

"I told you that PharmaForce has made a perfect product. It sticks to the target material so we don't have to breathe it in. The same company makes my heart medication. I'm alive only thanks to their incredible R&D department."

Runit raised his eyebrows and nodded as if this was indeed something to be impressed by and grateful for, but silently he wished the PharmaForce R&D department would spray themselves with Red-1953 and strike a match.

"Ready to fire, sir," one of the flame-suits announced.

"Commence at will," Krucks said loudly, and then lowering his voice and turning to Runit, added, "This is pretty amazing to watch."

The same man who'd informed Krucks of the burn-ready status pushed a button on a long silver tube, which resembled an old-fashioned vacuum cleaner attachment hose, and an orange laser shot out, immediately igniting the Red-1953. Flames spread down the shelves as if choreographed, clinging nearly perfectly to the bookcases. The fire emitted an eerie yellow smoke, which was quickly sucked into a large, portable filter machine about the size of a refrigerator that moved robotically on traction wheels.

"The cleanser actually senses and follows the smoke. Fantastic, huh?" Krucks asked rhetorically. "And the Red-1953 works on almost anything except concrete, stone, and most metals."

The nasty and powerful PharmaForce agent did its job shockingly well, and Runit watched the beautiful books reduced to fiery ash. *Who would do this?* he wondered. *Corrupt people fear books because they contain something more powerful than themselves: ideas. What were they afraid of? What did they think lay hidden in these volumes that warranted such destruction?*

CHAPTER SIXTY-NINE

The missing AOI agents troubled Drast. Something was wrong. He contacted his darkest informants, those that existed between the shadows of the Aylantik regime and the Rejectionists. Some of those slippery dregs of humanity surely had direct links to Rejectionists. Others likely believed PAWN existed, and so followed the noise, knowing a word or a face might prove valuable to the AOI. Drast tried to avoid this lot, as they were unreliable and often created reverse leaks and drama, but he needed this thing contained.

He was sure there were things going on in the Pacyfik that he didn't know of, but his career had been long enough, and his experience deep, so that he could feel the approach of terrible danger the way a veteran firefighter senses when an explosive flame lurks behind a quiet door. The situation wasn't unexpected. Drast had been chosen to head the most problematic region because of his ability to manage any situation. But, in some sense, his hands were tied. If it had been entirely up to him, Deuce Lipton and Blaze Cortez would have been arrested and placed in solitary confinement at one of the AOI's remote prisons, because this crisis was unlike any other.

Miner worried about peace and war because he was a business-man. Drast worried about survival because he was a soldier, and not just his own life, but survival of the human species.

He scanned the daily issue-reports: inoculations in two New Mexico Area communities where Creatives often protested, arrests of seven Rejectionists in Vancouver, hackers changing health records, and others manipulating transactions involving digis – both the work of another rogue and mysterious group known as "Trapciers" – an AOI agent caught selling secrets in Panama, a Rejectionist camp located in Peru, books to be burned at the Port-land library, an illegal school of pre-Banoff studies discovered in Belize, the investigation of the AOI headquarters firebombing, missing AOI agents, and, of course, the search for that damned PAWN woman. He took out a health-beam, a tiny sensor pad, and tapped it on his forehead, silently thanking PharmaForce for the handy little invention that made headaches a thing of memory.

Then the AOI Chief zoomed. "Polis, I understand you have people missing?"

"We believe it's connected to the firebombing."

"Which is connected to PAWN," the Chief said as if it couldn't be more obvious.

"That is the present theory."

"What about the books?"

Why was she so preoccupied with the damned Portland Library? "Agents have been on-site all morning. The books are being torched as we speak. That matter should be fully closed within hours."

"Excellent. And I have more good news. We have a name for the woman."

If she has a name, then either the Chief has her own agents working my region, or the woman's reach extends outside the Pacyfik, Drast thought. Both prospects terrified him. *If and when I am World Premier, I will find a way to oust you,* he mused, then he worried she might have neuron-mites on him, an experimental mind-reading, nano-sized

INU that once introduced into the body, typically without the target's knowledge, made reading his thoughts possible. "What is it?"

"Munna."

"Is that it? Sounds like a code name?"

"May well be. We picked up a woman on the island of Okinawa, off Japan, who gave us the information."

"How did she give it?"

"Said-scan. It's accurate." The method, postmortem brain scans, had been in use for nearly twenty years, and proved more than ninety-eight percent accurate. The challenge had always been getting a complete piece of data. The method had once been described by a technician as "trying to read words written on grains of sand located across the ocean while looking through a window screen."

"Any images?"

"No. Apparently she'd never met Munna. But it seems a rebellion is imminent."

"Why?"

"The woman had recently been in Tokyo and taken an allegiance oath to PAWN . . . with two thousand others."

Drast shuddered.

After a few more minutes, the Chief ended the zoom with her standard, "Peace prevails, always."

Drast didn't tell Miner about the call from the Chief. Instead, he reported that his agents had found nothing upsetting or controversial about the Denver Imp with which he'd chosen to work. He did caution, however, that many Imps had ties to Blaze Cortez, and in addition to the implied potential leak, it also meant parts of any Imps' past could have been hidden or created. Miner knew all that already, but those were chances he had to take.

He and Sarlo raced back to the outskirts of town to meet the "vampire" before he went to sleep. On the way, they viewed the latest report Drast had flashed on the AOI's ongoing search for the woman in the Pacyfik.

"They've got everything in the mix and they still can't find her," Miner said. "Sat-grids, swarm-drones, breeze-blowers—"

"Sat-grids use technology made by StarFly, right?"

"Yeah. One of Deuce's companies. Do you think he's interfering?"

"Isn't it possible?" Sarlo's father had been a farmer, her mother an attorney, and they had divorced when she was just four. Half of her childhood had been spent in the city, and the other time – on alternating weekends and most of the summers – were spent in the rural countryside. She always believed this gave her a unique perspective, and granted her the valuable traits of patience and balance. She also liked to remind Miner of her zodiac sign, Libra.

"Hell, anything's possible, but how are they beating swarm-drones and breeze-blowers? Deuce doesn't own manufacturers." Miner brought up a projected image of a swarm-drone and double-checked the maker. "You understand how they work – the bug-sized drones, equipped with cameras? They fly into an area like a swarm of bees, usually unnoticed, and instantly transmit live-stream, ultra-high-definition video. We can get in anywhere a flying insect can go. They're even as small as gnats now."

"They're remotely guided by GPS and enabled through INUs, both of which Deuce manufactures."

"AOI operations don't use Eysen-INUs, and I'll have to confirm which AOI division routes the GPS data to the swarm-drones, but I don't believe it's his," Miner said.

"What about breeze-blowers? I don't even know what they are."

"Breeze-blowers are dust-sized computers, also equipped with video transmitters, but they act with DesTIn and are much more autonomous. They literally blow in the breeze, and can continue to supply data and images for years."

She thought about how powerful anything is that utilizes the Design Taught Intelligence advanced artificial intelligence program and shuddered. "I had no idea such a thing existed. Who makes those?"

"They've been around for decades, but have only been used in non-scientific applications for the past twenty-two months. PharmaForce makes them. The original purpose was medical."

"Wow," she said, adding, "Scary-wow."

"Drast will find the woman."

"And when he does, is she the key to stopping PAWN?"

"That, and killing Deuce Lipton."

"What about the Council?"

"I'm just going to have to change their mind."

"And that's why we're in Denver? Because of Deuce's uncle?"

"Exactly. His being alive, the very fact that he was born in secret, is proof of a conspiracy. A conspiracy as old as PAWN. I believe I can tie the uncle to PAWN, and therefore the rebellion to Deuce, and that's treason of the highest order." Lance smiled. "The Council will kill Deuce Lipton for me."

CHAPTER SEVENTY

Somewhere on the outskirts of Denver, a district consisting of small rustic lodges, littered in the dense forest, had become an enclave for some of the most brilliant Imps. Sarlo worried that the long narrow driveway, through thick, snow-laden ponderosa pines, would prove difficult for their LEV to navigate, but just as the ramshackle appearance of the cabin belied the modern high-tech interior, so had the dirt and gravel concealed a LEV-capable private road. Almost thirty centimeters of snow blanketed the surrounding woods, but the structure's roof remained clear thanks to thermal radiation.

The Imp greeted them as Imps often did; an uncomfortably long eye-to-eye stare and a weak clap of his ghostly hands. Sarlo almost laughed, as the man appeared to be a stick figure in clothes. Even his black and gray hair was thin, and his face was long, gaunt, and ashen. He could have been cast in a vampire movie, if the film depicted the sick and aging variety.

Inside, the main room was awash in color from as many as thirty AirViews, floating around as if they were alive. Small pieces of equipment resembling modified INUs, connected together with visible nano-laser-links, filled one wall, and the only furniture consisted of two levitating tables and four air-filled conforms which, at first glance, seemed like giant beanbags, but were in fact high-tech custom sensory chairs.

"I've never seen these," Miner said, pointing to the tables.

"Of course you haven't. You've never been here before," the Imp said dryly.

"I meant anything *like* them," Miner corrected, slightly annoyed.

"Same technology as INUs, I just modified it for my use. Perhaps you'd like to market them."

"Maybe. They seem very functional."

The Imp scowled, as if the word "functional" took away from his creative wonder. "You have a problem that I might solve?" he asked, motioning to the chairs. "The digis have been moved?"

"They have," Sarlo answered. The Imp stared at her as if seeing her for the first time, and then pulled a private AirView in front of his eyes.

"Yes, I see that, good. Excellent. Proceed."

In something of a futuristic fortune-telling session, they sat around the floating table for the next fifteen minutes while Miner tried to get his answer without revealing the actual question.

Finally, frustrated, the Imp stood. "Mr. Miner, you're wasting my time, which you're entitled to do since you paid for it, but if you want to know something you *must* trust me."

Miner looked at Sarlo. She shook her head.

The Imp caught the exchange and began singing an old song from Miner's childhood, "Must trust, said the rusty bus, or we'll get crushed, must trust, said the rusty bus, or we'll get crushed." Miner remembered the jingle that, during the 2040s, had been meant to encourage people to modify old vehicles for use on the new roads, but sometime after that it became a playground chant.

"Would you trust an Imp?" Miner asked.

"What is misunderstood about my kind, Mr. Miner, is that we are perceived by the general population as somehow being less human. It is because of that misconception that we have become social outcasts which, by the way, suits us fine because you people bore us." He smiled momentarily at Sarlo, his stare lingering as if to exclude her from his observation. "But what is missed in that consensus is the fact that our accelerated intelligence has created vast amounts of mental capacity and mind expansion which, in turn, has led to something far deeper than someone without an implant could achieve. *Awareness*."

"Awareness?" Miner asked.

"There are so many things that you have no idea about, dreams which remain on your tongue when you speak, unappreciated in crossing the sea of imagination. Places to travel to when there is no one left to blame, hidden realms where invitations were long engraved but now gather dust unopened, power capable of twisting ambition and weapons into cake frosted with stars. " His eyes darted around, looking animated and alive for the first time since they'd arrived. The movement of his pupils seemingly caused the AirViews to shuffle and swirl around their heads as his hands remained still folded in his lap.

Sarlo watched the display like a kid at Disney. The moving AirViews caused some kind of static electricity, or at least she thought it was, as colored sparks and pops danced among the giant glowing forms. Later, she remembered hearing music in the background. An ethereal chanting mixed with soft, beautiful cries. But just then, all her senses could process were the colors and lights.

"You want to know about Lipton," the Imp whispered, but it came out as if it was spoken through a microphone, loud and crisp with the name "Lipton" echoing in reverberation.

"How do you know?" Miner asked, stunned. He'd been so careful.

"Must trust, said the rusty bus, or we'll get crushed, must trust, said the rusty bus, or we'll get crushed," the Imp sang.

The room quickly went still, the AirViews all changed, and from a hidden source, an aqua light emanated so that each of them and all the surrounding space was an inspiring hue of blue.

Sarlo repeated her boss's question. "How do you know?"

"That greater capacity of mind allows us not just to access all the knowledge of humankind, my dear. It also provides us the ability to find the channel and frequency to touch the source."

"The source?" she asked.

"The human mind, free of distractions, practiced and open, is capable of reaching the higher plane." His eyes locked onto hers. "I'm connected to the infinite knowledge of the *universe*."

"You're half-machine," Miner scoffed.

"The machine simply frees my mind," the Imp said. "Why do you think we get the implants? To get rich?" He motioned his arm around the modest cabin. "No. It's to find enlightenment."

Miner shook his head. He'd never considered Imps as anything other than a tool, marrying the best of human intelligence with that of a computer. He'd also never really thought about "enlightenment," or much of anything past material gain in this one, and all-too-short, lifetime.

"Tell him," Sarlo said.

Miner, desperate for the information, and just as desperate to guard his main strategic advantage, the secret of Booker Lipton's other son, didn't know what to do.

"I am a better man," the Imp said. "Accept that." He held Miner's eyes in his as if magnetized, hypnotized. "If I can help, then I must already know."

"Prove it," Miner said. "Tell me where my question begins."

The Imp, still keeping his stare, remained silent for almost a minute, then spoke in that broadcast whisper. "Booker Lipton. What happened while he was gone?"

Sarlo gasped.

"Torgon unbelievable," Miner said. "He had a second son. I need to know everything about him."

"They call him Cope," the Imp said, smiling, and proceeded to tell Miner everything he needed to know.

CHAPTER SEVENTY-ONE

Runit fought agony from bitter and familiar places, along with new fronts in his personal war with pain. The room looked oddly like a forest fire raging beneath an orange sky as the Red-1953, shifting strange yellow smoke, and flames turned everything a redish-orange hue.

"Kind of wish we had some marshmallows," Krucks said, with a chuckle.

Runit ignored him. The books he'd failed called at him, crying out in suffering, blaming him for every burning page. He felt the heat permeate his pores and, although the smoke was well away from him, the suffocating stench of Red-1953 and roasting book paper made him nauseous. He imagined the disintegrating stories, thoughts and ideas floating through the giant filter machine, tortured and mutilated.

Suddenly, he imagined he saw Harper's face screaming in the flames. These past few days, he'd begun to realize that her death hadn't been an accident. She'd died in a freak fire that spread from the chemistry lab below her classroom at the university where she taught. But there had been little damage then, and seeing the Red-1953 and knowing about her involvement with PAWN, it clicked.

The AOI had killed her. He'd always believed something hadn't been right. Ever since her death an unsettled feeling had wrapped him like a cold, slimy creature from a nightmare, but he'd written it off as desperate grief. But now he knew, and nothing could convince him otherwise. Maybe even Chelle or Nelson could confirm it. If not them, then Blaze Cortez or Deuce Lipton could surely find out. He looked at her screaming image in the flames, as if she were really in there, and swallowed back tears. Anger took hold. *I'm sorry, Harper,* he said silently.

If it hadn't been for Grandyn, he would have shoved Krucks into the flames or tried to lock the flame-suits out of the other areas of the library where books made of paper still breathed clean air and sat ready to enlighten and entertain. He might have even made a dash for the exit and . . . and . . . and done something, something radical and dangerous, but he didn't know what.

Instead, he stood there next to Krucks and watched his wife burn along with the books, powerless to save either one.

But as they moved to the other side of the building and the process began all over again, Runit vowed that he would not lose to the AOI a third time. As the flame-suits sprayed more books, he watched in detached satisfaction.

He had the most important books. They were going to all this trouble to burn what some corrupt high official had determined was a threat to their utopian world, yet what they feared most was locked safely away in a barn more than four hundred fifty kilometers away.

And the only two people he really cared about were there, Grandyn and Chelle. If the AOI didn't throw him into the flames or execute him at the end of the day, he would see them both tonight. All he had wanted to do had been done. He had saved the books and kept his son safe. He couldn't wait to get back to them.

Nelson might be there too. His oldest friend, the oldest story: best friend sleeps with wife. Damn them! His anger pulsed with the flames. Fumes from the burning paper, glue, and that toxic

PharmaForce chemical escaped the roving filter machines and started to make him truly nauseous. Or was that the stench of betrayal?

His martyred wife had been an adulteress. Part of him knew. He thought back and could almost pinpoint the day. She had so much passion, more than enough for both of them, he'd always thought. But there'd been something else in her eyes beyond the mystery and spark of rebellion. She needed adventure and creativity. Damn it, if only he'd written that book.

"Happerman?" Krucks called, alarmed.

Runit realized, while blaming himself, he'd wandered too close to the fire.

"Careful, man, we don't want a fatality here. All that extra paperwork would delay my vacation."

Runit nodded vaguely and his thoughts returned to Nelson. *Why do I even like that cranky, drunk writer?* Nelson once told him that certain scenes rewrote themselves in his head after a book was published and nearly drove him insane. He said that the characters could be even more difficult. They often kept talking to him long after a book was done, and sometimes while writing, characters would change a scene by what they said, which caused him considerable stress and time, reworking the plot to suit their needs. Every book Runit hadn't written haunted him, so he understood about the mental takeover from the craft of writing. Those unwritten books, locked inside a writer's head, make an inescapable noise, like murmurs from conversation one can't quite make out blended loudly with paper pages blowing in a disturbing wind.

"Writers must write, like painters must paint," Nelson told him. "But it's different for writers because until the story is down on paper, it will continue to expand in the writer's crowded mind, where it can't ever be contained." Nelson had stared at Runit with a look of terror and added, "And minds don't explode like you would think. They crack slowly, painfully, and with all kinds of distortion."

That's why he liked him. They shared the same pain. The question was, could he *forgive* him?

That answer was probably contained in the pages of one of the tens of thousands of books burning before him. Some author had no doubt written this plot, or something similar at least. What did they have the hero do? *Am I the hero?* Runit wondered. *Am I really brave and true?* He was there, wasn't he? Risking his life for the books, the urgent objective of the protagonist against the advice of the heroine. Is Chelle really the heroine? *Will I get the girl in the end?*

The books screamed as something in one of them popped, unexpectedly sending a flare out almost across to another shelf. *Reaching for a friend, trying to save a loved one,* Runit thought. One of the flame-suits went back and gave it a quick look, then continued moving forward, spraying more Red-1953.

Runit just wanted it to be over. He wanted to throw up. He wanted to die. But he *needed* to save more than the books. He needed to honor *his* promise and keep Grandyn safe. He needed to get the girl, to see how the story ends. And maybe, most of all, Runit Happerman needed to save himself from the mediocrity his life had become.

As he watched so much creativity go up in red, chemical-induced flames, he found his fire. This was his story to tell. Runit was the last librarian. He had his book. He'd never been able to finish a novel because they didn't contain enough truth. But this story, the burning books, the AOI, even Harper's betrayal, connected it all. The pre-Banoff world that fascinated him, the power of books, and a man standing up to whatever comes, a man being brave and true.

CHAPTER SEVENTY-TWO

Deuce had watched via Seeker as the books still in the library were incinerated. He'd seen it before, but this time two things were different.

This was the last library, and he'd managed to save the most important books.

He'd been meditating since watching the incineration, trying to control his urgently wandering mind. A chime interrupted his escape and an AirView lit up. Deuce smiled at the image. Another victory.

Two minutes later, the cause of his celebration entered his private office: two of the people he loved most.

The old man looked around the dimly lit room as if he were on a space ship. "Why do you need all this gadgetry?"

"Thanks for coming, Uncle Cope," Deuce said, hugging the old man and ignoring his question. At the same time he shot his son a look that said, *I don't know how you got him here, but you make me proud.*

Twain gave his dad a slight bow, knowing he actually didn't deserve much of the credit. His great uncle, the man he called "UC," didn't go anywhere he didn't want to, nor do anything that didn't have a purpose beyond what Twain might ever be able to understand.

"The promise of the Eysen was to do away with all of this," Cope said.

"Perhaps," Deuce replied. "I need to know more about the books. I need to know more about PAWN, about the revolution. Have you ever seen Munna?"

"You're asking things above your frequency."

"Am I?"

"I am not involved with the books, the revolution, or any of those things, so if you're asking *me* about *them*, then you're expecting answers from another source." Cope slowly rubbed his fingertips together. "I suspect you employ hundreds, maybe thousands of people who could gather information on such topics for you, but you need more, don't you? More than the current status of these things. More than even the history of it. You want to know the future."

"I *need* to know," Deuce said.

"You do have much of my father in you," he said, staring deeply into Deuce's eyes. "There are things that can only be known if the questions are truer than the answers. If the seeker isn't ready, all manner of chaos can ensue."

"I'm ready," Deuce said empathetically. "Cope, it's happening. I'm ready, the world's ready, and it wouldn't matter even if we weren't. The time is now."

"Time is a funny thing."

Deuce nodded.

"Forgetting," Cope said quietly. "Forgetting. That's where all this trouble began. People forgot where they came from. Took way more than they needed."

"Uncle Cope, please." Deuce had heard this talk before, many times, while walking in the redwoods. But with each breath he took he felt time running out. Even if this same old story, of humanity forgetting its true purpose and soul, was just a long introduction to the information he needed, he didn't have the patience. "With all due respect."

Cope nodded, then paused and took a deep breath. "There was a real Eysen once. The first one." He looked at Deuce and Twain. "My father didn't really invent it. He found it."

"UC, are you kidding? Where? What do you mean Booker didn't invent it?" Twain asked.

"Well he didn't actually find it, a friend of his did. Ripley Gaines, an archaeologist. He dug the first Eysen out of a cliff in the forested mountains of Virginia."

"What was it doing there? Where did it come from?" Twain asked.

Deuce remained silent.

"Someone had hidden it there, millions of years before."

"No way!"

"Yes," Cope said, smiling.

"How?" Twain asked.

"That conversation is for another day, but what you need to know now is this: all of what has happened, in these years since it was discovered, was predicted. A man named Clastier wrote it down. His prophecies told of the Banoff."

"Before it happened?"

"Nearly two centuries before."

"UC, that means we had warning!" Twain said, agitated. "And they still couldn't stop it?"

"Clastier's work has always been suppressed by one group or another," Cope said. "The Aylantik government is doing it again, even as we speak."

"Is that why they're destroying the books?" Twain asked.

"Only in part," Cope said. "Thousands of books concern them. They couldn't possibly find the source of their fear, so they must destroy them all."

"So what good is it if we hide all the books?" Twain asked. "We can't show them to everyone. People won't read thousands of books in order to glean some esoteric knowledge."

"Material things are not important. This struggle has persisted for millennia. It often appears lost, but the wisdom is older than I am, older than time, and there will be a moment of return."

"But it can be sooner, than later. We can influence it. We *can*," Deuce said.

Twain was somewhat lost, but let his great-uncle and his father have an uninterrupted, silent, communicative stare.

Cope nodded. "There are eight important works which may still exist in that library. Clastier, and seven others."

"Wow," Twain said.

"That we can do something with. What are the titles?" Deuce asked.

"Long ago they would have been concealed in other books."

"Wasn't there a better way to hide them?" Twain asked.

"It's difficult to understand, but this type of knowledge can't just be taught and learned. It must be discovered and felt. There is also the matter of timing . . . one cannot understand something until they're ready. Even an entire society is subject to this."

"We must find those eight books."

"It won't be easy. Someone would have to be so familiar with books that they would notice even a slight variation in the text," Cope said.

"Someone like a librarian?" Deuce asked rhetorically. *The last librarian*, he thought to himself.

"Booker lived before the Banoff. Did he know it was going to happen?" Twain asked.

"Yes, my father knew," Cope answered solemnly. "He did what he could. He got Clastier's prophecies out, and even spoke about them, but history hasn't done a good job of remembering what those times were really like. So much has been written about the Banoff period of plague and war, *the final war*, and the centuries that proceeded it, but that last decade, just prior to all the sadness and turmoil, has really been ignored, even hidden."

"Why?" Twain asked.

Cope looked at Deuce.

"It was a lot like where we are now," Deuce said. "We may have amazing technology and clean energy, disease under control, and so-called peace, but our paradise is on the edge of a great precipice. Much as theirs was then."

"The vibration of the two times is very similar," Cope added.

"History repeats itself," Twain mused.

"How can we find those eight hidden books?" Deuce asked. "Please tell me all you know about them."

Cope smiled and slipped a hand into his inside coat pocket, pulling out an old envelope, then handed it to Deuce.

He looked at his uncle, confused, then glanced at the address. In scrawled, faded black ink, it read, *Spencer Lipton, II – February 2098*

"Who is this from?" Deuce asked hopefully.

"My father," Cope said. "Booker wrote that letter to you more than fifty years ago, and asked me to give it to you when this day came."

Deuce stood stunned. "Fifty years ago I was a baby."

"Actually he gave it to me, addressed like that, when I turned eighteen, two years before you were born."

"But how could he have known?" Twain asked.

"Oh, well," Cope said, reflectively, as if staring back a hundred years into the past. "Booker Lipton knew many things."

CHAPTER SEVENTY-THREE

Deuce pleaded with Cope to go to the island with Twain, but he said he'd been away from his trees long enough. A Flo-wing dropped him off on the edge of the redwoods and went on to take Twain to a boat, although calling one of Deuce's many yachts simply a boat was something only the trillionaire did. He had watercrafts that might, one day, present real problems for the AOI if it ever came down to an all-out war.

Before he left, Cope tried to convince Deuce to take the peaceful path, but wouldn't reveal what, if anything, he knew about the looming rebellion or its outcome. He'd only looked long and penetratingly at Deuce, as he often did, and said, "Time will tell you everything, and it won't always be too late."

Chelle had told him where to meet them, but Runit hadn't spoken to her since she'd left . . . and those hours on the stairs. *Could that have been less than twenty-four hours ago? Does she know I'm alive?* he wondered, not so sure himself. *How much longer do I have?*

When Krucks told him goodbye on the library steps, he expected bullets, a bomb, or something terrible. But nothing had come, only a couple of flashes on his INU. The first was from the county, reminding him the security codes would be changed Monday morning, and to be sure his personal property had been removed from the library. It had. And one from the Aylantik Office of Employment promising a new job for him within ten days. He found that one optimistic. *Maybe they aren't going to kill me.*

Runit climbed into his LEV, a conservative, gray model that had just enough room to stretch out and sleep, which he planned to attempt during the long drive. He stated his desired destination, and the voice recognition system immediately announced the expected duration of his trip and the vehicle's readiness, awaiting his command to begin.

He hesitated a moment, remembering novels he'd read. *This is where the vehicle explodes. This is how they will kill me.* He looked out the window, debating. Finally, he gave the command anyway, and nothing happened other than the LEV moving. *Maybe this time is different.*

Deuce listened to the BLAXER report, then quietly switched the AirView off and let the INU project the far galaxies across the room. In seconds, the sensation of floating among the stars returned. He did his best thinking that way, fully reclined in a "creation chair," controlled by touch to rotate, float, and incorporate full sensory perception adaption.

Chelle had bothered him from the start. Now he confirmed what his instincts had been telling him all along, and it left him disturbed.

She wasn't just the connected widow of Beale Andreas, banker to the power-elite, and, Deuce believed, she sure wasn't loyal to

PAWN. Chelle Andreas had an agenda perhaps bigger than his own, and a tangled list of contacts that rivaled those of Blaze Cortez. There were many reasons to fear her involvement, the first being that much of this newly discovered information had come from the AOI data on her, and yet she had not been arrested.

Why? Someone with her past, her data, should have been watched twenty-four-seven, yet they didn't seem to know her present location. How could that be? Why would the AOI allow such a radical revolutionary to live?

He'd have to have a talk with her, but not until Monday. It was risky to allow her to go unchecked until then, but even riskier to chance a meeting between the two of them before the library business was finished and the books were safe.

Chelle complicated things. Deuce had to get word to Runit about Booker's letter. They needed to find the books that comprised the eight works, and to determine if they'd been among the 116,804 volumes smuggled out before the burn. But now, according to the plumber, Runit and Chelle were romantically involved. It made him even more suspicious of her, and it compromised the librarian. It also meant that Nelson could be a problem. Because he was her brother, his motives were now in question, but only the librarian could be expected to find the eight works in such a short time, and under such conditions.

Deuce's zoom woke Runit as the librarian's LEV was just south of Eugene.

"The books are gone," Runit said, sitting up sleepily at the surprise of seeing Deuce's image, while the windows still shaded out the world.

"No, they're safe," Deuce said.

"Not those," Runit said. "The ones left behind. A million worlds cremated. I watched them go. Ceaseless red and gray dust." He paused, overcome. "That dust may remain in that windless building. Oh, it was so eerily transformed. My library," he gasped, "it's now just a burnt out mausoleum. Filled with the scars of eternity."

Deuce remained silent for several moments, then said gently, "You saved so much, Runit. More than you know. You could not have done more. No one could have." Saying the last part to himself.

CHAPTER SEVENTY-FOUR

Runit shivered thinking back on the nightmarish visions he knew would haunt him forever. "What kind of person burns books? What are they afraid of?"

"You're a librarian. You should know that answer better than most," Deuce said. "They want certain things forgotten or hidden or never known, and the places where such things are recorded, like books, become dangerous to the corrupt. The ones who want to control what people think. The ones who feel safe only when everyone sees it all their way."

"I do know that, but the continuous shock of the last week is that the world is a far stranger place than I ever knew."

"Speaking of that, you're being tracked."

"They really are going to try to kill me, aren't they?"

Deuce admired Runit for using the word try. He knew of only one person the AOI had failed to execute: Munna. But her existence had been confirmed only in the last forty-eight hours, so all her years in hiding didn't really count. The AOI was the most efficient killing machine ever created. Part police force, part intelligence service, and part military, it had no equal in history, and certainly not in the present world. Deuce hoped Runit would live, and he needed Munna alive at least a little longer, but he had his doubts that either would be alive in a few days.

"They will kill you, when they're done with you."

"What use am I to them now? If they wanted me to lead them to the missing books, that would mean they knew about the books. Oh no! What if they did know about the books all along and they're using them to get to PAWN?"

Deuce was impressed with the librarian. "I have a LEV waiting for you at the rest area just past Roseburg. It's a heavily treed area. You'll pull in, use the bathroom, and someone will give you the code to it. Yours will be driven away in the opposite direction."

"Will that work?"

"Yes. It will buy us time, and time is the most important thing right now."

"Why are you helping us?"

"On the contrary. You're helping me. The man at the rest area will also give you an Eysen-INU. I will explain more, but I need you to find a list of books."

"Are those books the reason all this is happening?"

"Yes. You'll understand once you get the INU."

Runit found it ironic that even after everything that had occurred, he was still acting as a librarian, pulling books for a patron.

The LEV exchange at the rest area went smoothly. The AOI agents he'd been expecting to emerge from the trees with laser weapons never materialized. Runit was relieved to be in a new LEV, allegedly and momentarily safe from AOI trackers. The vehicle had already been programmed with a destination.

He opened the Eysen-brand INU, as soon as he gave the drive command. Holographic images of eight books appeared. They weren't all actual books that existed, only Clastier's Papers were published as their own work, but the remaining seven were books within books, hidden texts that had been purposefully concealed in other titles. Deuce said that if the books could be found, there might be a way to avoid a bloody revolution. The books could bring down the Aylantik government and destroy the AOI.

Is that possible? Could some old printed and bound paper and ink book actually have that much power in such a technologically advanced society? It won't be easy, but I'd like to find out.

An hour later Runit's tired Information Navigation Unit lit. Deuce again. "I'm sorry Runit, but I have some horrible news," Deuce said carefully. "The AOI has raided the location where your people were."

Runit felt the physical force of metal and concrete crushing in on him, the sting of hot polluted water filling his lungs as if the LEV had careened off the highway and into a stifling sewage swamp. He tried to imagine they were okay and he tried to think, but both efforts failed, as he wrestled through the crash taking place in his mind.

"I don't know if there were any survivors. I've got a force on the way."

"Who?" was all he could get out.

"Chelle Andreas, Nelson Wright, Vida Mondragon, and Grandyn were all at the location at the time of the strike."

Runit considered opening the door and leaping from the moving LEV, helpless in his distance. He glazed over and locked himself in that place he'd created when Harper died.

"They may have survived," Deuce said. His image suddenly larger, he stepped out of the AirView and sat next to Runit. "Listen to me Runit. PAWN had armed militia there, and there were a group of TreeRunners present. There's evidence that the

AOI didn't anticipate a level of response. The location has tunnels and hidden shelters."

Runit looked over hopefully at the digital image, which appeared as real as if it were Deuce himself sitting there.

"I'm not going to tell you they're alive," Deuce said, "but they might be. Some, or all of them, may have survived."

"Can you get me there any faster?"

"You're not going there at all. It's a fiery, smoking mess. More AOI agents are en route, my force too. The war has begun. But I promise you this, Runit. If they got out, my people will find them and bring them to you. We'll know more soon. Hang in there."

Alone again, Runit had the glass tint back to clear, and he watched the forested mountains sweep by as the LEV raced along at its maximum speed of 160 km/h.

"I'm going to find those eight books and destroy you," he said out loud. "Do you hear me, AOI? The last librarian has a weapon that should scare the torgon out of you . . . BOOKS!" he yelled.

CHAPTER SEVENTY-FIVE

Miner and Sarlo, once again in the air, flying to another city, sat across from each other, tense and tired.

"Those Imps are scary," Sarlo said.

"Absolutely frightening," Miner agreed. "Think what they can find on any of us. What they know. Technology has stolen our last secrets."

Polis Drast's face appeared projected into the air from Miner's INU. "I'm on my way to Portland," he said. "We've hit seven PAWN locations in Oregon Area, and we should have the woman in custody within hours. They call her Munna."

"Excellent. I want to speak with her myself. I'll be in Portland in less than an hour," Miner said.

"You don't need to come to Portland. You can view my interrogation on the Field just as easily," Drast said.

"I'm already on my way. This is too important. Munna is the key."

Miner didn't tell Drast that he had another reason for going to Oregon Area. Cope Lipton was believed to be in the region, and Miner's private forces, already scouring the area for Munna, were now including Cope in their search efforts. Miner believed it was even possible that the two could be found together, and he needed to be the first to find Deuce's mysterious uncle. "I'll let you know when I'm on the ground. Peace prevails, always," he said, ending the zoom.

"How could Booker Lipton have planned this revolution almost a century ago? Even before the Banoff? It's not possible," Sarlo asked, resuming their conversation.

"I really don't know," Miner said. "But our Imp friend didn't say Booker planned it, he said he knew it would happen. That's a big difference. If Booker Lipton had some kind of prophetic view into the future, that would explain how he developed the Eysen-INU. You may be impressed with its specs now, but let me tell you that when it first hit the market eighty years ago, it was worlds ahead of anything we had at that time. It was as if it had been plucked from a science fiction novel, or imported from a distant galaxy far, far away."

"Can someone really see into the future?"

"Hell, I don't know. Yesterday, I would have said no. But if the Imp is right, and it's hard to argue with all he knew, then Booker Lipton somehow saw at least one hundred years ahead of his time, and there is only one person left alive he would have trusted with that knowledge. We have to find him now."

"But if Cope Lipton knows Munna, then we might be underestimating PAWN and their chances," Sarlo said. "I mean, if they've had a hundred years to prepare . . . if they've waited all that time and are suddenly acting now. . . isn't it logical to assume that they believe they're finally in a position to defeat Aylantik?"

"Unless something else is forcing them to act now. Perhaps it's our surprising discovery of Munna after all these years. Or what if Munna is sick and close to death? Maybe the World Premier resigning unexpectedly, or the closing of the last library, or . . ." Miner pulled up an image of the Portland Library. "Wait, wasn't Deuce Lipton caught trying to save the books when the AOI shut down the library in Belgium?"

"Yeah. He's some sort of bibliophile," Sarlo said.

"What if he *isn't* a book collector? What if he's looking for something instead? Like a book of prophecies."

"Would the library have something like that?"

"Why not? Lots of rare books wound up at the larger libraries as families, estates, and smaller libraries dumped their physical books. If such a prophecy exists, we could use it to know what they know . . . to know what's going to happen."

"Well, if there was anything like that in the Portland Library, it's gone now." She brought up an AirView and displayed a report on the burning. "Entered by an agent Krucks and signed off by Drast himself. 'Entire collection of Portland library, last remaining physical books, burned.' Ironic if we destroyed the only thing that might save us."

"Maybe it wasn't destroyed. Deuce may have found it already. We need to find the librarian."

"Runit Happerman," Sarlo said, manipulating the virtual data in her INU.

The INU reported pertinent facts in an electronic voice that sounded smoother than any human. "Runit Happerman, age forty-three, widower, one son, Grandyn Happerman, known associate of Nelson Wright—"

"He's that controversial author," Sarlo interrupted.

"Wife deceased, Harper Happerman, AOI extermination," the INU voice continued. "Possible connections to Creatives, Rejectionists, and PAWN."

"Torgon-hell," Miner said, exasperated. "We killed the librarian's wife."

"Not only that," Sarlo said. "The librarian's friend, the author, he's the brother of Chelle Andreas, the widow of Beale Andreas."

Miner's eyes widened. Sarlo had never seen him so lost. For a moment, he couldn't find words, and looked as one might if stabbed by a friend.

"How was this missed? It's end-of-the-world type of information," he finally said. "The revolution is coming, and PAWN might be more prepared than we are!"

"What do you want to do?"

"Run everything on everyone connected to them. Find the matches, and see if anything leads back to Deuce." Miner pulled up his well-viewed screens on the Liptons. "And have the Force pick up our Imp friend in Denver and bring him to Portland. I want to talk to him again. There's obviously more to know about this little nightmare."

"What if it's already too late?" Sarlo asked.

"Only if there is war, is it too late," Miner said as the pilot announced their descent into Portland. "We must avoid war at all costs. Even if that cost is my entire fortune." Miner looked at the floating AirViews all around him, one showing the face of Runit and whispered firmly, "Find me that damned librarian!"

CHAPTER SEVENTY-SIX

The LEV got off the Interstate an exit early. Runit tried to change its course, but it would not take his commands. *Someone must be overriding,* he thought, hoping it was Deuce. Maybe he was going to see Grandyn and Chelle. *Maybe they are alive!* After twenty minutes of winding through narrow backroads, a prisoner of Deuce's LEV, he wondered if perhaps the AOI had found him again. Six minutes later, the LEV pulled over and stopped. Two women dressed in black and green Tekfabrik military-style fatigues jumped from the trees.

"Mr. Happerman, you need to come with us."

"Where? Who are you?"

"We work for Deuce. We're taking you to a safe place."

"Why didn't Deuce zoom me and tell me?"

"This entire sector is blanketed by intensive monitoring and surveillance. Breeze-Blowers, Crimers, Mapnots, Swarm-Drones, Sat-grids; AOI has thrown *everything* at us. LEVs are too susceptible."

Runit didn't know what she was talking about, or whether he should go, but they weren't pointing weapons at him, and if they were AOI they could have already killed him. "Where are we going?" he asked again, moving toward them.

"Not far. You'll need this." One of them handed him a Tekfabrik jumpsuit. He put it on and followed them.

Their definition of "not far" differed from his. After three hours of hard hiking through trail-less wilderness, they finally stopped.

One of them motioned Runit not to talk. The other took out an Eysen-INU and manipulated a holographic keypad until the tree closest to them opened, revealing a one-meter-wide shaft with a metal chain link ladder hung on the inside. One of the women entered and climbed down, the other motioned him to follow. Looking down into the tree, he saw a dimly lit opening, with a yellowish glow illuminated only a few meters down. Soon the woman's figure blocked it out as she disappeared into the darkness. Runit climbed inside the secret tree and descended on the swaying, chain ladder.

Once he reached the bottom, maybe ten or twelve meters down, the world before him seemed out of a futuristic sci-fi movie from the past. A corridor led away, glass walls on either side of it revealing rooms filled with floating AirViews, holographic people in conversation with real ones, and levitating light panels displaying a full spectrum of colored knobs, switches, and buttons.

"What *is* this place?"

"We call them POPs, for PAWN Operational Pod."

"Do people live down here?" Runit asked, still trying to take it all in.

"A few hundred live and work in this POP."

"How many POPs are there?"

The women looked at each other and apparently decided to ignore his question. They walked briskly down the long hall until a door appeared about fifty meters into the heart of the POP. Through the glass wall, he saw Grandyn.

He pushed past the woman and stumbled into the room, unable to stop the tears. He grabbed his son. "You're alive! I can't believe it! Are you okay?"

Grandyn held his father for several moments, then pulled back and looked into the eyes of the man who had raised him, feeling safe again. It was all there between them. Their history instinctively worked to decode the previous twenty-four hours, the desperate strain and toxic tension they'd endured, and the books were the least of it, although the books might be the only part that made any sense. The betrayal of memory, the lie of facts, the crumbling truths of what the government stood for and how the utopia they'd been cradled in since birth had turned out to be a crypt constructed of webs and dust. They saw themselves in each other's eyes and rejoiced in their bond, while at the same time wading through shards of reciprocal pain.

"Vida's dead," Grandyn finally said. His son's anguished face tore at Runit. It took him back to the blackness after Harper's death.

He knew that expression, that burning unquenchable emptiness, the torture of having the closest person in the world stolen from you. Justification was impossible. Grandyn suffering agony like that, losing someone he loved, put the burning books into perspective. Worse, it identified a cost to saving the books. An undeniable charge of guilt that Runit would forever bear – Vida's death had been the first. He owed more, and cringed at the weight of the karmic tax.

"I'm so sorry," Runit said hoarsely, his tear-filled eyes conveying unspoken understanding and comfort to his bereaved son.

"They killed Bo and Wade too," Grandyn said.

Runit closed his eyes, recognizing the name of two of Grandyn's longtime TreeRunner buddies. He'd watched them grow up. Youth robbed, casualties of a silent war which had never been declared and could not be won. "What happened?"

"The AOI has escalated," Chelle said, entering the room behind him.

Runit smiled at her voice, fearing she'd been lost too. He turned and she fell into his arms.

"Chelle saved me," Grandyn said. "She killed a man for me."

Runit looked at her, biting back tears of gratitude. "You saved my boy." He bowed his head to her, lips trembling, hands shaking. "Thank you."

"One less AOI agent," she said, as if it had been routine.

"Thank you," Runit repeated, pulling her tightly back into him.

"It's okay," she whispered, and then stepped back and massaged the air around her INU. "The Doneharvest, that's what the AOI is calling their crackdown, is unlike anything since pre-Banoff," Chelle explained, lighting up an AirView to show him footage.

Everyone knew the name Doneharvest, the first head of the AOI after the Banoff. He was credited with restoring peace, but his methods had been extremely controversial and harsh. It was rumored he'd been killed by an assassin, but in the more than fifty years since his death, no one had ever been arrested in connection with it, and the "murder" remained one of the AOI's many mysteries.

"They want to exterminate PAWN," Chelle continued. "They've been rounding up Creatives all day. We suspect strikes into the Amazon are imminent." The air filled with images of AOI agents arresting artists and writers.

"What's in the Amazon?" Runit asked.

"Rejectionists," Chelle said, as if he'd know just what she meant. "How'd it go at the library?"

"I'd rather not talk about it," Runit said. "You were right. I probably should have come with you."

"You might be dead now if you had," Chelle said. "I'm glad you're here now."

Runit suddenly remembered Nelson had been with them. "Is your brother okay?" he asked.

"He's fine. Once we found out about Doneharvest, he decided to go and try to plead with Deuce for full support, funding, and weapons," Chelle said.

"Isn't Deuce helping? His people led me here." He turned, looking for the women who'd escorted him, but they were gone.

"They were actually with PAWN, and only claimed to be sent by Deuce because we figured you wouldn't come otherwise."

"Why didn't they just tell me that Grandyn and you were here?"

"They didn't know."

A short, thin man dressed in Tekfabrik fatigues entered the room. "Chelle, it's time to go," he said.

"Where?" Runit asked. "Aren't we safe here?"

"We're not safe anywhere anymore," she said. "You need to meet someone."

"Who?"

"A woman I've only recently met, who might be able to make sense of all this for you. A woman who can answer all of your questions. They call her Munna."

CHAPTER SEVENTY-SEVEN

Chelle led Runit and Grandyn around a winding corridor in the expansive underground PAWN facility. At one point, Runit accidentally dropped his small pack, which contained a change of clothes, a few personal items, and the copy of *The Road* he'd taken from his library office. He retrieved it and had to jog to catch up. Chelle was in a hurry.

"Does PAWN stand a chance against the AOI?" Runit asked.

"Why don't you ask Munna that question? We'll be there in a couple of hours."

"A couple of hours? How big is this place?" Runit asked.

"Oh, she's not here. She doesn't like to live underground."

"Why do we have to risk going back out there with the Doneharvest going on? I don't *have* to meet Munna."

"Munna wants to meet *you*," Chelle said. "Anyway, I told you. We're not safe anywhere. It's better to keep moving."

They exited the POP from a different tunnel, which opened out from a stone hatch concealed in a very small cave on a cliff. They had to jump down off a two-meter high ledge.

They hiked hard for two hours through the damp forest without a break, constantly gaining elevation. Chelle checked their location several times on her INU. Conserving their energy, they hadn't talked much until Runit suddenly asked, "Where are the books?"

"Deuce Lipton has about half of them," Chelle said quietly.

"How did he get them?"

"I told him where to find them."

"Why?"

"He's in a better position to protect them."

"Why doesn't he have them all?"

"They had to do it in two trips. They got one shipment out right away, but once the Doneharvest grew so massive, it became too dangerous to risk revealing their location."

"I talked to Deuce hours ago. Why didn't he tell me?"

"You talked to Deuce?" Chelle asked, surprised.

"Yeah, didn't he tell you where I'd be?"

"No, we tracked you through your INU and then commandeered your LEV through a GPS interface."

"Why can't the AOI track me the same way?"

"We've taken countermeasures. It's complicated. I'll put you with a tech person as soon as we get to Mexico. You'll learn more than you ever wanted to know about surveillance."

"Mexico?"

"I'm getting ahead of myself."

"I'll say," Runit said.

Grandyn couldn't help but laugh.

"Where are the rest of the books?"

"Down there," she said, pointing. He could see an old barn in a meadow below them as they crested a ridge.

"Couldn't we have driven here?" Grandyn asked.

"I wish, but it's not safe with the Doneharvest," Chelle replied.

"Hey, look!" Grandyn said, holding his arm up. Ahead of them, a soldier was crouched by a tree.

"It's okay," Chelle said. "PAWN has the whole area surrounded.

"To protect the books?" Grandyn asked, impressed.

"The books, and Munna."

"She's here with the books?" Runit asked.

"I'm told she insisted on it," Chelle said, waving to the soldier, who clearly knew her on sight.

Inside the barn, Runit was relieved to see stacks of bundled books. After the horror of witnessing a million of them burning, these treasured relics, among the last of their kind, overwhelmed him, and he began to shake. Chelle touched his shoulder to steady him, but he pulled away, still upset that she had allowed Deuce to take the priceless volumes.

An old woman emerged from a corner with a book in hand. She looked older than anyone Grandyn had ever seen, even in books. Thick, powder-white hair appeared to be the only thing holding up her pale, crinkly, parchment-like skin, but her ocean-green eyes were bright and clear, and her walk, albeit with a cane, steady.

"Greetings," Munna said in a honeyed, gravel voice. "So you're the last librarian." She bowed slightly to Runit, then she extended her hand.

Her use of the long abandoned custom of shaking hands surprised him. "Yes, ma'am," Runit said self-consciously, not sure if he was in the presence of a natural fluke, a revolutionary, some kind of spiritual leader, maybe even an immortal goddess, or perhaps all of the above. Finally, he took her hand and gave it a careful shake, afraid to break the dainty thing. He was surprised by its worn, flannel-like softness.

"Please, everyone, call me Munna."

"Okay, Munna. This is my son, Grandyn."

She smiled at Grandyn and stared thoughtfully for a moment.

Grandyn felt uncomfortable as she continued staring, as if trying to memorize his face.

Runit noticed that Munna was missing several teeth. Everyone he'd ever seen had perfect teeth because the Aylantik provided free dental care to all. Munna obviously was not enrolled in Aylantik's mandatory Health-Circle.

"My dear, you're trembling," she said, turning back to Runit. "Here, take my shawl."

"No. Thank you," Runit said. "It's the books. They destroyed all the others."

"I know. I'm sorry. Back when I was young, books weren't rare at all. They were in almost every home, and libraries stood full, even in small towns."

"How old is she?" Grandyn whispered to Chelle.

"She was born in 1968. You do the math."

"How can anyone live to be one hundred and thirty years old?" Grandyn whispered urgently. He looked at her again, now seeing something beyond her incredible age. He saw power, a force like he'd never imagined possible.

CHAPTER SEVENTY-EIGHT

"Munna, it's not safe for you or the books to be here," Chelle said. "The AOI may be looking for the books, and they're definitely looking for you. Neither should be with the other."

"Lest we make it too easy for those bureaucratic thugs." Munna laughed.

"Yes, ma'am," Runit said. "The post Banoff author Towne Windom once said, 'Running is sometimes the best way to fight.'"

"Did he?" Munna said, not very familiar with the post-Banoff writer. "Well, Joseph Campbell said, 'The cave you fear to enter holds the treasure you seek.' Understand?" Munna smiled, then waited until Runit responded with an affirmative nod before continuing. "Well my friends, screw the AOI. I'm not only going to see these books, but I'm going to read some of them. Might even take a few with me. I've got an old library card. May I check one out?"

Runit looked at Chelle.

"You can't keep the last great library of books boxed up in a barn," Munna said. "We have a proper place, a safe place . . . with shelves."

"I'm afraid no place is safe from the AOI. Their eyes are everywhere," Chelle said.

Munna laughed. "They've been looking for me since before you were born. I think I'm a slightly better authority on the best way to hide something from Aylantik."

"Yes, ma'am," Chelle said, feeling properly admonished.

"It's not all the books," Runit said. "She gave half of them to Deuce Lipton."

"I know she did," Munna said, scowling momentarily at Chelle. "But no one ever had *all* the books, did they? Libraries of various sizes have always existed. Perhaps it's better to keep these books separated for a while, until we restore freedom to the world."

"Aren't we free now?" Grandyn asked.

"Dear boy, we weren't even free when we were free, but all we have now is a beautiful lie."

Grandyn nodded as if he understood, but the whole thing confused him. He looked to his father. Runit was the reason Grandyn was here, the reason he'd done just about everything in his life. Even when they didn't agree, he wanted to make him proud.

Runit caught his glance just then, and smiled that slightly crooked, sort of troubled smile that always put Grandyn at ease. There was something else too, carried in that exchange between Happermans: Runit conveyed understanding and comfort for the loss of Vida, and it felt real. It helped, because Grandyn knew, better than anyone, what his dad had been through.

"Can't we just leave the books here?" Chelle asked.

"Look where you are Chelle," Munna said. "We can't leave the last books in the world stacked up in a barn like bales of hay. If it were up to you, they'd probably be piled out in a cornfield." She shook her head. "Some place easy for that crafty Deuce Lipton to come pick up the rest of them."

"Whatever you want," Chelle said, leaving the barn.

Munna watched her go, and remained lost in thought for a moment before speaking. "Thank you, Runit, for all your sacrifice in saving these books. You have no idea how important this is to our cause, to humanity, to the truth."

She spoke her words as if giving a historic speech. She seemed accustomed to using her presence to motivate crowds, to giving inspiration to a revolution. The cause, as Chelle had pointed out, was one that Runit didn't fully understand. What little he'd gleaned from his meager knowledge of PAWN and their plight seemed to indicate these people wanted to return to some form of the pre-Banoff world. That didn't seem like a good idea to Runit, who knew too much about how harsh those days had been with war, poverty, crime, and disease.

"A smart man like you probably knows that the word revolution contains the word love. Interesting that the computers kept those two words from English for the Com language. Love and revolution," Munna said, knowingly.

"Kafka said, 'All language is but a poor translation.' Wouldn't you agree?"

"Yes, I would," Munna said, laughing. "I just knew I'd like you." She touched his face the way a proud mother would. "Of course, love is written backwards within revolution, but that's only to keep it hidden. That's the secret of all great rebellions . . . love."

"How so?" Runit asked. "What is this all about?"

"Oh my," Munna said, as if beginning to tell a magical story to a child. "It's about everything. If Aylantik hadn't wasted the last hundred years on greed, we could have been somewhere so very different."

"But is here so bad?" Runit asked. "There has always been corruption."

"No, not always. And yes, it is *so* bad when one considers what can be seen through the windows to your soul. If they weren't so interested in seeing our every move and grabbing every bit of power, they might have seen that the real power lies within."

"So this is about religion?" Runit asked.

"Not even remotely. It's about potential."

"I'm sorry, but what does that mean?" Runit asked.

"I'll show you." She stared at him, her lips slightly parted in neither a smile nor a frown. Her already bright eyes lit with a new vitality, her thumbs moved rapidly and softly on the insides of her index fingers, and then she took in a deep breath. "You're wondering how you can search for the books that Deuce told you about," she said, nodding. "And, hypocritically, you're upset with Chelle for letting Deuce take half the load. You're afraid for your son. You're not sure you'll live because of what happened in Belgium. Don't worry, I won't bring up the part about Nelson's indiscretion here."

"Are you tied into the Seeker?" Runit asked, unimpressed.

"No," Chelle answered, walking back into the barn. "Munna has developed the ability to maximize her brain capacity. She's tapped into the universal consciousness . . . and into her own cells. It's how she's lived so long."

"Whoa," Grandyn said.

Munna smiled.

Runit wasn't sure he believed it.

Munna nodded at him. "Please come here, Runit." She curled a bony finger. He walked over to where she stood against her cane. He noticed its carvings of unrecognizable symbols, which looked like an old, ancient language. Before he could wonder what they might mean, she beckoned him again. "Give me your ear," she said. He stooped his ear to her mouth. "I knew Harper. She was a fine woman," she whispered. "She deserved your devotion, even with her lapse. And you've kept your promise to her. Grandyn is strong. And you, dear man, are brave and true."

CHAPTER SEVENTY-NINE

Drast zoomed Miner, who by now was in a penthouse hotel suite overlooking Portland. Both Mount St. Helens and Mount Hood, promised the woman at the desk, would be visible in the morning. Miner loved views, and actually felt that he owned them as personal possessions.

"I've just interrogated a PAWN member and confirmed her answers through brain scans," Drast said. "Munna is real, she's alive, and she's one hundred and thirty years old!"

Miner stared at the image of Drast and considered telling him about Cope Lipton. The danger ate at him. Normally cool and in control, Miner felt anxious and unsure. His obsession with Deuce was giving way to his concern that the combination of Munna and Cope might overwhelm Aylantik. He'd always believed in the invincibility of the AOI, but Munna and Cope changed his perception of the prospects of war, the meaning of power, and of reality itself. "Torg," was the only response he could manage to Drast's news.

"The life expectancy for anyone born before the Banoff is around seventy. Everyone born as late as 2024 is already dead because of exposure to the infection. Even with the great drugs developed by PharmaForce, the elderly have weaker immune systems and are more susceptible, having lived closer to the Banoff," Drast said, telling Miner nothing he didn't already know. "I remember when the Aylantik announced that the last person born pre-Banoff had died. I don't think *anyone* has ever lived that long. How is this woman alive?"

"The question isn't a health matter. It makes no difference how she has survived, the problem is that she remembers life before the Banoff," Miner said.

Drast looked at him, realizing both the danger and the opportunity. "If her brain is still working right, don't you think she'd want to talk about it?"

"Only if she isn't afraid to die."

After the zoom, Sarlo looked at him. "Why don't we get his help? We're looking for three people: Munna, Cope, and Runit, now conspicuously and coincidentally missing. The AOI is the greatest surveillance apparatus in human history. Don't you think Drast can contribute?"

"The AOI is already looking for Munna. They've been searching for her for decades, and until today couldn't even prove she existed. The Enforcers are on it," Miner said, speaking of PharmaForce's security unit which operated more like his private secret police. The Enforcers were third in personnel under arms, lagging behind only Lipton's BLAXERS and the AOI. "With the Enforcers, I'm certain of loyalty and confidentiality. The AOI is too big and too easy a target for the leaching tentacles of Deuce Lipton and Blaze Cortez."

Blaze walked into Deuce's office in San Francisco. "Good idea, doing this in person," he said.

"Time is short," Deuce replied. "You and I are in a position to make this right."

"War is inevitable."

"Damn it Blaze, why do you say that?"

"Because you know it is. Delays are merely delays." Blaze combed his fingers through his long hair, which looked tangled from the wind.

"Maybe, but the longer we put it off, the more likely something else can take hold."

"The truth?" Blaze looked at him skeptically. "That's a dream. Something only you believe, Deuce. The truth is buried too deep beneath a mixture of lies and toxic mountains of greed."

"We *can* save it."

"Ha! You manage to save a hundred thousand dusty books, and now all of a sudden you can save the truth?" Blaze asked, manipulating the lights and symbols emanating from his INU until Deuce's private bar opened, a drink was dispensed, and a serving-bot brought it to him. "You really should encrypt your code."

"I do," Deuce said, knowing Blaze knew he did.

"Oh, my talent is so large that sometimes I forget to notice my own brilliance."

"Blaze, I know you want the truth to rule once again."

"The truth has not ruled in eons, so saying that it will *once again* rule, is a farce."

"Have some courage Blaze."

"Courage is not something a capitalist understands. It implies doing something for the right reasons. I do things in the pursuit of money, not for some moral idea, and certainly not for the greater good."

"Then, why did you come here today?"

"Because you're the richest man in the world, and you asked. Notice the financial aspect in my reasoning?" Blaze smiled.

"You helped get those books out."

"Purely a business proposition. I did it for the money."

"Then why didn't you sell them out to the AOI? That information would have been worth millions of digis."

"Any sucker can sell information when they get it. The art is selling it when it has the most value. I'm gambling that the payday is greater down the road. Some information, if not used, expires worthless. Some, like a decent wine, gets more valuable with age." As he spoke, Blaze manipulated a massive, floating Rubik's Cube, this one with nine hundred lighted squares per side, with sixty shades of various colors. He'd invented it, and no one, including Blaze himself, had ever been able to complete it.

"Fine, we'll do it your way. I need a piece of information to find its way to Lance Miner."

"Is it accurate? Because I do not trade in lies. Nothing robs a man faster than lies. It's a dark world, where no one trusts anybody," Blaze said, pontificating for his own pleasure.

Deuce looked up in the ceiling where the stars of the Andromeda galaxy were visible. Blaze seemed oblivious to the planetarium above them, but Deuce knew Blaze missed nothing, so had chosen to ignore the beautiful slice of the brilliantly recreated universe. "Do you know that the Andromeda galaxy is moving toward our own Milky Way at more than a million kilometers per hour?" Deuce said. "In five billion years, the two galaxies will collide."

"Andromeda is actually moving toward us at 1,078,260 kilometers per hour," Blaze corrected. "But not to worry. The human species will long be safely away from Earth as our sun, a 4.6 billion-year-old yellow dwarf star with a diameter of 1,392,684 kilometers, will, approximately 130 million years after it burns through all its hydrogen, become a red giant, engulf Mercury and Venus, and finally consume Earth."

Deuce smiled, finding it impossible not to like Blaze. He wondered, yet again, if his implant denials could possibly be true.

"Yes, the information I need Miner to receive is accurate. There is a PAWN facility in Colorado near Black Canyon. It's their largest." Deuce moved his fingers around holographic controls.

"I've just sent the details to your INU. You should sell this information to Miner."

"Indulge me with two questions."

Deuce nodded.

"Why are you betraying an organization that I've known you to support? And why Miner, instead of selling it to Polis Drast?"

"Do you really not know the answers?"

"There is a difference between knowing the answers and being sure of them," Blaze said. "I need to be certain how big the bang will be, and who is lighting the fuse."

"Sometimes in order to avoid war, a battle must be lost," Deuce said. "If the AOI sees how big the opposition is, they may throttle down. And if PAWN suffers such a blow, they will have to delay the rebellion."

"Those are big 'ifs,' and a risky strategy . . . but it might work," Blaze said. "What about my second question?"

"You know as well as I do that Polis Drast wants war. *Needs* it to fulfill his ambitions to become the next World Premier. If he gets the PAWN base info first, he'll turn it into a pretext for war. Miner, on the other hand, wants peace more than even I do, and he still has the power to prevent this silent war from turning into something loud and unstoppable."

"Consider it done," Blaze said, smiling. "I'm always happy to do a deal where I make money on both sides. Have one hundred million digis in my account in the next five minutes. And don't worry. I'll charge Miner ten times that amount. This is a big one. Many will die, the balance of power might shift, and war, at least for now, might just be averted."

CHAPTER EIGHTY

Runit and Grandyn spent hours searching for the secret books. The bundles provided some organization, but not much.

"Talk about a needle in a haystack!" Runit said.

Grandyn laughed. The old barn did, in fact, have plenty of hay bales, and the books were stacked haphazardly throughout. "Your system is something only a librarian could understand," he said, pointing to a pile near the center of the cavernous space where the truck had once been.

"If we'd only known about the eight missing books before we moved everything," Runit said while reading spines.

"Don't be so frustrated Dad. We'll find them."

"They may not have even made it out of the building. They may be ashes," he said, shuddering while remembering the horrifying scene of the books being burned. "The books we're looking for could even be in the batch Chelle let Deuce Lipton take."

"Where are Chelle and Nelson, anyway?"

"Meeting with some important PAWN leaders."

"I thought Munna was the leader," Grandyn said.

"She's just one of them. More of a figurehead really."

Grandyn nodded.

Later, after temporarily suspending the search for the missing eight books, Runit and Grandyn went to their lodgings for the night. They tried to sleep in the back room of the ancient building that, at one time, had been part of a large vineyard. The AOI had stepped up the Doneharvest throughout the day. Raids and arrests were happening all over the Pacyfik. More AOI personnel were arriving every hour, and the PAWN agents assigned to keep Runit and Grandyn safe thought it best to keep them in a dark and musty wine cellar, minus the bottles. It could have been a bomb shelter, and Runit might have felt safer if he didn't feel so isolated. The two front rooms above them were occupied by the three PAWN rebels.

The one who had brought them to the winery would continue on with them in the morning to another remote location in the long process of hiding and protecting the last librarian. Munna had requested it, and Chelle had convinced the leaders of her faction that there was no one else who could identify the important works hidden within the stolen cache. She refused to say how the information about secret books within books had been obtained, but her sway among the top rebels was strong. The books would be moved too, but it might be several more days until Runit could get another look at them.

Runit gave the precious copy of Cormac McCarthey's *The Road* to his son. It was like an old friend coming home. Grandyn had read it three years earlier at his father's urging. "It seems to have new meaning now," Runit said.

Grandyn nodded and silently reflected on the plot. "Do you believe it?" Grandyn asked. "That Mom was part of PAWN and that she might have discovered something?"

"I'm afraid so. There was a lot about your mother that she chose not to share with me," he said, thinking of the fling with Nelson. They talked well into the night about Harper, PAWN, the way to find codes or messages hidden in books, and about their new lives as rebels. Runit was tired, but he had much to process, and talking it through with the person he loved most in the world, as they lay there in the dark, made him feel much more sure about everything that had happened.

"Dad, you haven't said anything about watching the books burn," Grandyn said as they were on the verge of sleep.

"Half of me wants to pretend it never happened. The other half never wants to forget," Runit said quietly. "It was like watching evil."

"I grew up in that beautiful library with those wonderful books. I don't know how you could bear to watch it all burn. The books were my friends, always there teaching me, making me laugh, and taking me places . . . so many places."

"They were part of our family," Runit agreed and, after a long pause, added, "When the flames grew and the heat was really intense, I swear I could hear the books screaming."

"We saved all we could."

"But for how long?"

"People died for those books. Real people. Friends that I loved." Grandyn's voice cut through the blackness of the musty cellar. "I will not allow their deaths to be in vain. I'll fight forever to preserve them, until we get rid of Aylantik."

"I don't want you to become another victim of this cause," Runit said. "I couldn't survive losing you."

"I don't know what the plan is with PAWN and all of this, but I'm a TreeRunner, and we can survive undetected in the forests indefinitely."

"I'm afraid it may come to that."

"What is a life without meaning? A strange and empty walk alone in the cold."

Runit smiled, recognizing the quote from one of his favorite post-Banoff authors, Jean Van Ness. "Do good. Share love. Risk it all for something more than yourself," Runit said, finishing the quote.

"Even if I do die," Grandyn said, "it will be for the reason I lived." Neither spoke for almost a minute. "But don't worry," Grandyn said. "I'm eighteen, and I'm gonna live forever."

CHAPTER EIGHTY-ONE

Monday, February 5

Chelle slipped in next to Runit in the early hours, just as light filtered softly from the doorway. Runit couldn't help but smile as he felt her body against his.

"Do you forgive me?" she asked. "Deuce will protect his books. You don't have to worry about that."

Runit had thought about it, and wasn't sure whether Deuce wanted to save the books from being changed, or if he'd wanted them in order to find the eight missing works. Either way, he believed they'd be protected, at least until those lost were found, and the odds were they had at least some of the eight among PAWN's half.

"You're a difficult person not to forgive."

"I'll take that as a yes," she said, kissing him.

"Do you all mind," Grandyn said groggily. "I'd like to sleep for a few more days if possible."

"I wish it were," Chelle said, "but the AOI raided nine more locations last night. We barely got the TreeRunners out safely."

"I should be with them," Grandyn said, an argument he'd lost yesterday.

"We'll be joining up with them later," Chelle said.

Suddenly, they heard the rebels running and shouting above them.

"Could you have been followed?" Runit asked Chelle.

"I was careful." But even as she answered, she thought of the satellites, the vehicle traces, Seeker, Field displacements, drones, swarms, informants . . . *How had they survived this long?*

"Is there another way out?"

"I don't think so," she replied, trying to think but only able to recall concrete walls all around them. "We should go up there and see what's happening."

The sound of gunshots and lasers seemed louder and faster. They looked at each other. A scream: one of the good guys hit. Then the floor above collapsed on them in a fiery explosion of flashing lights and debris. Confusion, smoke, and moans filled the next few minutes, but Chelle was sure she saw two AOI agents killed by a surviving rebel. After that a smattering of shots was heard, and then silence.

Grandyn had been burned badly by the flash, but remained conscious. "Dad," he called out once he became convinced the fighting had ended. Only more silence answered him. "Dad, where are you?"

The smoke cleared, and it was eerily light as the sky was now visible. The remaining glow of the sunrise turned everything a dark orange hue. He screamed when he saw his father, feeling sure he was dead.

"No!" Somehow he dragged himself to Runit, who was covered in blood.

Grandyn lay there, holding his father's lifeless body. Shock and anger prevented Grandyn's tears from flowing. Grandyn looked up at Chelle, as if betrayed. She tried to give a comforting glance, but rage choked her efforts. Grandyn couldn't stand – the burns on his leg were too severe. In that empty moment, pushing past the torturing pain, and not knowing if his father was alive, he vowed to destroy the AOI. It would be his mission. In time, he'd try to make it less about revenge and more for the elevated purpose of setting the world free again, but for now, it was only vengeance that he sought.

"Is he breathing?" Chelle yelled.

Grandyn shook from his angry trance, and placed his cheek next to Runit's mouth. There was something . . . "Yes, I think he is still alive!"

"Then we can save him," Chelle said. "But we have to hurry!"

In the echoing silence of the blown-out cellar, a combat zone from a long-ago-started war that was only now being fought – and lost – Grandyn kissed his father's forehead softly.

"You're a hero," he whispered. "You saved the books . . . the world will know this one day and celebrate you. But you've always been my hero." A tear fell from his eye and he felt sure his throat was going to close off all his air. With a soft and cracking voice he breathed the words, "Brave and true."

"Can you walk?" Chelle called, trying to hold herself together, after seeing Runit's broken body.

"I don't think so."

Chelle's thoughts burst through her battered head. *We have to get out of here. The AOI has obviously penetrated PAWN and launched a full offensive against us. Maybe we can find Nelson. He might still be alive. He has to be alive!* She tried to regain her grip on the situation, to draw on the fiery inner-strength that drove her. *The AOI might have arrested Deuce Lipton . . . what about his books? Oh, Runit, I'm so sorry.* In spite of her reassuring words to Grandyn, she didn't really believe Runit could survive, and fought her welling tears. *How much time do we have until another AOI team arrives? Is Munna safe?* She scanned the rubble and saw nothing that could help her get Grandyn and Runit to safety. *Both Happermans might have to be left here, but the AOI will execute them on the spot. Maybe I can get them to the trees. They look to be only two hundred meters away.* She started to cry. *Damn it, how can I save them! The AOI could be here in seconds.*

Then she heard a Flo-wing.

CHAPTER EIGHTY-TWO

Chelle surveyed the bombed out ruin, wondering if escape was even possible. "Grandyn, we have to go now. Your dad would want you to live. It was his highest purpose." She braced for his rage. "Come on." Most of Chelle's left side, including her head, was bleeding, but she didn't let the pain slow her. She scrambled over bloody and torn bodies, found a laser rifle next to a dead AOI agents, checked its charge, and tossed it to Grandyn. "We can make it, but you have to forget the life you almost had. You're a soldier now, and we're at war." Chelle hardly recognized her voice, and tried to remain steady.

"Are you crazy? I'm not leaving my dad here!"

"His best chance is for the AOI to pick him up, they'll get him to a hospital. They'll want him alive."

"No, we fight here." Grandyn began to crawl to a corner where he'd have better cover. She took a conventional gun from one of the fallen PAWN rebels, knowing from her weapons studies it was an AK-47 assault rifle. As the Flo-wing's engines grew louder, she grabbed two extra magazines off the soldier and retreated to an area close to Grandyn that had become a pile of concrete slabs.

Grandyn, feeling the air rush as the Flo-wing landed, realized that he might die soon, and tallied the losses: his mother, Vida, and two TreeRunners, now maybe his father, himself. So many deaths resulting from the revolution he knew so little about. Some of that blood was on his hands.

What had his mother known so long ago? Had she realized the risks of never seeing her son again?

Footsteps and shouts. He steadied himself against the wall and readied his finger over the firing button, then stole a glance at Chelle. She was staring straight ahead into the collapsed opening of the building, weapon pointed, only a breath from shooting.

"Runit, are you in there?" The voice sounded familiar. "Are you okay?"

Whoever it was tossed an INU into the room. Chelle considered shooting it, knowing it would be filming them, but its floated images projected a two-way channel showing her who was out there. She recognized the plumber and placed his face with the voice. It must be one of Deuce's Flo-wings.

"Runit, we've come to get you out of here. There's no time. You have to come now," the plumber yelled.

Chelle looked at Grandyn. If it was a trap, they were dead anyway.

"We need help!" Chelle stood and yelled, weapon pointed to the ground.

"Okay Chelle. We're coming in." The plumber appeared a second later, flanked by fully outfitted soldiers in wavesuits, carrying laserstiks and pulse-rods.

"Grandyn's pretty bad," she said, pointing. "And Runit's worse." Her voice went thin on the final word.

The plumber shined a muted blue light toward Grandyn, and then said something into his wrist. A moment later four men appeared with two stretchers.

We're going to be all right, Grandyn thought, crawling back to his father. "Hold on a little longer, Dad." He knew Deuce would have the best medical team available. "They'll save you, Dad."

Against his protests, they loaded Grandyn first, explaining that the critical nature of Runit's injuries meant it would require a more methodical process to get him onboard. Chelle waited at the Flo-wing door, wanting to make sure they got Runit okay.

The area suddenly lit up with blasts and lasers in cascades of colors.

The sky was exploding, as if the lasers were cracking the atmosphere open. It seemed the air, itself was on fire. Through the impossible glow of countless bursting colors, Tech-crafts, and Air-gunships smothered in on them.

Grandyn tried to get up, as a full invasion was unleashed. "My dad! I've got to help him," he yelled, but the medics held him back. Lasers and powered ordinances rained around their position. He struggled to see through the smoke and constant flashes.

"Go!" Someone shouted to the pilot. "Now!"

Chelle started to run back to Runit, but the Plummer grabbed her and drug her into the Flo-Wing. They were airborne even before the door sealed. Out the window, she saw the two men carrying Runit's stretcher surrounded by AOI forces. She cleared the blur in her eyes and they were suddenly flying in a different direction, the scene and her beloved librarian gone.

After a harried four minutes of near misses, bumps, and treacherous maneuverings, the pilot announced they had lost their AOI pursuers. She'd find out later that they'd only been saved by satellite weapons taking out the best of the government's fleet.

"Mr. Lipton is looking forward to speaking with you Ms. Andreas," said a pleasant looking woman once things calmed down.

"Likewise," Chelle said, looking around as if the trillionaire might be onboard.

The Flo-wing had a lavatory, running water, and a tiny galley. A doctor attended to Grandyn's burns while a nurse cleaned up Chelle's wounds. Grandyn glazed over until they tried to inject him with a painkiller.

"No!" he said, "you've got to go back for him!" Grandyn's stretcher was pressed against several cartons of medical supplies, and fittingly, a stack of hardcover books salvaged from the battle. There were several rows of smart-seats, which contoured to one's body and provided instant stimulation, heat or cooling, whatever was needed. But most of the area they were in had been converted to an in-flight medical clinic. "Please, turn around," Grandyn cried.

"They'd shoot us down, before we even got close," Chelle said. "We'll find him, Grandyn. I swear to you, we will get him back."

Grandyn's eyes closed, having trouble focusing, as sheer agony overtook.

The doctor cut away what was left of Grandyn's clothing, revealing a lean, muscular body. Burns covered about thirty percent of his torso and twenty percent of his legs. A nurse helped administer a thick green cream on the worst of the wounds, and a brown powder on everything else. "I know it hurts. Let me give you the shot," the doctor said. "Please."

"No," he said, finally collapsing, unconscious.

The doctor readied an injection to make certain he stayed sedated.

"He said no!" Chelle barked from a few feet away.

"Okay," the doctor said meekly, putting the syringe away.

Chelle had a few deep wounds, which the nurse taped. She also refused any painkillers. A short time later, Crater Lake came into view and they started to descend, saving her the question of where they were headed. PAWN had long maintained a facility near the famous landmark. She didn't know Deuce had become involved with PAWN enough to be welcome at one of their most covert locations, but it could not be a coincidence. The remote lake had once been a national park, but after the Banoff, all such protected lands around the world had become known as Earth Parks. Many were expanded, including Crater Lake. The areas around Earth Parks were subject to rural controls, which, similar to old zoning laws, restricted development.

It had been a couple of years since her last visit to this PAWN compound, but she recognized it from the air. Later, she'd learn that the Lipton family had secretly owned the property since before the Banoff. It included a series of parcels, which were the closest privately owned lands to the famous lake.

The property was accessible only from the air, from where it appeared as a spacious mountain lodge. However, the real facility remained safely hidden underground, fifteen thousand square meters on three subterranean levels.

CHAPTER EIGHTY-THREE

Men escorted Chelle to a small tower, camouflaged into the trees so that Crater Lake could be seen from the large window, but the structure would be almost impossible to see from the lake.

"Where's Nelson?" she asked when Deuce entered. "Is he alive?"

"He's safe. We just located him. Somehow he managed to get a motel room in Ashland, under the name Bob Hauser."

She smiled. "He uses that alias sometimes, the name of a long-time childhood friend."

"It served him well. You'll meet up with him later this evening. PAWN has a safe house in Ashland." *Unless I detain you longer,* Deuce thought.

"Can't you bring him here?" *Or are you lying? Is my brother actually dead?*

"It's too dangerous to stay here." He paused. "Not dangerous for you, but for PAWN. We can't compromise this facility."

"Then why am I here?" She looked around with growing concern.

"I needed to meet with you, and there is no other location where we could both come and go undetected." He could see her mind working. "All kinds of special equipment has been installed here to thwart AOI detection." He pointed to her injuries. "They tell me you'll be okay. Are you in much pain?"

She had questions about his explanation, but decided not to waste time. "I'm fine. Where's Grandyn?"

"Resting."

"Why did you need to see *me*? This is a lot of trouble and risk."

"I wanted to know whose side you're on."

"I would think that would be obvious." *I sure hope it is.*

"Nothing in this struggle is obvious, and I think you know that."

She tilted her head.

"There aren't just two sides," he continued. "There are seven, maybe more."

Chelle did the calculations. She'd always assumed there were five, but with side deals and cross interests, it could easily be seven or more. It also wasn't lost on her that Deuce knew much more than she did about many things. "And now that you've seen me?"

"I'm still assessing. I certainly understand why people fall in love with you so easily."

"Why?" she asked, with enough sincerity that Deuce couldn't help but laugh.

"You're a dangerous woman, I am sure of that. To whom you pose that danger is my question. And it's an urgent one."

And you're a dangerous man, she thought. Chelle both feared Deuce and needed his support. "Why not let the AOI arrest me then? Or have one of your mercenaries kill me?"

"You and I both know that you're too important for that."

"You flatter me."

"I knew your husband."

"I know." *Why are you bringing that up?*

"I knew him quite well." *His secrets are keeping you alive.*

"Did you?"

"I like to think so. Beale Andreas was an impressive man. I held him in high regard."

"Yes, he was, and well you should. But I don't think you knew him as well as you think, or you and I would have met before this, and you would not be questioning my motives."

Although not surprised by her confidence, Deuce was impressed. *Why were you involved with the books? Why the allegiance to PAWN when you have other friends whom you value more?* "Terrible business, his death."

She steeled herself. "Yes."

"I know who ordered it. And I know why."

"I do too."

"Then we both have reasons for wanting the Aylantik reign to end."

"So it would seem." She pursed her lips. "Why are you doubting me then?"

"Oh, forgive me Chelle, I am not questioning your motives. I'm questioning your loyalties."

"I should question yours."

"Now we are back to where we began. It is a complicated struggle that the world is locked in, wouldn't you agree?"

"Are you going to let me go?"

"I have no choice. I am trying to avoid war, and something tells me that of the many things that could start this war, you're one of the surest."

Are you afraid of me, Mr. Lipton? You, the most powerful person on the planet, worried about little ol' me? "There's something special about the lake, isn't there?" Chelle asked, looking out at the glassy indigo water reflecting cotton clouds and two thousand foot high volcanic cliffs. The pines, firs, hemlocks, and the solitary Wizard Island rising out of the incredibly deep lake seemed otherwordly.

"Some think so." *Changing the subject. Not too subtle, but an interesting choice. I want to trust you Chelle, more than anything. I need to trust you.* Deuce knew nothing she said could be considered truth, so he was ignoring the questions likely to incite her, and instead chose to use his instincts.

"Do you?" Chelle asked. "Have you found the magic in this place?"

"Yeah. I like to walk around the lake. It makes me feel close to my grandfather. He loved it here."

"That's not what I meant."

"I know what you meant Ms. Andreas, I'm simply dodging your question."

She nodded once and the faintest smile formed on her lips.

"Runit Happerman should never have died," Chelle said, suddenly turning angry.

"We don't know for sure that he's dead," Deuce said. "I have every resource at my disposal searching." He couldn't accept that if the librarian was gone, the chance to find the wisdom and secrets contained in the missing eight works might have been forever lost. He would still try, but without Runit's knowledge of the volumes, he had no idea how anyone could find them. "If Runit is dead, we can preserve his memory by protecting the books. But I need all of the books. No one can protect them like I can. Will you help me with that?"

Chelle didn't immediately answer. Instead, she just stared out at the lake. Finally, just as the silence began to grow uncomfortable, she said, "I will, if you'll do something in return for me."

CHAPTER EIGHTY-FOUR

Nelson opened the motel room door and stood aside as Chelle stepped into the pine-paneled room. Grandyn remained in the doorway silently, too emotional to speak.

"Grandyn," he said, hugging his "nephew."

"We have to find him," Grandyn said tearfully into Nelson's shoulder. Until he saw his "uncle," He had subconsciously been holding his breath, breathing in that way one does when scared to use any more air than is necessary, afraid that if he breathes normally he might unravel into an unrecognizable entity, easily blown away and lost in a small storm.

"We will," Nelson said, holding Grandyn in a hug. "We've sent the word out." Nelson exchanged a quick, private glance with Chelle. "Come in," Nelson said, pulling Grandyn inside. Chelle followed.

"Have we learned anything?" Grandyn asked.

"Not much, but we haven't heard he's dead, so that's a very good sign. I believe they would make sure we knew if he hadn't survived his injuries."

"I need to—"

"You need to be patient and careful. Your father would not

want you dying to save him," Nelson said. "We have a lot of ways to find him. Deuce is also desperate to locate and rescue him."

Chelle sat on the edge of one of the beds, staring stoically at the floor. Grandyn had not been able to get the image of his father's broken body out of his mind. *Dad always said I was so smart, so strong, but it was him,* Grandyn thought. *He was the one who had all the strength. If I have anything, it came from him. Dad gave me everything! How can I go on without him?*

Grandyn looked at Nelson, who was all that remained of his former life, the happy one where his father would have done anything for Grandyn. Even with his refusal to admit Runit could be dead, he had seen the damage, held his still body. Grandyn knew the odds were high that his dad didn't make it.

Losing your best friend, your guiding star, the bedrock of your life, is a hollowing I'm not sure I can endure . . . He stared blankly at Nelson, lost and destroyed. *How does one live without unconditional love?* he wanted to ask, but no answer could satisfy his desperate emptiness. No explanation could staunch the bleeding of his soul. Instead he asked the simplest of questions.

"What are we going to do now?"

"We're going to finish what your dad started," Nelson said. "We are going to save what's left of the books, and we're going to use them to bring the bastards down."

"We'll make them pay, Grandyn," Chelle said. "The people who killed Vida, my husband, your . . . they will pay for their crimes. I promise you that."

Grandyn nodded. His tightly balled fists, raised shoulders, and swollen eyes didn't begin to tell of the fury and anguish consuming him from the inside, but she understood those feelings and the hardness they caused, chiseling away the softness of love and hope that every human carries until it's shaken and beaten out of them by an avalanche of loss.

She took one of his hands in both of hers and looked up into his bloodshot eyes. "This is not over. They do *not* get to decide. Do you understand?"

Grandyn nodded.

"We love your dad too," Chelle said. "Not like you, but Nelson and I love him in our own ways, and we're your family now. We're your family forever."

"We have to find my dad," he said, barely containing the rage in his words.

Nelson nodded.

Chelle put her hand on his shoulder, searched his eyes again. "We will."

"And I want to find them, all of them. The ones that did this," he said gritting his teeth. "Can you help me?"

Chelle looked at Nelson, and then back to Grandyn. "You remind me of your mother. She would have been so proud of you."

"You knew my mother?"

"She recruited me."

Grandyn looked puzzled.

"Your mother was a great woman who fought to bring down the same flawed system that has allowed these monsters to destroy so many lives. But there is a group that has endured for generations, quietly growing in power and size until it's now ready to challenge the Aylantik government to expose the truth and give control back to the people."

"I thought she was just a researcher for PAWN. I mean, I didn't know anything until this weekend when my dad . . . he didn't know either."

"Families often don't know," she said. "It's safer."

"Safer?" Grandyn howled. "That little secret stole my mother *and* my father. Who gets to decide? Maybe I was too young, but my father should have known. If he had, then this might all be different. One or both of them might still be alive."

"Your mother made that call," Chelle said. "But be careful that you don't start blaming the wrong people for your losses. The AOI has killed our loved ones." She motioned her hand to include Grandyn, Nelson, and herself. "*They* caused the misery. PAWN is just trying to get things back to right. We're the good guys."

"I don't have enough memories of my mom, but my dad . . . he's still in my lungs. I'm breathing his breath. I don't even want to believe he's dead!"

"Your mother was a strong and important voice in PAWN, and she helped teach thousands of us about how things used to be, how they should be, using history and lost documents to show the truth. Along the way, she uncovered many of the lies they use to control us." Chelle looked at Nelson for a moment as if waiting for him to jump in, but he remained silent. "And Runit made it possible for us to continue. He preserved the truth. Our fight would be much harder, if not impossible, without it."

"I know you lost your husband, and believe me, I can imagine your pain. But Chelle, I've lost everyone. *Everyone!*" Grandyn said. "Don't you see me choking here? I'm so full of torgon rage that each time I speak, it feels like I'm about to vomit glass, nails . . . blood, and fire."

"I understand," Chelle said softly.

"Your parents both sacrificed for the same crime, a crime that wasn't theirs," Nelson said. "Harper and Runit were simply trying to preserve the truth. Vida and your TreeRunner pals were just in the way. The AOI has always operated under the shoot-first-ask-no-questions-later policy."

"They don't care about anything except keeping power. They will kill anyone who even slightly challenges the status quo," Chelle said. "There's something else you need to know. Something about your mother." She looked at Nelson.

He pursed his lips, but stayed quiet.

"I wish I had been able to tell your father what I'm about to tell you," she continued, "but we . . . ran out of time."

CHAPTER EIGHTY-FIVE

"What is it?" Grandyn could feel the tension in the room, the weight of some tragic news about to be delivered. He could still recall the same feeling when, at eight years old, his father told him his mother would not ever be coming home.

"Harper Happerman was a hero of the rebellion for many reasons, but for one thing above all others. It is because of her that we have been able to expand and gain the support of so many. If and when we win and take back the light of the world from the greed-control-cartel, which now smothers our true potential, we'll have her to thank."

Chelle paused and looked at him for a lingering moment, as if to capture his last remaining moments of innocence before the truth forever shattered his perception of everything.

"Your mother proved something many others had long suspected. Something so horrific that it is nearly impossible to ponder. The AOI murdered my husband over the same secret. A *secret,*" she repeated, as if astounded that something that could be whispered had killed her husband and Grandyn's mother. But the truly astonishing part was what the secret had done. "A *secret* so horrible, it conceals the most gruesome crime ever committed . . .

The Banoff was no natural plague. It wasn't even some tragic accident. A group of people planned, and executed it, exterminating billions of innocent people."

Grandyn stared at her blankly, as a deaf person does when unable to read lips. Then, after almost half a minute, his head started slowly moving back and forth and his hands trembled.

"Who?" It was the only word he could force out, and it sounded like a screeching moan.

Chelle was shaking too, as she had done on each of the few occasions when she'd spoken of the secret out loud. "The founders of Aylantik, the earliest AOI, and a group called the A-Council. They slaughtered entire societies, almost wiped out our species for one simple reason . . . greed," Chelle said, answering not just who, but why. She recalled that when she had learned the truth, her first question had been why someone would do it. "They wanted riches and power, and believed they were more entitled than the rest of us. Than the *most* of us. Their descendants are still in power and are co-conspirators-after-the-fact in this massive crime against humanity because they know, they continue to perpetuate the lie, and they still kill anyone who threatens their horde."

"*The lie*," Grandyn said. "It's so big, it's unbelievable. How could they have concealed it all this time?"

"Forgive me Grandyn," Nelson began, "but if your dad were here, I think he would answer you with a line from *Fahrenheit 451*. 'But you can't make people listen. They have to come round in their own time, wondering what happened and why the world blew up around them.' Ray Bradbury was wise a hundred years too early."

Grandyn nodded at his closest living "relative," and the rage crept in again. "Does PAWN have enough weapons?" he asked. "Can they? Are we ready to strike back and drag these murdering torgs into the streets?"

"It's close," Chelle said. "However, 'close' is a relative term in relation to the decades that PAWN has been fighting this silent war. Realistically, we are a year away, but you can help make it happen sooner. After I saw how your TreeRunners helped save the books, I believe it can be quite a bit sooner."

"And the books," Nelson said. "There is proof of it, hidden in the books."

"Where? Which ones?" Grandyn asked.

"I don't know. It's in some kind of code or something. Your dad could have found it."

"We'll find it," Grandyn said. "I swear on all that I am, we will find the proof and we will end them."

They spent the remainder of the afternoon contacting TreeRunners and making plans. Chelle and Nelson watched in awe as Grandyn rose to the occasion and became the leader they knew would emerge. They weren't surprised, having known and loved his parents.

Tuesday, February 6

The next morning, Nelson left early to meet with PAWN officials, where they would review data from the latest crackdowns, determine the best course for the remaining books, and to seek any news on Runit. For the first time since it began, the Doneharvest had eased a bit overnight, and the rebels wanted to take advantage. Their options were either to retreat, or to bring on full war. Neither seemed a particularly wise choice at the moment, but one of those tumultuous paths would need to be taken.

Grandyn and Chelle were eating breakfast in the motel room, discussing how best to recruit the remaining TreeRunners. "They will all come," Grandyn said.

"But some of them have commitments to the Aylantik government, plans for school, futures . . ."

He finished a sip of fruit juice, and put the glass down hard.

"You don't understand TreeRunners. It is not a choice. Right is right. That is where they will go. A TreeRunner always goes on the right path."

"I hope—"

The door exploded. Smoke filled the room. Grandyn turned only in time to see a flash, and then everything went black.

One of the intruders reported into his INU. "Zero,eight-twelve hours. Targets secured. Taken alive."

CHAPTER EIGHTY-SIX

Wednesday, February 7

To Chelle, with all that had happened, their arrest had not been a surprise, nor had her separation from Grandyn. But staying in a cold, sterile isolation cell for more than thirty hours left her uncertain about her fate. So many plans had been put on hold. So much interrupted. The longer they kept her in isolation, the more likely she would be sentenced to execution without charges or trial.

She wondered who had her INU, and if they would be able to decode it. She'd been told many times by PAWN tech people that the safeguards built into Eysen-INUs were foolproof, and that only she would ever be able to access the data hers contained, but she had reasons to be extra concerned. For hours she worried what would happen if the wrong people saw her greatest secrets.

Chelle and Nelson's great-grandfather had been a gravedigger. That was before the Banoff, back when the Aylantik still put people in the ground and used headstones. With so many dead in the Banoff, they could barely keep up with burning the bodies, and burials never came back. The Aylantik had even made them illegal.

All bodies had to be burned to be sure any plague or related viruses were destroyed, but a story had passed down through her family that Nelson had fictionalized in one of his novels.

The gravedigger spent all his time in cemeteries, and claimed he often saw spirits comforting the bereaved. Chelle wondered if it could be true. Nelson had told her of his talk with Deuce about Fermi's Paradox, and it made her think. The paradox is about the thousands and thousands of planets orbiting stars that should be able to support life, and the millions of others which must exist among the trillions of stars out there. And yet even in 2098, no evidence has been found, no contact made.

In her desperation, the real possibility of her death, she applied the same thesis to souls. With all the billions of people who had died, if there really were an afterlife, where was the proof? Chelle wanted proof. Sitting in that cell, imagining the electron-sting from an AOI executioner, she wanted to know where she was going once the cold envelope of death took her. Would Beale and Runit be there?

Convinced, Runit was dead, Chelle cried until nothing was left, reviewing in her mind every step and encounter with Runit, and second-guessed all of it. She believed she could have saved him, should have saved him, and regretted his loss more than she'd ever have predicted.

If I live, I'll make it up to your son, she said silently to Runit. *I promise.*

But even as she made that vow, she questioned whether she had already screwed that up too.

Thursday, February 8

By the time forty-seven hours had passed since her arrest, she'd become convinced of her fate. When a guard finally appeared, she asked for pen and paper to write a letter to a man she wasn't sure was even still alive. Instead, they took her from the cell and headed for the roof. She knew something must have gone terribly wrong in the second or third wave of the AOI crackdown. So much was at stake, how could it not have? The layers and complications had been building for decades, the path out was too intricate, too much a maze, and no one could safely navigate the silent war anymore.

"Where are you taking me?" she demanded.

The AOI agents ignored her.

"Why are we on the roof?" she said, trying not to panic, her arms cuffed behind her back. Twenty-six floors up, the winds blew as on a stormy mountaintop. They were going to throw her off. "Who ordered this?" she yelled.

One of the men strapped a Tekfabrik around her mouth, rendering her mute. Now she knew it was over. Chelle didn't mind dying, but regretted not completing her mission. Her life had long ago been given for the cause. It had been so absolute that the idea of failing now gutted her.

What's happened? she wondered, but couldn't voice. There had always been risks, especially when working within both sides of the long silent war. She should have requested a meeting before they gagged her, but what good would it have done? Nelson must be dead too.

They pushed her toward the west side of the building. That area contained the solar collectors on the otherwise flat roof. Only a few meters from the edge, she could look down and see her fate. The hard ground below would come fast. Suddenly, she caught sight of a Flo-wing banking in. It landed quickly, and the men shoved her over to it. They weren't going to throw her over! But then she realized it might be too messy, even for the AOI, so they'd fly her out over the ocean and dump her for the sharks, a fitting end for such a prominent revolutionary.

The door to the Flo-wing opened and she saw the face of Polis

Drast. The two AOI men lifted her inside, and an agent already on board dismissed them with a salute and a nod. Once airborne, the agent released her from her cuffs and she moved to a seat next to the AOI Pacyfik Region Head.

"Are you okay?" Drast asked her.

"I am now," she answered, leaning over to kiss him.

CHAPTER EIGHTY-SEVEN

Polis Drast held Chelle. "I'm sorry you had to go through that. I could not risk getting you out any sooner."

Chelle pulled away from him, trembling. She gasped several times . . . as if coming up for air after a violent shipwreck, but her drowning had occurred in terror and time instead of storm-churned water. She looked at Drast, half wanting to slap him, and half wanting to be held and rocked like a baby. "I understand. These are dangerous times. You don't control everything, not even in the Pacyfik," she said with more than a touch of bitterness.

"Lance Miner suddenly wanted the librarian. It's hard to say why Runit Happerman became his priority. Miner has so many agendas, so many soldiers and spies. But I pushed to own any investigation in my region, and his people assured me that Miner wanted the librarian alive, for questioning." He noticed her tears and tenderly wiped them from her cheek. "It should have been a routine arrest. We still don't know why it went wrong."

"I loved him!" Chelle burst out, still shaking. Convinced he was dead, she thought of Runit, how bravely he'd ventured into the unknown, shadowy world of the revolution and did what had to be done. He had saved the books and kept his only son safe.

The ache of his absence stole at her stability, as if the ground would never seem solid again.

"I didn't know," he said in sadness.

Chelle looked at him, knowing his feelings, saying nothing. She doubted he could not have prevented it, but twice his employer had caused the death of the men she loved.

"Do you remember when I recruited you, and then we recruited Beale? Both times I told you we would lose people we loved."

"The fight is so large, the cause so great, of course I remember. But I have only loved three people outside of my family, and two of them are dead."

"I'm sorry you have lost them, and I hope they will be the last, but I fear they will not."

"Are they onto you?" she asked, a deep breath causing an involuntary shudder, not yet convinced she was really safe.

"I don't think so, but Miner has been in Denver talking to Imps, and he now has an unnatural fascination with the library closing. I fear he's learned something."

"What happened to Runit's body?" Chelle asked, suddenly realizing that Drast had never confirmed his death.

"Apparently Miner's people got there first."

"So he could still be alive?"

"Miner said he was killed."

"But he could be lying."

"Always possible with him, but he chewed me out about it. Furious that the Librarian had not been taken alive."

Chelle thought back to the attack. Grandyn easily could have imagined his father was still breathing. She recalled seeing one of the stretcher men shaking his head after trying to get a pulse. "I think we should be sure about Runit."

Drast looked at her skeptically.

"Not just because of my attachment," she clarified. "It's the books. If he is still alive—"

"All reports are he is not. However, I will seek to verify this. But I must be cautious, and can give Miner no more reasons to doubt me."

She nodded, then looked out the window lost in thought and still trying to recover from her death row incarceration. *It's over . . . at least for now,* she told herself. *I've escaped.*

"Are you . . . really okay?" He touched her arm. "So much has happened . . . "

"We are so close to war," she said trying to answer his unspoken question. There were so many layers to the intrigue she'd been lost in ever since Beale's death. Many of the people she trusted were scoundrels and this troubled her. Even now, Drast might not be telling her everything about Runit. Yet he had risked so much to save her, to protect her. "I thought the revolution was finally starting when the Doneharvest crackdown began."

"I tried with all my skill and capacity to push us over the brink into a conflict which could continue under its own momentum and eventually bring down Aylantik." He stared into his INU and swirled AirViews around them showing AOI troops moving into the Pacyfik. "Miner used influence, and the Chief sent resources from other regions."

"Damn her, 'Peace prevails, always,'" Chelle said, inadvertently pushing her hand through an AirView of the AOC Chief. "I can't stand that woman."

"Likewise."

But if they're using out-of-region agents, they must suspect you," Chelle said, as the Flo-wing reached top speed, blowing through low clouds.

"Maybe not. I am still here, which might not prove Miner doesn't have suspicions, but I'm good with the Chief." He looked into Chelle's bloodshot eyes, wanting to kiss her, but he didn't think the timing was right. "Miner could be using me in some other way. But assuming he hasn't yet learned of my true allegiances, then the move by the Chief can be seen simply as a preemptive step to avoid an escalation, something we all know she doesn't want to risk. So we don't get our war yet. I'd also thought we were there, but Miner is so desperate to continue the peace, and I'm not yet free of his power."

"But in mere months . . ."

"Yes." He smiled. "Once I am World Premier.

"If we live that long," Chelle said, wiping tears and sweat from her face. "I've almost been killed twice in three days."

"Dangerous times . . . I'm doing all I can, but I am under the same warning I gave you. Any time, I can lose someone I love . . . but our cause, to undo the great injustices done, horrendous things that have distorted our world, is worth any sacrifice. It must be, or we will not win."

"You sound like a candidate from the banned history books, back when statesmen pontificated on matters of consequence, human rights, the cruelty of poverty, and war."

"Things we dare not speak of while in the presence of voters in these *modern* times," he said, looking out the window as Portland came into view. "Were you able to speak to Munna?"

"You know that in my time working with PAWN, I really never believed she was real. I mean, one hundred and thirty years old? Come on. And no one ever let me see her, not even Harper. I assumed she was just made up to keep everyone unified." Chelle paused and stared off, then lowered her voice. "But, Polis. . . Munna *is* real. She is greater than even her legend. She makes me believe."

"In what?" he asked, slightly annoyed.

"In everything."

He didn't respond, and they remained in their own thoughts for several minutes.

"Where was it left?" he finally asked.

"PAWN has grown large and powerful. They're close to forming a coalition between the Creatives, the Rejectionists, and the List Keepers."

"The List Keepers will never join with PAWN. They have different objectives."

"But similar enough: the end of Aylantik rule," Chelle said. "And now, with the TreeRunners, there is another opportunity."

"Which is?"

"They're of the perfect age and skill level to infiltrate the AOI in a fairly large way. And they're fiercely *loyal* to one another." She knew his three words – logic, loyalty, love – and understood the effect they had on him.

"Can they be convinced?" he asked, clearly sparked by a *loyal* army of young people, for he knew the TreeRunners' reputation.

"Many have already signed on. The AOI killed some of them. I think their participation will be big. And I believe that a coalition of the other powers will also happen, under Munna."

"Even if Munna can pull that off, will she live much longer? It can't be held together without her, or someone like her. Even if she has another year or two, the Doneharvest has made things desperately difficult for all the dissenters," Drast said.

"They have weapons."

"Primitive things from another century. They shoot ammunition, for torg's sake.

"Deuce Lipton will provide modern weapons."

"Has he promised this?"

"Not yet, but he will." She touched his hand. "Don't worry so much, Polis. We will have this war. One way or another, our day will come."

CHAPTER EIGHTY-EIGHT

Munna walked slowly through the trees. Her deliberate steps, with the steadiness of her carved cane, a constant companion, might lead someone to guess she was in her eighties, but never that she was fifty years beyond that milestone.

"There are many sides to this conundrum," she said to Nelson as they made their way down the narrow path. "Polis Drast, head of the AOI in the Pacyfik and possibly the next World Premier, wants war, unbeknownst to his benefactor Lance Miner, who needs peace at any price. And then there's your pal, Deuce Lipton. He would like fantastic change, wouldn't he? Beginning with how that change is to come about, a complete realignment of how we live without violence."

"That seems obvious. Lipton is an idealist," Nelson said.

"Ah, yes, but do you know why? Has your fast writer's mind worked out that plot detail yet?"

"He also wants peace."

"Perhaps," she said. "But he might be willing to accept a brief war, if it quickens the purpose to which he was born."

"Which is?"

"To continue the work of Booker Lipton."

"With Eysen and StarFly and all the money in the world?" Nelson asked in a slightly sarcastic tone.

"Oh, there was so much more to Booker than just making a fortune and creating the Eysen-INUs. I knew him quite well once, a long time ago, for too brief a moment," she said. Her face clouded, making her look closer to her age of one hundred thirty, but it quickly recovered. "Booker wanted to bring the true age of enlightenment to the world. Instead he, and all of us, got tangled in the brutality of the Banoff and our subsequent utopian dark ages, called Aylantik." She stopped to poke her cane at some mushrooms. "But Booker never lost his vision for a world on a higher and more beautiful level, instead of one run by fear."

"And Deuce is meant to carry that to fruition?" he asked, momentarily distracted by the elaborate carvings on her cane.

"Yes, and he may just succeed if the stars align with him. Never discount the alignment of stars when you're seeking to make the world a better place."

"And PAWN, are they trying to make the world a better place?"

"PAWN, well, like a good game of chess, one cannot expect to win without the judicious use of pawns." She laughed at her well-used line. "But our PAWN, or at least its leadership, desires a full revolution, and cares very little about what form it is to take, so long as they win."

"And is that what you want?"

"Oh, goodness, no. PAWN latched onto me long ago because of my notoriety."

"Because of your power?"

"Yes, I suppose that too," she said, breathing heavily at the exertion of their walk.

"But now, with so much of PAWN ravaged through the Doneharvest, it looks like Lance Miner and his giant PharmaForce has won."

"It would appear that way, but with his victory comes even more power. His man, Polis Drast, will become the next World

Premier, and so war, averted for now, may yet occur in my lifetime."

Nelson looked at her with a raised eyebrow.

"Oh, yes," Munna said, smiling. "I may live a bit longer yet."

"I expect you'll outlive us all," Nelson said.

Munna stabbed at another mushroom. "Oh, good," she said. "Those are my darlings. Be a chum and pick those for me." She handed Nelson a small fabric bag from a pocket. "People wonder how I live so long. The secret is due in no small part to my life-long habit of eating sprouts and medicinal wild mushrooms."

"I survive on a slightly different diet," Nelson said, carefully filling her bag and handing it back.

"Yes, I know," she said sadly.

"Where are we going now? How can we be expected to rebuild PAWN from this forest where there isn't even access to the Field?"

"Haven't you been listening?" she asked sternly. "PAWN uses me, I don't use them. We have a chance to win only as long as there is no war."

"So you're allied with Lance Miner's interests?"

Munna took and exhaled a deep breath. "This isn't one of your novels Nelson. We're not in the pages of a thriller where it's the good guys against the bad guys. This is real life, or something like that." She chuckled. "There is more than one protagonist, and certainly more than one villain. Even more than two sides."

"If that's true, I might be out of a job."

"Oh, you're definitely not out of a job. You're just changing your medium and your target audience. But you'll still be writing. I have a new assignment for you, and this is more important than the bestseller lists. I'm going to introduce you to the real power in this conflict, the way to take the dream and make the change. Think you can handle that? You should probably quit smoking if you want to live long enough to see it happen." She winked.

He thought that an awful idea, but nodded anyway. "We lost so much when Runit was killed. I'm not sure we can—"

She smiled. "I've heard tell that the librarian lives."

"Runit is alive? Where?"

Munna reached out a hand as if to steady him. "Careful. Emotions can be wild things in dangerous times. And Runit's condition and whereabouts are not fully known to us yet."

"But he's alive?"

"I believe he is, but it is a complicated business. Speak not of it until I learn more."

"You'll let me know, any little shred?"

"Of course."

He looked at her for a long moment, silently in awe of her existence. "So, if we're not out here in the middle of nowhere to help PAWN, then what is this all about? Where are we going?" he asked again.

"Not *where* we're going," Munna corrected. "But *whom* we are going to. And aren't these trees the most beautiful things you've ever seen?"

Before Nelson could answer, an old black man, wrapped in a thick, mud-colored linen cape, stepped onto the path.

"Nelson," Munna said, holding out her hand, "meet Cope Lipton."

"Lipton?" Nelson said, clearly surprised. "I'm sorry, who are you?"

"Didn't Munna just say?" Cope asked with a wink.

"He's Booker Lipton's son," Munna said. "He had two sons."

Nelson, not sure the world needed anymore Liptons, was struck by an aura of wisdom emanating from the old man. "I suppose you're going to tell us how to win the revolution."

"There are more important things than revolution."

"Not when the Aylantik is in charge," Nelson said.

"Who is running he world matters less than the energy of the world."

"You'll have to explain that one to me," Nelson said, reaching for a bac.

Cope gently took the bac from his hand, and rubbed it in his old bony fingers until it disintegrated. "I'll be happy to explain it to you Nelson. In fact, I have lots to teach you and little time left in which to do it."

Nelson looked at the two ancient people standing before him, the oldest ones he'd ever known, and felt suddenly completely at ease, confident, and renewed. "Then let's get started."

CHAPTER EIGHTY-NINE

Drast bid farewell to Chelle. Sadly, it was not safe for them to be together. The best hope for the revolution rested with Drast heading the Pacyfik AOI and Chelle leading PAWN. They planned to try to find moments, yet each knew that a single contact in any form would bring enormous risks and must be put off until victory or death.

Drast, stood inside a small dark closet on the lower level of his spacious residence. The cramped space was outfitted with all the anti-surveillance technology available to a top AOI official and several more that were not. He opened a tiny AirView and exchanged a few encrypted words with someone he'd never spoken with before, but trusted completely. Less than a minute after it had begun, the conversation ended and Drast was content, even excited that they now possessed a secret weapon which could ensure the right side won. *We have the librarian,* he said to himself, knowing he must keep this vital information from Chelle, from everyone. Although the report had been clear—his injuries were severe—the next twenty-four hours were critical. Still, Drast was one of only three who knew the librarian lived. *Within a matter of days, I will have everything I've ever wanted.*

Grandyn didn't know his location or who was holding him, but he figured, based on the length of the trip and the mountains he could see out of the small window, that he was still somewhere in the southern Oregon Area.

The young woman looked at Grandyn. "So you're a TreeRunner?"

Grandyn didn't answer.

"That might just keep you alive."

Grandyn didn't care about being alive. He wasn't sure what that even meant anymore. All he wanted to do was to kill every last AOI agent.

"You're full of hate, aren't you Grandyn Happerman?" the List Keeper asked, studying him carefully.

"Who are you?" he sneered.

"I'm your only friend at the moment. I'm the best chance you have to avoid being executed today . . . or tomorrow, for that matter. In fact, I may be the person who keeps you alive for the next few years. After that, you'll be on your own."

"What happens after that?"

"We will have won . . . or we'll all be dead."

Grandyn was intrigued, but still unsure. "Who are you?" he repeated.

"I'm a List Keeper. You don't know what that is yet, but we're a special organization, not unlike the TreeRunners. Except that instead of physical survival skills, we practice virtual survival techniques, and we're so secret that not even the AOI knows we exist."

"And how's that going to save me?"

"I have the ability to give you an entirely new identity."

"Why do I need that?"

"Hmm, I thought you were supposed to be smart." The List

Keeper shook her head, eyeing him coldly. "Maybe you're not worth the effort. Because, let me tell you, it is a *lot* of trouble."

"It's because I helped get the books?"

"It's because your father was the last librarian, because your mother was Harper Happerman, and because you're practically related to Nelson Wright and Chelle Andreas."

"Where are they now?" Grandyn asked, looking out the round window in the tiny cell, avoiding eye contact, trying to see something beyond out there. His father, Nelson, the truth . . .

"Nelson and Chelle are probably dead. The AOI arrested Chelle yesterday, and Nelson is also missing, presumed in custody," she replied like a hardened soldier, with no visible emotion.

"How did I get away?" he asked, refusing to consider the possibility of having lost another loved one. Nelson was all he had left, if he was even still alive.

"Your father is a hero to the revolution . . . he had two missions, and both were completed."

"Missions?"

"He saved the books, and he saved you," she paused allowing a moment for that statement to register. "Your family has a few powerful fans. I'm not at liberty to say which one arranged for your rescue and paid for the chance you're being offered."

"Offered? You mean I have a choice?"

"Well, if you can call it that. Your parents, your girlfriend, and at least two of your fellow TreeRunners are dead. You can walk out of here today and you'll join them before the sun sets, or you can decide to let us work our magic and simply wait for your real life to begin."

"Do you know for a fact my father is dead?"

"My superiors claim he was killed in a raid. Weren't you there?"

"He was breathing when I last saw him."

"But horribly injured, and surrounded by AOI?"

Grandyn nodded.

"I'm sorry," she said, seeing his distress.

"Will you help me find out what happened to him?"

She stared at him for a moment. "The world is not going to be like you remember it . . . before the books were taken."

"That's not an answer."

"Many people will help you. I will be among them. You'll see. If your father somehow made it, we will find him."

"Thank you." He took a deep breath, trying to control his fears, his anger, and his hope. "What about the TreeRunners who worked with us to get the books?"

"Four of them were compromised. We have them as well. They're being briefed."

"And they'll be offered new identities?"

She nodded. "We're working on it. TreeRunners are a special case."

"Which four?" Grandyn asked.

She slid her fingers around her INU and photos of four familiar faces beamed out.

He nodded, seeing his oldest friends. People he could trust above all else. Hopeful that they would be joining him. For in that moment, he decided to accept a new identity. Something about the young woman made him trust her. Maybe it was the way she talked. She had the same determination as he did, the same fire. And he had survived. Whether his father had lived or not, Grandyn realized that just by staying alive he could honor all the sacrifices, and the life of the Last Librarian.

"What will I have to do?"

For the first time, she smiled. "Change the world, Grandyn Happerman . . . that's all."

END OF BOOK ONE

The Lost TreeRunner, book two of the Justar Journal is available now at your favorite store.

The Lost TreeRunner, the thrilling follow up to The Last Librarian - Three years after the AOI burned the books, Grandyn Happerman is missing. For more than one thousand days, Lance Miner, Deuce Lipton, Blaze Cortez, PAWN and the AOI have been searching for him. And, although no one has seen or heard from Runit, stray whispers indicate, impossibly, that the last librarian could still be alive. There are rumors that some books survived, books that contain the truth. As Grandyn desperately struggles to stay one step ahead of his pursuers, he attempts to piece together the clues, which will lead to the Justar Journal. Get it now at your favorite store.

A SPECIAL NOTE FROM THE AUTHOR

Thanks to the thousand or more readers who have contacted me about the previous ending of this, my bestselling book. Although, I replied to you at the time, I want to acknowledge again how much your comments, and especially your passion about the story, meant to me. However, I do want to single out several of the earliest people who wrote to me about the original ending, Leeanne Accetturo, Frank C. Klock, Gregory Juckett, MD, Samantha Jackson, Paula Graham, and Aline.

When I was deliberating on whether or not to revise this book, I consulted with several loyal fans of *The Last Librarian*: LA Dumas, Bob Dumas, Ingo Zen, Melanie Hansen, Robyn Shanti, Peggy Gulli, and Robert Zorger. They each gave me their thoughtful insights and opinions for which I am grateful. It was Rob Zorger, though, who cited an excellent example from the late William Peter Blatty, author of *The Exorcist*. Upon explaining his decision to revise the book that had made him famous, the legendary writer mused that with years to think about it, the new edition would have added material, a polish, an extra very spooky scene, and even a new character. Then Blatty said, "This is the version I would like to be remembered for." And that is how I feel about the tweaks and changes I have made to *The Last Librarian* and the other two books in *The Justar Journal*, remember me for this.

Thanks for sharing the adventure!
Help spread the word
If you enjoyed this book, please take a minute to
post a review wherever you purchased it
(even a few words).
Reviews are the greatest way to help an author.
And, please tell your friends.

I'd love to hear from you1
Questions, comments, whatever.
Email me through my website.
I'll definitely respond (usually within a few days).
Join my Inner Circle
If you want to be the first to hear about my new releases, advance
reads, occasional news and more,
join my Inner Circle at: BrandtLegg.com

ABOUT THE AUTHOR

USA TODAY Bestselling Author Brandt Legg uses his unusual real life experiences to create page-turning novels. He's traveled with CIA agents, dined with senators and congressmen, mingled with astronauts, chatted with governors and presidential candidates, had a private conversation with a Secretary of Defense he still doesn't like to talk about, hung out with Oscar and Grammy winners, had drinks at the State Department, been pursued by tabloid reporters, and spent a birthday at the White House by invitation from the President of the United States.

At age eight, Legg's father died suddenly, plunging his family into poverty. Two years later, while suffering from crippling migraines, he started in business, and turned a hobby into a multi-million-dollar empire. National media dubbed him the "Teen Tycoon," and by the mid-eighties, Legg was one of the top young entrepreneurs in America, appearing as high as number twenty-four on the list (when Steve Jobs was #1, Bill Gates #4, and Michael Dell #6). Legg still jokes that he should have gone into computers.

By his twenties, after years of buying and selling businesses, leveraging, and risk-taking, the high-flying Legg became ensnarled in the financial whirlwind of the junk bond eighties. The stock market crashed and a firestorm of trouble came down. The Teen Tycoon racked up more than a million dollars in legal fees, was betrayed by those closest to him, lost his entire fortune, and ended up serving time for financial improprieties.

After a year, Legg emerged from federal prison, chastened and wiser, and began anew. More than twenty-five years later, he's now using all that hard-earned firsthand knowledge of conspiracies, corruption and high finance to weave his tales. Legg's books pulse with authenticity.

His series have excited nearly a million readers around the world. Although he refused an offer to make a television movie about his life as a teenage millionaire, his autobiography is in the works. There has also been interest from Hollywood to turn his thrillers into films. With any luck, one day you'll see your favorite characters on screen.

He lives in the Pacific Northwest, with his wife and son, writing full time, in several genres, containing the common themes of adventure, conspiracy, and thrillers. Of all his pursuits, being an author and crafting plots for novels is his favorite.

For more information, please visit his website, or to contact Brandt directly, email him: Brandt@BrandtLegg.com, he loves to hear from readers and always responds!

BrandtLegg.com

BOOKS BY BRANDT LEGG

Chasing Rain

Chasing Fire

Chasing Wind

Chasing Dirt

Chasing Life

Chasing Kill

Chasing Risk

Chasing Mind

Cosega Search (Cosega Sequence #1)

Cosega Storm (Cosega Sequence #2)

Cosega Shift (Cosega Sequence #3)

Cosega Sphere (Cosega Sequence #4)

Cosega Source (Cosega Sequence #5)

CapWar ELECTION (CapStone Conspiracy #1)
CapWar EXPERIENCE (CapStone Conspiracy #2)
CapWar EMPIRE (CapStone Conspiracy #3)

The Last Librarian (Justar Journal #1)
The Lost TreeRunner (Justar Journal #2)
The List Keepers (Justar Journal #3)

Outview (Inner Movement #1)
Outin (Inner Movement #2)
Outmove (Inner Movement #3)

ACKNOWLEDGMENTS

Thanks to the readers. I've been fortunate to have heard from a great many of you and that's what pushes me on those days when the writing doesn't come so easily. I very much appreciate those sharing the journey with my characters and me. It means a great deal when you drop a kind word across the Internet and it finds its way onto my screen at just the right moment. Love to you all!

Ever since this series came to me in a dream, I've raced to get the story down. Along the way, the usual suspects helped get the finished pages out on time: Roanne Legg listened to the initial ideas that day up on Grizzly Peak and then read the first few drafts. In addition to those important duties, she did just about everything else so that I could have more time to write. My mother, Barbara Blair, wore out a wrist, while writing notes on one draft, yet her constant enthusiasm never wavered. Bonnie Brown Koeln is a wonder; sometimes she must feel like she is making the same corrections from book to book, but her patience is endless. Elizabeth Chumney volunteered for another run and got it in on time . . . thirty-some years! Also, I want to thank, Melanie C. Hansen, for reading it again, and making sure the revised edition was ready. And finally to Teakki, who patiently waited for his own story, until I finished writing each day.

PS - Can acknowledgements have a PS? Apparently they can, at least in revised editions. Extra thanks go to Teakki who read every word of the three books with me to decide on exactly what changes would happen and often helping choose just the right words. Love you forever!

This book is dedicated to Teakki and Ro

GLOSSARY

A-Council – Secretive group that controls the economy and decides who will be elected.

ACE – Aylantik Commission on the Environment.

ADAM – Atom-Displacing-Adjusted-Molecule technology – Reduces the weight of objects.

AirSlider – Jet-propelled scooter, sometimes equipped with laser munitions.

AirView – Virtual INU (computer) monitors.

AOI – Aylantik Office of Intelligence.

AOI Chief – Top AOI official.

Android – An artificial being, advanced robot, with approximate human appearance. Manufactured to replace humans in many jobs.

Aylantik Government – Group running the world since the end of the Banoff War.

Aylantik Records Circle (ARC) – Manages ID chips.

Aylantik region – One of twenty-four regions governed by the Aylantik.

Bacs – Privately made cigarettes.

Banoff Pandemic – Plague which wiped out more than half the world's population in 2025.

Banoff War – War which followed the plague. In which the Aylantik coalition secured power.

Bearing rights – Rights to have one child could be sold for up to 20,000 digis after age eighteen.

BLAXERs – Deuce Lipton's private "security" army.

Breeze-Blowers - Dust-sized computers, equipped with video transmitters, that blow in the breeze.

CAAP – Corporate Assets Acquisition Parity Board.

Chamber-slot – Plan to breach all AOI prisons at once.

Chiantik region – One of twenty-four regions governed by the Aylantik.

Chicago85 – Company that sells spy, intelligence, and surveillance technologies to the government.

CHRUDEs - Cloned Human Replacement Unit DesTIn Enabled – Human-like robots.

Collins-HG3 – Autonomous flying weapon.

Com – Universal language that has replaced all other languages, including English.

Courier – People who personally deliver confidential messages or small parcels.

Creatives – Writers, artists, musicians, etc., who tend to have liberal views and prefer total freedom.

Cyborg – Cybernetic Organism constructed from organic and biomechatronic parts.

DACAR – Data Arts Correction And Revisions Project.

DesTIn - Design Taught Intelligence, or "DesTIn," an advanced artificial intelligence program.

Digi-link – World Central Bank.

Digis – Form of digital currency.

Digital-drapes – Where people download books, movies, music, or whatever data they desire.

Doneharvest – AOI martial law style crackdown.

Earth Parks – Replaced National parks and protected lands.

ELS – Equidistant Letter Sequence – Type of code for hiding messages in text.

Enforcers — Security unit of PharmaForce and Lance Miner's private army.

Exchange – Code word for the second start of the revolution.

Eysen-INU – Leading type of Information Navigation Units.

FA – False Audio equipped micro-whistler-FAs.

Field – What the Internet evolved into – Everything is connected.

Field-View – Secure videoconference.

Flash – Equivalent to email/text/instant message.

Flo-wing – Super-fast vertical takeoff mini aircraft – The evolution of helicopters.

FRIDG – Facial Recognition Identification Grid.

Grunges – Slang for AOI agents.

Health-Circle – Or AHC – Aylantik government agency responsible for health care.

Hops – State run health and fitness facilities.

ID chip - Secured into every Aylantik citizen. Details all personal data.

Implant – AI computer brain interface implanted in humans resulting in super intelligence.

Imps – Slang for people who have computer implants.

INU – Information Navigation Units – Powerful marble-sized computer/communications device.

InvisiLine – Secret bank and currency control.

ISBN – International Standard Book Number – Unique book identifier system.

Lasershod – Advanced handgun.

Laserstiks – Advanced, highly accurate, long-range weapon.

LEVs – Levitating Electro Vehicles – Solar-propelled floating vehicles.

Micro-whistler-Mimics (MWM) – Device that fits into mouth – Blocks conversations, broadcasts a false audio.

Micro-drones – Bug-sized drones, used individually or in swarms.

Media no-list – Topics not allowed to be covered by the media – PAWN, Rejectionists, etc.

Medical Sensor – Small coin-sized patch worn to monitor all health data.

Monitoring-mimic-drones – Bird-sized, sophisticated drones. Almost impossible to detect.

Nano-camo – Tarps that automatically change to the surrounding landscape like a chameleon.

Nano-tracers – Seeker-defeating microscopic decals applied to the face.

Neuro-cap – Erases data and memory from both human, cyborg, CHRUDE, and Imp brains.

Neuron-mites – Mind reading nano-sized INUs.

Nusun – Single nation utopian Earth.

Over-hold – Instantly contouring chair/gliding sofa, which applies massage and aromatherapy.

Pacyfik region – One of twenty-four regions governed by the Aylantik.

PAWN – People Against World Nation – Leading revolutionary group.

Phantom-Shield Nano-device – Sends holographic image into the same path and trajectory.

PharmaForce – World's largest pharmaceutical company, controlled by Lance Miner.

Plantik – The naturally derived plantik that replaced plastic.

POPs – PAWN Operational Pods – Underground PAWN facilities.

Proof – A-Council's name for the generation that survived the Banoff.

Pulse-rods – Communication-disrupting weapon.

Q-lifts – Ultra fast elevator that uses atom-displacing-adjusted-molecule technology.

Red-1953 – Chemical used to burn books.

Rejectionists – People who rejected Aylantik rules and modern society.

Retina-synch - Allows wearer to access data through what amounts to a micro-contact lens.

Said-scans - Postmortem brain scans.

Sat-grids – Satellite monitoring system.

Scram Network – Emergency, secret communications system that operated apart from the Field.

Seeker – AOI camera network.

Shockers – A hand-held laser-powered pulse bomb about the size of a hand grenade.

Slide – Thumb drive-like data carrying device for INUs.

Sonic-bomb – Vibration frequency device that can shatter everything within a specified radius.

Sophisticated-GPS – Tracking program able to predict where an object is heading or came from.

StarFly – Largest company in the world's fourth biggest industry: Space. Owned by Deuce Lipton.

Swarm-Drones – Bug-sized drones, equipped with cameras – Can go anywhere a flying insect can.

Tech-tracing – Can track the fingerprint of any electronic device from the web of satellites.

Tekfabrik – Multipurpose nano-fabric capable of changing color, size, and texture. Self-cleaning.

Thread – High capacity memory stick about the size of a short piece of angel hair pasta.

Torgon – Curse word in the com language. Also used as torg, torgged, or torging.

Traditionals – Name used to describe ordinary humans without implants, etc.

Trapicers – Mysterious revolutionary group.

Tru-chair – Chair that conforms to the sitter's anatomy and delivers acupressure. Uses energy by harvesting body heat.

Wavesuits – Tekfabrik suits equipped with tracking-blocking capabilities.

Whistler – Tiny device and app that blocks AOI monitoring of INUs.

World Premier – Elected leader of the United Earth and head of the Aylantik government.

Zoom – Similar to a phone call with video.

Printed in Great Britain
by Amazon

79819470R00230